Romance readers around the world were sad to note the passing of **Betty Neels** in June 2001. Her career spanned thirty years, and she continued to write into her ninetieth year. To her millions of fans, Betty epitomized the romance writer, and yet she began writing almost by accident. She had retired from nursing, but her inquiring mind still sought stimulation. Her new career was born when she heard a lady in her local library bemoaning the lack of good romance novels. Betty's first book, *Sister Peters in Amsterdam*, was published in 1969, and she eventually completed 134 books. Her novels offer a reassuring warmth that was very much a part of her own personality. She was a wonderful writer, and she is greatly missed. Her spirit and genuine talent live on in all her stories.

BETTY NEELS

Discovering Daisy &
Off with the Old Love

HARLEQUIN® SPECIAL RELEASE

ISBN-13: 978-1-335-04511-9

Discovering Daisy & Off with the Old Love

Copyright © 2019 by Harlequin Books S.A.

The publisher acknowledges the copyright holder
of the individual works as follows:

Discovering Daisy
Copyright © 1999 by Betty Neels

Off with the Old Love
Copyright © 1987 by Betty Neels

Recycling programs
for this product may
not exist in your area.

Printed in U.S.A.

CONTENTS

DISCOVERING DAISY

Chapter 1

It was a blustery October afternoon and the dark skies had turned the sea to a dull grey, its sullen waves eddying to and fro on the deserted beach. Not quite deserted, for a girl was walking there, stopping now and again to stare seawards, stooping to pick up a stone and hurl it out to sea and then walk on again. She looked small and lonely with so much emptiness around her, and certainly she was both, but only because there was no one there to see.

She marched along at a furious pace, making no attempt to wipe away the tears; they didn't matter; they relieved her feelings. A good weep, she told herself, and everything would be over and done with. She would present a smiling face to the world and no one would be the wiser.

She turned back presently, wiped her eyes and blew her nose, tucked odds and ends of hair back under her headscarf, and assumed what she hoped was her normal cheerful expression. Climbing the steps back onto the sea front of the little town, she waved to the porter of the Grand Hotel across the road and started up the narrow, steep main street. The season was pretty well over and the town was settling down into its winter sloth; one could walk peacefully along its streets now, and chat unhurriedly with the shopkeepers, and the only cars were those of outlying farmers and the owners of the country properties dotted around the countryside.

There were narrow lanes leading off the street at intervals, and down one of these the girl turned, past a row of small shops converted from the old cottages which lined it; chic little boutiques, a jeweller's, a tiny tea room and, halfway down, a rather larger shop with a sign painted over its old-fashioned window: 'Thomas Gillard, Antiques'. The girl opened the door of the shop and the old-fashioned bell jangled.

'It's me,' she called ungrammatically, and pulled off her headscarf so that her nut-brown hair tumbled around her shoulders. She was an ordinary girl, of middle height, charmingly and unfashionably plump, her unassuming features redeemed from plainness by a pair of large hazel eyes, thickly fringed. She was dressed in a quilted jacket and tweed skirt, very suitable for the time of year but lacking any pretentions to fashion. There was no trace of her recent tears as she made her way carefully between the oak clap tables, Victorian Davenports, footstools and a variety of chairs: some very old, others Victorian button-backed balloon chairs.

Ranged round the walls were side cabinets, chiffoniers, and a beautiful bow-fronted glass cabinet, and wherever there was space there were china figurines, glass decanters and scent bottles, pottery figures and small silver objects. She was familiar with them all. At the back of the shop there was a half-open door leading to a small room her father used as his office, and then another door opening onto the staircase which led to the rooms above the shop.

She dropped a kiss on the bald patch on her father's head as she passed him at his desk, and went up the stairs to find her mother sitting by the gas fire in the sitting room, repairing the embroidery on a cushion cover. She looked up briefly and smiled.

'It's almost teatime, Daisy. Will you put the kettle on while I finish this? Did you enjoy your walk?'

'Very much. It's getting quite chilly, though, but so nice to have the town empty of visitors.'

'Is Desmond taking you out this evening, love?'

'We didn't arrange anything. He had to meet someone or other and wasn't sure how long he would be gone…'

'Far?'

'Plymouth…'

'Oh, well, he'll probably get back fairly early.'

Daisy agreed. 'I'll get the tea.'

She was fairly sure Desmond wouldn't come; they had gone out on the previous evening and had a meal at one of the town's restaurants. He had met some friends there. Being in love, she saw very little wrong with him, but some of his friends were a different matter; she had refused to go with them to a nightclub in Totnes and Desmond had been icily angry. He had called her a spoilsport, prudish. 'Time you grew up,' he had told her, with a nasty little laugh, and had taken her home in silence.

At the door he had watched her get out of the car and shot away, back to his friends, without saying another word. And Daisy, in love for the first time, had lain awake all night.

She had lost her heart to him when he had come into the shop, looking for glass goblets, and Daisy, being Daisy, twenty-four years old, plain, heartwhole and full of romantic ideas, had fallen instant prey to his superficial charm, bold good looks and flattering manners—all of which compensated for his lack of height. He was only a few inches taller than Daisy. He dressed well, but his hair was too long—sometimes, when Daisy allowed her sensible self to take over from romantic dreams, she did dislike that, but she was too much in love to say so.

He was a conceited man, and it was this conceit which had prompted him to invite Daisy out for dinner one evening, and that had led to more frequent meetings. He was a stranger to the little town, he had told her, sent by a London firm on a survey of some sort; he hadn't been explicit about it and Daisy had supposed him to be in some high-powered job in the City, and that had given him the excuse to get to know her.

She helped her father in the shop, but she was free to come and go, so that first dinner soon led to him being shown the town. His apparent interest in it had encouraged her to take him to the local museum, the various churches, the row of cottages leading from the quay, old and bowed down with history. He had been horribly bored, but her obvious wish to please him was food for his ego.

He'd taken her out to tea, plying her with witty talk, smiling at her over the table, and she'd listened to him egotistically talk about himself and his important job, laughing at his jokes, admiring a new tie, or the leather briefcase he always carried, so necessary to his image.

That he didn't care for her in the least didn't bother him; she served as a distraction in the dull little town after the life he'd lived in London. She was a stopgap until such time as he could find the girl he wanted; preferably with good looks and money. And a good dresser. Daisy's off-the-peg clothes earned her nothing but his secret mockery.

He didn't come that evening. Daisy stifled disappointment, and spent the hours until bedtime polishing some antique silver her father had bought that day. It was worn smooth by the years, and usage, and she thought how delightful it would be to eat one's food with such perfection. She polished the last spoon and laid it with the rest in a velvet bag, then put it in the wall cupboard where the small silver objects were housed. She locked the cupboard, shot the bolts on the shop door, locked it and set the alarm and went back upstairs. She had gone to the kitchen to make their evening drink when the phone rang.

It was Desmond, full of high spirits, apparently forgetful of their quarrel. 'I've a treat for you, Daisy. There's a dinner-dance at the Palace Hotel on Saturday evening. I've been invited and asked to bring a partner.' He turned on the charm. 'Say you'll come, darling, it's important to me. There'll be several people I've been hoping to meet; it's a good chance for me…'

When Daisy didn't speak, he added, 'It's rather a grand affair; you'll need a pretty dress—something striking so that people will turn round and look at us. Red—you can't ignore red…'

Daisy swallowed back excitement and happiness as she said sedately, 'It sounds very nice. I'd like to come with you. How long will it last?'

'Oh, the usual time, I suppose. Around midnight. I'll see you safely home, and I promise you it won't be too late.'

Daisy, who if she made a promise kept it, believed him.

Desmond said importantly, 'I'm tied up for the rest of this week, but I'll see you on Saturday. Be ready by eight o'clock.'

When he rang off, she stood for a moment, happy once more, planning to buy a dress fit for the occasion. Her father paid her a salary for working in the shop and she had saved most of it… She went to find her mother to tell her.

There was only a handful of dress shops in the town, and since her father didn't have a car, and the bus service, now that the season was over, had shrunk to market day and Saturday, Totnes and Plymouth were out of the question. Daisy visited each of the boutiques in the high street and to her relief found a dress—red, and not, she considered, quite her style, but red was what Desmond wanted…

She took it home and tried it on again—and wished she hadn't bought it; it was far too short, and hardly decent—not her kind of a dress at all. When she showed it to her mother she could see that that lady thought the same. But Mrs Gillard loved her daughter, and wanted her to be happy. She observed that the dress was just right for an evening out and prayed silently that Desmond, whom she didn't like, would be sent by his firm, whoever they were, to the other end of the country.

Saturday came, and Daisy, in a glow of excitement, dressed for the evening, did her face carefully and pinned her hair into a topknot more suitable for a sober schoolteacher's outfit than the red dress, then went downstairs to wait for Desmond.

He kept her waiting for ten minutes, for which he offered no apology, and her mother and father, greeting him civilly, wished that Daisy could have fallen in love with any man but he. He made a great business of studying the dress. 'Quite OK,' he told her airily, and then frowned. 'Of course your hair is all wrong, but it's too late to do anything to it now...'

There were a great many people at the hotel, milling around waiting to go into dinner, and several of them hailed Desmond as they joined them. When Desmond introduced her, they nodded casually, then ignored her. Not that she minded that. She stood quietly listening to Desmond. He was a clever talker, knowing how to keep his listeners interested, and she could see that he was charming them.

She took the glass of wine she was offered and they made their way through the crowded foyer, stopping from time to time to greet someone Desmond knew, sometimes so briefly that he didn't bother to introduce her. They sat with a party of eight in the restaurant, and presently Desmond, already dominating the talk at the table, made no attempt to include her in it. The man on her other side was young, with a loud voice, and he asked her who she was.

'Came with Des? Not his usual type, are you? Cunning rascal wants to catch the eye of the guest of honour—he's an influential old fellow, very strait-laced—thinks all young men should marry and settle down with a little woman and a horde of children. The plainer the better.' He laughed. 'You're just the ticket, if I may say so.'

Daisy gave him a long, cold stare, suppressed a de-sire to slap his face, and instead chose a morsel of what-ever it was on her plate and popped it in her mouth. If it hadn't been for Desmond's presence beside her she would have got up and walked out but he had impressed upon her the importance of the evening; his chance to meet the right people...

She sat through dinner, ignoring the awful man on her left and wishing that Desmond would speak to her. Only he was deep in conversation with the elegant woman on his right, and, from time to time, joining in talk with other people at the table. Perhaps it would be better once they started the dancing...

Only it wasn't. True, he danced the first dance with her, whirling her around in a flashy fashion, but then he told her, 'I must talk to a few people once this dance is over. Shan't be long; you'll get plenty of partners—you dance quite well. Only do, for heaven's sake, look as though you're enjoying yourself. I know it's a bit above you, Daisy, but don't let it intimidate you.'

He waved to someone across the ballroom. 'I must

go and have a word, I'll be back,' he assured her, leaving her pressed up against a wall between a large statue holding a lamp and a pedestal holding an elaborate flower arrangement. She felt hemmed in and presently, when Desmond didn't come back, lonely.

One side of the ballroom was open onto the corridor leading to the restaurant, and two men strolling along it paused to look at the dancers, talking quietly together. Presently they shook hands and the older man went on his way. His companion stayed where he was, in no hurry to leave, his attention caught by Daisy's red dress. He studied her at some length. She didn't look as though she belonged, and that dress was all wrong...

He strolled round the edge of the ballroom towards her, vaguely wishing to help her in some way. Close to her now, he could see that she wasn't pretty, and looked prim, definitely out of place on the noisy dance floor. He stopped beside her and said in a friendly voice, 'Are you like me? A stranger here?'

Daisy looked up at him, wondering why she hadn't noticed him before, for he was a man who could hardly go unnoticed. Tall, very tall, and heavily built, with handsome features and grey hair cut short. He had a commanding nose and a rather thin mouth, but he was smiling at her in a reassuring way.

She said politely, 'Well, yes, I am, but I came with someone—he has friends here. I don't know anyone...'

Jules der Huizma was adept at putting people at their ease. He began a gentle rambling conversation about nothing in particular and watched her relax. Quite a pleasant girl, he reflected. A shame about the dress...

He stayed with her until presently he saw a man

making his way towards them. When Desmond reached them, Mr der Huizma nodded in a friendly fashion and wandered away.

'Who was that?' demanded Desmond.

'I've no idea—another guest?' Daisy added with unexpected tartness, 'It was pleasant to have someone to talk with.'

Desmond said too quickly, 'Darling, I'm sorry,' and he gave her a smile to quicken her heartbeat. 'I'll make it up to you. I've been asked to go on to a nightclub in Plymouth—quite a jolly crowd. You can come too, of course. Another one won't matter.'

'Plymouth? But, Desmond, it's almost midnight. You said you would take me home then. Of course I can't go. In any case I wasn't invited, was I?'

'Well, no, but who's to mind? Another girl won't matter, and good Lord, Daisy, let yourself go for once—' He broke off as a girl joined them. A pretty girl, slim and dressed in the height of fashion, teetering on four-inch heels, swinging a sequinned bag, tossing fashionably tousled hair.

'Des—there you are. We're waiting.'

She glanced at Daisy and he said quickly, 'This is Daisy; she came with me.' He spoke sharply, 'Daisy, this is Tessa.'

'Oh, well, I suppose one more won't matter. There'll be room for her in one of the cars.' Tessa smiled vaguely.

'It's kind of you to ask me,' said Daisy, 'but I said I would be home by midnight.'

Tessa's eyes opened wide and she laughed. 'A proper little Cinderella, though that frock's all wrong—you're too mousy to wear red.' She turned to Desmond. 'Take Cinderella home, Des. I'll wait here for you.'

She turned on her ridiculous heels and was lost among the dancers.

Daisy waited for Desmond to say something, to tell her that he wouldn't go with Tessa.

'OK, I'll take you home, but for heaven's sake be quick getting your coat. I'll be at the entrance.' He spoke in an angry voice. 'You're doing your best to ruin my evening.'

Daisy said woodenly, 'And what about my evening?'

But he had turned away, and she wasn't sure if he had heard.

It took her a minute or two to find her coat under a pile of others in the alcove close to the entrance. She was putting it on when she became aware of voices from the other side of the screen.

'Sorry you had to hang around for me, Jules. Shall we go along to the bar? There is still a great deal to talk about and I'm glad of the chance to see you after all this time. Wish it had been quieter here, though. Not much of an evening for you. I hope you found someone interesting to talk to.'

'I found someone.' Daisy recognised the voice of the man who had been so pleasant. 'A plain little creature in a regrettable red dress. A fish out of water…'

They moved away, and Daisy, not allowing herself to think, went to the entrance, where Desmond was waiting. He drove her home in silence, and only as she was getting out of the car did he speak. He said, unforgivably, 'You look silly in that dress.'

Funnily enough, that didn't hurt her half as much as the strange man's opinion had done.

The house was quiet, with no light showing. She went in through the side door, along the passage to her father's office and up the stairs to her room—small, but charmingly furnished with pieces she had chosen from the shop, none of it matching but all of it harmonising nicely. There was a patchwork quilt on the narrow bed, and plain white curtains at the small window, and a small bookshelf bulging with books.

She undressed quickly and then parcelled up the red dress to hand over to the charity shop in the high street. She would have liked to have taken a pair of scissors and cut it into shreds, but that would have been a stupid thing to do; somewhere there must be a girl who would look just right in it. Daisy got into bed as the church clock chimed one and lay wide awake, going over the wreck of her evening. She still loved Desmond; she was sure of that. People in love quarrelled, even in her euphoric state she was aware of that, and of course he had been disappointed—she hadn't come up to his expectations and he had said a great many things she was sure he would regret.

Daisy, such a sensible, matter-of-fact girl, was quite blinded by her infatuation, and ready to make any excuses for Desmond. She closed her eyes, determined to sleep. In the morning everything would be just as it had been again.

Only it wasn't. She wasn't sure what she'd expected—a phone call? A quick visit? He seemed to have plenty of time on his hands.

She busied herself arranging a small display of Coalport china, reflecting that she knew almost nothing about his work or how he spent his days. When he took her out in the evenings he would answer her queries as to his day with some light-hearted remark which actually told her nothing. But, despite the disappointment and humiliation of the previous evening, she was quite prepared to listen to his apologies—might even laugh about the disastrous evening with him.

Even while she consoled herself with these thoughts, good sense was telling her that she was behaving like a naive teenager, although she was reluctant to admit it. Desmond represented romance in her quiet life.

He didn't phone, he didn't come to see her, and it was several days later that she saw him on the other side of the high street. He must have seen her, for the street was almost empty, but he walked on, to all intents and purposes a complete stranger.

Daisy went back to the shop and spent the rest of the day packing up a set of antique wine glasses which an old customer had bought. It was a slow, careful job, and it gave her ample time to think. One thing was clear to her; Desmond didn't love her—never had, she admitted sadly. True, he had called her darling, and kissed her and told her that she was his dream girl, but he hadn't meant a word of it. She had been happy to believe him; romance, for her, had been rather lacking, and he had seemed like the answer to her romantic dreams. But the romance had been only on her side.

She wedged the last glass into place in its nest of tissue paper and put the lid on the box. And at the same time she told herself, I've put a lid on Desmond too, and I'll never be romantic again—once bitten...!

All the same, the next weeks were hard going. It had been easy to get into the habit of seeing Desmond several times a week. She tried to fill the gaps by going to films, or having coffee with friends, but that wasn't entirely successful for they all had boyfriends or were engaged, and it was difficult to maintain a carefree indifference as to her own future in the face of their friendly probings. She got thinner, and spent more time than she needed to in the shop, so that her mother coaxed her to go out more.

'There's not much doing in the shop at this time of year,' she observed. 'Why not have a good walk in the afternoons, love? It will soon be too cold and dark, and there'll be all the extra custom with Christmas.'

So Daisy went out walking. Mostly the same walk, down to the sea, to tramp along the sand, well wrapped up against the early November wind and rain. She met a few other hardy souls; people she knew by sight, walking their dogs. They shouted cheerful greetings as they passed and she shouted back, her voice carried away on the wind.

It was during the last week of November that Daisy met once more the man who had likened her to a fish out of water. Jules der Huizma was spending a few days with his friend again, at his house some miles out of the town, enjoying the quiet country life after the hurry and stress of London. He loved the sea; it reminded him of his own country.

He saw her some way ahead of him and recognised her at once. She was walking into the teeth of a chilly wind bearing cold drizzle with it, and he lengthened his stride, whistling to his friend's dog so that it ran on ahead of him. He had no wish to take her by surprise, and Trigger's cheerful barks would slow her down or cause her to turn round.

They did both. She stopped to pat his elderly head and looked over her shoulder; she greeted him politely in a cool voice, his words at the hotel still very clear in her head. And then forgot to be cool when he said, 'How delightful to meet someone who likes walking in the rain and the wind.'

He smiled at her as he spoke, and she forgave him then for calling her a fish out of water—a plain fish too. After all, in all fairness she had been both. Indeed, when it came to being plain she would always be that.

They walked on side by side, not talking too much for the wind was too fierce, and presently, by mutual consent, they turned back towards the town, climbed the steps and walked up the main street. At the corner of the lane, Daisy paused. 'I live down here with my mother and father. Father has an antiques shop and I work there.'

Mr der Huizma saw that he was being dismissed politely. 'Then I hope that at some time I shall have the opportunity to browse there. I'm interested in old silver...'

'So is Father. He's quite well known for being an expert.'

She put out a wet gloved hand. 'I enjoyed the walk.' She studied his quiet face. 'I don't know your name...'

'Jules der Huizma.'

'Not English? I'm Daisy Gillard.'

He took her small damp paw in a firm grip. 'I too

enjoyed the walk,' he told her gently. 'Perhaps we shall meet again some time.'

'Yes, well—perhaps.' She added, 'Goodbye,' and walked down the lane, not looking back. A pity, she thought, that I couldn't think of something clever to say, so that he would want to see me again. She remembered Desmond then, and told herself not to be so stupid; he wasn't in the least bit like Desmond, but who was it that wrote 'Men were deceivers ever'? Probably they were all alike.

She took care for the next few days to walk the other way—which was pointless since Mr der Huizma had gone back to London.

A week or so later, with the shops displaying Christmas goods and a lighted Christmas tree at the top of the high street opposite the church, she met him again. Only this time it was at the shop. Daisy was waiting patiently by the vicar, while he tried to decide which of two Edwardian brooches his wife would like. She left him with a murmured suggestion that he might like to take his time and went through the shop to where Mr der Huizma was stooping over a glass-topped display table housing a collection of silver charms.

He greeted her pleasantly. 'I'm looking for something for a teenage god-daughter. These are delightful—on a silver bracelet, perhaps?'

She opened a drawer in the large bow-fronted tallboy and took out a tray.

'These are all Victorian. Is she a little girl or an older teenager?'

'Fifteen or so.' He smiled down at her. 'And very fashion-conscious.'

Daisy held up a dainty trifle of silver links. 'If you should wish to buy it, and the charms, Father will fasten them on for you.' She picked up another bracelet. 'Or this? Please just look around. You don't need to buy anything—a lot of people just come to browse.'

She gave him a small smile and went back to the vicar, who was still unable to make up his mind.

Presently her father came into the shop, and when at last the vicar had made his decision, and she'd wrapped the brooch in a pretty box, Mr der Huizma had gone.

'Did he buy anything?' asked Daisy. 'Mr der Huizma? Remember I told you I met him one day out walking?'

'Indeed he did. A very knowledgeable man too. He's coming back before Christmas—had his eye on those rat-tailed spoons...'

And two days later Desmond came into the shop. He wasn't alone. The girl Daisy had met at the hotel was with him, wrapped in a scarlet leather coat and wearing a soft angora cap on her expertly disarranged locks. Daisy, eyeing her, felt like a mouse in her colourless dress; a garment approved of by her father, who considered that a brighter one would detract from the treasures in his shop.

She would have liked to have turned away, gone out of the shop, but that would have been cowardly. She answered Desmond's careless, 'Hullo, Daisy,' with composure, even if her colour was heightened, and listened politely while he explained at some length that they were just having a look round. 'We might pick up some trifle which will do for Christmas...'

'Silver? Gold?' asked Daisy. 'Or there are some

pretty little china ornaments if you don't want to spend too much.'

Which wasn't a polite thing to say, but her tongue had said it before she could curb it. It gave her some satisfaction to see Desmond's annoyance, even though at the same time she had to admit to a sudden wish that he would look at her—really look—and realise that he was in love with *her* and not with the girl in the red coat. It was a satisfying thought, but nonsense, of course, and, when she thought about it, it struck her that perhaps she hadn't loved him after all. All the same, he had left a hole in her quiet life. And her pride had been hurt...

They stayed for some time and left without buying anything, Desmond pointing out in a rather too loud voice that they were more likely to find something worth buying if they went to Plymouth. A remark which finally did away with Daisy's last vestige of feeling towards him...

During her solitary afternoon walks, shorter now that the Christmas rush had started, she decided that she would never allow herself to get fond of a man again. Not that there was much chance of that, she reflected. She was aware that she was lacking in good looks, that she would never be slender like the models in the glossy magazines, that she lacked the conversation likely to charm a man.

She had friends whom she had known for most of her life; most of them were married now, or working in some high-powered job. But for Daisy, once she had managed to get a couple of A levels, the future had been an obvious one. She had grown up amongst antiques, she loved them, and she had her father's talent for finding them. Once she'd realised that she'd studied books about them, had gone to auctions and poked around dingy little back-street second hand shops, occasionally finding a genuine piece. And her father and mother, while making no effort to coerce her, had been well content that she should stay home, working in the shop and from time to time visiting some grand country house whose owners were compelled to sell its contents.

They had discussed the idea of her going to a university and getting a degree, but that would have meant her father getting an assistant, and although they lived comfortably enough his income depended very much on circumstances.

So Daisy had arranged her future in what she considered to be a sensible manner.

She thought no more about Desmond. But she did think about Mr der Huizma—thoughts about him creeping into her head at odd moments. He was someone she would have liked to know better; his calm, friendly manner had been very soothing to her hurt feelings, and he seemed to accept her for what she was—a very ordinary girl. His matter-of-fact manner towards her was somehow reassuring.

But there wasn't much time to daydream now; the shop was well known, Mr Gillard was known to be an honest man, and very knowledgeable, and old customers came back year after year, seeking some trifle to give as a present. Some returned to buy an antique piece they had had their eye on for months, having decided that they might indulge their taste now, since it was Christmas.

Daisy, arranging a small display of antique toys on a cold, dark December morning, wished that she was a child again so that she might play with the Victorian dolls' house she was furnishing with all the miniature pieces which went with it. It had been a lucky find in a down-at-heel shop in Plymouth—dirty and in need of careful repair. Something she had lovingly undertaken. Now it stood in a place of honour on a small side-table, completely furnished and flanked by a cased model of a nineteenth century butcher's shop and a toy grocery shop from pre-war Germany.

All very expensive, but someone might buy them. She would have liked the dolls' house for herself; whoever bought that would need to have a very deep pocket…

Apparently Mr der Huizma had just that, for he came that very day and, after spending a considerable time examining spoons with her father, wandered over to where she was putting the finishing touches to a tin-plate carousel.

He bent to look at the dolls' house. She wished him good morning, then said in her quiet voice, 'Charming, isn't it? A little girl's dream…'

'Yes? You consider that to be so?'

'Oh, yes. Only she would have to be a careful little girl, who liked dolls.'

'Then I'll buy it, for I know exactly the little girl you think should own it.'

'You do? It's a lot of money…'

'But she is a dear child who deserves only the best.'

Daisy would have liked to have known more, but something in his voice stopped her from asking. She said merely, 'Shall I pack it up for you? I'll do it very carefully. It will take some time if you want it sent. If you do, I'll get it properly boxed.'

'No, no. I'll take it with me in the car. Can you have it ready in a few days if I call back for it?'

'Yes.'

'I shall be taking it out of the country.'

Going home for Christmas, thought Daisy, and said, 'I'll be extra careful, and I'll give you an invoice just in case Customs should want to know about it.'

He smiled at her. 'How very efficient you are, and how glad I am that I have found the house; presents for small children are always a problem.'

'Do you have several children?'

His smile widened. 'We are a large family,' he told her, and with that she had to be satisfied.

Chapter 2

Packing up the dolls' house, wrapping each tiny piece of furniture carefully in tissue paper, writing an inventory of its contents, took Daisy an entire day, and gave her ample time to reflect upon Mr der Huizma. Who exactly was he? she wondered. A man of some wealth to buy such a costly gift for a child, and a man of leisure, presumably, for he had never mentioned work of any kind. And did he live in England, or merely visit England from time to time? And if so where did he live?

Mr der Huizma, unaware of Daisy's interest in him and, truth to tell, uncaring of it, was strolling down the centre of the children's ward of a London teaching hospital. He had a toddler tucked under one arm—a small, damp grizzling boy, who had been sobbing so loudly that the only thing to do was to pick him up and comfort him as Mr der Huizma did his round. Sister was beside him, middle-aged, prematurely grey-haired and as thin as a rail. None of these things were noticed, though, for she had the disposition of an angel and very beautiful dark blue eyes.

She said now, 'He'll ruin that suit of yours, sir,' and then, when he smiled down at her, asked, 'What do you intend to do about him? He's made no progress at all.'

Mr der Huizma paused in his stride and was instantly surrounded by a posse of lesser medical lights and an earnest-faced nurse holding the case-sheets.

He hoisted the little boy higher onto his shoulder. 'Only one thing for it,' He glanced at his registrar. 'Tomorrow morning? Will you see Theatre Sister as early as possible? And let his parents know, will you? I'll talk to them this evening if they'd like to visit...'

He continued his round, unhurried, sitting on cot-sides to talk to the occupants, examining children in a leisurely fashion, giving instructions in a quiet voice. Presently he went to Sister's office and drank his coffee with her and his registrar and the two housemen. The talk was of Christmas, and plans for the ward. A tree, of course, and stockings hung on the beds and filled with suitable toys, paper chains, and mothers and fathers coming to a splendid tea.

Mr der Huizma listened to the small talk, saying little himself. He would be here on the ward on Christmas morning, after flying over from Holland in his plane very early, and would return home during the afternoon. He had done that ever since he'd taken up his appointment as senior paediatrician at the hospital, doing it without fuss, and presenting himself at the hospital in Amsterdam on the following day to join in the festivities on the children's ward there—and somehow he managed to spend time with his family too...

A few days before Christmas he called at the shop to collect the dolls' house. Daisy, absorbed in cleaning a very dirty emerald necklace—a find in someone's attic and sold to her father by its delighted owner— glanced round as he came into the shop, put down the necklace and waved a hand at the dolls' house shrouded in its wrappings.

'It's all ready. Do take care not to jog it about too much. Everything is packed tightly, but it would be awful if anything broke.'

He wished her good evening gravely, and added, 'I'll be careful. And we will unpack it and check everything before Mies sees it.'

'Mies—what a pretty name. I'm sure she will love it. How old is she?'

He didn't answer at once, and she wished she hadn't asked. 'She is five years old,' he said presently.

She wanted to ask if he had any more children, but sensed that he wasn't a man who would welcome such questions. Instead she said, 'I'll get Father to give you a hand—have you a car outside?'

When he nodded, she asked, 'Are you going back to Holland today?' She sighed without knowing it. 'Your family will be glad to see you...'

He said gravely, 'I hope so. Christmas is a time for families, is it not?' He studied her quiet face. 'And you? Do you also attend a family gathering?'

'Me? Oh, no. I mean there isn't a family—just

Mother and Father and me.' She added quickly, 'But we have a lovely Christmas.'

Mr der Huizma, thinking of his own family gathered at his home, wondered if that were true. She didn't seem a girl to hanker after bright lights, but surely Christmas spent over the shop with only her parents for company would be dull. He dismissed a vague feeling of concern for her as her father came into the shop; theirs had been a chance meeting and they were unlikely to see each other again.

He and Mr Gillard carried the dolls' house out to his car, and before he drove away he came back into the shop to thank her for her work with it, wish her a happy Christmas and bid her goodbye.

There was an air of finality about his words; Daisy knew with regret that she would not see him again.

She thought about him a good deal during Christmas. The shop was busy until the last minute of Christmas Eve, and Christmas Day was filled to the brim, with the morning ritual of opening their presents, going to church and sitting down to the traditional dinner in the late afternoon. On Boxing Day she had visited friends in the town and joined a party of them in the evening—all the same, she found time to wonder about him...

And of course on the following day the shop was open again. It was surprising what a number of ungrateful recipients of trinkets and sets of sherry glasses and china ornaments were anxious to turn them into cash. And then there was a lull. Money was scarce after Christmas, and customers were few and far between, which gave Daisy time to clean and polish and repair with her small capable hands while her father was away for a few days at an auction being held on one of the small estates in the north of the country.

He came back well satisfied; not only had he made successful bids for a fine set of silver Georgian tea caddies and a pair of George the Second sauce boats, but he had also acquired a Dutch painted and gilt leather screen, eighteenth-century and in an excellent condition—although the chinoiserie figures were almost obscured by years of ingrained dirt and dust. It had been found in one of the attics and had attracted little attention. He had paid rather more than he could afford for it, and there was always the chance that it would stay in the shop, unsold and representing a considerable loss to him. But on the other hand he might sell it advantageously…

It fell to Daisy's lot to clean and restore it to a pristine state, something which took days of patient work. It was a slow business, and she had ample opportunity to think. It was surprising how often her thoughts dwelt on Mr der Huizma, which, considering she wasn't going to see him again, seemed a great waste of time.

It was towards the end of January, with the screen finished and business getting brisker, when two elderly men came into the shop. They greeted her with courtesy, and a request that they might look around the shop, and wandered to and fro at some length, murmuring to each other, stooping down to admire some trifle which had caught their eye. Daisy, whose ears were sharp, decided that they were murmuring in a foreign language. But they spoke English well enough when her father came into the shop, passing the time of day with him as they continued their leisurely progress.

They stopped abruptly when they saw the screen, right at the back of the shop. For two calm, elderly gentlemen they exhibited a sudden interest tinged with excitement. There was no need for her father to describe it to them; it seemed that they knew as much about it as he did, possibly more. They examined it at length and with great care, asked its price, and without further argument took out a chequebook.

'I must explain,' said one gentleman, and Daisy edged nearer so as not to miss a word. 'This screen— you tell me that you bought it at an auction at the Kings Poulton estate? I must tell you that an ancestress of ours married a member of the family in the eighteenth century and brought this screen with her as part of her dowry. It was made especially for her. You will have seen the initials at the edge of the border—her initials. When we were last in England we enquired about it but were told that it had been destroyed in the fire they had some years ago. You can imagine our delight in discovering that it is safe—and in such splendid condition.'

'You must thank my daughter for that,' said Mr Gillard. 'It was in a shocking state.'

The three of them turned and looked at her. She smiled nicely at them, for the two elderly gentlemen were friendly, and she was intrigued by the screen's history and the chance discovery they had made of it. 'It is very beautiful,' she said. 'I don't know where you live, but you'll need to be very careful with it; it's fragile...'

'It must return, of course, to our home in Holland—

near Amsterdam. And we can assure you, young lady, that it will be transported with great care.'

'In a van, properly packed,' said Daisy.

The elder of the two gentlemen, the one with the forbidding nose and flowing moustache, said meekly, 'Most certainly, and with a reliable courier.' He paused, and then exchanged a look with his companion.

'Perhaps you would undertake the task of bringing the screen to Holland, young lady? Since you have restored it you will know best how it should be handled, and possibly you will remain for a brief period to ensure that no harm has come to it on the journey.'

'Me?' Daisy sounded doubtful. 'Well, of course I'd love to do that, but I'm not an expert, or qualified or anything like that.'

'But you would do this if we ask you?'

She glanced at her father.

'A good idea, Daisy, and you are perfectly capable of doing it. You'll need a day for travelling, and another day for the return journey, and a day or two to check that everything is as it should be.'

'Very well, I'll be glad to do that. I'll need a couple of days in which to pack the screen…'

The moustached gentleman offered a hand. 'Thank you. If we may return in the morning and discuss the details? I am Heer van der Breek.'

Daisy took the hand. 'Daisy Gillard. I'm glad you found your screen.'

His companion shook hands too, and then they bade her father goodbye.

When they had gone, Daisy said, 'You're sure I can do it? I can't speak Dutch, Father.'

'No problem, and of course you can do it, a sensible girl like you, my dear. Besides, while you're there you can go to Heer Friske's shop in Amsterdam—remember he wrote and told me that he had a Georgian wine cooler I might be interested in? Colonel Gibbs has been wanting one, and if you think it's a genuine piece you might buy it and bring it back with you.'

'Where will I stay?' asked the practical Daisy.

'Oh, there must be plenty of small hotels—he will probably know of one.'

It was surprising how quickly matters were arranged. In rather less than a week Daisy found herself sitting beside the driver of the small van housing the screen on her way to Holland. She had money, her passport, and directions in her handbag, a travelling bag stuffed with everything necessary for a few days' stay in that country, and all the documents necessary for a trouble-free journey. She was to stay at Meneer van der Breek's house and oversee the unpacking of the screen and its installation, and from there she was to go to Amsterdam and present herself at Mijnheer Friske's shop. A small hotel close by had been found for her and she was to stay as long as it was necessary. Two or three days should be sufficient, her father had told her.

Excited under her calm exterior, Daisy settled back to enjoy her trip. Her companion was of a friendly disposition, pleased to have company, and before long she was listening with a sympathetic ear to his disappointment at missing his eldest daughter's birthday. 'Though I'll buy her something smashing in Amsterdam,' he assured her. 'This kind of job is too well paid to refuse.'

They crossed on the overnight ferry, and since Mijnheer van der Breek had made all the arrangements for their journey it went without a hitch and in comfort.

It was raining when they disembarked in the early morning, and Daisy, looking around her, reflected that this flat and damp landscape wasn't at all what she had expected. But presently there was a watery winter sun, and the built-up areas were left behind. They stopped for coffee, and then drove on.

'Loenen aan de Vecht,' said the driver. 'The other side of Amsterdam on the way to Utrecht. Not far now—we turn off the motorway soon.'

He bypassed Amsterdam and emerged into quiet countryside, and presently onto a country road running beside a river. 'The Vecht,' said Daisy, poring over the map.

It was a delightful road, tree-lined, with here and there a pleasant house tucked away. On the opposite bank there were more houses—rather grand gentlemen's residences, with sweeping lawns bordering the water and surrounded by trees and shrubs.

Before long they came to a bridge and crossed it.

'Is it here?' asked Daisy. 'One of these houses? They're rather splendid…'

They turned in through wrought-iron gates and drew up before an imposing doorway reached by stone steps. There were rows of orderly windows with heavy shutters and gabled roofs above the house's solid face, and an enormous bell-pull beside the door. Daisy got out and looked around her with knowledgeable eyes. Seventeenth-century, she guessed, and probably older than that round the back.

The driver had got out too and rung the bell; they could hear its sonorous clanging somewhere in the depths of the house. Presently the door was opened by a stout man, and Daisy handed over the letter Mijnheer van der Breek had given her in England.

Invited to step inside, she did so, prudently asking the driver to stay with the van, and was led down a long, gloomy hall to big double doors at its end. The stout man flung them open and crossed the large and equally gloomy apartment to where Mijnheer van der Breek sat. He handed him the letter and waved Daisy forward.

Mijnheer van der Breek got up, shook hands with her and asked, 'You have the screen? Splendid. It is unfortunate that my brother is indisposed, otherwise he would have shared my pleasure at your arrival.'

'It's outside in the van,' said Daisy. 'If you would tell me where you want it put the driver and I will see to it.'

'No, no, young lady. Cor shall help the man. Although you must supervise its removal, of course. We have decided that we want it in the salon. When it has been brought there I will come personally and say where it is to go.'

Daisy would have liked five minutes' leisure, preferably with a pot of tea, but it seemed that she wasn't to get it. She went back to the van, this time with Cor, and watched while the men took the screen from the van and carried it carefully into the house. More double doors on one side of the hall had been opened, and she followed them into the room beyond. It was large and lofty, with tall narrow windows heavily swathed in crimson velvet curtains. The furniture was antique,

but not of a period which Daisy cared for—dark and
heavy and vaguely Teutonic. But, she had to admit, a
good background for the screen.

Time was taken in getting the screen just so, and
she finally heard Mijnheer van der Breek's satisfied
approval. What was more, he told her that she might
postpone unwrapping it and examining it until after
they had had luncheon. It was only after he had seen
his treasure safely disposed that he sent for his housekeeper to show Daisy her room.

Daisy bade the driver goodbye, reminded him to
drive carefully and to let her father know that they
had arrived safely, and followed the imposing bulk of
the housekeeper up the elaborately carved staircase.

She was led away from the gallery above and down
a small passage, down a pair of steps, along another
passage, and then finally into a room at the corner
of the house with windows in two walls, a lofty ceiling and a canopied bed. The floor was polished wood,
with thick rugs here and there. A small table with two
chairs drawn up to it was in one corner of the room,
and there was a pier table with a marble top holding
a Dutch marquetry toilet mirror flanked by a pair of
ugly but valuable Imari vases. The room was indeed
a treasure house of antiques, although none to her liking. But the adjoining bathroom won her instant approval. She tidied her hair, did her face and found her
way downstairs, hopeful of lunch.

It was eaten in yet another room, somewhat smaller
than the others, but splendidly furnished, the table laid
with damask cloth and a good deal of very beautiful

silver and china. A pity that the meal didn't live up to
its opulent surroundings.

'A light lunch at midday,' explained Mijnheer van
der Breek, and indeed it was. A spoonful or two of
clear soup, a dish of cold meats, another of cheeses,
and a basket of rolls, partaken of so sparingly by her
host that she felt unable to satisfy her appetite. But the
coffee was delicious.

Probably dinner would be a more substantial meal,
hoped Daisy, rising from the table with her host and,
since he expected it of her, going to examine the screen.

She spent the afternoon carefully checking every
inch of the screen; removing every speck of dust, making sure that the light wasn't too strong for it, making
sure that the gilt wasn't damaged. She hardly noticed
the time passing, and she stopped thankfully when the
housekeeper brought her a small tray of tea. She worked
on then, until she was warned that dinner would be at
seven o'clock. She went to her room and changed into a
plain brown jersey dress which did nothing to improve
her appearance but which didn't crease when packed…

Both elderly gentlemen were at dinner, so that she
was kept busy answering their questions during the
meal—a substantial one, she was glad to find; pork
cutlets with cooked beetroot, braised chicory and large
floury potatoes smothered in butter. Pudding was a
kind of blancmange with a fruit sauce. Good solid fare.
Either the gentlemen didn't have a good cook or they
had no fancy for more elaborate cooking. But once
again the coffee was delicious. Over it they discussed
her departure.

'Perhaps tomorrow afternoon?' suggested Mijnheer

van der Breek, and glanced at his brother, who nodded. 'You will be driven to Amsterdam,' she was told. 'We understand that you have an errand there for your father. We are most grateful for your help in bringing the screen to us, but I am sure that you would wish to fulfil your commission and return home as soon as possible.'

Daisy smiled politely and reflected that, much as she loved her home, it was delightful to be on her own in a strange country. She would see as much of Amsterdam as possible while she was there. She would phone her father as soon as she could and ask him if she might stay another day there—there were museums she dearly wanted to see…

She was driven to Amsterdam the next day by the stout man in an elderly and beautifully maintained Daimler. The hotel her father had chosen for her was small and welcoming, down a small side-street criss-crossed by canals. The proprietor spoke English, and led her up a steep staircase to a small room overlooking the street. He reminded her that the evening meal was at six o'clock, then went back to his cubby-hole by the entrance.

It was a gloomy afternoon, already turned to dusk. Too late to visit Heer Friske's shop, so Daisy contented herself with tidying her person, unpacking her few clothes and then sitting down in the overstuffed chair by the window to study a map of the city. Complicated, she decided, as she found the small square where Heer Friske had his shop. But she had all day before her on the morrow and, since her father had had no objection to her staying for a second day, she would have a whole further day sightseeing before going back on the night ferry.

She went downstairs presently, to the small dining room in the basement, and found a dozen other people there, all of them Dutch. They greeted her kindly and, being a friendly girl by nature, she enjoyed her meal. Soup, pork chops with ample potatoes and vegetables, and a custard for pudding. Simple, compared with the fare at Mijnheer van der Breek's house, but much more sustaining...

She slept well, ate her breakfast of rolls and cheese and cold meat, drank several cups of coffee and, thus fortified, started off for Heer Friske's shop. The hotel didn't provide lunch, and in any case she didn't intend to return before the late afternoon. As she started to pick her way through the various streets she saw plenty of small coffee shops where she would be able to get a midday snack.

She missed her way several times, but, being a sensible girl, she didn't get flustered. All the same, she was glad when she reached the shop. It was small and old and the window was crammed with small antiques. She spent a minute or two studying them before she entered the shop. It was dark inside, lighted by rather feeble wall-lights, and extended back into even deeper gloom. The whole place was crowded with antiques. Daisy made her way carefully towards the old man sitting at a desk in the middle of it all.

She said, 'Good morning,' and offered a hand, guessing quite rightly that he wasn't the kind of man who would waste time on unnecessary chat, for he barely glanced at her before resuming the polishing of a rather fine silver coffee pot.

'Daisy Gillard,' said Daisy clearly. 'You told my father that you had a Georgian wine cooler. May I see it, please?'

Heer Friske found his voice and spoke in strongly accented English. 'You are here to buy it? You are capable?'

'My father thinks so.'

He got up slowly and led her further into the shop, where the wine cooler stood on top of a solid table. He didn't say anything, but stood back while she examined it. It was a splendid specimen, in good condition and genuine. 'How much?' asked Daisy.

His price was too high, but she had expected that. It took half an hour's bargaining over several cups of coffee before they reached an amount which pleased them both. Daisy made out a Eurocheque, said that she would return on the following day to make arrangements to convey the unwieldy cooler to the station, and took her leave, pleased with herself and happy to have the rest of the day in which to do exactly what she liked.

By the time she got back to the hotel in the late afternoon she was tired but content; she had crammed the Rijksmuseum, two churches, Anne Frank's house and a canal trip into her time, stopping only for a brief while to consume a *kaas broodje* and a cup of coffee.

At dinner she told her companions where she had been and they nodded approval, pointing out that the evening was when she should take the opportunity of walking to the Leidesplein to get a glimpse of the brightly lighted square with its cafés and hotels and cheerful crowds.

Daisy, a cock-a-hoop over her successful day, decided that she would do just that. It was no distance, and although it was a chilly night, with a sparkling frost, there was a moon and plenty of people around. She found her way to the Leidesplein easily enough, had a cup of coffee at a street stall while she watched the evening crowds, and then started back to the hotel.

However, somehow she mistook her way, and, turning round to check where she had come from, took unguarded steps backwards and fell into a canal.

She came to the surface of the icy water and her first thought was thankfulness that she hadn't had anything valuable about her person; the second was a flash of panic. The water wasn't just cold, it smelled awful— and tasted worse. There were probably rats... She opened her mouth and bawled for help and swam, very hampered by her clothes, to the canal bank. Slippery stones, too steep for her to scramble up. She bawled again, and, miracle of miracles, a firm hand caught her shoulder while a second grabbed her other arm, almost wrenching it from its socket. She was heaved onto the street with no more ado.

'Not hurt?' asked her rescuer.

'Ugh,' said Daisy, and was thankfully sick, half kneeling on the cobbles.

'Only very wet and—er, strong-smelling,' added a voice she knew.

He bent and set her on her feet. 'Come with me and we'll get you cleaned up.'

'Mr der Huizma,' said Daisy. 'Oh, it would be you,

wouldn't it?' she added wildly. It was nice to have been rescued, but why couldn't it have been by a stranger? Why did it have to be someone who, if he'd remembered her at all, would have thought of her as a quiet, well-mannered girl with a knowledge of antiques and a liking for walks by the sea. Now it would be as a silly, careless fool.

'Indeed it is I.' He had her by the arm. 'Across this bridge is the hospital where I work. They will soon have you clean and dry again. You didn't lose anything in the canal?'

'No. I didn't have more than a few *gulden* with me. I only turned round to see where I was...'

'Of course,' agreed Mr der Huizma gravely, 'a perfectly natural thing to do. This way.'

The hospital was indeed close by. He led her, squelching and dripping, into the Casualty entrance and handed her over to a large bony woman who clucked sympathetically and led Daisy away before she had time to utter a word of thanks to Mr der Huizma. Her clothes were taken from her, she was put under a hot shower, her hair was washed and she was given injections. The sister, who spoke good English, smiled at her. 'Rats,' she said, plunging in the needle. 'A precaution.'

She was given hot coffee, wrapped in a hospital gown several sizes too large and a thick blanket, and sat on a chair in one of the cubicles. She felt quite restored in her person, but her mind was in a fine jumble. She had no clothes; her own had been taken away, but even if they were washed they would never be dry enough, and how was she to get back to the hotel? No one had asked her that yet. She rubbed her long mousy hair dry and began to worry.

The cubicle curtains were parted and Sister appeared; looming beside her was Mr der Huizma. Daisy stared up at them from the depths of her blanket.

'My clothes? If I could have…?'

Sister interrupted her in a kind, forceful voice. 'Mr der Huizma will take you back to your hotel and explain what has happened. Perhaps you would be good enough to bring back the blanket, slippers and gown in the morning?'

'Oh! Well, thank you. I'm a great nuisance, I'm afraid. Shall I take my clothes with me?'

'No, no. They are being washed and disinfected. You may collect them in the morning.'

Daisy avoided the doctor's eye. 'I'm sorry I've been so tiresome. I'm very grateful…'

Sister smiled. 'It is a common happening that people— and cars—should fall in the canals. You will come to no harm, I think.'

Mr der Huizma spoke. 'Shall we go, Miss Gillard?'

So Daisy, much hampered by the blanket and the too-large slippers, trotted beside him, out of the hospital, and was shoved neatly into the dark grey Rolls Royce outside.

It was a short drive, and beyond expressing the polite hope that she would enjoy the rest of her stay in Amsterdam, he had nothing to say. And as for Daisy, it seemed to her it was hardly the occasion for casual conversation.

At the hotel he ushered her across the narrow pavement and into the foyer, where he engaged the proprietor in a brief conversation, not a word of which Daisy could understand. But presently he turned to her, expressed the hope that she was none the worse for her ducking, and bade her goodbye.

Daisy, at a disadvantage because of the blanket, thanked him again, untangled a hand from the blanket and offered it. His large, cool hand felt strangely comforting.

The next morning, her normal, neatly dressed self, not a hair out of place, she took a taxi to the hospital, handed over the blanket, the gown and the slippers in exchange for her own clothes, and made a short speech of thanks to Sister, who nodded and smiled, wished her a happy day and a safe return home and warned her to be careful.

There was no sign of Mr der Huizma, and there was no reason why there should have been; he was obviously a senior member of his profession who probably only went to Casualty when his skills were required. All the same, Daisy lingered for as long as possible in the hope of seeing him.

Mijnheer Friske had the wine cooler packed up ready for her to take. She arranged to collect it that evening, when she went to get her train to the Hoek. It would be unwieldy, but no heavier than a big suitcase, and there would be porters and her father had said that he would see that she was met at Harwich. She assured Heer Friske that she would be back in good time, checked the contents of her handbag—ticket, passport, money and all the impedimenta necessary for her journey—and set off to spend the rest of the day window shopping, exploring the city and buying one or two small gifts.

Being a girl of common sense, she left her clothes, including those the hospital had returned to her, with the kindly Heer Friske, taking only her coat with her which she presently left at a dry cleaners to be collected later. Everything was going very smoothly, and she intended to enjoy her day.

And she did, cramming in as much as possible; another museum, a church or two, antique shops, browsing round the Bijnenkorf looking for presents.

It was late afternoon, after a cup of tea and an elaborate cream cake, when she started on her way back to Heer Friske's shop.

She walked through the narrow streets, thinking about her stay in Holland—a very enjoyable one, despite the ducking in a canal that had been the means of meeting Mr der Huizma again. Not quite the meeting she would have chosen. Aware of her lack of looks, she was sure that a soaking in canal water had done little to improve them. And there was nothing glamorous about a hospital blanket.

She was almost at Heer Friske's shop, walking down a narrow quiet street with no one to be seen, the houses lining it with doors and windows shut, when she was suddenly aware of danger. Too late, unfortunately. Someone snatched her handbag, and when she struggled to get it back someone else knocked her down. She hit the cobbles with a thump, was aware of a sudden terrible pain in her head, and was thankfully unconscious.

The two men disappeared as swiftly and silently as they had appeared. It was ten minutes or so before a man on a bicycle found her, and another ten minutes before an ambulance arrived to take her to hospital.

Chapter 3

Mr der Huizma, leaving the hospital in the early morning after operating on a small baby with intus-susception, met Casualty Sister in the foyer, also on her way home. He paused to wish her good morning, for they had known each other for some years, and enquired after her night.

'Busy—as busy as you, sir. By the way, the English girl is back…'

He paused in his stride. 'She was to return to England last night. What has happened to her?'

'Mugged. She was brought in about five o'clock. Concussion. No identification, of course—they took everything. They traced her name from the admissions book and notified the hotel. The proprietor couldn't give much information, only that she had paid her bill and intended to leave for England that evening.'

Mr der Huizma sighed and turned on his heel. 'Perhaps I can be of some assistance. Her father must be told…'

The sister of the ward to which Daisy had been taken was in her office. She got up as he came in. 'The English girl—we have tried to telephone her family but there was no reply…she is still unconscious, sir. You would wish to see her? Dr Brem is with her now.'

Daisy looked very neat lying in bed. Her hair had been plaited and lay on her pillow; her arms were neatly arranged on the coverlet. She was rather pale, and now and again she frowned.

Mr der Huizma nodded to his colleague. 'No fracture? No brain damage?'

'Not as far as we can see. Rather a deep concussion, but all her reflexes are normal. You've seen Sister?'

'Yes.' Mr der Huizma bent over the bed. 'Daisy, Daisy, can you hear me?'

The frown deepened, but she didn't open her eyes. She mumbled, 'Go away, I'm asleep.' And then added, 'My head aches.'

Mr der Huizma took a hand in his. 'My poor dear. You shall have something for that at once, and when you wake up you will feel better.'

He spoke very softly. 'Is your father meeting you at Harwich?'

'How else am I to get the wine cooler halfway across England? Go away.'

Which he did, to retire to Sister's office and pick up the phone.

Her father, waiting patiently for the ferry to dock, was surprised to hear his name on the loudspeaker. 'A phone call from Holland,' he was told, and was ushered into a small office to take it.

'Daisy?'

'Jules der Huizma, Mr Gillard. Daisy has had an accident. She is not seriously hurt but she has a concussion. I have just come from her bedside and she has regained consciousness. She is being well cared for and I can assure you that you have no need for anxiety. She will be kept in hospital for a few days and I will personally arrange her return to you.'

'How did it happen?'

'She was mugged. Her handbag was taken, so it will be necessary for her to obtain a new passport and money. Someone will give her assistance with this.'

'Should I come over? Or my wife?'

'There is no need, unless you have a strong wish to do so. She must be kept quiet for a few days, and you would only be allowed to visit her for a brief period. I will phone you each day and let you know how she is getting on. One other thing—she spoke of a wine cooler. Is this something which can be dealt with?'

'Yes, yes. Heer Friske… I'll explain…'

When he'd finished, Mr der Huizma said, 'I'll see to the matter for you,' before bidding him a civil goodbye.

He went home then, wondering why he had saddled himself with offers of help to a comparative stranger. Heaven knew his days were busy enough, without hunting wine coolers and the self-imposed task of phoning Daisy's father each evening. He let himself into the tall narrow house which was his home, climbed the carved staircase at the end of the narrow hall, showered and dressed and went down to his breakfast.

He was met in his dining room by an elderly man, thin and stooping, with a severe expression, who wished him good morning and observed in accusing accents that Mr der Huizma had been out half the night again. 'It's not right,' he grumbled, 'having you out at all hours, and you an important man.'

Mr der Huizma, looking through his post, made light of it.

'It's my job, Joop, and I enjoy it.' He smiled at him. 'I'm famished...'

He had a busy day ahead of him, with no time to think about Daisy, but in the early evening on his way out of the hospital he went to see her.

She was having long periods of consciousness, Sister told him, and had obediently drunk the variety of beverages offered her. She had spoken very little.

'She seems worried about something called a wine cooler.'

'Ah, yes, that is something I can deal with on my way home. I'd like to see her for a few minutes if that is convenient?'

Sister beamed at him—such a nice man, and always so courteous and thoughtful. She led the way to Daisy's bed and, being a sentimental woman, thought how charming she looked lying there quietly, her hair in a neat plait, her pale face devoid of make-up. She glanced at Mr der Huizma, wondering if he thought the same. He might be engaged to marry, but surely his heart would be touched...

Mr der Huizma, his heart quite untouched, looked

down at Daisy with a professional eye. Dr Brem had assured him that she was doing nicely. A few days in bed and she would be perfectly fit.

And Daisy, looking back at him, could see that his look was wholly professional, not the friendly look of the nice man she had walked with on the beach at home. She said politely, 'Good evening, Mr der Huizma. I am quite recovered.'

'In a few more days,' he cautioned her. 'I am going to see Heer Friske this evening. Is there anything you wish me to say to him?'

'That's very kind of you. I expect he may be wondering why I haven't been to collect the wine cooler and my things. Would you please tell him that I'll come in a few days' time and get it, and take it home with me.'

'An awkward thing to travel with, surely?'

'Well, a bit, but I'll manage. Thank you for going to see him.' She frowned. 'How did you know about it?'

'Your father told me. I phoned to tell him that you were delayed and the reason for it.'

'Thank you. I'm sorry to be such a nuisance.'

'It is no trouble. I'm glad to see that you have recovered so well.' He smiled then. 'Sleep well.'

He turned away and then paused. 'I should have told you at once. Your mother and father know that you are quite safe and in good hands; they send their love. They would have come here but I said that there was no need, that you would be home again in a few days.'

When he had gone, Daisy closed her eyes and went over their conversation. It had been brief, impersonal, and he had been impatient under his perfect bedside manner. Probably he considered her a nuisance and

would be glad to see the last of her. Her spirits, already
at their lowest, sank without trace, and two tears rolled
slowly down her cheeks. Before she could wipe them
away Sister was by her bed, on her evening round.

'Daisy? In tears? Has Mr der Huizma upset you?'

'No, no. He's been most kind.' Daisy managed a
smile. 'I've got a little headache…'

She swallowed tablets, drank a warm drink, assured
everyone that she felt perfectly all right and closed her
eyes. She didn't think she would sleep, but if she kept
them shut Sister would report to the night staff that she
was asleep. They were all so kind… It would be nice
to be home again, and when she was she would forget
Mr der Huizma.

Satisfactory arrangements having been made with
Heer Friske, Mr der Huizma went home, remembering
with a twinge of annoyance that he was dining with
friends that evening and that his future bride would
expect him to call for her so that they might arrive together. Before then he had a good deal to do; the post
to read, phone calls to make, patients' notes to study.

He went to his study, closely followed by Joop with
a tray of coffee and a small dog of nondescript appearance. He thanked Joop for the coffee, received delighted
greetings from the dog and sat down behind his desk.

There were biscuits on the tray, which he offered the
dog while he drank his coffee. 'I have to go out this
evening, Bouncer. I do not particularly wish to do so.
I am coming to the conclusion that I am not a socially
minded man. When I return we will have a pleasant
walk before bed.'

Bouncer hung out his tongue and panted, ate the last of the biscuits and made himself comfortable on his master's feet. He was a unique specimen of dog, as Mr der Huizma frequently told his friends. Long and thin in body, and covered with a silky coat, he possessed short legs and large ears. He had beautiful amber eyes and the heart of a lion. And he loved his master with an undemanding devotion. He closed his eyes now and dozed while Mr der Huizma opened the first of his letters.

Presently he got up and went through the house to let Bouncer out into the narrow walled garden behind it. It was a cold night, but the sky was clear and there was a frost. Walking up and down its length while Bouncer raced to and fro, Mr der Huizma found himself thinking of his walk along the shore in England. Daisy had been a good companion, saying little and when she did talking sense. He sighed for no reason at all, whistled to Bouncer, and went to dress for the evening.

Helene van Tromp, the lady who had every intention of marrying him, lived with her parents in a vast flat in the Churchillaan. She was hardly in the first flush of youth, being only a year or so younger than Mr der Huizma—and he had turned thirty-five—but she was considered a handsome woman by her friends; very fair, with large blue eyes, regular features and a fashionably slender figure, kept so, as only her dearest friends knew, by constant visits to her gym instructor and the beauty parlour. She was always exquisitely dressed, with never a hair out of place, and Mr der Huizma, arriving at her home, was given a cheek to kiss and told not to disarrange her hair.

'You're late,' she told him. 'I had hoped that we might have had a talk with Mother and Father; you see them so seldom.' She smiled enchantingly at him. 'Of course when we are married we shall be able to spend more time with them…'

'I shall be just as busy then as I am now,' he pointed out.

She gave a little laugh. 'Don't be silly, Jules. You can give up all that hospital work once we're married and build up your private practice. We shall have time and leisure to see more of our friends.'

Mr der Huizma thought privately that that was the last thing he wished to do; he had friends of his own, sober, married men with families and comfortable wives, as involved in their work as he was in his. He didn't particularly like Helene's friends, although he had done his best to do so, and he had thought in a vague way that once they were married she would take an interest in his friends and his work. It struck him forcibly now that that didn't seem likely. It seemed hardly the time to argue about it; he made his polite goodbyes to Helene's parents and drove with her to the dinner party.

'A wasted evening,' he told the faithful Bouncer much later, walking with him round the quiet streets near his house. There must be something wrong with him, since he had been unable to enjoy the light-hearted dinner table talk. Some of it had been malicious, and some of it had sparkled with wit, but no one there had said anything which meant anything. To be amused and amusing was all that was required.

It was some time later, as he was on his way up to

bed, that he paused on the staircase to wonder why he had wanted to marry Helene and if he had ever been in love with her. It was a sobering thought to take to his bed. It should have kept him awake, but he was a tired man, and strangely enough it was Daisy's face which imposed itself upon his last waking moments.

Two days later Dr Brem pronounced Daisy fit to go home, and, meeting Mr der Huizma on his way into the hospital, told him.

'Not immediately?'

'No, no. She has arrangements to make, of course, but her new passport came today and she has received money for her journey. Another couple of days, I should think. You're going to see her again?'

'Yes. I'm off to Utrecht this evening, but I'll be back before she leaves.'

'Nice little thing,' said Dr Brem. 'We shall miss her—been no trouble at all.'

Daisy, setting about the business of getting herself and the wine cooler back home, wondered if Mr der Huizma would come to see her again. By the end of the following day, all ready to leave the next morning, she had to admit that he wasn't coming. She had told Sister that she had arranged to leave on the night ferry, and when that lady had wanted to know where she intended to spend her day until then had said, not quite truthfully, that she would be with a friend of her father's.

'Well, take care,' said Sister the next day, and shook hands briskly. After all, Daisy was a grown woman, and able to look after herself—despite her regrettable way of encountering accidents.

Ten minutes after Daisy left the hospital, Mr der Huizma parked his car in its forecourt, went to have a word with his registrar and then to see Daisy.

'She left not half an hour ago,' Sister told him. 'Dr Brem told her she could go home, though he advised her to stay another day or two. But she had everything arranged within a day—said she wanted to get back to England. She's going over on the night ferry.'

'It's only eleven o'clock in the morning,' Mr der Huizma pointed out.

'Yes, I know. I asked her what she intended doing all day and she said she would spend it with a friend of her father's.'

Mr der Huizma had a moment's regret for the pleasant free day he had planned for himself. Daisy would most certainly go to collect the wretched wine cooler, and he had a fleeting vision of her transporting it and herself back to England. And probably having another accident...

When he went into Heer Friske's shop, he was standing on one side of the wine cooler, now wrapped in sacking and stout cardboard, and Daisy was on the other side. They both looked round as he went in. Heer Friske said nothing, but Daisy said, 'Oh', in an annoyed voice.

Undeterred by this cool reception, Mr der Huizma crossed the small shop to join them.

'Wondering what on earth to do with it?' he asked cheerfully.

Daisy shot him a cold look. 'Certainly not. All my arrangements are made.'

Mr der Huizma glanced at Heer Friske, who

shrugged his shoulders. 'Miss Gillard is happy to take the wine cooler with her—who am I to stop her?'

Mr der Huizma smiled a little. 'I am travelling to England by the midnight ferry from the Hoek,' he said smoothly. 'I shall be happy to take Miss Gillard and the wine cooler in the car with me.'

'Quite unnecessary,' said Daisy quickly. 'Thank you all the same. I'm quite able to travel as I have already planned.'

'Oh, I'm sure of that. I have no doubt you are capable of doing anything you wish, but why be pig-headed about it? It's of no consequence to me if you come or not; I'm merely making a practical suggestion.'

He didn't wait for her answer. While she was seeking one he nodded again at Heer Friske, who picked up the wine cooler and carried it out of the shop.

'Where is he taking it?'

Daisy started after him, but somehow Mr der Huizma was in the way.

'To my car. Be sensible, Daisy.'

'That's all very well, but I don't know where you're taking it.'

'We will take it to my house, where you will remain as my guest until it is time to leave for the ferry.' He sounded so reasonable.

'Indeed I won't,' said Daisy roundly. 'Whatever next? You must have no wish to have me as a guest, and what about your wife…?'

'I am not married,' said Mr der Huizma mildly, 'and I can't think why you should imagine that I don't want you as a guest. I don't remember ever saying so.'

He uttered this in such matter-of-fact tones that she believed him. 'Well, it's very kind of you.'

'Not at all. We will go to my home now, and if you wish to spend the day shopping or sightseeing, feel free to do so. Although perhaps it would be sensible if you were to lunch with me so that we can discuss the journey. We shall need to leave soon after eight o'clock this evening.'

She found herself on the pavement outside the shop, watching Heer Friske stowing the wine cooler and her suitcase in the boot of the Rolls, and presently, after suitable goodbyes had been exchanged she was in the car, sitting beside a silent Mr der Huizma.

It wasn't an unpleasant silence, rather she found it reassuring, so that she allowed her thoughts to simmer gently without bothering her too much. It had all happened rather quickly, and soon she would probably have second thoughts, but of course by then it would be too late to do anything. Besides, the wine cooler was in the car, and getting it out again would present a problem even if she decided to change her mind. Upon rather dreamy reflection about this, she decided that it would be foolish to do that.

Mr der Huizma drew up before his house, got out of the car and opened her door. She stood for a moment on the pavement and looked up at it. It was very old, in a row of old houses each with a different gable, their windows gleaming, their paintwork pristine. She mounted the stone steps beside him and the heavy old door with its handsome transom was opened as they reached it.

Mr der Huizma, who usually let himself into his home, hid a smile. He bade Joop good morning in his own language and turned to Daisy. 'This is Joop, who runs my home with his wife, Jette. He speaks English, and if I am not around he will help you in any way.

'Miss Gillard will be travelling over to England with me this evening, Joop. On the night ferry.'

Joop's severe expression didn't alter. 'Very good, *mijnheer*. I will bring coffee to the drawing room. If Miss Gillard would like to come with me, I will fetch Jette.'

Mr der Huizma had picked up a pile of letters from the console table against one wall and was leafing through them. 'Yes, do that, Joop.' He nodded at Daisy. 'See you in five minutes or so, Daisy. Joop will show you where to go.'

Daisy was handed over to a stout middle-aged woman with a round cheerful face and small dark eyes who trotted her off to a cloakroom tucked away at the end of a long hallway, smiled and nodded, and shut the door on her. Daisy tidied her already tidy person, peered for a brief moment in the mirror and decided that she looked plainer than usual, then went into the hall again to find Jette waiting for her. She in turn handed her over to Joop, who led the way back down the hall to a pair of splendid double doors which he opened with all the pomp one would have expected for the entrance of the fairy queen.

Daisy slipped past him and stood for a moment looking around her. The room appeared empty except for a small, unusual-looking dog who came to meet her, looking pleased.

Daisy stooped to pat him. 'What a splendid fellow you are,' she told him, and advanced a few steps into the room. It was large and high ceilinged, with two tall windows draped in claret velvet curtains. There was a scattering of comfortable chairs and small tables, a very beautiful rent table between the windows, and two display cabinets on either side of the great fireplace. Daisy, her small nose twitching with interest, took a few more steps.

'Eighteen-century marquetry and in perfect condition,' she informed the dog.

She squeaked with surprise when Mr der Huizma observed, 'Quite right. Rather nice, aren't they?'

He had been standing in a doorway at the end of the room, watching her, and added, 'I see Bouncer has made friends. You like dogs?'

'Yes, yes, I do. I'm sorry—I didn't mean to pry.'

'Hardly that, surely. Now if you had opened one of the cabinets and taken out some of the contents I might possibly have taken umbrage.'

Daisy said. 'You speak such good English. I mean, you use words which quite a few English people don't often use.'

'Thank you, Daisy. That is probably because I'm a Dutchman. Here's Joop with the coffee. Come and sit over here and decide what you wish to do with your day.'

'Don't you have to work?'

She chose a small armchair covered in tapestry and Bouncer came and sat at her feet.

'No. I have been in Utrecht. Now I have a day or so free.'

She poured coffee from a very beautiful little silver coffee pot. Early eighteenth century? she thought. And the cups and saucers—fine, paper-thin porcelain. She handled them delicately and supposed it would be rude if she were to ask about them.

'The coffee pot is 1625 and the cups and saucers are later—around seventeen-hundred.'

'They're very lovely. Are you not afraid of breaking them?'

'No. They are in constant use. Jette doesn't allow anyone else to wash them but herself.'

'So many people hide their treasures away in cupboards…'

'In which case they might just as well be smashed. Have one of these biscuits—Jette is a splendid cook.'

Daisy drank the delicious coffee and ate the biscuits. She felt that she should be feeling awkward or annoyed at having her plans changed so ruthlessly—or even shy…but she felt remarkably at ease. In fact, she was enjoying herself…

Presently Mr der Huizma begged to be excused while he saw to his letters and made some phone calls. 'If you don't wish to go out, feel free to do what you want here. There's a library across the hall, with books and papers and magazines, and if you would like, Joop will show you the door into the garden.'

'A garden? Here behind the house? I'd like to see it, if it's not a bother.'

'Joop shall take you to the garden door.'

She was led through a narrow door beside the staircase, down a couple of steps and along a paved passage. The house went back a long way from the street, with windows in the oddest places. When Joop opened the door onto the garden she could see that although it was narrow it was a good length. Beautifully laid out, too, with narrow brick paths on either side of a small lawn and on either side of the paths flowerbeds backing onto high brick walls. She walked down to the end and found a little arbour and a small pond with a fountain—not running water, of course. The pond was sheltered by a trellis of roses.

In summer it would be a delightful place in which to sit and do nothing, reflected Daisy, and despite the chilly day she sat down in the arbour. This was a lovely house. She corrected herself—a lovely home. A grand house, splendidly furnished, but lived in and loved. When Mr der Huizma married—and of course he would—his wife would be the happiest woman on earth. Daisy, quite carried away, started to daydream aloud.

'Fancy sitting here on a summer's day. There would be a baby in a pram, and two or three children running around, and Bouncer, and perhaps a cat and kittens...'

Mr der Huizma, pausing on the path to listen to this, observed mildly, 'It sounds delightful, but surely rather crowded?'

Daisy felt a fool. 'I was just pretending. Don't you ever pretend?'

'Not enough. I must cultivate the habit. Do you like my garden?'

'It's perfect.'

'Come with me; I'll show you something.' He took her to an ancient door in the end wall, drew its bolts, turned its great key, and opened it. Outside there was a paved space, and beyond that a canal. There were steps too, and at the bottom of them a small boat.

'Your back door?' hazarded Daisy, and, when he

nodded, 'Of course, long ago it must have been a sort of tradesman's entrance. What a splendid idea. Do you use it?'

'Seldom—although when I was a small boy I used to row myself out into the main canals.'

Daisy stared at the still dark water. 'Your mother must have been terrified.'

'So she has frequently told me.'

She wanted to ask him about his boyhood, his mother, his family, but instead she asked how far away the main canal was, and listened intelligently when he explained.

They went back into the garden presently, and then into the house to sit in his lovely drawing room and sip sherry and talk about any number of things.

Daisy, her tongue loosened by the sherry, her annoyance forgotten, told him a good deal more about herself than she realised, and Mr der Huizma, enjoying himself, egged her on.

They lunched in a rather grand dining room, with a rectangular table, lovely ribbon-backed chairs, a massive side-table and family portraits on its panelled walls. Daisy, undeterred by the ancestors looking down upon her, ate her toast and pâté, scrambled eggs and smoked salmon, and thin slices of cheese with croissants warm in their basket, drank the coffee Joop offered her, and then, at her host's suggestion, followed him into the library.

A smallish dim room, lined with bookshelves, with a large leather-covered table ringed by comfortable chairs—and a set of George the Third library steps, which her professional eye lighted upon with interest.

There were books in abundance, and the table was covered with newspapers, magazines and a variety of journals; she could have spent the day there very happily. She roamed round while Mr der Huizma settled himself into a chair, waiting patiently until she had had her fill. Only then did he get up.

'I've a history of this house. Would you like to see it?'

'Oh, yes, please. Is it a first edition?'

'Yes, and written in Dutch, but some of the drawings are interesting.'

They were bending over it, Daisy absorbed while he translated from the Dutch, when the door was opened. He looked up and said, 'Why, Helene, this is a surprise,' and crossed the room to meet the woman who had entered.

Daisy had looked up too. Here was the living image of what she so longed to be. Perfection, no less—tall, blonde and beautiful, dressed exquisitely with simple elegance, slim as a wand. Daisy added the thought that she was *too* thin, bony in fact. Just a little more shape would have made her quite perfect. Perhaps, thought Daisy, Mr der Huizma liked very thin women.

She glanced down at her own well-rounded person and sighed.

Mr der Huizma was speaking. 'Daisy, come and meet Helene van Tromp—my fiancée.' He had a hand on Helene's arm. 'Helene, this is Daisy Gillard, who has been here dealing with the buying and selling of antiques—she is an expert.'

Daisy offered a hand and smiled. Helene smiled too, only the smile didn't reach her eyes. 'How interesting.

Have you bought something from this house? I do hope so; I dislike all this old furniture.'

Daisy said in a shocked voice, 'But no one would want to sell anything in this house; it's full of treasures.'

Helene looked at Mr der Huizma. 'So why is she here?'

'Daisy is here because I am giving her a lift back to England on the night ferry.'

Helene, for a split second, didn't look beautiful. 'Oh?' She glanced at Daisy. 'Did you fall under Jules's car or faint on his doorstep?'

Daisy said matter-of-factly, 'No, nothing like that. I fell in a canal and Mr der Huizma hauled me out and took me to the hospital. Oh, and then I got mugged. He heard that I was going back to England today and offered me a lift, that's all!'

Helene stared at her for a moment, and then smiled. A dull girl, with no looks to speak of, and obviously she hadn't succumbed to Jules's charm, nor was she impressed by his obvious wealth. Daisy was dismissed as not worth bothering about.

Mr der Huizma was called away then, to take an urgent phone call, and Helene seized her chance. 'You must be tired,' she said sweetly. 'Why don't you go and have a rest? You have a long journey before you.'

She took Daisy's arm, led her to the door and opened it. 'There's a small sitting room no one uses; you can curl up on a sofa and have a nap. I'll tell Joop to bring you a cup of tea later.'

Daisy wasn't in the least tired, but it was obvious that Helene wanted to get rid of her—which in all fairness was quite understandable. Daisy supposed that if she were engaged to someone like Mr der Huizma she would want to keep him to herself. She allowed herself to be drawn across the hall and into another room.

'No one will disturb you,' said Helene softly, and shut the door on her.

The room was, comparatively speaking, small. It was also delightfully cosy, with comfortable chairs, a little writing desk and a round table upon which was a bowl of flowers. It was pleasantly warm too, and Daisy sat down in one of the chairs and looked around her. Helene had said it was a room which was seldom used, but it seemed to her to be very lived in. There were books scattered around, and magazines, but she didn't bother with them; she had plenty to occupy her thoughts.

She didn't like Helene, for a start, which seemed unkind considering how gracious that lady had been. She didn't think that Mr der Huizma would be happy with her, despite her beauty and elegance. It was no concern of hers, though. And probably they were ideally suited; Helene would undoubtedly grace this lovely old house and be a perfect hostess. Her thoughts became rather muddled with worrying about the wine cooler and how she was to get home once they reached England. She really should have settled the matter before agreeing to go with Mr der Huizma, although, come to think of it, she hadn't been given the opportunity...

Joop came presently with a tray of tea, enquiring if her headache was better and if there was anything she required. Daisy, who hadn't got a headache, thanked him politely and said, 'No, thank you.'

She drank her tea and wondered how long she should

stay in the room—until they left that evening? Was she to have her dinner on a tray as well?

Questions which were answered by Mr der Huizma, who came in quietly and sat down opposite her.

'You must forgive me. I had no idea that you had a headache and were feeling tired.'

Daisy spoke without thinking. 'Oh, but I'm not in the least tired, and my head doesn't ache. Helene—you don't mind me calling her that?—was kind enough to suggest that I might like to rest for a bit.'

She wasn't sure if she liked the look on his face, but he said pleasantly, 'In that case shall we have a drink before dinner?'

'That would be lovely. I like this room.'

'My mother uses it when she visits me…'

Daisy smiled. 'There, I had a feeling that it was lived in, if you know what I mean—writing letters and sewing and knitting, and just being happy.'

He looked at her thoughtfully. 'You are quite right, of course.'

They had their drinks, and presently dined, and then Daisy was led away by Jette so that she could get ready for the journey. The wine cooler was checked, her case put into the boot, and she herself stowed neatly in the car. Such luxury, thought Daisy happily, and then wondered not so happily if she would need to sustain a conversation all the way to the Hoek.

She need not have worried. Beyond making sure that she was comfortable, Mr der Huizma seemed happy enough with his thoughts; his austere profile certainly discouraged small talk.

Chapter 4

After a while Daisy discovered that the silence between them was a restful one; the kind of silence between old friends who had no need to talk. She gave a small sigh of content and allowed her thoughts to wander. Father would be pleased about the cooler. Getting it from Harwich might be a bit difficult, but at least she would be back in England. Perhaps it would be a good idea to phone him and ask him to drive up to Harwich and collect her and it. It struck her then that she hadn't thought about that before, and Mr der Huizma had been a bit arbitrary, hadn't he? Still, never look a gift horse in the mouth. The most difficult part of the journey would be over by the time they got to Harwich.

At the Hoek he bade her stay in the car in a pleasant voice which none the less brooked no argument. He was gone for some time and she began to get uneasy. Just as she was wondering if she should go and look for him, he reappeared.

'We can go on board,' he told her.

'I haven't shown anyone my ticket…'

'I have tickets. You can cash yours in when we get to Harwich.'

'And pay you back,' said Daisy smartly, not wishing to be beholden.

'As you wish.' He had joined the queue of cars going aboard, and presently she found herself being urged up the stairs to the deck above. She would have paused here, but he told her, 'The top deck,' and led the way, carrying her overnight bag.

It was quiet there, with only a stewardess in sight to lead them to their cabins. Mr der Huizma nodded briefly as the woman opened a door. 'I'll see you in the restaurant in ten minutes,' he said and went on down the corridor to his own cabin.

Daisy looked around her. The cabin was small but very comfortable. First class, she supposed and wondered how much it would cost. And where was the restaurant? And supposing she hadn't wanted to go to it?

She brushed her mousy hair smooth, did her face and sat down on the bed. The ten minutes was already up but she really didn't see why she should go to the restaurant if she didn't want to. The trouble was, she did want to. She was hungry, for one thing, and for another, despite his silence, she quite liked being with Mr der Huizma.

He was there, waiting for her, very much at ease, coming to meet her as she hesitated in the doorway.

'A drink? It might be a good idea as the crossing is sometimes rough at this time of year.'

'Thank you,' said Daisy. 'It was quite rough when I crossed with the screen, but I wasn't sick.'

His thin mouth twitched slightly. 'How about a dry sherry? And it is always a good idea to have a meal.'

They ate presently, talking a little about one thing and another, never once mentioning her stay in Amsterdam, and as soon as their meal was finished Daisy said that she would like to go to her cabin.

He made no attempt to keep her. 'We dock around seven o'clock. Someone will bring you some tea and toast about half past six. We'll have breakfast later.' He didn't give her the chance to say anything but bade her goodnight abruptly. This question of breakfast would have to be settled in the morning. Once they were at Harwich she would collect the wine cooler and find somewhere quiet, phone her father and do whatever he thought best.

It was going to be a rough crossing. She got into her narrow bed feeling squeamish, but she was tired too; she was asleep before she could decide whether she felt seasick or not.

She was awakened by the stewardess with tea and toast and warned that the ferry would be docking shortly. 'A nasty rough crossing,' said the stewardess.

Certainly the ferry was still rolling around, making dressing a lengthy business, but the tea and toast stayed down and she felt her usual self. Finding her way on deck, she wondered if Mr der Huizma had slept too, and decided that he had. Somehow she couldn't associate him with being sick...

She saw him at once, leaning over the rail watching the ferry edging its way into the harbour. But he must have had eyes at the back of his head, for he turned round to look at her as she crossed the deck.

There was something about her, he reflected, which intrigued him. Certainly not her looks, although she had a delightful smile and her eyes were lovely; large and sparkling and… He sought for a word—kind. Helene had dismissed her as a dull girl, badly dressed and too reserved, but he knew that wasn't true. There was nothing dull about Daisy, and although her clothes were off the peg they were in good taste and she wore them with elegance. He found himself wishing that he knew more about her.

He went to meet her and they stood together watching the quay getting nearer. Presently they went down to the car deck and got into the Rolls. There would be a short delay before they could disembark; the opportunity Daisy was hoping for.

'If you wouldn't mind letting me get out once we are through Customs—and the wine cooler, of course?'

'And then what will you do, Daisy?' he wanted to know.

'Phone Father…'

'I phoned him yesterday before we left. I'm driving you home—you and your wine cooler.'

She turned to look at him. 'But it's miles; you can't possibly do that.'

'I'm spending the night with friends—remember I have stayed with them before? When we went walking on the shore?'

'Oh, well. That would be nice. Why didn't you tell me before?'

'Because I rather think that you would have flatly refused to come.'

She considered this. 'Yes, I think that perhaps I might have.' She smiled at him. 'But I'm really glad to have a lift all the way home. Thank you.'

'Don't thank me. I'm glad of the company.'

'Are you really? But you don't talk. I thought you were annoyed at having to offer me a lift.'

'Not at all, Daisy. But you are not a girl who expects to be entertained with small talk, are you?'

'No. And I don't mind if you don't say a word. There's always such a lot to think about.'

Mr der Huizma glanced at her and agreed gravely. He had a lot to think about too.

They were through Customs and on the way to Colchester when he suggested that they might stop for breakfast. He took her to Le Brasserie and they ate a splendid breakfast before going on to Chelmsford, Brentwood and the ring road. The M25 was busy as he skirted round the north of the city to join the M3, and presently the A303. 'I'll turn off at Salisbury,' he told her.

They stopped at Fleet for coffee, and took the A303. There wasn't a great deal of traffic now that they were well away from London, and Mr der Huizma drove fast, saying little, leaving Daisy to look out at the wintry landscape. Once he had turned off to Salisbury she allowed her excitement at coming home to take over. She hadn't been away for long, but such a lot had happened;

it would be nice to settle down to her usual quiet life. At least, she amended, for a time. Her visit to Amsterdam had given her a taste for foreign travel...

Once through Salisbury Mr der Huizma slowed the car's pace and Daisy gave him an enquiring look. They still had a long way to go. Surely it would have been quicker to keep to the A303?

'Lunch,' he told her briefly. 'There's a good restaurant just before we rejoin the A303.'

He stopped in a smallish village and turned in through the open gates of a large house in its centre. Inside there was a welcoming fire in the bar and a pretty dining room. Daisy sighed with pleasure and went off to the Ladies, then rejoined him at the bar to drink sherry and peruse the menu.

The food was excellent. There were other people lunching, just enough to make the place feel cosy, and the log fire made nonsense of the cold grey day. And Mr der Huizma, abandoning his silence, became once again the man who had been such a pleasant companion walking along the shore...

They drove on then, turning off before Exeter and making for the coast through narrow Devon lanes.

'Mother will be delighted to give you tea,' said Daisy as he turned the car into the country road which would lead to her home.

'That is very kind, but I should get on. I shall be staying with my friends for a couple of days.'

Daisy blushed, for he had spoken in his usual quiet manner but she sensed a snub. She had been silly; of course he wouldn't want to stay for tea. He had given her a lift home but that was no reason to suppose that he would wish to take the matter further. She said, 'Yes, of course,' in a wooden voice, and added the remark that it would soon be dark.

Mr der Huizma had seen the blush and had a very good idea of what Daisy was thinking. He need not have been quite so brusque; indeed, he would have enjoyed meeting her father again, and her mother, and he had to admit that he regretted that he wouldn't see Daisy again. Which was a good thing, he reminded himself. He was beginning to find her too interesting…

The main street of the little town was deserted when he stopped outside the antiques shop. The window was still lighted, and the door was opened at once and Mr Gillard came out to the car.

Mr der Huizma got out and opened Daisy's door, and stood quietly while Daisy was hugged and exclaimed over. But then Mr Gillard turned to him and wrung his hand. 'So good of you,' he declared, 'we are so grateful. Come along in—there's tea waiting.'

Mr der Huizma gave a mental shrug. Another half-hour of Daisy's company would do no harm. After all he would never see her again. He followed the older man into the shop.

Daisy had run upstairs to her mother. 'It's so lovely to be home,' she declared. 'And I've such a lot to tell you…'

She broke off as her father and Mr der Huizma came into the room and smiled widely at him, because he had changed his mind after all. And he, seeing the smile, wished very much that their paths would not lie so far apart. He had a fleeting image of Helene then, reminding him that such a wish was something he must forget.

They had tea, and he sat by Mrs Gillard, answering her questions about Daisy, assuring her that no harm had been done and then telling Mr Gillard about Heer Friske and the wine cooler—which remark led easily enough to a brief chat about antiques. And all the time Daisy sat quietly, saying very little, wishing that time would stand still so that Mr der Huizma could stay for ever.

But of course it didn't. Presently he got up, thanked her mother for his tea, offered to unload the wine cooler and then shook Daisy's hand and wished her goodbye too, in a friendly voice devoid of warmth.

Then he had gone.

Daisy started to clear away the tea things and her mother went to the window to watch their guest drive away. 'A lovely car,' she observed, 'and what a very nice man, love. I suppose his being a doctor makes him have such beautiful manners.'

Daisy said that, yes, she supposed so, in such a quiet voice that her mother gave her a quick glance and added, 'Well, you'll be able to tell us all about it this evening, dear. You run along and unpack your things and I'll see about supper. You must have a great deal to tell us.'

And indeed Daisy spent the rest of the evening giving a faithful account of her stay in Holland, making much over the delivery of the screen and her visits to Heer Friske, but glossing over her encounters with Mr der Huizma.

* * *

Mr der Huizma, dining with his friends that evening, told them his version of his various encounters with Daisy. 'You didn't mind my coming at such short notice? I knew Daisy from my previous visit—you remember that hotel where we dined together? We met there, and as you know I saw her several times while I was staying here. I felt that the least I could do was to see her safely back home with this wine cooler.'

His hostess said gently, 'Poor girl, falling in the canal and then being mugged. Such a nice sensible girl too. She is very well liked, you know, but funnily enough as far as I know she hasn't any boyfriends. Of course young men want pretty faces...'

It was at breakfast the following morning that Mr der Huizma was asked by his hostess if a date had been set for his wedding.

'Helene is in no hurry to marry; she leads a busy social life—she will be going to Switzerland to ski, and then some friends of hers have invited her to go to California.'

His host chipped in. 'A pity. I don't suppose Gillard told you last night—he's not a man to boast—but when I was there last week he showed me a really beautiful diamond brooch—a perfect bow—just the kind of gift a bridegroom would give his bride. Funnily enough I thought of your Helene—such a beautiful woman. He bought it from the Lancey-Courtneys; they've been selling a good deal of stuff lately. It belonged to a great-great-grandmother, I believe, and no one in the family liked it.' He chuckled. 'I was tempted to mortgage this house and buy it for Grace.' He smiled at his wife. 'But she persuaded me not to.'

Mr der Huizma passed his cup for more coffee. 'It sounds exactly the kind of thing Helene would like to have. Perhaps I'd better take a look at it.'

It would mean seeing Daisy again. He smiled at the thought…

Daisy, tying price tickets on a collection of small china figures, looked round at the tinkle of the door-bell. Her father was in his office, she had slipped back into her accustomed routine, and already Amsterdam seemed a dream. The sight of Mr der Huizma, wander-ing through the crowded shop towards her, made the dream reality. She put down the china ornament, aware that her hand wasn't quite steady, but she wished him good morning in a normal voice.

His good morning was friendly. 'Busy already, Daisy? Do you not take a holiday from time to time?'

'Well, going to Holland was like a holiday. Do you want to see Father?'

'I've been told he has a brooch I would like to see…'

She fetched her father then, and went back to her pricing, and the two men went into the office. She won-dered why; perhaps her journey home had cost more than her ticket, and then there had been their meals. Her father would probably insist on paying for them. But why should Mr der Huizma come to the shop? She was sure her father hadn't suggested it on the previ-ous evening.

The office door opened and her father called, 'Daisy, come here, will you?'

The two men were standing at his desk, looking down at the brooch lying in its bed of dark blue velvet. It shone and sparkled and she said involuntarily, 'Oh, what a pretty thing.'

Her father touched it with a gentle finger. 'Yes, it is. It's also very dirty.' He glanced at Mr der Huizma. 'I couldn't let you have it in this state. When did you want it?'

Mr der Huizma's voice sounded remote. 'It is to be a wedding gift to my bride. There is no great hurry, however, we are unlikely to marry before the summer. But I should like to buy it.' He paused, and the sudden idea in his head became vital action. 'I shall be returning home later today, but may I leave it with you to clean? I see no chance of coming this way for some time, though. Perhaps Daisy could bring it over when it is ready?' He smiled suddenly. 'She has proved herself a splendid custodian for the screen and the wine cooler, and the brooch wouldn't be difficult to transport.'

'Well, I don't see why she shouldn't do that. The brooch will take some time to clean—a couple of weeks...'

The two men looked at Daisy, Mr der Huizma with his eyebrows gently raised, her father fondly. She saw that she was supposed to say something.

'Yes, of course I'll take it,' said Daisy, and at the same moment Mr der Huizma knew that nothing on earth would allow him to let Daisy travel alone with the brooch—she could be mugged again, injured. He realised that the brooch didn't matter, but Daisy did. Behind his placid features his clever head was already full of half-formed plans.

But for the moment he said nothing. Ways and means were discussed, and presently the two men went upstairs to talk over the idea with coffee. Daisy stayed in the shop and sold a pair of brass candlesticks and a copper bed-warmer to a young American couple honeymooning in England. She let them have the bed-warmer for less than the price on the ticket because they were so obviously happy and delighted with their purchases.

She felt happy too. She hadn't allowed herself to dwell too much on the fact that she wouldn't see Mr der Huizma again, but she had been aware of disappointment, almost sadness at the thought. But now she would go to Amsterdam again, and even if their meeting was brief, it would mean that she would see him once more. Their paths had crossed several times, she reminded herself, and she had come to regard him as a friend. She thought of the brooch then—a splendid gift for his Helene. 'If I were Helene,' muttered Daisy to the empty shop, 'I'd be head over heels in love with him.'

When he and her father came back into the shop she was buying a small Wedgwood teapot from an elderly lady. A genuine piece, with the model of the widow on its lid, and worth a good deal more than the lady had asked for it. By the time she had paid the delighted owner its true value, Mr der Huizma had gone…

The task of cleaning the brooch fell to her lot; she had patience with finicky jobs and she spent part of each day restoring it to its original sparkle, so that she was constantly reminded of Helene and Mr der Huizma. She didn't hurry over it. There was no need, her father had pointed out, and besides the shop had to be attended to if he was busy elsewhere. A week went

by, and a second, and midway through the third week
the brooch was ready. Minutely examined by her father and carefully packed up. Any day now, as soon as
it was convenient, she would go over to Holland. Or
so she thought!

Back in Amsterdam Mr der Huizma had immediately immersed himself in his work, and only some
days following his return did he visit Helene.

'So you're back again,' she greeted him. 'Really,
Jules, you must cut down on your work. Give up some
of the hospitals where you have beds. Oh, I know you
need to keep your hand in with the children on the
wards, but you would have a far bigger private practice if you did. There are plenty of other doctors who
could take over from you…'

She was looking very beautiful that evening, beautifully dressed and made up and ready to charm him.

But he discovered that he wasn't charmed. He was
fair enough to realise that he did spend many of his
days and quite often his nights with his small patients,
but Helene had known that when she had said that she
would marry him. He saw now that she had no real interest in his work; she would cavil at interrupted meals,
broken nights and urgent flights to other countries,
she would be quite unable to visualise the kind of life
they would lead together, and certainly she wouldn't
be willing to give up the social round which was so
important to her.

But he was an honourable man. He had asked her
to marry him believing that he had loved her. He *had*

been in love with her, but that wasn't enough and that wasn't her fault...

He said now, 'Helene, my work is my life. My patients matter to me—if you were to come to the hospital and see some of the little ones you would understand that.'

Helene crossed the room and sat down beside him on the sofa. 'You're tired because you're working too hard. Of course you enjoy your profession, it must be most interesting, but why wear yourself out? Life's too short. I've been invited to fly down to Cannes for a week—the van Hoffmans. Come with me; they told me to bring you if you were free.'

'But I'm not free,' said Mr der Huizma quietly.

Helene frowned. 'Nonsense. Really, Jules, you're deliberately annoying me...'

'No, Helene.' He sounded tired and remote, and she had a sudden feeling that she had gone too far. She didn't love him, but he would suit her as a husband—money, an old family, making a name for himself in his profession. She had thought that her future was secure with him, but now she felt a faint prickle of doubt. She laid a hand on his arm.

'Don't be angry, Jules. I do know how much your work means to you, but I worry that you don't have enough leisure.'

He went home presently, and sat for a long time in his study with the faithful Bouncer for company. He saw nothing but unhappiness for himself and Helene if they were to marry. He was aware that she didn't love him, had never even *been* in love with him, but she had seemed so suitable.

'I'm a fool,' said Mr der Huizma to Bouncer, who wagged his tail and whined in sympathy. It was late when he at last went up to bed. The half-formed plans he had allowed to simmer at the back of his head had resolved themselves. Tomorrow he would go and see Heer Friske.

It was early evening before he reached the antiques shop. His day had been long, and there were several sick children who were concerning him. He was tired, but this was something he had promised himself he would do.

The shop was still open, and when he walked in Heer Friske came to meet him.

'The wine cooler has arrived safely; I have heard from Mr Gillard. It was good of you to give Daisy a lift back, *mijnheer*.'

'It was no trouble. It would have been an awkward journey for her by ferry and train, although she seems a sensible young woman.'

'Indeed, and a knowledgeable one too. She has the instincts of a good antiques dealer. I dare say she will find work with one of the big firms in London…'

This was the opening Mr der Huizma sought. 'She is most interested in Dutch antiques. Did she not tell you? But of course she doesn't know anyone in Holland who would train her…'

'She knows me,' observed Heer Friske. 'I wouldn't mind having her for a couple of months. The tourist season will be starting shortly, and I was thinking of getting someone.'

Mr der Huizma murmured in a disinterested voice and went to look at an attractive small enamel box, a pretty trifle, pale green and painted with roses. He bought it without speaking of Daisy again, and presently went home. Perhaps nothing would come of it, but Heer Friske had risen to his bait.

And Heer Friske was thinking about it, pondering the pros and cons. He decided that he would write to Mr Gillard.

He was a cautious old man, and he deliberated over the matter for some time and then finally wrote his letter.

Mr Gillard read it several mornings later over his breakfast. He read it twice before remarking, 'This letter will be of interest to you, Daisy. Heer Friske asks if you would like to work for him for a short period. He was impressed by your knowledge of antiques and thinks that a month or so in his shop will broaden it.'

Mr Gillard took off his spectacles and looked at Daisy. 'You will do as you wish, of course, but if my opinion is asked then I would say that it is a good idea. One can never know enough, and although you have no qualifications there is no reason why you shouldn't carry on here when I retire.'

'You're not going to retire for years,' said Daisy, 'but I see what you mean.'

She had a mental picture of herself in middle age, plain of face, slightly dowdy as to dress, and absorbed in her work. Well, there wouldn't be anything or anyone else to be absorbed in, would there? No husband or children, dogs, cats or ponies, all living in a comfortable house as happy as the day is long…

She brought her thoughts back to the present. She

would like to go to Amsterdam, and not only for the reasons her father had mentioned. She would be in the same town as Mr der Huizma, she might meet him again, which was something she very much wanted to do.

'Yes, Father, I should like to go. When does Heer Friske want me to start?'

'He doesn't say. He writes that he will wait for your decision before he goes into details. I suppose it will be fairly soon, for the tourists will be arriving in Holland to see the bulb fields and I believe he does good business at that time.'

'I don't speak Dutch,' said Daisy.

'Well, probably most of his customers are American or English. You will be an asset in the shop. Of course, there is a good deal to discuss before you agree. Are you to be paid, I wonder, and what free time can you expect and where will you live?'

Her mother said quietly, 'Surely all that can be sorted out in one letter? And of course Heer Friske isn't going into details until he knows that Daisy will go to Amsterdam.' She added, 'You'll need some new clothes, dear.'

Something elegant, thought Daisy, so that Mr der Huizma would notice her—that was if they should meet...

Heer Friske was pleased at her decision; she would receive a small salary, he wrote, and commission on anything she might sell from his shop. She would be free on Sundays and Mondays, but on her working days she was not to expect any time off. She would have a room in his house; he and his wife would be glad to have her company. The date of her arrival was to be arranged within the next week or so.

Daisy took herself off to Plymouth. Spring might be in the air but it was still chilly. She bought a jacket and skirt in a warm brown tweed, a couple of woolly jumpers and a sober grey dress suitable for the shop. And, since her father had been generous with a cheque, she bought a three-piece in dark green jersey just in case she should encounter a social occasion.

She went back home, tried everything on before packing them tidily, and waited to see what would happen next.

Mr der Huizma had allowed ten days or so to elapse before calling in at Heer Friske's shop once more. This time he bought an antique baby's rattle—coral and silver bells; it would doubtless make a handsome christening present for some baby or other later on. While he was purchasing it Heer Friske, in an unusually expansive mood, told him that he had engaged Daisy.

'That was a good idea of yours,' he observed, 'and it seemed worth asking her. She is glad to come, and I shall teach her all I can while she is here. She has her future to consider—probably she will take over her father's shop in due course. A nice girl, but not pretty, and unlikely to marry.'

'When is she to come?' enquired Mr der Huizma idly.

'As to that, as soon as it can be arranged...'

Mr der Huizma's manner was casual. 'I'm going over to England next week, I could give her a lift back here.'

'You would do that? It would not inconvenience you?'

'Not in the least. Would you let her know? I shall be in England on Saturday and will call at her home early on Sunday morning. We should be back here late on Sunday evening.'

He went home then, to make arrangements for the journey, and after due thought telephoned Mr Gillard.

'It is so fortunate,' he pointed out in his placid voice, 'that I shall be in England next week. I can collect the brooch and Daisy at the same time, provided you have no objection to her leaving early on the Sunday morning. I must be back for a Monday morning clinic.'

'I'm sure Daisy will be glad of a lift,' said Mr Gillard, 'and I'm grateful. I wasn't too happy about her taking that valuable brooch. I'll let her know and she will be ready—eight o'clock and many thanks.'

Daisy's eyes sparkled when she was told. Kindly Fate was giving her a treat. Mr der Huizma loomed large in her mind, but she didn't allow herself to think too much about him. He was the nicest man she had ever met, and she liked him, but he was going to marry Helene and that fact prevented her from allowing her thoughts to wonder about him. To see him again would be delightful, though. Probably he wouldn't speak more than half a dozen words to her, but they would be together for several hours.

She packed her case, rubbed a face cream guaranteed to bring beauty to the dullest visage into her cheeks, and washed her abundant hair. The cream made no difference at all, but she felt better for it and on the strength of its supposed magic qualities bought a new lipstick.

She was to stay with Heer Friske for as long as either she or he wished. Two or three months, she supposed, perhaps longer. Of course there was always the possibility that his wife might not like her, or that she wouldn't pull her weight in the shop. She hoped that would not happen; there was so much to see and learn.

Daisy wrinkled her small nose with pleasure—all those marvellous museums, and those narrow streets lined by antiques shops to explore, as well as getting familiar with the contents of Heer Friske's shop.

She was up early on Sunday morning, eating a hasty breakfast, wearing the new jacket and skirt, pale with excitement, listening to last-minute instructions from her father and quiet sensible comments from her mother.

When Mr der Huizma arrived she hardly spoke beyond replying to his pleasant greeting. He had a cup of coffee, examined the brooch and stowed it away in a pocket, complimenting her on the work she had done on it, then professed himself ready to leave. So she bade her mother and father goodbye and got into the car beside him. Now that the moment of departure had actually come she had the sudden urge to get out of the car again; to stay at home, return to the security and quiet of her life there. Even if she had voiced her wish she would have had no chance to carry it out, for Mr der Huizma drove away without loss of time so that she had only a moment in which to wave goodbye.

'Comfortable?' His voice was calmly reassuring and she relaxed.

'Yes, thank you. It is kind of you to give me a lift…'

'Well, I thought it a good idea to get you and the

brooch at the same time, since I was in England. You're happy at the idea of working for Heer Friske?'

'Yes. I liked him; I don't know his wife, though.'

'I'm sure you will be happy with them. You will be kept quite busy, I dare say. His shop is popular with tourists who are looking for genuine antiques; he refuses to sell anything else.'

After that they lapsed into silence—which she had expected anyway. They stopped for coffee mid-morning, and were nearing Harwich before he stopped again for lunch.

'Aren't we a bit early for the ferry?' asked Daisy.

'We're crossing on the new fast ferry—three and a half hours—saves a good deal of time. A catamaran. I came over on it. You'll find it very comfortable.'

When she saw it, Daisy didn't think it looked very safe. But once on board she changed her mind about that. It was warm and comfortable, and there were easy chairs and plenty of space. It seemed a long time since she had got up that morning; she curled up in a chair and went to sleep.

As a travelling companion she was ideal, decided Mr der Huizma.

She woke instantly at his touch when they docked, her hair slightly tousled, her face shiny with sleep, and she skipped away to tidy herself, to return in good time, once more immaculate, to get into the car again and sit quietly while he drove through the town and onto the motorway.

It was early evening by now, and den Haag, looming ahead of them, looked inviting in the dusk. Daisy was surprised when Mr der Huizma turned off the main road.

'We will have a meal,' he told her. 'You will probably be too tired to eat once we get to Heer Friske. There's a quiet restaurant here, where we can get a meal.'

Daisy was hungry, and did justice to the grilled sole and the massive pudding which followed it—besides, it meant that she could be with him for just a little longer. But they didn't linger over the meal; she sensed that he wished to get home as soon as possible. They drove on presently, and it was with regret that she saw Heer Friske's shop at last. This is the end, she thought.

Chapter 5

Mr der Huizma told Daisy to stay where she was, then got out of the car and rang the bell beside the small door next to the shop. Which gave her ample time in which to wish that she had never come, that she was home again—and then, at the sight of Mr der Huizma's large person standing there, to feel a wave of pleasure at the sight of him.

The door was opened and Heer Friske stood there, smiling. Mr der Huizma came back to the car and opened her door, and got her case from the boot. Her moment of panic was over. She got out and greeted Heer Friske, and was borne indoors and up the stairs to where he and his wife lived, with Mr der Huizma following with her case.

The room they entered was cosy, lived in and warm,

and Mevrouw Friske was just as cosy. She made Daisy welcome, and offered coffee. Mr der Huizma refused, with his beautiful manners, and after a few minutes' talk made his farewells. With her hand in his, Daisy thanked him for her lift.

'It was a very pleasant journey,' she told him, aware that she sounded stiff and reserved. 'It was so kind of you to bring me here.'

He stared down at her, not smiling. 'But I wanted the brooch,' he reminded her, 'and since the car was empty it made sense to bring you with me.'

He was still holding her hand. 'I hope that you will be very happy while you are in Amsterdam. Please give my regards to your mother and father when you write. Don't worry about phoning them this evening. I'll do that when I get home.'

He went away then, and Mevrouw Friske bustled her up another flight of stairs to a pretty little room at the front of the house. It was simply furnished but comfortable, with a patchwork quilt on the bed and thick curtains to keep out the winter's cold. There was a shower across the landing, Mevrouw Friske told her, and added anxiously that she hoped Daisy didn't mind being on her own on the top floor. She waited while Daisy took off her coat, and then went back to the living room with her where Heer Friske was waiting.

She was to start work on Tuesday morning; breakfast was at half past seven, the shop opened at half past eight and stayed open until six o'clock—although if there was a customer in the shop it remained open until he or she had gone. Lunch-hour was brief, but there would be a substantial evening meal once the shop had closed. Tomorrow, being Monday, he pointed out, the shop would be closed. 'Which will give you time to settle in,' said Heer Friske in his correct English. 'And now you will be tired. Coffee and a biscuit with cheese, and you will wish to go to your bed.'

So Daisy spent a short while giving him news of her father and mother and the shop, while Mevrouw Friske sat and knitted, only half understanding but ready with a smile or a motherly word or two, and presently she bade the nice old couple goodnight and went up the steep little staircase to her bed.

And later, tucked up cosily under the quilt, she thought about Mr der Huizma. He would be with Helene, she supposed, and the brooch would be sparkling on Helene's too thin bosom. No doubt they would discuss the date for their wedding. It would be a grand affair; she felt sure that Helene had any number of friends and family. About Mr der Huizma she wasn't so sure; he had barely mentioned his family, never discussed anything to do with his private life, in fact. Perhaps he wasn't close to his family...

In this she was mistaken. He was even at that moment sitting at his ease, with Bouncer lying on his feet, in a great chair on one side of a vast fireplace in a large and elegant room in a house in the country close to Hilversum. It was a square, solid house, with green shutters at its many windows and a vast door reached by double steps, and it stood in large well-kept grounds. The other occupant of the room sat on the other side of the cheerful fire, placidly knitting. A small, rather

plump lady, with an elegant hairstyle, no looks to speak
of but dressed with great good taste.

She nodded to the elderly woman who had brought
in the coffee tray and observed, 'Well, Jules, now that
you are here, you must tell me about your trip to England. Your phone call was brief...'

'Dearest, all my phone calls are brief, otherwise
I'd never get through my days. I should be home now,
catching up on tomorrow's case-sheets, but it seems
some time since we saw each other...'

'A month ago,' said his mother, rather tartly. 'You
had intended to come a week ago, but Helene had arranged something.'

'Yes. I'm sorry about that. She will be going to California shortly; I'll make it up to you then.'

His mother smiled. 'Jules, dear, it is unkind of me
to grumble—I know what a busy life you lead. Tell
me, did you have a good journey? You went rather
suddenly.'

He began to tell her then. 'The brooch is very beautiful; I must let you see it. And since I was going to
fetch it, it seemed sense to bring Daisy back with me.'

'Daisy?'

'I must explain about her...' Which he did, at some
length. 'I think you would like her.'

'Is she pretty?'

'No, but she has lovely eyes, a great deal of brown
hair and a pretty voice.'

His mother kept her eyes on her knitting. 'She
sounds a very nice girl. Quite clever at her work too,
I expect.'

'Yes, she is.'

She peeped at her son and saw his smile. 'How did you meet?'

He told her that too. 'And we met again by accident out walking. She doesn't mind the wind and the rain.'

'Then she should like Holland!' said his mother, and they both laughed.

His mother asked presently, 'You will be seeing Helene as soon as possible, of course? I am sure she will be delighted with the brooch—or do you intend giving it to her on your marriage?'

'I think that for the moment I will keep it safe. Helene hasn't decided on a date yet.'

His mother murmured something vague in reply and hoped secretly that Helene would never decide. She had accepted her as a future daughter-in-law because she was devoted to Jules and wanted him to be happy, but she had never liked her—although she had to admit that she was beautiful and, when she wished, charming. She hadn't wasted much charm on her future mother-in-law, though, and barely suppressed her boredom when she visited with Jules, making it plain that she found the house old-fashioned. But she had been careful to do this when Jules hadn't been there. She thought sadly that Helene would do nothing to encourage Jules in his work, nor would she put up with the continuous interruptions which were all part and parcel of his life.

He got up to go then, with a promise that he would visit her again as soon as he could.

'Do, Jules. If Helene is away and you are free on a Sunday we could spend the day together.'

He went back home then, with Bouncer sitting beside him, and found himself wishing that it was Daisy sitting there.

When Daisy went down to breakfast the following morning she was told to go and enjoy herself. 'Time enough to start work tomorrow,' said Heer Friske. 'It is your chance to buy stamps and postcards, and see where the nearest shops are.'

So Daisy made her bed, tidied her room, helped Mevrouw Friske with the washing up and then took herself off to explore. She remembered from her first visit where the nearest shops were. There were shops all round Heer Friske's; shops given over to antiques, like his, shops selling the kind of thing tourists wanted to buy—pictures, Delft china, modern silver—but the kind of shops she sought were at the end of the street some five minutes' walk away. A post office, a stationer's, a shabby little shop selling wool and haberdashery and cheap souvenirs, a bakery and a small supermarket.

Quite sufficient for her needs, she decided. There would be little chance to go to the Kalverstraat or Leidestraat and look in the elegant shop windows there, but since she had very little money she didn't suppose that would matter. She bought stamps, postcards and an English newspaper, and went back to the shop. It was almost noon, and there was a delicious smell coming from the kitchen. She took her things to her room and offered to set the table for lunch. Presently Heer

Friske came in and they sat down to thick pea soup, full of tiny pieces of sausage and pork, accompanied by thick slices of bread.

'My wife makes the best *echte* soup in Amsterdam,' observed Heer Friske, offering second helpings.

The shop opened the next day at eight-thirty, but there were only a few customers; Daisy looked and listened and stored away any amount of useful information. An old lady came in with a Delft plate. It was in mint condition and Heer Friske asked Daisy what she thought its value might be. She examined it carefully, looking for damage and repairs and finding neither, and named a sum, thankful for hours she had spent poring over *Miller's Antiques* and the close attention she had always paid at auction sales.

Heer Friske looked pleased. 'A fair estimate,' he told her. 'When the shop is closed this evening we will look at what Delftware I have and you will learn more...'

So that evening, after a substantial meal of pork chops, red cabbage and boiled potatoes, followed by something Mevrouw Friske called 'pudding' but which Daisy rechristened custard, they went back downstairs and inspected the Delft china. There wasn't a great deal of it, but what there was was genuine and valuable. Daisy went to bed a good deal wiser about it, and lay in bed going over everything that Heer Friske had told her. She could see that there was a great deal that she must learn—but that was why she had come, wasn't it?

Almost asleep, she amended that. She had come not only to increase her knowledge of antiques but so that she might have a chance of seeing Mr der Huizma once in a while. Amsterdam wasn't such a very large city, and the hospital wasn't far from the shop…

The week went quickly, and if the long hours in the shop were tiring, she knew that she was learning all the time. She had waited upon one or two customers— Americans, glad to find someone who spoke English and was willing to chat for a little while while they looked through the silver intent on taking back something from Holland. They were only small sales, but Daisy was delighted; she had broken the ice and felt that she was worth her small salary.

She had been told that she was to come and go as she wished on Sunday. The Friskes seldom went out, but family and friends visited them, and occasionally they spent the day with Mevrouw Friske's sister. Daisy was given a key and told to get herself a meal if she felt inclined and there was no one home.

On that first Sunday she didn't venture far. After breakfast she walked to the Oude Kerk and went back for the midday meal with the Friskes. She went out again in the afternoon, and took a tour of the canals in one of the glass-topped boats, and afterwards found a small café where she had tea and a cream cake of gigantic proportions. And all the while she kept an eye open for Mr der Huizma…

She spent the evening watching Dutch television with the Friskes and went to bed early. Next week she would venture further afield. Perhaps take a train or a bus to Delft or den Haag. There were endless possibilities, she told herself.

She was getting into the swing of things now, and the next week went quickly. She was making herself useful in the shop, and when there were no customers she listened to Heer Friske explaining the history of marquetry and examining one or two fine specimens which were in the shop. And when Saturday came she made careful plans for Sunday. She would take a bus to Vollendam, a favourite venue for tourists, and a kind of showplace of Holland as it had been. The buses went from Central Station and she knew where that was. She would have a snack lunch there and come back in the afternoon, and then if there were still some hours to spare, she would go and look at the shops in Leidesgracht and Vijselstraat.

The last customer went and she started to take the more valuable antiques out of the window while Heer Friske locked up the takings and the valuable silver. When the phone rang he called her over. 'For you, Daisy.'

She picked up the phone quickly; her mother had telephoned during the week, and there was no reason for her to ring again unless there was something wrong. She said, 'Hullo,' in a worried voice, and then 'hullo' again, in a quite different voice, when she heard who it was.

'Jules der Huizma. I have a free day tomorrow; do you care to have a drive with me so that I can show you something of Holland?'

'Oh, yes, please. I'd love to do that.' Daisy was breathless with delight.

'Good. I'll pick you up at ten o'clock.'

'I'll be ready.' And then, as a thought struck her, she said, 'But don't you want to spend it with Helene? Is she coming too? She might not like it...'

He sounded faintly amused. 'Helene is in California, but I am quite sure that she would have no objection to me taking you on a sightseeing trip.'

'Oh, well. If you are sure…'

'Quite sure,' said Mr der Huizma. He put the phone down and addressed Bouncer. 'We are going to have a day out, Bouncer, and we are going to enjoy every minute of it.'

He had spent two weeks thinking about Daisy. Sooner or later she would go back home and he need never see her again—indeed he *must* never see her again. He must forget her, or do his best to do so; she must never intrude into the future. A future with Helene as his wife. But he was not yet married.

Daisy was up early on Sunday morning, taking pains with her face and her hair, glad that it was a dry day, even if chilly, so that she could wear the coat and skirt. Sensible shoes, she decided, in case they did some walking, and the silk scarf her mother had given her to tie over her hair. There was always a wind in Holland, or so it seemed to her. She ate her breakfast under the Friskes' kindly eyes and went pink with excitement when the doorbell rang.

Mr der Huizma came upstairs and spent ten minutes talking to the Friskes before asking her if she was ready, then whisking her down to the car and popping her into it. Bouncer was already there, pleased to see her, and he sat squashed between her and his master's bulk.

'He can sit in the back if you prefer?'

Daisy patted the silky head. 'He would be lonely;

besides, I like him. I wish we had a dog at home, but he would be needing walks and company…'

She looked around her as he drove through the quiet streets away from the centre of the city. 'Where are we going?'

'To the coast first. Zandvoort. We'll have coffee there. Tell me, Daisy, are you happy with Heer Friske?'

'Oh, yes. They are both so kind to me, and the shop's quite busy—he's well known, isn't he? And I'm learning a lot—marquetry and Beidermeyer and I didn't know that Holland had such an enormous variety of Delft blue. Heer Friske has an almost perfect eighteenth-century ewer, and some beautiful tiles. Father hasn't any of those. Perhaps Heer Friske will let him have some; I could take them back when I go.'

Mr der Huizma glanced at her. 'You are already thinking of returning to England?'

'Heavens, no. I'd like to stay for a couple of months, if Heer Friske will have me. There's so much that I don't know.' She turned a beaming smile on him. 'Isn't it lucky that it isn't raining? Are we going to take Bouncer for a run?'

'Of course, but coffee first.'

Daisy, quite at her ease now, said, 'I have a door key; the Friskes are going to visit friends and my dinner is all ready for me to warm up. Mevrouw Friske is so kind, and we get on so well. It's a bit difficult sometimes, when we don't quite understand each other, but I'm learning fast—just useful words. Dutch is a frightful language, isn't it?'

'So I have been told, but since it is my mother tongue I don't feel qualified to comment.'

Daisy had gone bright pink. 'I'm sorry, that was rude of me—although I didn't mean it to be.'

'I do know that, Daisy, and surely we are sufficiently acquainted by now to be at ease with each other?'

'Well, I suppose we are acquainted, but it's not like being friends.' She frowned. 'It's difficult to explain, but you're you and I'm me...'

He didn't pretend not to understand her. 'Nevertheless, I believe that we are friends, Daisy.'

They were travelling along a country road and he pulled in onto the grass verge. He offered a large hand. 'Friends, Daisy?'

She shook the hand and beamed at him. 'Oh, yes, please.'

'And now that is settled once and for all, you might call me Jules?'

'All right, I will,' she went on. 'You know, I have always felt that we were friends, only I didn't think you had thought about it.'

Mr der Huizma reflected that he had thought about it a great deal during the last two weeks or so, but he didn't say so. He said briskly, 'We're going to Leiden now. I was a student at the medical school there; it's a charming little town. We won't stop, though, since we shall lunch in Delft.'

All the same he did stop obligingly so that she might see the Burcht, a twelfth-century mound with a fortress on the top, right in the middle of the town, and he stopped again so that she might have a glimpse of the Rapenburg Canal and the university and the museum.

'Were you happy there?' asked Daisy.

'Yes. I go back from time to time; it's full of pleasant memories.'

He drove on to Delft then, parking near the Grote Markt and taking her to a small restaurant where she could see both the town hall and the Nieuwe Kerk standing facing each other across the market square.

He didn't ask her what she would like to eat. 'This is a typical Dutch meal,' he told her. 'I hope you're hungry.'

She was, which was a good thing, for presently a waitress brought two large plates covered by vast pancakes dotted with tiny bits of crisp bacon. She also brought a big pot of dark syrup.

Mr der Huizma ladled the syrup onto the pancakes. 'It looks crazy but it tastes delicious,' he told her. And it was.

Daisy ate all of it with an enjoyment which brought a gleam of pleasure into Mr der Huizma's eyes. They drank a pot of coffee between them before he took her across to the Nieuwe Kerk. 'William of Orange is buried here, as well as other members of the royal family. You must come again and spend some time here; it's a delightful little town and very Dutch. And now is the time of year to see it, before the tourists come.'

They got back into the car and he told her, 'We're going to drive across to Hilversum. We'll pass Alphen aan de Rijn on the way—there's a bird sanctuary there—and we will pass Gouda too—that's for another time—there are some lakes close by—Reeuwijk Meer—you'll get a glimpse of them.'

She supposed after that they would return to Amsterdam. It was almost four o'clock now, and the afternoon had grown grey and chilly, but presently they joined a main road and she saw the signpost to Hilversum.'

'You're going the wrong way,' said Daisy. 'Amsterdam was that road on the left.'

'We must have tea first.' He didn't enlarge on that, and she presumed that there was a café or tea room he particularly wanted to go to. The country was pretty, even on this rather bleak day. There were small woods and narrow roads, and here and there a glimpse of a large house behind the trees. The trees and bushes soon thinned out along the side of the road, and she had a fine view of a large square house standing well back from the road, backed by trees. It was white with green shutters, and its many windows climbed up to a steep roof.

'Oh, look,' said Daisy, 'what a lovely house. It looks as though it's been there for ever, and it looks cosy although it's rather large. And look, the windows are lighted. I expect it houses a family with children and dogs and cats.'

Mr der Huizma swept the car between tall gateposts. 'Well, not at present,' he observed, 'but possibly one day. And it is a cosy house; I was born in it.'

Daisy turned to look at him. 'But you have a lovely house in Amsterdam.'

'This is the family home. My mother lives here; we are going to have tea with her.'

'But she doesn't know me.'

'Well, no. She hasn't met you yet, has she?'

He stopped the car before the house, and got out and opened the door for her.

'I'm not sure,' began Daisy doubtfully.

He said bracingly. 'Come, come, where is your British phlegm? And I'm sure you would like a cup of tea.'

He greeted the elderly woman who opened the door as they went up the steps, and then said, 'This is Katje, our housekeeper. She doesn't speak English but understands a few words.' So Daisy shook hands and smiled, and was smiled at in return. 'Let her have your jacket; she will show you where the cloakroom is.'

Daisy followed Katje to the back of the square hall and was ushered into a small room equipped, as far as she could see, with everything a woman might need. Having tidied her hair and powdered her nose she went back into the hall to find Jules standing there, where she had left him.

He opened an arched double door, and with a hand on her shoulder walked her into the room beyond. His mother was sitting in her usual chair by the fire, and she got up as they went in.

'Jules, how nice to see you—and so punctual too.' She offered a cheek for his kiss and turned to Daisy, smiling.

'Mother, this is Daisy Gillard, over here to learn something of our antiques.' His mother, already aware of that, smiled and offered a hand. 'My mother,' said Mr der Huizma, and watched them shake hands, still smiling, and then he smiled himself, because it was all right; they liked each other...

Tea, to Daisy's relief, wasn't just a cup of weak tea and a tiny biscuit. The tea was a fragrant Assam and there were tiny sandwiches as well as scones and a fruitcake. Sitting there by the fire, listening to her hostess's quiet voice going from one unalarming topic to another, was a delight. Beyond a few casual questions about herself, Mevrouw der Huizma made no attempt to cross-examine her. The talk was desultory and un-forced; it was as if the three of them had known each other all their lives. Well, of course Jules and his mother had, hadn't they? reflected Daisy, biting into a second slice of cake, but somehow she seemed to be included in the family.

But she couldn't presume on such kindness; when the great *stoel* clock struck six she suggested that she should go back to Amsterdam. 'The Friskes expect me back in the evening,' she pointed out, which wasn't quite true but it sounded all right. So presently she bade Mevrouw der Huizma goodbye, thanked her for her tea, and got back into the car with Jules and Bouncer.

And if she was secretly disappointed that he hadn't urged her to stay longer, she squashed the thought at once as being ungrateful. He had, after all, spent the whole day driving around Holland with her, when he might have spent it doing something more exciting.

To her relief there were lights from the Friskes' up-stairs windows, so that her fib appeared justified. As Mr der Huizma stopped before their door she began the little speech she had thought about on their way, but she didn't get far with it. He interrupted her with, 'Daisy, spare me the thanks I'm sure you have been rehearsing. I have enjoyed my day with you; you're a good companion, you know. You don't talk unless you have something to say, and then it's good sense, and you're blessedly silent...'

Daisy said, 'Oh, am I?' in a surprised voice, not sure

if she liked the bit about her being silent; had she talked too much? She was aware that, whereas she was usually reserved with people, with Jules she felt so much at ease that she might have let her tongue run away with her.

He got out and opened her door and they crossed the cobbles to the door.

'If I am free next Sunday we will drive up to the Frisian lakes and take a look at Leeuwarden.'

He took the key from her hand and opened the door, then stood looking down at her, and she smiled at him, delighted that she would see him again. Despite himself he kissed her upturned face, then gave her a gentle shove through the door and closed it before she had the chance to say goodnight. Which was just as well for she was too astonished to speak.

She made her way upstairs to the Friskes' sitting room in a bemused manner, answered their questions as to how she had spent her day and presently sat down to *echte* soup and smoked sausage and *zuurkoel*. And all the while she was thinking about his kiss. Of course everyone kissed these days, she told herself sensibly, but it hadn't been a social kiss, had it? It had been warm and lingering; there had been nothing social about it. She decided to forget it.

Easier said than done, she discovered, but as the next Sunday approached she warned herself sternly to let Jules see that it had made no impression upon her, that it had been something easily forgotten. Moreover, she decided that if he should suggest any more outings she would refuse. It was no good saying that she was spending the day with friends, for she had none as yet. She could have a heavy cold—so much more plausible than a headache…unless it was a migraine. But perhaps he wouldn't ask her out again; Helene would be coming back from California and he would spend his spare time with her. It was quite natural, Daisy told herself, that a man should spend his free time with a companion if his fiancée wasn't there with him. Which was where she ought to be, thought Daisy.

She had expected to feel awkward when he called for her on Sunday, but his quiet friendliness dispelled that at once.

It was a damp grey day, with the threat of rain, but the car was warm and comfortable and Bouncer was glad to see her again.

'We shall go to Alkmaar, and then on to the Afsluit-dijk to Friesland,' he told her, 'and we shall come back for part of the way through the reclaimed land from the Ijsselmeer. The reclaiming is still going on, and the country isn't very interesting, but there are any number of farms there and they're prosperous.'

After that he didn't say much, only asking from time to time if she had enjoyed her week. She answered him briefly, mindful of his remarks about being silent, and asked instead if he had had an interesting week.

It struck him that Helene had never asked him that, and he began to tell her a little of his work. Daisy asked questions: How many children were in his wards? Did he operate? Were the children happy in hospital? What happened when they were discharged home? And did he like the babies or the toddlers best?

And he answered her questions in detail, realising what a pleasure it was to talk about his work to someone who was really interested and not just polite. Of course he talked to his mother, but he saw her infrequently and there was always family news to discuss so that he seldom did more than touch lightly on his work, but now, with Daisy all ears beside him, listening eagerly to his replies, he told her all that she wanted to know and found himself enjoying talking of it.

In Alkmaar they stopped for coffee and a brisk walk through the little town as far as the cheese market and the Weigh House with its carillon, before driving over the Afsluitdijk into Friesland. He drove through Harlingen and Franeker and on to Leeuwarden, where they had lunch at a hotel and another quick walk for Bouncer's benefit and for a view of the statue of the cow—the sign of Friesland's prosperity.

And then it was on again to Sneek, and the lakes, and on to Meppel and so to Lelystad, one of the small towns on the reclaimed land, and thence to Naarden and Hilversum.

'Mother is expecting us for tea,' said Mr der Huizma, turning in between the pillars.

And it was all just as delightful as the previous Sunday had been, sitting in the grand room, with Bouncer close to his master, scoffing the odd pieces of cake or biscuit, and a large ginger cat sitting beside Mevrouw der Huizma in her chair, so that the room didn't seem grand at all, just a room where people were happy and content. Daisy, unable to put it into coherent thought, felt a quiet happiness. Heart's ease, she thought, that's what I'm feeling.

She took care not to outstay her welcome. Mevrouw der Huizma kissed her goodbye. 'I'm sure we shall see each other again,' she observed—something which

Daisy secretly hoped for. But Jules said nothing about a
further meeting when they reached Heer Friske's house.
Nor did he kiss her, but bade her goodbye in a cheerful
brisk manner and told her not to work too hard.

So I'm not going to see him again, Daisy told herself, getting ready for bed. Helene would be coming
back. He would give her the diamond brooch and they
would marry. She was almost asleep before she voiced
her thoughts. 'But they won't live happily ever after!'

The shop was unusually busy the following week,
and Daisy, having mastered some essential Dutch,
found herself fully occupied. The tourists were beginning to drift in, and each evening Heer Friske taught
her all he knew about marquetry and Dutch porcelain.

When the weekend came, Daisy took herself off
to various small side-streets lined by antique dealers' shops, and studied their windows before having
an early lunch in a café and spending the afternoon in
the Rijksmuseum. She had a cup of tea there, and stayed
until it closed. As she left its entrance she saw Mr der
Huizma in his car. Helene was sitting beside him, but
Bouncer was on the back seat. He didn't see her; indeed, both of them were looking ahead, not speaking...

So Helene was back. At the back of her mind Daisy
had had the vague hope that she might like California
so much that she had decided to stay there. So now I
can stop being silly, Daisy told herself, walking briskly
back for her supper. It was nice knowing him, but now
I can forget him.

Which should have been easy, but Fate sometimes
disregards the best of intentions.

It was on a morning towards the end of the next

week that Daisy, rubbing up some silver candlesticks while Heer Friske was talking a customer into buying some Dutch tiles, was distracted by a great deal of noise in the street outside. Heer Friske was occupied, so she put down her cloth and went out of the shop to take a look.

A car had stopped close by, and an elderly woman was sitting on the cobbles clutching a large black cat while the driver stooped over her. He looked up as Daisy reached them.

'Do you speak English? I wasn't driving fast but the cat ran across the street and she came after it.'

'I'm English,' said Daisy, and mustered a few Dutch words. The woman shook her head. No, she wasn't hurt, nothing was broken; she was just sore. Daisy put two and two together, patted her shoulder reassuringly, stroked the cat and said, 'Look, I think you'd better take her to hospital. It's not far. Wait a minute while I speak to Heer Friske.'

The car driver mopped a worried brow. 'Will you come? I'm very grateful—I'll pay.'

Heer Friske, having sold his tiles, came hurrying out on Daisy's heels, explained to the woman, helped the driver get her into the car, still holding the cat, and told Daisy to go with them. He turned to the man. 'And bring her back when everything is settled.'

So Daisy got into the car beside the driver and steered him through the streets to the hospital. Once there, she went into Casualty and found the sister. She remembered her, so that explaining what had happened wasn't difficult. The woman was led away and Daisy, having been handed the cat, wondered what to do next.

The driver was talking to the receptionist and they were soon joined by a large police officer. She held the cat securely and joined them.

'Will someone tell the patient that I'll take the cat back to her home? Only I must know her address and have a key to get in.' She turned to Sister. 'Could you explain that I'm at Heer Friske's and that I'm quite honest. I'll get a taxi—I can't wait any longer.' She looked at the driver and the officer, deep in talk. A few minutes later she had the key and the address and was on her way to the hospital entrance. And a few yards from it she met Mr der Huizma, also on his way out.

Chapter 6

There was no avoiding Jules, nor, apparently, had he any intention of letting her try to do so.

'Daisy…' He took in the cat tucked under her arm with a quick glance. 'You're leaving the hospital? I'll drive you back.'

Anyone else would have bombarded her with questions, thought Daisy, but not Jules. She took a firmer grip on the cat, gave a brief resumé of events and waited to see what he would say.

'We will take the cat back home,' said Mr der Huizma without hesitation, 'warn a neighbour, if possible, and return you to Heer Friske's shop. He must be worried. This lady is in Casualty? Is she injured?'

And when Daisy said that she didn't know he said, 'Well, never mind that now; I can find out easily enough. Just leave it to me.'

He swept her out to the car, glanced at the address Sister had written down for Daisy, and drove off. It was a small house in a row of small houses, very neat, with gleaming windows and spotless curtains, and inside the whole place shone with polish. The furniture was old, but cared for, and behind the tiny kitchen there was a garden, very small and as neat as the house. The cat went at once to a chair in the corner of the living room, curled up and prepared to sleep, quite untroubled by the goings-on around it. Daisy found a saucer, filled it with cat food and put it on the kitchen floor, and Mr der Huizma went next door to talk to a neighbour.

He came back presently. 'We are to leave the kitchen window open so that the cat can get in and out; the neighbour will feed him if necessary.'

'The key?' asked Daisy.

He took his phone from his pocket and she waited patiently while he talked and listened and talked again. 'The patient is to come home presently. She isn't seriously hurt—bruises and a small cut on her leg. Let me have the key and I will see that she gets it. I shall be going back to the hospital.'

Something which hadn't been his intention but he was a kind man. He added, 'Come along, I'll drive you back to Heer Friske.'

Daisy had barely spoken; delight at seeing him again had rendered her speechless. He had taken command of the situation and she had been willing to do as she was told. Now she said, 'You've been very kind, but I can walk back; it's not far…'

He had gone to open the little window in the kitchen. 'I shall be going past the shop,' was all he said.

He left her there presently, bidding her a brisk goodbye and driving away before she could utter thanks. Back to the hospital which he had so recently left for a few hours before he saw his private patients in the evening. He reflected ruefully that on almost all of the occasions when he and Daisy had met she had disrupted his plans. And now she had popped up again to disturb him. They had exchanged barely a dozen words, and yet he had enjoyed every minute of her silent company. He frowned, remembering that he had resolved not to see her again. Her small, quiet person had begun to fill his thoughts, something which had to be stopped.

He went into the hospital and sought out the sister in Casualty, who told him that the woman was ready to be discharged and then asked him if Helene was back from California. She was a long-standing friend and colleague, anxious to see him happily married. She didn't like Helene, whom she had met at various hospital functions, but thought she seemed entirely suitable. She was surprised to see the look on Mr der Huizma's handsome face when he told her that she had recently returned home. Surely a man shouldn't look like that when speaking of the woman he was to marry?

She prudently said nothing more, but went to fetch the cat's owner.

Mr der Huizma drove her home, gave her back her key and listened with pleasure to her gratitude towards Daisy. 'Such a kind young lady. Came to help me at once, and understood how I felt about my cat. And her a foreigner too.'

The temptation to stop at Heer Friske's shop on the way home was great, but he resisted it. Meeting Daisy had been unavoidable, but to seek her out deliberately was quite another thing.

He went home, and later to his consulting rooms, and when he finally got back to eat a late dinner there was a message from Helene. She would expect to hear from him in the morning.

Mr der Huizma looked through his diary. He had a busy few days ahead of him; there would be very little time to see Helene and certainly no chance to take her out to dinner or the theatre, which he thought she would expect. He made a note to have flowers sent to her home and settled down at his desk to continue writing an article on infant malnutrition. He had been asked if he would go to the famine areas in Africa and advise on the feeding of the starving babies and children there, and he had decided to go. It was something dear to his heart, and he had contrived to arrange his work so that he could go for a month. He paused in his writing and sighed; Helene wasn't going to like his decision. It was a pity he hadn't been able to arrange it while she was in California…

On the following Monday morning Daisy called on the woman with the cat. She had been to the post office, bought herself a newspaper, some toothpaste and a bottle of shampoo and, as an afterthought, a tin of cat food. The woman came to the door when she knocked; she recognised her and asked her in.

Daisy, at a loss for words, held out the cat food, and right on cue the cat came into the room and walked over to her, weaving round her feet. The woman beamed, keeping up a flow of talk, none of which Daisy understood. When the woman paused for breath Daisy ventured, 'Better?' and, since it was a word very similar to its Dutch counterpart, the woman nodded and smiled, waved Daisy to a chair and went out of the room to return with a letter in her hand. She gave it to Daisy and pointed and nodded so Daisy took it out of its envelope. It was in English, and was from the man who had knocked the woman down. There was money inside too. She read the letter and then, dredging up the words she knew, explained that the money was compensation for the accident. Her accent was shocking, but with a good deal of hand-waving and nodding she made her companion understand.

She gave the letter and the money back, and when she would have got up was waved back to her seat. 'Coffee?' said her hostess, and since Daisy had an hour to spare, and the cat had scrambled onto her lap, she stayed in the neat little room, carrying on what passed for conversation with the woman.

When she got up to go she realised that she had enjoyed herself, and learnt quite a few more Dutch words. Never mind the grammar, she decided. Knowing what everything was called in Dutch was the priority. Never mind the accent either; Heer Friske would put her right with that. She went back to the shop feeling that perhaps she was making a little niche for herself; perhaps she would meet people and make friends.

Mr der Huizma, preparing for his journey, working early and late and making up in part for his forthcoming absence, had told Helene of his intention.

She had phoned him and told him that he could take

her out to dinner. 'There's that new restaurant in the Leidesgracht,' she had said. 'We'll go there; you'll have to book a table…'

She had rung off before he could speak.

The dinner hadn't been a success. They had almost finished their meal before she'd asked him if he had been busy. 'Your boring job,' she'd said, laughing at him across the table. 'We must go out more…'

'I'm going away,' he had told her quietly, and had explained why he was going.

'But it will be ghastly,' she'd exclaimed. 'You'll pick up one of those horrible diseases. There are dozens of young doctors willing to go, I'm sure. Really, Jules, I can't allow you to do it.'

His eyes had been cold. 'I'm afraid there is no question of your allowing me to do anything, Helene. This is my work and I intend to do it. I thought you might have understood…'

She had been pale with annoyance. 'Understood? I'm not some GP's wife, meekly accepting a dreary life of interrupted nights and uneaten meals. Life's meant to be enjoyed and I intend to enjoy it.'

He had stayed silent for a moment, and then said quietly, 'If that is how you feel, Helene, perhaps we should reconsider…'

She had seen that she had gone too far. 'Jules, I'm sorry. Of course you must do what you think right. Only you frightened me for a moment…' She'd smiled at him, the picture of contrition. 'Forgive me?'

'Of course, but I do not intend to change my mind, Helene.'

She had said quickly, 'No, no, of course not. You must tell me about it—how long will you be gone?'

She had infused interest into her voice. For a few moments she had been afraid that she would lose him; as a husband he was all, or almost all, that a woman could wish for.

She had kissed him warmly when they parted, but for Jules it could have been as unimportant as something half felt and brushed away with no further thought. He was aware now that Helene didn't love him, never had, perhaps, but knew he represented everything that she wanted from life. She had no intention of releasing him from their engagement, and for his part would have been content with that—until he had met Daisy, whom he must forget, and who would go back to England and eventually marry some man or stay single. She had never been more than friendly, he reflected ruefully; it had been his misfortune to fall in love with a girl who didn't care twopence about him.

He was to leave in a week's time, and every minute that he could spare he spent with Helene, trying to rekindle his feelings for her. But she, secure as to her future, brushed aside his suggestions that they should marry.

'For heaven's sake,' she had told him impatiently, 'I'll have years of being a wife, running our home and planning our social life. I mean to have some fun before then.' She'd pouted prettily. 'Jules, if only you would have fun too. You're thirty-five, and as far as I can tell your life's one dreary round of hospitals and patients and giving lectures.'

'But that is my life and I'm happy with it, Helene. You can always change your mind...'

Once again she'd had a moment's uncertainty, but she was too self-centred to let it worry her. 'Dear Jules, of course I won't change my mind. When you get back we'll fix a date for the wedding.'

He said nothing to his mother when he visited her, but that lady, watching him on one of his rare visits, saw that something wasn't right. She had enquired about Helene, as she always did, and received his vague replies in silence. But when she asked if he had seen Daisy and saw the look on his face she felt troubled. Unless Helene gave him a good reason for doing so Jules would never break their engagement—and Helene wasn't likely to do so. But that, reflected Mevrouw der Huizma silently, is what I hope and pray will happen.

Daisy was up early on the morning Jules was to leave for Africa. She had neither seen nor heard anything of him, which should have made it easy to forget him, only it hadn't. She thought about him a good deal, despite her resolution not to do so, and now, on this bright spring morning, she was in the shop packing up some china a customer was to call for on his way to the airport. Mevrouw Friske was upstairs, getting breakfast, and Heer Friske was still in bed. The street outside was empty save for early tradesmen.

She had her back to the door when the old-fashioned bell tinkled, and she glanced at the clock as she hurried to open it. The customer was early; he would have to wait for a few minutes.

She pulled up the blind as she opened the door, and stood back wordlessly as Mr der Huizma walked in.

'We're not open,' said Daisy, and, as an afterthought, 'Good morning.'

He made no reply to either of those remarks. 'I'm going away—for a month, perhaps longer.' His eyes searched her face. 'I didn't want to go without saying goodbye. I'm going to Africa.'

'But you'll be back?' Her heart had sunk into her shoes, but she was glad to hear her voice sounding normal.

'Oh, yes. Will you be gone?'

'I don't know. Perhaps. Why are you going to Africa?' she added. 'It's a long way.'

'I'm going to organise a hospital and feeding centre for the children in a famine area.'

'Yes, of course; they must need someone like you. If I were a nurse I'd have liked to have gone with you.' And when he said nothing she added, 'Helene must be sorry that you're going.'

As indeed she was—but for all the wrong reasons.

He said harshly, 'Helene has a great many interests to keep her happy while I'm away. Will you miss me? Daisy?'

She studied his calm face. 'Yes, of course I shall. One always misses friends, and we are friends, remember? But I don't see you often—hardly at all, and then it's by accident.' She sighed. 'But, yes, I'll miss you. But I wish you success,' she added, 'and a quick return home.' She put out a hand, suddenly aware that if he stayed much longer she would burst into tears. 'Goodbye.'

He took her hand and held it carefully, as though it might break, then he swept her into his arms and kissed her. It was a kiss not to be easily forgotten. Indeed Daisy hadn't known kisses like that existed outside romantic novels.

'I have to have something,' said Mr der Huizma in a goaded voice, and released her so violently that she nearly fell over.

'Well,' said Daisy, but she spoke to an empty shop. The Rolls was already on its silent way.

It would never do to burst into tears, although she very much wanted to. Instead she sucked in her breath like a hurt child, and finished packing the china. Presently, called to her breakfast by Mevrouw Friske, she went upstairs and drank her coffee. To eat would have choked her; she pleaded a headache which she was sure would soon go, and agreed with Mevrouw Friske that she would make up for her lack of appetite at their midday meal.

Mr der Huizma, handing over the car to Joop, who had accompanied him to Schipol, boarded his plane and allowed his thoughts to dwell on Daisy. She had been pleased to see him, he was sure of that, but she had said nothing which would allow him to hope that she had any warmer feelings for him. And a good thing too, he reminded himself. That she should be made unhappy was something he would not be able to bear. He hadn't intended to kiss her, that had been a mistake, but one which he realised he had been powerless to prevent. He hoped that she would consider it as a farewell kiss and nothing more. He didn't think that she was a girl

who had been kissed very often, and she would probably think that it was a normal goodbye. After all they
were friends; she had said so.

And now he must forget her, and consider the work
ahead of him. He got out his paperwork and began to
study it, dismissing Daisy from his mind. He hadn't
thought once about Helene. For the moment his personal problems must take second place.

Daisy got through her day somehow. She knew how
awful it was to love someone who didn't love you. True,
he had kissed her quite savagely, but he hadn't really
minded when she had told him that she would probably be gone by the time he returned. If she had been
other than a sensible girl, who had learned that she
wasn't particularly attractive to men, she might have
built her hopes on that kiss. As it was she decided that
he had been upset at leaving his home and Helene and
had needed to express his feelings.

A sensible conclusion, which didn't prevent herself
from crying till she fell asleep that night. It was so
awful that she wouldn't see him again—she would be
home before he returned, she felt sure—but what was
worse was that she had no idea where he had gone, nor
would she hear news of him. And how silly of her to
fall in love with a man who was on the point of getting
married to a very beautiful woman, and who lived in
a different world to her own.

Hearts didn't break, Daisy assured herself, and life
must go on, and in a little while she would be able
to think of him as one thought of a pleasant dream.
She would apply herself wholeheartedly to the study

of Dutch antiques, strive even harder to acquire some knowledge of the Dutch tongue, and on her free Sundays see as much of the country as she could.

These high-minded resolutions took her through the week following Jules's departure, and she planned a whole day's outing on Sunday. It would involve buses and trains, and she would probably get lost, but it would keep her fully occupied and it would be something to write home about…

There was a letter for her on Saturday morning; a vellum envelope, and addressed in a fine, spidery handwriting. Her heart had leapt at the sight of it and then common sense had taken over. Mr der Huizma had no reason to write to her, and she doubted if expensive notepaper was readily obtained where he was living now. She opened it, and spread out the sheet of fine notepaper it contained. It was from Mevrouw der Huizma. Would she have lunch and spend the afternoon with her on Sunday? Joop would fetch her and bring her back. Perhaps she would phone and let her know.

Daisy read the letter twice, and then sat thinking about it. She would love to go, she liked Mevrouw der Huizma and she wanted to see Jules's home again, but would it be better if she were to refuse? Going to his home would keep alive the memories she was trying so hard to forget. But he wasn't there, she reminded herself…

She went to tell Heer Friske, and then telephoned her acceptance.

Joop came to fetch her soon after eleven o'clock. Daisy had spent some time searching her scanty wardrobe for something suitable for the occasion, but really there wasn't anything there to match the magnificence of his home. It would have to be the jacket and skirt again, and a plain silk blouse. Not that it mattered, reflected Daisy, studying as much as possible of her person in the small looking glass in her room. Jules wasn't there, and even if he was, he wouldn't notice what she was wearing.

Joop, driving an elderly Daimler, greeted her in a fatherly fashion and looked pleased when she got in beside him. He drove well, but at a discreet pace, which gave her time to practise her Dutch on him. He replied in the same language, gently correcting her when her verbs became too tangled. At the house he ushered her out of the car and into the house. Katje took her jacket and led the way to the drawing room.

Mevrouw der Huizma was sitting in her usual chair, Bouncer beside her. She got up to greet Daisy with every sign of pleasure.

'Sit down, Daisy. Katje will bring coffee in a moment. This is kind of you to bear me company. I wondered if you would like to see round the house presently? There are some rather nice pieces, and I know you are interested in antiques. But first let us have coffee and chat. How are you getting on?'

They talked comfortably over coffee, but Jules wasn't mentioned. Daisy, who had been hoping to hear something of him, was disappointed, but perhaps later…

They began a tour of the house presently. 'For there is a lot to see,' explained her hostess. 'The ground floor will take us until lunch time.'

Daisy would have liked to have spent more time in

the drawing room; it held some splendid specimens of marquetry and a collection of porcelain she could have spent hours over, but she followed Mevrouw der Huizma out of the room to linger in the dining room, with its magnificent Regency sideboard and panelled walls hung with family portraits in heavy frames. Daisy, peering up at them, thought that Jules looked very like his ancestors, even though he didn't wear a wig. But she didn't say so as she followed her hostess into a small room with striped wallpaper, comfortable chairs and a round games table under the window. There was nothing modern there, but it would be a delightful room in which to sit and do nothing…

'I sit here a great deal,' said Mevrouw der Huizma, 'sewing and knitting and writing letters. The grandchildren call it Granny's Room.'

'Oh—do you have many? Grandchildren?'

'Five, so far. I have two daughters. I hope for more grandchildren when Jules marries.'

Daisy said steadily, 'I'm sure you must do. Children are such fun, and this house is made for them, isn't it? I mean, it's rather grand and large, but it's home…'

Mevrouw der Huizma gave her a look of deep approval. Here was a girl after her own heart, and, she suspected, Jules's heart too. She sighed and led the way to the library, and the study, and then into the vast conservatory at the back of the house.

Presently, drinking sherry before lunch, once more in the drawing room, she said, 'You must come again, Daisy, and roam around as much as you please. Everything is catalogued, which may help you.'

'I should like that very much, *mevrouw.* But I'm not sure how much longer I shall be at Heer Friske's…'

They lunched in the dining room, sitting together at one end of the long table; melon balls, jellied lobster, salad, and a sponge pudding swimming in sherry and thick cream. Daisy, undeterred by the eyes of Jules's ancestors staring down at her from the walls, enjoyed every morsel.

It was as they sat drinking their coffee in the drawing room that Mevrouw der Huizma observed, 'I was glad to hear from Jules this week. A brief note brought by one of the nurses returning to Holland. He says very little, but I gather that there is a tremendous amount of work to be done there and they need skilled men such as he. I shall be glad to see him again, though.'

She bent to pat Bouncer, curled up at their feet. 'Jules brought Bouncer here while he is away; he's company for me and he does miss his master. Joop, too, comes here whenever I need him. Both my daughters live some distance away—Ineke in Goningen and Lisa in Limburg. They both have young children and homes to run, and it isn't easy for them to visit me very often. They telephone me several times a week, though.' She smiled. 'You see that I am very well cared for by my family.'

She put down her coffee cup. 'Would you like to see the rest of the house, Daisy? It will take some time, and then we can have a nice chat before tea.'

It certainly took time; Daisy could have spent hours lingering in the bedrooms. Especially the vast principal bedroom, with its four-poster and massive tallboy, and the dressing table under the bow windows, all of

mahogany inlaid with tulip wood, and there was a silver ewer on a side-table which she would have liked to
examine at her leisure. But politeness forced her to follow her hostess from room to room, some large, some
small, all splendidly furnished.

'There are attics too,' explained Mevrouw der
Huizma, 'crammed with more furniture, but that would
take too long…'

She led the way downstairs, and as they reached
the hall the doorbell clanged and Joop went to open
the door.

'Who can that be?' She frowned. 'I was not expecting anyone to call.'

Certainly not Helene, who brushed past Joop and
crossed the hall, smiling, her hands held out as though
she were about to embrace Mevrouw der Huizma.

'Mevrouw der Huizma. I come unannounced, but
I thought we might have a talk together. You must be
missing Jules and there is so much for us to discuss.'

Mevrouw der Huizma took one of the outstretched
hands and shook it.

'Helene, this is a surprise. You have news of Jules?'

'Oh, just a note saying that he had arrived safely. I
don't expect to hear from him, and really there's nothing of his work there which would interest me.'

'So I would imagine,' said Mevrouw der Huizma,
and spoke in English. 'I believe that you have met Daisy
at Jules's house?'

Helene gave Daisy a cursory glance. 'Have we? Oh,
yes, you're the girl from the antique shop.' She added
sharply, 'Are you looking over the furniture here?'

She was being deliberately rude, but Daisy ignored that. She didn't answer.

It was Mevrouw der Huizma who spoke. 'Daisy has spent the day with me.' She added deliberately, 'She has been here before, with Jules; he has shown her something of Holland while she is here.'

'Oh,' Helene's fine blue eyes were cold. While she had been in California, of course. This nondescript girl had gone behind her back—though heaven knew what he saw in her. Something would have to be done about that, but not at the moment.

'You couldn't have a better person to show you the country,' she said, and smiled at Daisy. 'Are you going to be here long?'

'I'm not sure, but I expect I'll go home in another month or so. It depends on Heer Friske.'

They had walked as they talked, and now seated themselves in the drawing room. Helene curled up on one of the sofas, as if to demonstrate how at home she was. Bouncer went over to her, and she put out a beautifully shod foot and pushed him away. She laughed as she did it. 'Jules's awful dog—I'm always telling him that it should live in the kitchen. Has he given it to you?'

Mevrouw der Huizma said levelly, 'No, Bouncer stays with me while Jules is away. He is splendid company.'

'Well, I shall persuade Jules to give it to you when we marry. A dog is such a nuisance.'

Mevrouw der Huizma ignored that. 'Will you stay for tea? We are just about to have ours?'

'Just a cup of tea. I must lose a few pounds; I got positively fat while I was in California and I've brought some lovely clothes back with me so I don't dare to eat too much.' She gave a satisfied little laugh and looked down at the elegant outfit which emphasised the boniness of her person.

Flat as a board, reflected Daisy. That dress would look better on a coathanger. She felt better for the thought. She wasn't given to unkindness, but really Helene was a horrid woman, and how Jules could possibly want to marry her Daisy couldn't imagine. At the thought of him she smiled a little, and Helene, watching her, felt a little prickle of disquiet. What had the girl got to smile about? she asked herself with sudden suspicion. 'Has Jules written to you?'

'Me? No, why should he? I'm sure he's far too busy to write to anyone except his nearest and dearest.'

Helene pouted. 'Well, I think it is too bad of him to go off like this.'

Mevrouw der Huizma said quietly, 'But that is what you must expect if you are a medical man's wife, Helene.'

'Oh, I'm sure I shall be able to alter that once we are married. Jules has suggested that we marry soon, but there is no hurry. After all, I shall be spending the rest of my life as a housewife…'

Daisy wondered if she had any idea of how to be a housewife. True, she would know how to give orders to servants, but would she be a good wife and mother? It seemed unlikely. Daisy thought of the cold, unloving future lying in wait for Jules. Only perhaps he wouldn't notice that if he loved Helene.

She accepted a cup of tea from Mevrouw der Huizma and made polite conversation, reminding herself that loving Jules gave her no right to wish him to give up Helene. Thinking about it made her feel a little sick.

Helene showed no signs of leaving, and Daisy wondered if she should suggest that she herself should go back to Heer Friske's shop. But before she could think up a suitable excuse Mevrouw der Huizma observed, 'Daisy and I will be busy this evening. We are going to study the history of this house. There are any number of books, and diaries over a long period. Some of the invoices and bills are most interesting. They are housed in the attics and I dare say we shall get very dusty and chilly.' She smiled at Helene. 'Would you like to join us?'

'No—no, thank you. I'm going out to dinner and I must be leaving. If Daisy had been going back I could have offered her a lift…'

She made her farewells presently, and Mevrouw der Huizma said, 'Let me know if you have news of Jules…'

'Oh, I don't expect to. And I'm sure he won't have time to read letters from me.'

She glanced at Daisy, and Daisy held out a hand which was ignored.

When Helene was gone Mevrouw der Huizma said gently, 'I am sorry that Helene was rude, Daisy. Let us go upstairs to the attics and look around. I believe you may be interested.'

'I should go back…'

'Unless you wish to return to Heer Friske, I had hoped that you would have supper with me.'

'Oh. I'd like that very much. I thought that you said that about the attics…you know…' Daisy stopped and went red.

Mevrouw der Huizma laughed. 'In order that Helene might go away? Well, yes, but I had intended asking you to stay, my dear, so please do so. Joop shall drive you back after supper.'

They spent a delightful hour or so up under the gabled roof of the house, looking through the books and papers arranged on shelves in one of the larger attics.

'I seldom come up here now,' said Mevrouw der Huizma, 'but when my husband was alive we would spend hours up here.'

'It's fascinating,' said Daisy. 'Here's an invoice for a hundred-piece dinner service. There must have been a great deal of entertaining.'

'Undoubtedly. You must come again, Daisy, and look your fill. Now we will go downstairs for our supper.'

Mevrouw der Huizma dusted down her fine wool dress and led the way down.

Later that evening Joop drove Daisy back. It had been a lovely day; she had told her hostess so and had been warmly kissed.

'And we must repeat it,' Mevrouw der Huizma had said.

When Daisy had gone she sat down at her desk and wrote a letter to Jules, with Bouncer at her feet and the ginger cat sitting on her knee. As she wrote she wondered if Helene would write to him too; it seemed unlikely. Mevrouw der Huizma nibbled the end of her pen, frowning.

Helene had had no intention of writing to Jules; he had written briefly to her but she saw no point in answering his letter. She had no wish to know about his work, and the social life she so much enjoyed wouldn't interest him. He had tolerated her way of life, expecting her to change when they married—something which she'd had no intention of doing. But now, since her visit to his mother, she felt a faint doubt creeping into her complacency. Daisy, that dull girl, had wormed her way into Mevrouw der Huizma's graces, and was probably scheming to attract Jules. Of course, the idea was laughable, but one couldn't be too careful. Helene had no wish to marry him yet, life was pleasant as it was, but she must make sure that she held his interest...

So she wrote a long letter to Jules, with almost no mention of her own activities but containing an embellished version of her visit to his mother. Daisy, she wrote, had been there—such a sweet girl and so clever about antiques. She would be going back to England very shortly, and did Jules know that she was hoping to marry later in the year?

Helene was clever enough to write no more about Daisy; she had said just enough to make him forget the girl. She posted the letter and then made her plans. A little chat with Daisy would do no harm.

Chapter 7

Halfway through the week Daisy was surprised to have a phone call from Helene, proposing that she should call for Daisy on Sunday and drive her to the sea. 'We can have lunch somewhere,' said Helene, 'and come back here for tea. Since you will be going back to England shortly, you must see as much as possible of Holland before then.'

Daisy was too taken aback to say anything for the moment. She didn't want to spend the day with Helene, but how could she refuse without seeming rude? Excuses flew through her head; none of them would hold water. She said finally, 'That would be delightful. Thank you, I'd like to come…'

'I'll call for you at eleven o'clock,' said Helene. 'Don't bother to dress up; we'll take pot luck.'

Since I've nothing to dress up in, thought Daisy, that need not worry me. I wonder why she is so friendly? Perhaps Jules had written to her and suggested it. But why would he do that? And surely Helene had a better way of spending her Sunday than driving her around, sightseeing? Especially as Daisy was only too well aware that Helene didn't like her. Or perhaps I've mis-judged her, thought Daisy, and felt guilty because of her dislike of the woman…

Helene arrived a little after eleven o'clock, driving a bright red sports car, wearing a white leather jacket over a red trouser suit. She looked lovely, and Daisy, getting into the car beside her, could quite see why Jules was in love with her. She hadn't got out of the car and had ignored Heer Friske and his wife waving from their living room window. Daisy looked up and waved as they sped away and hoped that they hadn't felt offended at Helene's indifference. But Helene was disposed to be friendly. 'Did Jules take you to Scheve-ningen? We'll go to Zandvoort first; we can have cof-fee there and then drive up the coast.'

Daisy, a little bewildered by this sudden show of friendliness, told herself that she had misjudged He-lene, and readily answered her casually put questions.

'How fortunate that Jules was there to pull you out of the canal,' said Helene, 'and what a coincidence that you had already met. Did you see much of him in En-gland?'

And Daisy, her doubts lulled by Helene's friendly manner, told her about their meeting, and the walk they had had along the shore. 'It was such a pleasant surprise to meet him again,' she said, and something in her voice made Helene look at her sharply. 'He has been very kind to me while I've been here.' She gave a little laugh. 'It's funny how we kept on meeting without meaning to.'

Helene, putting in a word here and there, encouraged her to talk. The girl was in love with Jules, that was obvious, and probably he had been flattered by that. Something which must be nipped in the bud before he got back to Amsterdam.

She had driven up the coast after they had had their coffee and presently stopped at Egmond-aan-Zee. She had deliberately chosen a rather splendid hotel, much frequented by the well-to-do and young, leisured men and women—something Daisy realised as they entered the restaurant. Her clothes were all wrong; she saw the faintly amused glances cast at her tweed jacket and skirt—adequate for Amsterdam, even if a bit wintry now, but here, amongst so many smartly dressed people, she stuck out like a sore thumb. She wished that Helene had chosen somewhere more modest as they were ushered to a table in the centre of the room, but Helene appeared not to see her unease.

'The menu is in French,' she said rather too loudly. 'Shall I translate for you?'

Daisy, whose French was more than adequate, felt a faint prickle of annoyance. Helene had seemed friendly, but now she was patronising her...

'I think I can manage,' Daisy said, and gave her order in nicely pronounced French, adding, 'We learn French in school, you know. I don't know why it should be French in preference to any other language.'

'I suppose it's considered necessary in a basic education.' A remark which Daisy told herself hadn't been intended unkindly.

She enjoyed her lunch. There was no point in allowing her surroundings to ruin her appetite.

They turned inland after leaving the hotel, to go through Alkmaar and cross to the other side of the country.

'You must see Vollendam,' said Helene. 'All the tourists go there; the villagers still wear the national costume. Of course it's a great attraction. Foreigners like to think of us wearing clogs.'

She stopped the car for a while so that Daisy could look around her and buy a postcard to send home.

'Of course, you're a tourist yourself,' remarked Helene, and laughed. 'You will have plenty to tell your family when you go back. Do you know when you are going?'

Helene had asked her that at Mevrouw der Huizma's house only a few days previously, and Daisy wondered why she was so eager to know.

'I haven't any idea. A few weeks, I dare say, perhaps longer.'

Helene didn't say any more, but then started talking about California and the fun she had had there. A conversation which lasted until they were once more back in Amsterdam.

Once in the city, Helene drove away from its heart and Daisy said, 'I don't think I've been this way before. Is it a short-cut to Heer Friske's house?'

'No, no, we'll have tea at home and then I'll drive you back. It's still quite early and I'm sure you're longing for tea.'

'Well, that would be nice.' It would be interesting to see where Helene lived. In another lovely old house like Mr der Huizma's, perhaps.

Helene stopped outside a block of imposing flats in Churchillaan.

'Here we are.' She swept Daisy through the entrance guarded by a porter and got into the lift. 'We're on the second floor.'

The lift stopped and they walked along a wide carpeted corridor. Helene took out a key and opened a door at its end.

It was nothing like Mr der Huizma's house. There were vast rooms, heavily furnished, thickly carpeted, the windows swathed in vast curtains. Not an antique in sight. Helene led the way, opened double doors and urged her into the room beyond. There were two persons there, an elderly man and a woman somewhat younger. They both looked round as Helene and Daisy went in. Helene said something in Dutch and then added in English, 'This is Daisy, a girl Jules befriended on one or two occasions.'

She looked at Daisy. 'My parents, Daisy.'

Neither of them moved towards her. She took a step forward, a hand outstretched, and realised that neither of them intended to take it. She said, 'How do you do?' and waited to see who would speak first.

'Well, sit down,' said Mevrouw van Tromp. 'I expect you would like some tea. Ring the bell, Helene.' She stared at Daisy, her face devoid of expression.

'You are visiting here?'

'No. I work for Heer Friske, who has an antique shop.'

'Indeed, and why did you come to Amsterdam to work?'

'To gain experience...'

Helene had gone out of the room and came back without the leather jacket. 'Take your coat off, Daisy. It's getting rather warm for winter clothes. I don't suppose you have much, though. Do you go out at all?'

Daisy took off her jacket. She said quietly, 'No. I work all day, and in the evening I learn what I can about Dutch marquetry and china.'

Mevrouw van Tromp's voice was sharp. 'Do you work in a shop in England?'

Daisy said 'Yes, my father deals in antiques.'

'Indeed?' There was silence as tea was brought in. Daisy was offered a cup of weak, milkless tea and a small biscuit, and while she nibbled at it she wondered if Mijnheer van Tromp was going to speak to her. Or was a shopgirl beneath his notice?

Mevrouw van Tromp sipped her tea. 'You have met Mr der Huizma?'

'Yes, several times, both here and in England.' Daisy nibbled again and wished she was anywhere other than where she was. Helene's parents were dreadful; how could Jules contemplate being their son-in-law? And this flat, almost vulgar in its ostentation. She supposed that if you loved someone well enough nothing else mattered...

She refused a second cup of tea and remarked, 'I've had a delightful day, Helene. Thank you for taking me for such a splendid trip. Would you mind taking me back to Heer Friske? We usually play bridge on Sunday evenings—a neighbour comes in and makes a fourth.'

Mevrouw van Tromp asked, 'You play bridge?' Her tone implied that shopgirls wouldn't know how.

Daisy had been holding her temper in check. Another remark like that and she might lose it. So she smiled and got up, and thanked her reluctant hostess for her tea and bade her goodbye. Mijnheer van Tromp still hadn't spoken, so she nodded to him and followed Helene back to her car.

Walking back to the flat's entrance, Helene said over her shoulder, 'I expect it's all rather overwhelming…'

'Why should I be overwhelmed?'

'Such a difference in lifestyle. It must seem like another world to you.'

'No.' Daisy choked back the reply she would have liked to have made. 'I am aware of the difference, but it doesn't overwhelm me. Why should it?'

Helene said sweetly, 'Jules was afraid that you might feel awkward…' And, before Daisy could open her mouth to answer that one, 'We intend to marry within the next month or two. I did suggest that we might invite you to the wedding, but he is so thoughtful—it would mean a decent outfit—nothing off the peg—and there would be your fare here and a hotel—even the smaller hotels are expensive in Amsterdam.'

They had reached the door and got into the lift. 'You must think I'm horrid, saying things like this to you—' Helene sounded sincere '—but neither Jules nor I would want you to feel awkward.'

They were out in the street now. Daisy paused on the pavement. 'I'd like to walk back…'

'It's quite a long way…'

'But I like walking.' Daisy held out a hand. 'Such

an interesting day,' she said, in a voice which revealed nothing of the surge of feelings threatening to burst from her person at any moment.

Helene hadn't expected that; she shook Daisy's hand and began, 'Oh, but…' But Daisy was already walking away. For the moment she was lost, but she looked as though she knew where she was going.

It took her some time to find her way back to Heer Friske's house. Mevrouw Friske was in the kitchen, arranging little biscuits on a dish. She looked up and smiled as Daisy went in, asked in her mixture of English and Dutch if Daisy had had a pleasant day, and added that there were five people coming presently to spend the evening. 'My sister and her husband and their three daughters. We shall enjoy a happy evening; there will be young people for you, Daisy.'

After Helene's barbed remarks, Mevrouw Friske's cosy voice was soothing. And the evening proved enjoyable too; the three girls, all about her own age, were friendly, their English a good deal better than Daisy's Dutch, and their skill at the card table was on a par with her own so that the bridge session was light-hearted.

As they wished her goodbye they voiced the hope that they would see more of her. It was Heer Friske who remarked that Daisy would be going back to England shortly. A remark which rather surprised her. She thought no more about it, though, but went to bed to go over and over in her mind Helene's remarks. Daisy knew that there had been no real friendliness on her part. Indeed, it was as if Helene had wanted to impress her with the difference in their lifestyles. She found it hard to believe that Jules had said the things Helene had told her, although she could see no reason for her to have lied about it. Possibly Jules had realised the difference in their way of life, but he would have meant it kindly, and he wouldn't have taken her to an ultra-smart restaurant if she had pointed out that her clothes were all wrong... Perhaps it was a good thing that he might not be back before she went home. Although to see him just once more was her dearest wish.

Where's your good sense? 'You're a silly girl,' Daisy told herself, 'to dream of Jules. Forget him and go to sleep.' Which eventually she did.

She went out in the morning to post her card home and poke around the row of small shops. She would buy presents to take home, but she wasn't sure what, and there was nothing there which she liked. She would beg a half-day from Heer Friske and go to the Kalverstraat. There was plenty of time to do that...

Only as it turned out there wasn't. Another week went by, and it was late the following Tuesday, when the last customer had finally gone after half an hour of browsing and buying nothing, that Heer Friske called her into his office.

He offered her a chair. 'We must have a talk,' he began. 'You have done well here, and I believe you have learned a lot. I had intended to ask you to stay until the end of the summer, but now a situation has arisen.'

He peered at her anxiously, but she returned his look placidly although she had a nasty suspicion of what was to come.

'Mevrouw Friske's niece—the eldest, Mel—you met her last week—she wishes very much to work for me, to be trained to a good knowledge of antiques. She has an aptitude already. And, as my wife says, it would be a good thing to have a member of the family working here in the shop, perhaps in time taking over when I retire. So, Daisy, she will replace you as soon as you wish to return to England. We have liked having you here with us, but you have a good home and a career before you. You must not think that we are turning you out; make your arrangements to suit yourself. We shall miss you; you have done well. I will write you an excellent recommendation. You do not mind that I say all this?'

He looked so upset that Daisy said at once, 'Of course not, Heer Friske. It's a splendid idea to have Mel work here with you. And I was going back home quite soon anyway, wasn't I? I've been very happy here and I've learnt a great deal. I'm grateful to you, and to Mevrouw Friske. When would Mel like to come? If I could have a day or two...'

He heaved a sigh of relief. 'If she should come on Saturday, is that too soon for you? You may have as much free time as you need. You will want to get your ticket and perhaps say goodbye to friends.'

'That suits me very well. I haven't many friends, and I'll write to them or telephone. If I could have a few hours off to make arrangements?'

'Of course, and you will wish to telephone your parents. I also will speak to your father and explain. You do not find me unkind for doing this?'

He looked so woebegone that she leaned forward and kissed his cheek.

'You're one of the kindest men I've ever met,' she told him.

She would fly back, she decided, and her father

would meet her at Heathrow. She had very little luggage, and getting to Schipol would be quick and easy.

She booked on the Friday morning flight, spent a morning shopping—cigars for her father, a silk scarf for her mother—and she wrote a letter to Mevrouw der Huizma. It was brief and stilted, for it was difficult not to mention Jules. She thanked her again for the pleasant visits she had paid, sent her love to Bouncer, expressed her pleasure at returning home and sent good wishes.

She would have liked to have said goodbye personally, but it was better this way; to go away quietly and be the more easily forgotten.

Saying goodbye to the Friskes wasn't easy. She had grown to like Heer Friske and his wife, but, as she told herself over and over again, it was a good thing that she was leaving Amsterdam. She was leaving Jules and all her dreams too, but that was another matter. Out of sight, out of mind, Daisy told herself stoutly, and, clutching the carefully wrapped china figurine Heer Friske had pressed into her hands at the last minute, she got into the taxi.

A bus took her to Schipol, and as she got out of it she was momentarily taken aback by the size of the place. She went through the entrance and found its vast reception area teeming with people. Unlike her, they all appeared to know where they were going. She had plenty of time, she told herself, and stood for a moment reading the signs and directions, rotating slowly, anxious not to miss something vital. She must go to the left; she checked that she had her ticket ready and picked up her case, and then put it down again as she saw Mr der Huizma coming towards her.

She should have pretended not to see him, picked up her case and lost herself in the crowds… She stood waiting for him to reach her, schooling her face to polite surprise.

'What are you doing here? And why have you a case with you?'

He hadn't said hullo, or bothered with some conventional remark about meeting her again.

'I'm catching a plane home,' said Daisy, quite giddy with delight at seeing him just once more. He seemed larger than ever, and although he was as immaculately dressed as always he looked tired and somehow older.

'Was it awful?' asked Daisy. 'And were you able to help?'

'Yes and yes.' He smiled at her then. 'Why are you leaving, Daisy?'

'I'm going home,' she told him again. 'I must go and get my boarding pass or I shall miss the plane.'

'But you had a reason to leave?' he persisted.

She blushed, but didn't avoid his eye. 'I've learnt a lot and I've enjoyed living here. Heer Friske has a niece who is going to take my place in the shop…'

'That is the only reason? Did you visit my mother?'

'Yes, I had a lovely day with her. And Helene took me out for a Sunday—it was kind of you to ask her to do that. We had a most interesting day.'

His face hadn't altered, but she thought that he was angry. 'I really must go. Father will be waiting for me at Heathrow.'

She offered a hand and he ignored it, but gathered her in his arms and kissed her. As far as Daisy was concerned, Schipol had become paradise, planes and an anxious parent and boarding cards meant nothing.

He let her go slowly and gently, picked up her case and took her arm.

'You'll need to go along here.' He sounded as calm as usual—perhaps she had dreamt that kiss…

She joined the queue and got her pass and he handed her case over.

'Over there. I can't come any further.'

'No, no, of course not. Thank you. Goodbye!'

He put out a hand and touched her cheek. 'Have a safe journey,' was all he said.

She joined another queue and didn't look round, and presently she was on the plane and Holland was far below, giving way to the North Sea and presently to the English coast.

Heathrow was as busy as Schipol, but had the advantage of English signs and directions. She found her way without difficulty to the entrance and found her father waiting.

He wasn't a demonstrative man, but he was delighted to see her again and she was glad to see him, for she loved him very dearly. She would never be able to tell him or her mother about Mr der Huizma, but they both loved her and with them she would go back to her quiet life and in time Holland would be a distant dream. She gave her father a tremendous hug. 'It's so nice to be home again,' she told him.

There was much to tell them when she got home, and there was no need to mention Jules's name—although she did tell them about her visits to Mevrouw der Huizma's house.

'And did you see much of the doctor?' asked her mother.

Daisy said steadily, 'Very occasionally. He was kind enough to drive me around on one or two Sundays, so that I could see a little of Holland. Oh, and we met by accident...' She recounted the incident of the old lady and her cat and they all laughed about it, but something in her face made her mother give her a sharp glance. There were shadows under Daisy's eyes, and from time to time she looked sad...

Once she had settled in again, there was plenty to keep Daisy busy. Her father had bought a quantity of early Victorian furniture, in perfect condition but woefully uncared for. It fell to Daisy's lot to clean the heavy chairs and cabinets and what-nots, then polish them to perfection. She was glad to have something to do, and spent long, patient hours in the small room at the back of the shop with soft brushes and cloths and the special polish her father made for himself. At the end of two weeks or so she had finished, and some of the furniture was put on display. Her father, arranging a balloon-back chair in the window, paused to look at Daisy, giving a final polish to a walnut Davenport, and thought uneasily that he had been working her too hard; she was pale and rather quiet.

Later, as they were having their lunch, he said, 'You've been working too hard for the last week or two, Daisy. I've been so anxious to have that furniture ready to sell that I haven't given you a moment to yourself. You're quite pale, my dear. You must have more free time. How about starting those walks of yours again? Morning or afternoon—whichever you'd rather have.'

'But there are quite a few customers…'

'Mostly in the afternoon. The browsers and tourists come in the mornings, but they never stay long and buy only the small stuff.'

'Then I'll go in the morning, Father. I'd like that. If I go after breakfast I'll be back well before lunchtime.' She added, 'And if we get really busy I won't go.'

'It seems as though you've never been away,' said her mother, 'and you've been home almost three weeks.'

Three weeks since I saw Jules, thought Daisy, and she seemed quite unable to forget him, even banish him to the back of her mind. If he hadn't kissed her it might have been easier…

Mr der Huizma had watched Daisy's small person until she was out of sight and then gone out into the street where Joop had been waiting with the car. He'd greeted him pleasantly, enquired after his health and the well-being of his household, not forgetting Bouncer, and taken the wheel.

'Bad, was it?' asked Joop, with the respectful familiarity of an old and devoted servant. 'You'll need a bit of a holiday, *mijnheer*.'

'Yes, it was bad, but not quite as bad now as when I arrived there. As for a holiday, that must wait until I've got my work organised here.'

Joop glanced at his master's profile. It looked grim and there were tired lines. He decided not to mention that Juffrouw van Tromp had phoned to ask when the doctor was returning. She wanted to know, she'd explained to Joop, so that she could arrange a party for him. 'So let me know immediately,' she had ordered sharply. Joop had done nothing of the sort; he had had a message from his master that very day, and if he hadn't chosen to let his fiancée know that wasn't Joop's business.

Joop frowned as they crawled through the city's traffic. Juffrouw van Tromp wasn't at all to his liking, nor to anyone else in Mr der Huizma's house.

Once more in his home, Mr der Huizma greeted Jette and Bouncer, and then went to his study to go through his pile of post and make several telephone calls. That done, he went to his room, showered and changed and came downstairs to find coffee waiting for him.

He sat drinking it, thinking of Daisy. He wasn't sure if she'd been pleased to see him; she had been surprised, of course, just as he had been, but she had been on edge to go. He had tried to detect any sign of pleasure at seeing him but her face had shown nothing but polite surprise. He told himself that he should be glad of that; in the face of her indifference to him he could put her out of his mind.

He went back to his study and settled down to work his way through the papers on his desk. And after lunch he returned to his study once more, to phone his mother before resuming work.

He had told Joop to let his mother know that he was coming home, and there had been a message from her saying that she would be back from visiting one of his sisters shortly after lunch. When he dialled the number she answered at once.

'Jules, you're back. I'm so thankful. You're busy, of

course, but when you can spare an hour come and see me. Was it bad?'

He told her a little of his work, and added, 'I'm going to be busy for several days, Mother, but I'll come and see you just as soon as I can.' And, unable to help himself, he added, 'I saw Daisy at Schipol, going home.'

'Yes, dear. I had a letter saying she was leaving Holland. Her reasons seemed vague. Did you have time for a talk?'

'No. A couple of minutes only. Are you well?'

So Daisy wasn't to be talked about. 'Very well, dear. Don't let me keep you gossiping; I'm sure you're busy enough.'

He ate a solitary dinner presently, took Bouncer for a walk and went back to his study. Not to work, but to contemplate a future which for him held no happiness. He had every intention of going over to England and seeing Daisy. There was no question of forgetting her. He had fallen in love with her, and he loved her, and he wanted her for his wife. If she could love him a little he would ask Helene to release him...

He had forgotten Helene; it was too late to go and see her, or even phone her. He would have to go to the hospital in the morning but the afternoon should be free. They could talk; they hadn't talked for a long time. Dining, meeting at friends' houses, going to a play had never offered the opportunity to talk.

He forgot his own problems once he entered the hospital the next morning. He became immersed in his little patients' problems, and the afternoon was well advanced by the time he got home to eat a late lunch and then get into his car and drive to Churchillaan.

Juffrouw van Tromp was home, the correct maid told him, and led the way to the drawing room. At the door he said, 'No, don't announce me,' and went quietly in.

Helene was there, sitting on one of the overstuffed sofas, talking to a man he didn't know. She saw him first and jumped to her feet, flustered, but covering it with cries of delighted surprise.

'Jules—you're back. What an unexpected—'

He cut her short. 'Yesterday. How are you, Helene?' He glanced at the man who had got to his feet.

'This is Hank Cutler—we met when I was in California. He's over here on business and came to see me. Hank, this is Jules der Huizma, my fiancé.'

She had recovered her usual air of casual sophistication and added, 'Come and sit down, Jules. I'm so glad you have come; we were discussing the party I was planning to welcome you back.'

Mr der Huizma stood quietly, not speaking, and Hank got to his feet again. 'I have to be going; you must have a lot to say to each other. Been in Africa, haven't you? Must have been interesting...'

'Interesting if one likes to watch small children and babies die,' said Mr der Huizma. A remark which sped Hank on his way.

When he had gone Helene said angrily, 'Really, Jules, did you have to be so pompous?'

She was looking very beautiful, exquisitely turned out, her make-up faultless, and anger had heightened her beauty.

'My apologies.' He sat down. 'I must learn to keep my opinions to myself.'

'Yes, you must,' she said sharply, 'if they are miserable ones—upsetting my friends.' She grumbled, 'I dare say he won't come to my party now.'

'I dare say I won't either!' said Jules smoothly. 'What have you been doing with yourself while I've been away?'

'I had a week at that hydro—really, I was exhausted. And there was that exhibition I told you about—everyone was there—and of course shopping is so tiring... Oh, and I had tea with your mother. That girl Daisy was there, looking at your furniture, or so she said. I don't trust these quiet girls—worming her way into your mother's good books...'

He said quietly, 'Why should she do that?'

'Ambitious, I dare say, hoping to get something, or get someone like your mother interested in her. I took her out for the day—thought I would let her see how different her world was from ours.' Helene gave him a defiant look. 'I told her that we were going to get married within the next month or so.'

And when he didn't answer, she added, 'Well, before you went away you seemed anxious to get married...'

'And are you? Anxious?' He sounded casual, and he looked positively placid.

Helene said slowly, 'Since you ask, no, I can't see that there is any hurry. You have your work and I have my friends. In the autumn, if you like.'

He asked idly, 'Why did you take Daisy out for the day?'

She laughed. 'I told her that you had asked me to do so. I said that you wanted her to have a treat before she went home.'

'Why did you say that?' His voice was quiet but she

frowned a little at the look on his face. 'Oh, I suppose I wanted her to realise that she wasn't one of us. I think she enjoyed herself; she told me all about this faithful boyfriend waiting for her to say yes.'

She gave him a quick look. He had minded that. She felt sudden fury that he should have been interested in such a dull girl when she herself was a woman everyone admired, who was lovely to look at, exquisitely dressed, fun to be with, a splendid hostess… She said, with a flash of anger, 'Oh, forget about her, Jules. She was one of those girls clever enough to know how to better themselves.'

He got to his feet. 'You're wrong, Helene. Daisy, was—is—someone you don't often come across. She was kind and honest and warm-hearted. Beauty is only skin-deep, you know.'

That frightened Helene. She crossed the room to him and put her arms round his neck. 'Oh, Jules, I don't mean half I say—you know that. I hope she will be very happy now that she is back with her young man. We'll send her a wedding present.' She smiled charmingly at him. 'Take time off, darling, let's go somewhere and celebrate. I'm really sorry; don't hate me for it. We'll marry at once if you want.' She looked into his face. 'You do want that, don't you, Jules?'

He looked at her lovely face. 'I've a backlog of work. I'd rather not make plans for a time.'

She had to be content with that, and after he had gone she wondered if her future was as secure as she had supposed it to be. She would take care not to mention Daisy again. Out of sight, out of mind, Helene decided, and, going to take a look at her reflection in the wall mirror, felt confident that she could arrange her life as she wanted it.

As for Mr der Huizma, he went back home to sit at his desk and study the days ahead; it would be a while before he could be free for two or three days. Time enough to go over to England and see Daisy.

Chapter 8

On the Sunday evening Mr der Huizma went to see his mother. He had dealt with the most urgent aspects of his work at the hospital and now got into his car once more and drove to his family home. He was still tired, and although he greeted her with his usual warmth he looked stern. Something was worrying him, and she thought that it was something other than his experiences in Africa. But she said nothing, and told him to pour himself a drink and sit down and tell her of his mission. It took some time, for she was interested and interrupted frequently. He fell silent at last. 'It was good to be able to talk about it,' he told her.

At supper they talked about the family, and finally his work. 'I suppose you will be busy now for the next few weeks,' said his mother.

'Yes, but I intend to take a couple of days off as soon as I can manage it. I'm going to England.' He glanced at his mother. 'To see Daisy.'

So that was the reason for his stern face. 'Yes, dear. She came here and spent the day. We had a delightful time up in the attics. It was a pity that Helene called—we had to leave some most interesting old books about this house. I had hoped to invite her again, but of course she returned rather suddenly to England.'

'Did she say why?'

'Heer Friske had a niece who wanted to join his business. It was a short note; I had the impression that it wasn't the usual kind of letter she would have written. I telephoned Heer Friske. He sounded really sorry that she had gone home, and observed that she had at least seen something of Holland before she went. Helene took her out for the day—perhaps you knew that?'

'Helene told me. She also told me that she had told Daisy that we were to marry very shortly.'

Mevrouw der Huizma said slowly, 'And are you, Jules? Going to marry soon?'

'No. It seems that Helene told Daisy that for reasons of her own. She has no wish to marry in the foreseeable future.'

His mother breathed a hidden sigh of relief. 'Well, dear, since you are so busy for weeks ahead that might be a good idea.'

He said harshly, 'Was Daisy happy? Here in this house with you?'

'Yes, Jules. And a delightful companion. A clever girl, I fancy, able to hold her own in any situation and, to use an old-fashioned word, modest about her knowledge.'

They began to talk of other things, and Daisy wasn't mentioned again.

Jules went back to Amsterdam. He would phone his mother before he went to England, he told her.

She sat, long after he had gone, thinking about him. He was a grown man, capable of running his own life, and had indeed made a success of it. She dared not meddle. He would do what was right, she was sure of that, but at what cost to his happiness? There was always the chance that Helene would release him from his promise, but she had to admit that it was a slim one.

And she was right; Helene, anxious now that she had lost whatever love Jules had had for her, did everything she could to recapture it. She did it in the only way she knew how; phoning him in the evenings, asking him to join her at some friend's house for dinner, suggesting that they should drive out into the country and dine at some popular restaurant, go to a play, spend a Sunday at Keukenhof, laughing off his protests that he had no time to spare. So from time to time he spent an evening with her, a pleasant companion listening to her chatter, admiring her dresses. That there was no warmth in his manner didn't worry her. She was an undemonstrative woman, not capable of loving deeply. She was confident that in time she would be able to arrange their future exactly as she wanted it.

It was a shock when he told her one evening that he would be going to England in a few days' time.

'To one of the hospitals?'

'I have two hospitals to visit, yes. I am going to see Daisy.'

She managed to keep her face composed. 'Give her my love. I dare say she is getting ready for her wedding. Perhaps you could find time to get her a present from us?'

'I doubt that.' He began to talk of something else then.

Daisy, now that summer was here, made the most of her daily walks. In another few weeks her father would need her more often in the shop, and her outings would have to be curtailed, even stopped for the height of the tourist season. She had a little colour in her cheeks now, but she had grown thinner and there were violet shadows under her eyes. But although she was quiet she was unendingly cheerful. That she longed to see Jules was something she kept to herself. She talked readily enough about her stay in Holland but Jules she never mentioned, something her mother had noticed with a troubled heart.

It was a bright, blustery day when she set out for her usual walk, but the sky was blue, even if overshadowed from time to time by great billowing clouds. She put on a cardigan over the sober dress she wore in the shop, tied a scarf over her neat head, and set out. She was a little later than usual, for her father had asked her to clean and polish a small silver-framed hand mirror; a delicate trifle which, arranged in the window, would draw the attention of passers-by. She would take her usual walk, she decided, go as far as the tumble of rocks at the far end of the beach and then climb the short distance to the coast path and go home along the low cliffs.

She was halfway to the rocks when she saw someone coming towards her. He had a dog with him, Trigger, who lumbered up to meet her with delighted barks. Daisy stood still. If she could have run away she would have done so, despite the happy beating of her heart at the sight of the vast figure coming so rapidly towards her. But there was nowhere to run...

He had reached her before she had her breathing under control. She said, inanely, 'It's a lovely day.'

He smiled slowly. 'The loveliest day of my life.'

'How funny that we've met again here on the beach.' She bent to pat Trigger, trying to get her self-possession back, wishing she could think of a few sensible remarks to make, casual and rather cool...

She need not have bothered; he said briskly, 'It's such a splendid day for a walk, isn't it? Are you going as far as the rocks?'

And when she nodded he said, 'Then may I join you? I'm over here for a few days and am giving myself a short break between hospitals. How are you liking being back home?'

He was friendly, with the casual friendliness of an old acquaintance, and Daisy fell into step beside him, torn between delight at seeing him once again and regret that he had shown no great pleasure at meeting her once more. Well, why should he? she asked herself silently, skipping to keep up. He had Helene... To maintain a conversation was essential, so she asked about his work in Africa.

He told her at some length, knowing that she was interested and listening to what he was saying, now and then making intelligent observations. But presently he said, 'Now it's your turn, Daisy. What are your plans for the future?'

She answered him seriously. 'Well, it's funny you should ask—we were talking about it this morning. In fact we've talked about it quite a lot lately, but nothing is decided.'

She didn't say more than that. Why should he be interested in her plan to get taken on by one of the big firms dealing in antiques so that she might learn even more? She thought that perhaps she had been rather abrupt and added, 'Of course it would mean father would have to get an assistant.'

A fragmented and misleading remark which left Mr der Huizma no better informed than he had been. But he was a man of infinite patience and he was here for another two days. He began to talk about nothing in particular in his friendly way, and Daisy, blissfully happy for the moment, threw sticks for Trigger, her face rosy from the wind, uncaring of the tendrils of hair escaping from her scarf. Somehow it didn't matter how she looked when she was with Jules. And anyway, he wasn't really looking at her—a quick glance from time to time, that was all.

They had reached the rocks, and she would have liked nothing better than to climb round them and go on walking, but it would soon be midday and she was to take over the shop that afternoon. She said urgently, 'I must go back…'

'The morning is quickly over,' he said easily. They didn't say much on their way back, and at the corner of the lane he bade her goodbye. She longed to know if he would meet her again, but, Daisy being Daisy, she didn't say anything, just bade him goodbye in her turn and ran to the shop and went inside without looking back.

Helping her mother lay the table for their lunch, she reflected that it was a good thing they wouldn't meet again. Perhaps it would have been better if they hadn't met this morning, upsetting all her efforts to put him out of her mind…

'Did Mr der Huizma find you?' asked her father as they sat at table. Daisy, caught unawares, went a bright pink although she sounded composed.

'Yes, Father, it was pleasant seeing him again. He's here for a day or two…'

And her mother said, 'He was so kind to you while you were in Holland…'

Daisy didn't want him to be kind; she wanted him to love her…

She thought about him during the afternoon, waiting patiently while a customer dithered between a Sèvres plate and a Rockingham milk jug. Would he be on the beach tomorrow? she wondered. He had said goodbye without saying that they might meet again. She would take her usual walk, she decided as she wrapped up the milk jug. Their meeting had been by chance, and if he had wanted to see her again he would have said so.

He was there, waiting at the bottom of the steps on the sea front, Trigger weaving happily to and fro. His good morning was cheerfully friendly as they started off towards the rocks. 'But I believe we're in for some bad weather,' he added.

She glanced uneasily at the sky. It was clear overhead, but out to sea the clouds were grey and threatening.

'Do you suppose these clouds are coming this way?'

'Yes, I'm afraid so. Perhaps you would rather go home?'

'No. No. I like the rain, only sometimes we get really bad weather here.'

They were walking side by side, content in each other's company, and Mr der Huizma looked at her small face, rosy from the wind, and thought how beautiful she was. 'Well,' he said, 'if you don't mind the rain…'

The clouds didn't appear to be moving and the wind had died down; they walked briskly, not saying much. There was still a day left, he reflected, and until then he was determined to remain nothing but a casual friend. But tomorrow he must ask her about the future—this man she was to marry. She wasn't wearing a ring…

They were almost at the rocks when he glanced out to sea. The sky had darkened but they hadn't noticed; now the clouds which had been hovering on the horizon were creeping towards them. His eyes narrowed.

'I'm not sure, but I think there's bad weather coming fast. We can sit it out among the rocks.' He whistled to Trigger and took her hand.

He had explored the rocks several times and knew where to go, between two great outcrops facing inland. Almost there, Daisy stopped to look out to sea. 'Oh, look,' she cried. 'Isn't that extraordinary…?'

'A whirlwind,' said Mr der Huizma calmly. 'Most interesting. But come along now.' He had Trigger on his lead and a vast arm round Daisy.

They settled with their backs to the rock which encircled them and Daisy asked, 'Will it last long, the whirlwind?'

'No. A bit noisy and rough, but we're secure here. I'm sorry; I should have seen it earlier.'

Daisy, feeling his arm around her, was glad that he hadn't.

It grew darker and noisier, and all at once the whirlwind was upon them—and gone again before Daisy had the time to feel frightened. But it was followed by great peals of thunder and flashes of lightning. She had always been frightened of storms; now she buried her face in his shoulder and kept her eyes tight shut.

She muttered into his Burberry, 'I'm terrified of storms. So sorry.'

She was surprised to hear his rumble of laughter, but all he said was, 'It will soon pass. We're quite safe here.'

Positively cosy, reflected Daisy, her head on his shoulder, Trigger's doggy warmth pressed up against her legs... She swallowed down her fright and thought how happy she was, sitting here hidden from the storm and Jules's arm holding her close. There was a great deal of him, and he was very solid. This, she thought, was a moment to remember for the rest of her life.

The whirlwind had passed, the storm was blowing itself out, and the thunder was a rumble in the distance. Jules took his arm away and stood up. It was raining, but there was a clear sky out to sea where the last of the clouds were hurtling away.

He hauled her to her feet, took her arm and walked her briskly back along the beach, Trigger walking soberly beside them. It was raining still, and the sea was boisterous, but Daisy, happy in her own particular heaven, didn't notice. Mr der Huizma, looking down at her blissful face, sighed and wished for a miracle. To break his promise to marry Helene wasn't a thing he would contemplate, but surely there was some way in which she might decide that to marry him was a mistake?

'I'm going back to Holland tomorrow evening,' he told her as they climbed the steps to the promenade. 'Could you get a few hours off? We might drive into the country and have lunch?'

She stood beside him amidst the litter the whirlwind had caused. 'Well, I usually walk for a bit each morning, but I go to the shop after lunch…'

'Then if I call for you around ten o'clock we could lunch early and have you back in good time.'

'I'd like that—if I could be back here before two o'clock…'

'That's a promise.'

He walked with her up the main street and waited at the corner of the lane until she had gone into the shop. She hadn't looked back.

For Daisy the rest of the day was endless; she washed her hair, did her nails, pleased in a modest way that she had pretty hands, inspected her face for spots, and went to bed early—but not to sleep immediately. The morning's events had to be gone over; every word, every smile!

She saw with pleasure in the morning that the weather was on her side; hardly a cloud, and warm enough for her to wear the jersey dress. She was ready long before ten o'clock, but all the same when she heard the car stop outside she stayed in her room until her mother called her. Mr der Huizma was in the living room, looking very much at home, discussing the weather. His, 'Good morning, Daisy,' was pleasant, but if her mother was looking for any warmer feeling she was to be disappointed. He was a man who had complete control over his features—an asset in his profession.

'Where are we going?' asked Daisy as he got into the car beside her.

'Dartmoor. I've booked a table at Gidleigh Park, just outside Chagford. They will give us lunch at half past twelve, which gives us plenty of time to get back by two o'clock.'

He took the road to Two Bridges, and then on to Postbridge, stopping for coffee at a small café there and driving unhurriedly along the narrow roads, pausing to watch the ponies and sheep with their lambs.

'Oh, this is lovely,' said Daisy as they sat in the car, patiently waiting for a ewe and her lambs to cross the road.

'Would you like to walk for a while?'

'Oh, yes, but is there time?'

'We can spare twenty minutes or so. We can go as far as that tor...'

The sun was warm and the air fresh; they walked briskly, and after a minute, since the rough grass was awkward to walk on, he took her hand. To Daisy, her fingers curled into his large palm, it seemed the most natural thing in the world to do.

Gidleigh Park was a hotel close to Chagford, in its own splendid grounds with the North Teign river running through them. It was an elegant place, offering unostentatious luxury and delicious meals. They had a table by one of the windows in the half-filled restaurant; the tables close to them were, as yet, empty. Daisy studied the menu and gulped back shock at the prices. Mr der Huizma, watching her face, said matter-of-factly, 'Shall I choose for you, or is there something you would particularly like?'

'Oh, yes, please, you choose...' She added with the unselfconsciousness of a child, 'I'm hungry.'

'Good, so am I. How about spinach tarts, lamb cutlets, and choose our pudding from the trolley?'

The tarts were delicious, and the cutlets came with new potatoes, baby carrots, petit pois and broccoli.

'Heavenly,' said Daisy, daintily polishing off the last of the carrots.

The pudding trolley was something to drool over. She chose chocolate mousse laced with brandy and topped with cream, accompanied by small paper-thin biscuits, while Mr der Huizma ate cheese.

Pouring coffee for them both, she beamed across the table at him.

'I'm having such a glorious day...'

He took his cup from her. 'Daisy, I am in love with you, do you know that?'

She put her coffee cup very carefully back into the saucer. She felt the colour creep into her face but she gave him a direct look.

'I didn't know, but I had begun to wonder if you were. I've tried not to think about it. You're going to marry Helene—quite soon, she told me.' She steadied her voice. 'It's because we keep meeting unexpectedly, don't you see? I mean, falling in the canal and being mugged and helping me with the wine cooler and...' She stared at his quiet face. 'If you saw me every day you wouldn't even notice me.'

When he still didn't speak she went on desperately, 'You're going back to Holland tonight; we shan't see each other again and you'll forget me.'

He said then, 'And that is what you would like? That I should forget you?'

When she nodded, he added, 'Well, it is a most sensible suggestion and, given the circumstances, the right one. We are both of us tied by circumstances, are we not?'

He smiled at her, looking quite unworried, so that she asked, 'But we're still friends?'

'Of course. I can't imagine that Helene or your future husband could object to that. Especially as our friendship will be of necessity a long distance one.'

'My future husband? I haven't got one. I mean no one has ever asked me to marry them.' She stared at him.

A slow smile spread over Mr der Huizma's handsome features. 'I was told that you were to marry shortly—some young man here.'

'I don't know any young men,' said Daisy. 'Desmond was the only one, and I can't even remember what he looked like...'

She looked at Mr der Huizma and thought that he looked ten years younger all at once.

'There is a great deal that I should like to say,' he told her. 'But it must wait for the moment. This has been a most illuminating conversation, Daisy.'

'Well, yes, but you do understand about you and me? I'm sure that once you get back to Amsterdam you'll have so many other things to think about—getting married…'

'Ah, yes. Now that is something about which I must think very seriously.'

He looked so cheerful, almost smug. Perhaps he was already falling out of love with her—and indeed there was nothing lover-like in his manner. She reflected sadly that his falling in love with her had been a moment's fantasy. A pity that she couldn't dismiss her own love for him with the same ease.

They went back to the car presently, and drove back along the main roads. Mr der Huizma chatted about this and that, for all the world as though he had never said that he was in love with her…

At the shop he got out with her, stayed to chat for a while with her mother and father, and then bade them goodbye. Good manners took her to the door with him.

'I hope you have a good journey home,' she said quietly. 'Please remember me to your mother and Helene. And thank you for a lovely morning and my lunch.' And then, 'Oh, Jules…'

This was what he had wanted to hear—the sudden longing in her voice. Her stoic front of friendliness was just that—a front. But he didn't say anything, only took her in his arms and kissed her. A long, slow kiss full of tenderness and love. Neither did he say goodbye, but got into his car and drove away without a backward glance.

And Daisy, regardless of the fact that she should be in the shop, went to her room and cried her eyes out.

When she had no more tears left she washed her face, tidied her hair and went down to the shop, red-eyed, but perfectly composed, and sold a Victorian chamber pot, a walnut what-not and a warming pan to successive customers.

Her enthusiasm for work astonished her father, who put it down to her pleasure at being back in England but her mother wasn't deceived.

'Do you suppose that you will hear from Mr der Huizma again, dear?' she asked casually several days later. 'I dare say he will send you a wedding card or something similar. After all you did know his fiancée, didn't you?'

'Not very well, Mother. I don't expect to hear from either of them. They have so many friends of their own.' Daisy took an apple from the dish on the table and bit into it—it was something to do, and would perhaps divert her mother from questioning her. But Mrs Gillard didn't ask any more questions; she was sure that Daisy was unhappy, and that Mr der Huizma was the cause of it. A pity she had ever gone to Amsterdam... Mrs Gillard loved her daughter dearly, and longed to see her happy again.

Daisy, aware of this, did her best. But sometimes when she looked in a mirror she wondered how it was possible to look exactly the same as usual when one's heart was broken.

Mr der Huizma had gone back to Amsterdam, phoned his mother to tell her that he was back, but had made no effort or plans to phone or meet Helene. He was extremely busy, and he needed time to find ways and means whereby he could sort out his future. At the moment he could think of nothing, but that didn't deter him from his determination. Daisy loved him, he was sure of that now, and she held his heart in her hands. That was enough for him for the moment. He put her out of his mind and concentrated on his small patients.

His ward was full, it always was, and his clinics were larger than ever. He kept his mind on his work until some ten days after his return, when he had the time to go and see Helene. He had seen none of his friends, not even his mother, and had immersed himself so deeply in his work that Joop took it upon himself to remonstrate with him. 'Work yourself into an early grave,' he predicted. 'Not an hour's leisure have you had, excepting for taking Bouncer for his walk. It's not natural.'

'Don't worry, Joop, I intend to visit Juffrouw van Tromp this evening,' he had replied. Which satisfied his old servant but not entirely. Ten days his master had been home and not so much as a phone call from the lady. Joop shook his head and went along to the kitchen to discuss his doubts with Jette.

As it happened there was a phone call from Helene waiting for Jules on his answering machine when he got home. She had just heard that he had been back home for ten days, so why hadn't he been to see her or at least telephoned? But, since he was home again, perhaps he could spare the time to see her that evening. He listened to the cross voice and admitted that she had reason to be annoyed. He picked up the phone and dialled her number.

He wasn't free early enough in the evening to take

her out to dinner. 'I shall be having drinks with friends and dining with them. You'd better come about nine o'clock. There are several parties during the next week or so and I've accepted for both of us; I'll let you know the dates. And don't be late. I have to be up early— I'm going to Amersfoort for the weekend with the de Groots.'

She rang off and he went to the dinner table and ate the excellent meal set before him. He took Bouncer for a walk, and then got into his car and drove to Churchillaan. Helene was waiting for him in the ornate drawing room.

'So here you are at last. Why wasn't I told that you were back?' She offered a cheek and he kissed it briefly.

'If you had phoned the hospital or my house, you would have been told,' he said mildly.

'My dear Jules, I can't spend my time on the phone; you know how full my days are.'

'My days are full too.' He sat down opposite her. She had thrown herself down on a sofa and she looked very beautiful.

'Well, don't be so gloomy. Wait while I tell you about these parties...'

'While I was in England I went to see Daisy. Helene, why did you tell me that she was to be married? A joke? A mistake?'

'A joke, of course. A girl like Daisy hasn't a chance of marrying—no looks, no decent clothes, her nose buried in old furniture.' Helene looked at him sharply. 'Anyway, she's back where she belongs; you can forget her.'

She realised that she hadn't got his full attention

and had a moment of panic. Had someone told him that she'd been seeing rather a lot of Hank Cutler? She said sweetly, 'She is such a nice girl. Really I'm sure she'll find a husband. Now tell me, Jules, have you been busy at the hospital? Have you had any news of that new clinic you started in Africa?'

She could be charming when she wished, and she exerted every scrap of that now. 'Shall we have coffee and I'll tell you about the parties I've promised we'll go to.' She saw his frown. 'At any rate I've promised for myself, but I said that you would come with me if you were free…'

He saw that the African clinic and his work there were already forgotten. He said quietly, 'I think it is unlikely that I shall be free for much social life for some time to come.'

'You're not going back to that clinic, Jules? I won't allow it. You've only been back a few weeks; you should be here, free to escort me, take me out to dinner, meet my friends…'

His eyes were cold. 'Did you not realise when we became engaged that I am not always free to do as I choose? Children are taken ill at the most inconvenient times; they don't wait until I am at the hospital to break arms and legs, scald themselves or fall ill for no reason at all.'

He had spoken in his usual calm way but she saw that he was angry. It wouldn't do at all; she would lose her hold over him.

'Jules, dear, I don't mean to be so thoughtless. Of course your work must come first. I promise you that I'll be a model wife. I'll entertain for you, so that you meet all the most influential people. I'm so proud of you, and I want you to be famous worldwide, not just here and in Europe. I shall be such a help to you.'

She talked on, but Mr der Huizma wasn't listening, nor did he see Helene lying so beguilingly on the sofa opposite him. All he saw in his mind's eye was a quiet girl with beautiful eyes and a quantity of brown hair...

It would have been useless to talk to Helene about their future at that moment. He would have to wait until she was in a more serious mood, get her to listen to him. She was still talking about parties and the wonderful weekend she hoped to have, and when he got up to go she stayed on the sofa, knowing what a delightful picture she made, and held out a hand.

'I'm far too tired to get up, Jules!' She smiled up at him. 'Phone me when you have a free evening; we could dine. I'll be back on Monday morning.'

'Enjoy your weekend, Helene.'

'Oh, I shall—although so much more if you were with me, Jules.'

He went home then, to take Bouncer for his last walk and then go to his study to work. It had been impossible to get Helene to listen to him, or to be serious about their future. He wondered if she had given serious thought to their marriage and the life they would lead together. She seemed unable to imagine any other way of life than a round of social pleasures. Somehow he must make her understand that her life would be utterly different from the one she now enjoyed, and then perhaps she might consider breaking off their engagement.

He drew the first of a pile of case-sheets towards him and began to read.

It was late on Sunday evening when he went to visit his mother.

'I thought you might bring Helene with you, Jules,' his mother observed. 'I haven't seen her since she was here, oh, some weeks ago, when Daisy was spending the day with me.'

'Helene has gone away for the weekend,' he told her. 'I saw her on Friday evening.'

'You haven't discussed the wedding yet?' persisted his mother gently.

'No. She has any number of social engagements, and I have a backlog of work.'

Katje came in with the coffee and Mevrouw der Huizma busied herself with the coffee tray. 'Did you see Daisy while you were in England, Jules?'

'Oh, yes.' He smiled suddenly. 'Mother, I can't talk about that—not yet! You don't mind?'

'No, dear. Now tell me about your work. That child with the dislocated hip you were so worried about— did you operate?'

'Yes—successfully, I'm glad to say. There's a small boy being admitted this week. I hope I shall be able to help him. Now tell me, how are the rest of the family?'

It was the middle of the week before he had a free evening. He phoned Helene. He would take her out to dinner somewhere quiet and they could talk...

Only Helene was going to a charity ball in Scheveningen. 'Something I can't cancel. It's a big event— two of the princes will be there. I simply can't miss it. Phone me later this week—perhaps we could spend Sunday together?'

He put the phone down and looked through his appointments book. He should have a free afternoon on Friday; he would go and see her then. There was a good chance that she would be at home; she had mentioned that she was going to the theatre in the evening so she would probably spend a quiet afternoon.

Helene was out when he arrived, soon after three o'clock. The maid who admitted him wasn't sure when she would be back, but if he cared to wait?

Mr der Huizma went to the drawing room and made himself comfortable in an oversized wing chair, refused the proffered tea or coffee and allowed his thoughts to wander; Daisy would be in the shop, wearing her serviceable dress, her hair very neat, no doubt selling some trifle to a customer or cleaning and polishing some small treasure which had come into her father's hands…

Half an hour later Helene returned home, bringing Hank with her. She spoke sharply to the maid as she entered the apartment and the woman, chivvied or ignored as the case might be, saw her chance for revenge. She said nothing to Helene about Mr der Huizma's presence in the drawing room.

He heard Helene's voice and Hank's laughter before they opened the door. Helene was speaking. 'Darling Hank, of course I'm going to marry him. He's got everything I want: money, the right ancestors, a brilliant career, and so engrossed in his work that I'll be free to do exactly as I want. We shall be able to go on seeing each other as often as we please. I shall have the best of both worlds…'

Mr der Huizma got out of his chair; a large man, he looked even larger now. He said mildly, 'I'm afraid I must disappoint you, Helene. You may have one world to your liking, but I'm afraid the second one won't be available.'

Helene had gone white. 'Jules, why wasn't I told that you were here? I was joking.' She turned to Hank. 'It was a joke, wasn't it, Hank?'

'Well, now, I rarely disagree with a lady, Helene, but it seemed to me that you meant every word. Mind you, Jules here might be prepared to overlook it, but somehow I don't think so. And I may not have any ancestors worth mentioning, but I've a nice place in California, as you know—and money.'

Mr der Huizma walked to the door. 'It does sound eminently satisfactory. I'm sure you're happy to release me from our engagement, Helene. I wish you both a happy future.'

He paused at the door. 'I will send an announcement to the papers. My regards to your mother and father.'

The maid, opening the door to him, wondered why he was smiling to himself. A nice, kind man, who deserved better than Juffrouw van Tromp. He bade her good day and got into his car and drove away to his home, where he ate a splendid tea, took Bouncer for a walk and then sat down at his desk to rearrange his schedule so that he could be free to go to England as soon as possible.

Chapter 9

Daisy had gone to Exeter for an interview with one of
the directors of a well-known firm of antique dealers
there. They had an auction room and a quite large staff.
If she accepted their offer she would start in a lowly
way, cleaning pictures and silver, widening her knowledge of the antique trade. She had taken the morning
bus and, with time on her hands, gone window shopping. The windows were full of clothes for summer—
such pretty clothes—some of them affordable. But she
went out so seldom they would hang in the wardrobe
until they were last year's models.

It was a pity, she reflected, that when Jules had come
she had been wearing an old skirt and cotton blouse.
True, she had been able to wear the jersey dress on their
day out together. But that was a year old and not this

season's colour… She bought a lipstick under the eyes
of a rather young lady on the other side of the counter,
and searched for her mother's favourite soap—violet,
in a pretty box with ribbons. She had a cup of coffee
and a sandwich, spent half an hour wandering round
the cathedral, and exactly on time presented herself at
the antique dealers.

She was interviewed by a youngish man who made
it obvious from the start that her chances of getting
the job were small. He sat back in his chair behind
the enormous desk, listening to Daisy's matter-of-fact
recital of her experience. Which, he had to admit to
himself, was adequate for the job. But the girl was too
reserved. Too quiet…

He cut her short rather rudely, told her that he would
let her know and thanked her in a perfunctory manner.
Nor did he bother to get up as she got out of her chair.
At the door she turned to look at him.

'I wouldn't like to work for you,' she told him politely, 'You have no manners.'

She closed the door behind her, leaving him with
his mouth open.

She would have to wait until the five o'clock bus to
go home; she went to the tea rooms in the cathedral
close and ordered a pot of tea and scones. Her trip to
Exeter had been a waste of time and money, and she
knew that her father would be disappointed. She would
have to think of something…

But she had no need to do that; there was a letter
for her when she got home. She didn't open it at once,
but gave her father an accurate account of her inter-

view. 'Of course I shan't be offered the job,' she told
him. 'I'm sorry, Father, but there are plenty of other
opportunities...'

She opened her letter then, and read it, and read
it again before she said, 'It's from Janet—' the only
cousin she had, daughter of her father's brother, and
married with two children '—she wants me to go and
stay for a week or two. Jack has been sent abroad by
his firm, both children have the chickenpox and she
isn't well.'

She looked at her mother, who nodded her head si-
lently. 'Of course you must go, dear. Poor Janet. Your
father can get someone in to help for a week or two.'
As he grumbled an answer she went on, 'There's Mrs
Coffin—utterly reliable even if she can't sell anything.
She can keep the shop open and do the odd jobs.' Mrs
Gillard added in a wheedling tone, 'It's only for a week
or two, dear.'

So Daisy packed a bag and took the bus to Totnes
and walked up the hilly high street, under the arch,
and turned down a narrow road leading away from
it. Janet and Jack lived in a nice old house in a row of
similar houses; they had been built more than a century ago and stood, solid and secure, lining the road
going downhill. There were no front gardens, but they
each had a long garden at the back, backing onto open
country.

Daisy thumped the door knocker and opened the
door, calling, 'It's me...'

Janet came running down the narrow stairs. 'Oh,
Daisy, you angel. I hated having to ask you but there's

no one else. I've friends, of course, but none of their children have had chickenpox so I couldn't ask them.' She asked anxiously, 'You have?'

'Yes, ages ago. They're in bed? And you? You look as though you should be in bed too.' Daisy put down her bag and took off her jacket. 'Well, now I'm here you can do just that, Janet. Just tell me if you need any shopping—and does the doctor call?'

'There's enough in the house for today. The doctor said he'd call this afternoon.'

'Good, so he can take a look at you at the same time as the children. I'll bring you a cup of tea when you're in bed, and see to James and Lucy.'

Janet in bed, and drinking her tea, Daisy went to look at the children. They were small, hot and cross, and very grizzly. She washed their little tear-stained faces, made their beds and found clean nightclothes, and went to inspect the fridge. There was plenty of ice cream; she spooned it into two small mouths and saw with satisfaction that they were dozing off.

It gave her time to take her bag to the small bedroom at the back of the house and then get a belated lunch for Janet and herself.

The doctor came later in the afternoon, pronounced the children progressing in the normal fashion, recommended that they stay in their beds for another day at least, and then went to take a look at Janet.

'Flu,' he diagnosed. 'Not severe, nothing that a few days of paracetemol and plenty of fluids won't cure.' He observed that he was glad that Janet had help, and bade her good day. He would call again in two days' time, but if she was worried she could ring him at any time.

Daisy doled out the pills, saw to the children, got supper and took a tray up to Janet. And, since everyone seemed comfortable and disposed to settle down for the night, went to bed herself. She had phoned her mother, had had a phone call from Jack, anxious for news, and there was nothing more to be done until the next day.

The next few days went quickly seeing to the invalids, the housework, the shopping, the washing, and cooking the kind of food needed to tempt poor appetites kept Daisy busy. It was hard work but she didn't mind; the more she had to do the less time she had to think about Jules.

All the same, at bedtime, when there was nothing else to be done but get into bed and go to sleep, she allowed her thoughts free rein, going over every moment of their day together and his kiss. She had never meant to let him see how she felt when they had said goodbye; she would regret that for as long as she lived. Although it didn't matter now that they wouldn't see each other again. She wondered what he was doing, picturing him with Helene, dining and dancing or at the theatre. And Helene would be more beautiful than ever, and most certainly wearing the diamond brooch…

Her reflections, although vivid, were quite inaccurate. Mr der Huizma was at that very moment making his final preparations to travel to England.

Janet was back on her feet, rather pale and wan, and the children had been allowed out of their beds, which meant that they needed amusing for a large part of the day. Daisy, although she loved them dearly, couldn't help wishing that they could have had a few more days in the beds. Their spots were fading and they were more cheerful now, and beginning to eat their meals, but their increasing liveliness made Janet's head ache, so that she spent a good deal of time on her bed. Shopping was difficult, because it meant rousing Janet to look after the children while she was out, and there was always a small mountain of washing and ironing waiting.

It had been a trying morning. Lucy had been sick and James had flung his breakfast onto the floor; Janet had crept back to bed with a splitting headache. Daisy, mopping up and wiping tearful little faces, hoped that the day would improve. And certainly there was a bright spot—Jack phoned to say that he would be home in two days' time. Daisy assured him that all was well, settled the children with their toys, took a cup of coffee up to Janet and went to inspect the fridge. Scrambled eggs for lunch, she decided, and there was enough ice cream for the little ones. If Janet felt better later in the day she could go out to the shops…

She took a tray up to Janet presently, and then sat down at the kitchen table with James in his high chair and Lucy on her knee, spooning in the scrambled egg. They would have their afternoon nap presently, and she would make herself a pot of tea and some toast.

She frowned as the front door knocker was thumped in a no-nonsense manner. The milkman had been, and so had the postman; it would be someone wanting to read the meter or sell her some dishcloths. She ignored it, and popped another spoonful of egg into a small pink mouth. But whoever it was wasn't going to take no for an answer.

She hoisted Lucy onto her shoulder, bade James be a good boy for just a minute and went to the door.

Mr der Huizma stood there, large and relaxed.

Daisy heaved Lucy into a more comfortable position. She said in a disbelieving voice, 'How did you get here?'

He looked down at her; anything he had intended to say to her was obviously something which must wait. He said, in a voice which held reassurance and a certainty that he was there to help, 'Hullo, Daisy,' and took Lucy from her. 'May I come in?'

'We're having lunch—scrambled eggs,' said Daisy. 'If you don't mind…'

He walked past her into the kitchen, sat down at the table, arranged Lucy comfortably on his knee and began to spoon egg into her mouth.

'Well,' said Daisy astonished.

'You forget,' he said smoothly, 'that I am a children's doctor.'

Janet's voice from upstairs wanted to know who it was. Daisy said, 'I'd better go and tell her,' then added, 'She's my cousin. Her husband isn't coming back until the day after tomorrow—she's been ill and the children have had chickenpox.'

'Ah—a family crisis; they do occur. Have you had your lunch?'

'Me? No. I'll have something later.' She blushed. 'I will make you some scrambled eggs and a cup of coffee if you don't mind waiting until I've put these two down for their nap.'

He said matter-of-factly, 'Go and tell your cousin that I'm here, and then see to these two. I'll go and get us something to eat and you can tell me how I can help.' When she hesitated, he said, 'No, don't argue, dear girl.'

So she went upstairs and told Janet, who watched Daisy's face as she talked and drew her own conclusions. 'How kind,' she commented. 'You could do with some help. If he likes to stay for tea I'll crawl down and meet him.'

And when Daisy went downstairs Mr der Huizma went quietly out of the house; by the time she got downstairs again, after putting the children down for a nap, it was to find that he was back, the table cleared and set with knives and forks and plates, one of the local butcher's famous pork pies on a dish and a bowl of salad beside it. There was a bottle of wine too.

'Come and sit down and tell me about it,' he invited. 'I hope your cousin doesn't find me a nuisance.'

Daisy eyed the pork pie. 'She says she'll come down to meet you if you would like to stay to tea.'

'Good. This isn't much of a meal, but if you're hungry...'

'Oh, but I am,' said Daisy and fell to!

Mr der Huizma resisted a strong desire to snatch her off her chair and carry her off somewhere quiet and tell her that he loved her, but he could see that his desires must take second place to the pork pie. His darling Daisy had obviously not been eating enough to keep a mouse alive...

He poured her a glass of wine and said soothingly, 'Drink this; it's a very light wine, just right for the pie.'

And when they had eaten he helped her clear the table and then washed up.

Daisy, drying plates, said, 'I'm sure you never wash up at home.'

'No, but I know how to do it.' He emptied the water away, wiped the sink tidily and hung up the teatowel. 'Now, let us sit down and see if we can improve this situation.'

'Well,' began Daisy, 'you're very kind, but shouldn't you be with your friends? Where you stay when you come down here?'

'I shall return there this evening, but in the meantime may I suggest that I do any necessary shopping for you? There is nothing much in the fridge, is there?'

She looked at him doubtfully. 'I can't think why you're here. How did you know?'

'I called on your mother and father. Let us keep to the point. What do these toddlers eat other than scrambled egg? Make a list and I'll fetch whatever you need.'

'Now?'

'Now, Daisy. And when I come back perhaps your cousin will feel well enough to come downstairs and we can have a cup of tea together.'

She had the feeling that he was taking over the household whether she liked it or not. Upon reflection she decided that she liked it. She sat down and made a list.

'You're very kind. I'll give you some money...'

'No, no. We can settle up later.'

When he had gone she went upstairs and explained to Janet, who declared that she felt better and was all agog to hear what Daisy had to say.

'You mean to say,' she said, when Daisy had given her a brief resumé of her visitor, 'that he's come over here to see you?'

'No, of course not. He comes to England quite often to the London hospitals. I told you he had met Mother and Father; I dare say they mentioned that I was staying here and he's just called on his way to somewhere or other.'

'Well, when he is back and tea's ready, I'll come down,' said Janet. 'And I'll see to Lucy and Jamie when they wake.'

He'd be gone for an hour at least, decided Daisy, and got out the ironing board.

Unlike the average housewife, going from shop to shop with an eye on the household purse, Mr der Huizma had walked into the nearest grocer's and asked for everything necessary to keep a small household with two children supplied with suitable food. 'Enough for two or three days,' he'd added.

Janet had come downstairs and was there to open the door to his knock. He introduced himself and was led into the kitchen, where Daisy stood ironing diminutive garments. She looked up as he went in.

'I'm going to make tea as soon as I've finished this...'

He put his carrier bags down on the table. 'I dare say you'd like to put these things away?' he asked Janet. 'And I'd love a cup of tea when Daisy's finished.'

Daisy went on ironing, listening to him and Janet chatting as they stowed the food away, and then the children woke up and Janet went to bring them downstairs.

'I'll put the kettle on,' said Mr der Huizma.

'You're very domesticated,' said Daisy tartly. She was tired, and he was behaving like a big brother or an uncle or someone equally dull.

'Only when I am obliged to be! You're cross, aren't you? Tired too. There's a steak pie in the fridge; it only needs to be warmed up. And a milk pudding for the children. Go to bed early, Daisy.'

Janet came down with the children then, and he sat down with them on his knee until Janet had made tea. Daisy, ironing the last nightdress, could see that he was quite at ease with them. She supposed that he had plenty of practice on his wards…

After tea he got up to go, waving away Janet's thanks. At the door he said, 'I'll fetch you tomorrow evening, Daisy. I have to go to Plymouth in the morning but I should be here around six o'clock.'

'I won't…' began Daisy.

'Yes, you will!' he assured her, and smiled so that her heart missed a beat.

When he had gone, Daisy said, 'I was going to stay until Jack got here. Can you manage, Janet?'

'Of course I can. I'm feeling quite well again, and the children are themselves once more. Jack will be home in the morning and I'll have everything ready for him. You've been an angel and that Mr der Huizma of yours is marvellous. Are you sure he isn't in love with you, Daisy?'

'Well, perhaps he is a bit, but he's going to marry someone in Holland.'

'Holland's a long way off and you're here,' said Janet. 'Now, let's get supper and go through the fridge. He wouldn't let me pay for anything, said it was a small return for accepting him as a friend...'

Daisy was ready when he arrived the following evening. He had flowers for Janet and a soft woolly toy for each of the children, and when Janet invited him to come and see them any time he was in England, he accepted with the charming good manners which came naturally to him. He had greeted Daisy with a casual friendliness which lasted for their journey back to her home. He didn't talk much, and when he did it was about impersonal matters, and Daisy, facing another goodbye, was in no mood to make polite conversation. When they reached her home he went in with her and spent a short time talking to her mother and father. Going to the door with him at last, Daisy offered a hand. Another goodbye, she thought unhappily, and this must really be the last one. Perhaps he would kiss her...

He didn't. He shook her hand briefly and got back into his car. Daisy went back to the living room and gave her mother and father a long and elaborate account of her stay with Janet, making light of Mr der Huizma's visit.

Her mother, listening to her bright chatter, said presently, 'Well, darling, you've earned a day or two's holiday. Mrs Coffin is coming in for the rest of this week so you can do whatever you want to do.'

Daisy cried herself to sleep and woke early. She couldn't think of anything she wanted to do; she would potter around at home, helping her mother and doing the shopping. She didn't want to go near the beach. To see Jules again didn't bear thinking of.

She collected her basket and her mother's shopping list after breakfast and set off for Pati's supermarket up by the church. It wasn't really a supermarket but Mr Pati, hard-working and a good businessman, liked to keep up with the times, and although it was small, it was an exact model of the vast supermarkets in Plymouth and Exeter.

It was still early, and there were no customers. Daisy asked after his wife's asthma, his small son's tonsils and his own aches and pains, which all took some time, but since time was something to pass as quickly as possible that didn't matter. Presently she took a trolley and got out her list.

She was reaching for Assam tea, always on the top shelf and almost out of reach, when a large hand lifted it down.

'One or two?' asked Mr der Huizma.

Daisy turned to face him. It really was too much. Why couldn't he just go away? She voiced the thought out loud.

'I came to England—and it was most inconvenient too—to talk to you, Daisy. That was impossible at Totnes, so I am reduced to going shopping with you.'

Daisy put two tins of Italian chopped tomatoes into

the trolley. 'Well, whatever it is you want to talk about, we can't do it here.'

'Oh, but we can! It is hardly the ideal surroundings, but I haven't the time to look for a suitably romantic background.'

He tossed two tins of asparagus tips into the trolley, and then added a packet of ravioli. Daisy reached for a jar of coffee and he, not to be outdone, added three tins of cat food.

'We haven't got a cat,' said Daisy.

'Then we will take it back with us; Jette has a cat and kittens.'

They were going slowly along the shelves, the list forgotten, although from time to time Mr der Huizma added some item or other to the growing pile in the trolley. At the end of the narrow aisle he put a hand over hers on the trolley handle.

'My darling girl, will you stand still just long enough for me to tell you that I love you? I've come all this way just to tell you that.'

Daisy looked at him. 'Helene,' she said in a sad voice.

'Helene has broken our engagement; she will eventually, I believe, go to California with someone called Hank.'

'You loved her…?'

'No. I may have been a little in love with her when we were first engaged. And then, when I saw you walking along the shore—you have been in my heart and my head ever since, my dear love. And I thought I had no chance with you, and then, that last time when we said goodbye, and you said, "Jules," in such a loving, unhappy voice… Will you marry me, Daisy? And learn to love me as much as I love you?'

'Oh, Jules,' said Daisy, an entirely satisfactory answer which swept her into his arms to be kissed and kissed again. Presently, when she had her breath back, she said, 'Yes, I'll marry you, Jules, of course I will. I've loved you for weeks.'

He kissed her again, and Mr Pati, watching from a discreet distance, crept a bit closer and stealthily wheeled the trolley back to the check-out desk. He was a romantic man at heart, and he liked Daisy, but business was business, so he began to tot up the goods in the trolley. A most satisfactory start to the day.

* * * * *

OFF WITH THE OLD LOVE

Chapter 1

The operation, a lengthy one, was, to all intents and purposes, over.

The man who had been bending over the still figure on the table for two hours or more straightened himself to his great height, spoke a few words to his registrar facing him, made sure that the anaesthetist was satisfied, peeled off his gloves and turned to his theatre sister.

'Thanks, Sister. I believe we caught him in time.' His voice was deep and quiet and rather slow and there were wrinkles at the corners of his eyes because he was smiling beneath his mask.

Rachel handed a needle holder to the registrar and a pair of scissors to the house surgeon assisting him. She said, 'Yes, sir, I'm glad,' and meant it. It had been a finicky case and she had watched Professor van Teule patiently cutting and snipping and plying his needle in his usual calm fashion. If he hadn't been successful she would have been genuinely upset; she had worked for him for two years now and they got on splendidly together. He was a first-rate surgeon, a brilliant teacher and a stickler for perfection, all of which he concealed under a laconic manner which new house surgeons sometimes mistook for too easy-going a nature, an error they quickly discovered for themselves. Rachel liked him and admired him; they had a pleasant relationship at work but where he lived or what kind of a life he led away from the operating theatre she had no idea, nor had she ever bothered to find out. His tall vast person, his handsome face and his pleasant voice were as familiar to her as the cloak she wrapped around herself going on and off duty: comfortable and nice to have around but taken for granted.

She nodded to one of the theatre nurses now and the girl slipped out of the theatre behind the Professor to take his gown and mask and warn Dolly, the theatre maid, that he would want his coffee. It was the last case on the morning's list and he had a teaching round at two o'clock. It was going on for one o'clock already and Rachel, with three brothers, had grown up with the conviction that a man needed to be fed regularly.

The registrar cast down his needle and put out a hand for the dressing and then stood back. 'You do it, Rachel. You're handy at it.'

He pulled off his gloves. 'That was a nice bit of needlework,' he commented. 'If ever I'm unlucky enough to be mown down by a corporation dustcart, I hope it'll be the Professor who is around to join the bits together again.'

'Refuse collector,' said Rachel, a stickler for the right word, 'and don't be morbid, George, you'll frighten Billy.'

She twinkled at the young house surgeon as she arranged the dressing just so and then stood away from the table while the patient was wheeled away to the recovery room.

'Coffee?' she asked, taking off her mask and gloves and standing still for one of the nurses to untie her gown. 'It'll be in the office…'

She went over to where her staff nurse was supervising the clearing away of the used instruments. She was a young woman, but older than herself, a widow with two children at school, and her firm friend.

'Norah, I'll be in the office. Professor van Teule wants his next list altered; I'll try and pin him down to doing it now before he disappears. Send Nurse Smithers to her dinner, will you? And Nurse Walters. Mr Sims's list isn't until two-thirty and we've got Mrs Pepys coming on at two o'clock.'

They exchanged speaking looks—Mrs Pepys, one of the part-time staff nurses, was tiresome and gave herself airs, talking down to the student nurses and reminding them all far too often that she was married to a descendant of the famous Samuel. 'We'll go to second dinner—at least, you go on time and ask them to keep mine for me, will you? And you scrub for the first case, I'll take the second and Mrs Pepys can take the third—' Rachel's pretty face assumed a look of angelic innocence '—ingrowing toenails!'

A subdued bellow from the other end of the theatre corridor gave her no time to say more. She joined the Professor and his colleagues in her office and listened without rancour while the registrar and Dr Carr, the anaesthetist, made pointed remarks about women gossiping.

'Go on with you,' said Rachel mildly, on the best of terms with them both, and poured her coffee and then replenished the Professor's mug.

He was sitting on a quite inadequate chair which creaked alarmingly under his weight. 'That will give way one day,' she pointed out kindly. 'Won't you sit in mine, sir?'

'Only when you are not here, Rachel.' He watched her settle in her own chair. 'And now, this list of mine...'

They discussed the changes amicably. The Professor did not offer his reasons for starting his list at eight o'clock in the morning in three days' time, nor did Rachel evince the slightest curiosity as to why he expected her to struggle with her nurses' off duty rota and juggle it to suit. He took it for granted that she was prepared to be scrubbed and ready for him at an hour when she was usually in her office, coping with paperwork while her nurses got the theatre ready.

He got up to go presently, taking his registrar and the house surgeon with him. At the door he turned to ask casually, 'Your weekend off, Rachel?'

'Yes. The theatre's closed for cleaning, sir.'

He nodded. 'Well, enjoy yourself.'

He wandered off to cast a sharp eye over his patient in the recovery room and Rachel began to enter details of the day's work into her day book, dismissing him completely from her mind.

That done, she went along to theatre, to find Norah on the point of going to her dinner and the two junior nurses back on duty. She spent the next half-hour instructing them; they were very new to theatre work and a little scared and clumsy, but they were keen and they admired her hugely. A highly successful lesson was brought to its end by the appearance of Mrs Pepys, looking, as always, far too good for her surroundings. She bade Rachel good day and ignored the nurses.

'Hello,' said Rachel. 'We've laid up for the first case—staff's back in a few minutes, she'll scrub. You lay for the second case, please, and take the third...' She paused on her way to the door. 'Ingrowing toenails.'

Mrs Pepys' exquisitely made-up face screwed itself into distaste. 'Sister, must I?'

Rachel's thick dark brows lifted. 'Staff's off duty early, I've a pile of book work, but if you don't feel you can cope...'

'Of course I can cope, Sister.' Mrs Pepys was furious at having her capabilities questioned but she didn't say so. Rachel was a calm, good-tempered girl, slow to anger and kind-hearted, but she was also a strict theatre sister and her tongue, once she was roused, had a nasty cutting edge to it.

With the two nurses safely in the anaesthetic room, making it ready, and Mrs Pepys huffily collecting instrument packs ready to lay up the second case, Rachel went off to her dinner.

There were only two other sisters still in the dining room: Lucy Wilson from the accident room, who, since accidents never occurred to fit in with the day's routine, was seldom at meals when everyone else was, and Sister Chalk, verging on retirement but still bearing the reputation of being a peppery tyrant. Rachel, who had trained under her on Men's Medical, still treated her with caution.

Conversation, such as it was, was confined largely to Sister Chalk's pithy opinion of the modern nurse, with Lucy and Rachel murmuring from time to time while they gobbled fish pie—always fish on Fridays—and something called a semolina shape. Presently they excused themselves and went their different ways. Dolly would have put a tray of tea in the office and Rachel, with five minutes to spare, was intent on reaching it as quickly as possible.

She took the short cut along the semi-basement passage, thus avoiding the visitors who would be pouring into the entrance hall and the wards, then took the stairs at the end two at a time to teeter on the top tread as Professor van Teule, appearing from the ground under her feet, put out a large arm to steady her.

'Oh, hello, sir,' said Rachel and beamed at him. He towered over her, but, since she was a big girl herself and tall, she had never let his size worry her. 'Short cut, you know.'

'I often use it myself,' he told her placidly and let her go. He stood aside so that she could pass him and with another smile and a nod she started off along the passage which would bring her out in the theatre wing. He stood and watched her go, his face impassive, before he trod down the stairs.

Rachel hadn't given him a second thought; she had

five minutes more of her dinner time still. She hurried into her office, saw with satisfaction that the tea tray was on her desk, and stationed herself before the small square of mirror on the wall, the better to powder her nose and tidy her hair beneath her frilled cap. Her reflection was charming: big dark eyes, a straight nose—a little too long for beauty—and a generous mouth, the whole framed in glossy dark brown hair, wound into a thick plaited bun. She pulled a face at herself, rammed a hairpin firmly into place and sailed into the corridor on her way to theatre, where Norah was dealing competently with Mrs Pepys's airs and graces and the junior nurses' efforts to be helpful. There was a good ten minutes in hand. The two staff nurses joined her for tea and then went back to theatre so that the two student nurses might have theirs.

Rachel settled down to her desk work, interrupted almost at once by the arrival of Mr Sims and the anaesthetist who, of course, wanted tea as well. They were joined presently by Billy, who, since there was no more tea in the pot, contented himself with the biscuits left in the tin.

'What is the first case, Rachel?' asked Mr Sims, who knew quite well.

'That PP—left inguinal hernia. Norah's scrubbing.'

'I want you scrubbed for the second case.'

'Yes, I know, sir,' said Rachel tranquilly. 'It's that nasty perf.'

'And the last?' Mr Sims was a shade pompous but he always was.

'Ingrowing toenail. Mrs Pepys will scrub.' She added, 'Is Billy doing it?'

'Good idea. That will allow me to leave George to keep an eye on him.'

The afternoon went well with none of the hold-ups which so often lengthened a list. Norah went off duty at four o'clock, and the heavy second case was dealt with by five o'clock, leaving Billy to tackle the ingrowing toenail. By six o'clock everyone but Rachel and one nurse had gone and, leaving her colleague to finish cleaning the theatre and readying it for the night, Rachel sat down once more to finish her books. She would be off duty at eight o'clock and had every intention of driving home that evening. She allowed her thoughts to stray to the two days ahead of her and sighed with anticipatory pleasure before finishing her neat entries.

She had a bed-sitting room in the nurses' home because, although she would have preferred to live out, there was always the chance that she might be needed on duty unexpectedly. She sped there as soon as she had handed over the keys to the night staff nurse, and tore into the clothes she had put ready—a tweed skirt and a sweater, for the evenings were still chilly at the end of March—snatched up a jacket and her overnight bag, and, pausing only long enough to exchange a word here and there with such of her friends as were off duty, hurried down to the car park where her car, an elderly small Fiat, stood in company with the souped-up vehicles favoured by the younger housemen and divided by a thin railing from the consultants' BMWs, Mercedes and Bentleys. As she got into the Fiat she glanced across to their stately ranks; Professor van Teule's Rolls Royce wasn't there. Fleetingly, she wondered where it was and then dismissed the thought as she concentrated on getting out of London and on to the M3 as quickly as possible.

Her home was in Hampshire, some fifty miles distant—a pleasant old house on the edge of the village of Wherwell, with a deep thatched roof and a garden full of old-fashioned flowers in which her mother delighted. She had never lived anywhere else; her father had been the doctor there for thirty years and, since her eldest brother intended to join him in the practice, she supposed that it would always be home.

The streets were fairly empty and Rachel made good time. Once on the M3, she pushed the little car to its limit until she came to the end of the motorway and took the Andover road, to turn off at the crossroads by Harewood Forest. She was almost home now. She drove through the quiet village and presently saw the lights of her home.

She turned in at the open gateway and stopped at the side of the house. Her father had the kitchen door open before she had got out of the car and she went joyfully into the warmth of the room beyond. Her mother was there and her eldest brother, Tom.

'Darling! So nice to see you.' Her mother gave her a great hug. 'You'll want your supper...'

Her father kissed her cheek. 'Had a good trip from the hospital?' he wanted to know. 'You look very well.'

Tom gave her a brotherly slap. 'Revoltingly healthy,' he pronounced, 'and putting on weight, too.'

'No—am I? There's too much of me already.' She grinned cheerfully at his teasing. 'How are Edward and Nick?'

'Doing well.' It was her father who answered. 'Edward's done excellently in his exams and Nick's settling down nicely.'

They had sat down at the old-fashioned table with its Windsor chairs at each end and the smaller wheelbacks, three each side. They were joined by Mutt, the labrador, and Everett, the family cat, who sat quietly while they had the soup and cold ham, taking a long time over them for there was so much to talk about.

'How's Natalie?' Rachel wanted to know, passing her cup for more tea.

'Fine. She's coming over tomorrow.' Tom had got engaged to a girl in the next village—the vet's daughter and someone they had all known for most of their lives. 'How about your Melville?'

Melville was a producer in television and it was because of him that Rachel neither noticed nor encouraged the advances of quite a few of the medical staff at the hospital. She was quite prepared to be friendly but that was all; she was wholly loyal to Melville and, being a modest girl, had never quite got over her delight and surprise when he had made it clear, after they had met at a party, that he considered her to be his. True, he hadn't mentioned getting married, but he took her out and about, sent her flowers and, when she had firmly refused to spend a weekend at Brighton with him, had taken her refusal with good grace and no hard feelings. Indeed, he had somehow made her feel rather silly about it and she was honest enough to agree with him. She was, after all, twenty-five and sensible. Too sensible, perhaps. She smiled. 'Up to his eyes in work but he's collecting me for a drink on Sunday evening.

I've got to be back because Professor van Teule wants to operate at eight o'clock on Monday morning.'

Her father lifted an eyebrow. 'Working you hard? Something tricky?'

'No, the usual list—most of his cases are tricky, anyway. I expect he wants to get away early.'

'You like working for him still, darling?' asked her mother.

'Oh, yes. He's always good-natured and easy—we get on famously.'

Her mother gave an inward regretful sigh. She had met Melville only once, and she hadn't taken to him. This Professor sounded nice—he would be married, of course, and probably middle-aged... She asked, 'How old is he?'

Rachel bit into an apple. 'Do you know, I've no idea? Anything between thirty-five and forty-five, I suppose. I've never looked to see.'

They cleared the supper dishes and then, since it was now late, went to bed.

The weekend went too quickly. Rachel, country born and bred, wondered for the hundredth time what on earth had possessed her to choose a job which forced her to live in London. But she had never wanted to do anything else and her family had let her go at eighteen to train at one of the big London teaching hospitals and made a great success of it, too. They were proud of her, although her mother's pride was thinned by the wish that Rachel would marry, but she never mentioned this.

Rachel drove back after tea; Melville wouldn't be free until half-past eight and she had plenty of time. It was a blustery evening and there was little traffic, even on the motorway. She parked the Fiat and made her way to her room where she changed into a dark brown suit and a crêpe blouse and exchanged her sensible low-heeled shoes for high heels. Melville liked well-dressed women; indeed, he didn't care for her job since, as he explained to her in his well modulated voice, it necessitated her wearing the most outlandish clothes.

'Well, I'd look a fool tripping round the theatre in high heels and a smart hat,' Rachel had pointed out reasonably, not really believing him.

She had ten minutes to spare; she nipped along to the little pantry the sisters shared in their corridor and found Lucy making tea. Melville had said drinks, which probably meant nothing but bits and pieces to eat with them and she had had no supper. 'Mother gave me a fruit cake,' she said. 'Bring that pot of tea with you and have a slice.'

Lucy followed her back to her room and kicked the door shut. 'Going out? It's a beastly night but I suppose Melville will see you don't get cold and wet. I like the shoes—new, aren't they?'

Rachel agreed guiltily. Since she had started going out with Melville she had spent more on clothes than she could afford, and they were the kind of clothes she wouldn't normally have bought. Her taste ran to tweed suits and simply cut jersey dresses with an occasional splurge on something glamorous for the hospital ball or some special occasion.

She drank her tea and gobbled up her cake. 'I must fly...' She took a last look in the mirror and Lucy said laughingly, 'Do him good to be kept waiting, and you needn't bother to prink; you look good in an old sack.'

Rachel gave her jacket a tug. 'I'm getting fat,' she worried. 'It doesn't notice because I'm tall, but it will—Melville doesn't like fat girls.'

'You're not fat.' Lucy picked up the teapot, preparatory to departing to her own room. 'Just generously curved. There is a difference. Have fun, love.'

Melville's car wasn't in the forecourt. Rachel peered round hoping to see him and then took a backward step back into the entrance hall. Her heel landed on something yielding and she turned sharply to find herself face to face with Professor van Teule's solid front.

She said guiltily, 'I'm so sorry—have I hurt you badly? I had no idea...'

He glanced down at his elegantly shod foot. 'I scarcely noticed.' He eyed her deliberately. 'You're very smart. Going out for the evening? If he's not here you'd better come inside—you'll catch a cold standing here.'

She obeyed his matter-of-fact advice, and, when he enquired if she had had a pleasant weekend, said that yes, she had. 'But over too soon—it always is.' She glanced at his placid face. 'Is there a case in theatre? You're here...'

'There was. I'm on my way home.'

She hardly heard him. Melville's Porsche had stopped outside and he was opening the entrance door and coming towards them. She half glanced at the Professor, a polite goodbye on her tongue, only he wasn't going away; he stood, completely at ease, watching Melville who caught her hand and cried, 'Darling, I'm late. Do forgive me—I got caught up at the studio. You know how it is.'

She said hello and added almost crossly, 'This is

Professor van Teule—I work for him. Professor, this
is Melville Grant—he's in television.'

'How very interesting,' observed the Professor.
'How do you do, Mr Grant.' He didn't shake hands,
only smiled in a sleepy way and patted Rachel on a
shoulder. 'Don't let me keep you from your free evening.'

He went on standing there, so that after a minute
Rachel murmured a goodbye and went to the door with
Melville at her heels.

It shouldn't have been like that, she thought pee-
vishly—he should have walked away instead of seeing
them off the premises like a benevolent uncle.

Melville opened the car door for her with something
of a flourish. He gave a quick glance behind him as he
did so to see if the Professor was watching. He was.

'Sleepy kind of chap, Professor What's-his-name.
Don't know that I'd care to have him nod off over my
appendix or whatever.'

Womanlike, Rachel sprang at once to the defence
of the man who had annoyed her. 'You couldn't have
a better surgeon,' she declared roundly, 'and he's far
too busy to do appendicectomies—he specialises in
complicated abdominal surgery and he's marvellous
with severe internal injuries; even when it seems hopeless, he…'

Melville drove out of the forecourt. 'My dear girl,
spare me the gruesome details, I beg you. Tell me, did
you have a happy time with your family? I can see that
it did you good, you're more beautiful than ever.'

Something any girl would like to hear and, to a girl
in love, doubly welcome. 'Lovely, but far too short.'

He had turned the car in the direction of the West End. 'I thought we might have a drink…' He named a fashionable club. 'I had dinner with the producer and you will have had a meal, of course.'

Rachel had her mouth open to say that she hadn't but she had no chance to speak, for he went on, 'There's a party next week—you simply must come, darling. Buy yourself something eye-catching; everyone who's anyone will be there.'

She thought guiltily of the dresses she had bought in the last few months, worn a few times and then pushed to the back of the wardrobe because Melville had hinted, oh, so nicely, that to be seen more than a couple of times in the same dress just wasn't on. She said quietly, 'I'll have no chance to go shopping and I'll be too whacked to go to any parties.' She turned to smile at him. 'You'll have to find another girl, Melville.'

She had meant it as a joke; his easy, 'It looks as though I'll have to,' took her by uneasy surprise. She spent the next minute or two mentally reviewing the next week's lists and the off-duty rota. It was take-in week, too; there was no way in which she could alter the unalterable schedule.

'Well, let's worry about it later,' said Melville and parked the car.

The club was brightly lit and very full. It was also elegantly furnished. They were ushered to a table a little to one side and Melville at once began to point out the well-known people around them. When a waiter came he turned to Rachel. 'You need bucking up, darling. How about vodka?'

She could hardly mention her empty stomach. Instead she murmured that it gave her a headache and could she have a long cold drink?

Melville shrugged in tolerant good humour. 'Of course, my sweet. What shall it be?'

'Tonic with lemon and ice, please.' She sat back and looked around her. The suit she was wearing had no chance against the ultra-chic women there, but that didn't worry her overmuch, just as long as Melville liked what she wore.

Their drinks came and with them a dish of *crudités*, some salted nuts and potato straws. None of them filling, but better than nothing. She nibbled a few carrot sticks and crunched a potato straw while Melville turned his head to wave to an acquaintance. He turned back presently and began on a long and amusing story about the production he was working on. He was handsome and entertaining and paid her extravagant compliments which she never quite believed. Not that that mattered, for he was in love with her; he had told her so many times. One day he would ask her to marry him and she was sure she would say yes. Her eyes shone at the thought so that Melville paused in what he was saying; she really was a remarkably pretty girl, although she was proving disappointingly stubborn about taking more time off. 'Let's go somewhere and dance?' he suggested.

She said with real regret, 'Oh, Melville, I can't. We start work at eight o'clock tomorrow morning and I'll have to be on duty before then.'

He frowned and then laughed and caught her hand. 'You really are the most ridiculous girl I've ever met. I could get you a part in my next production, or find you some modelling work, but you choose to spend your days in your revolting operating theatre.'

'I don't want to do anything else. It's not revolting, either.'

He picked up her hand and kissed it. 'You dear creature, so earnest. Tell you what, I'll pick you up tomorrow evening when you're off duty and we'll go somewhere and have a meal.'

'It's take-in week. I might get held up, but I'd love that. Somewhere where I won't need to dress up, Melville.'

'The nearest Lyons,' he assured her laughingly. 'And now, before you say it, you want to get back, don't you? Duty calls and so on.'

They took some time to get out of the club; Melville stopped so many times to greet people he knew. Rachel felt very proud of him. Sometimes, but not always, he introduced her with a casual, 'Meet Rachel,' and she smiled at faces which showed no interest in her and listened politely to what they had to say, although none of it made much sense to her.

At the hospital he leaned over and opened her door and then kissed her. 'I won't get out, darling,' he told her. 'I must go back to the office and work for a while.'

She was instantly worried. 'Oh, not because you took me out?' she wanted to know. 'Now you'll have to stay up late working...'

'I'd stay up all night for you, darling.' He smiled as he closed the door and with a wave shot away.

Rachel went to her room, made a pot of tea, ate the rest of the cake and put her uniform ready for the morning. Lying in a hot bath she mulled over her evening;

it had been delightful, of course, because Melville had been with her, but hunger had taken the gilt off the gingerbread. It was a pity, she mused, that she was in love with a man who didn't always remember to ask her if she were hungry, while there were several young men on the medical staff who would have whisked her off to the nearest café for a meal at her merest hint… She frowned. It was strange that, whereas she would have no hesitation in telling any one of them that she was hungry, she found herself unable to tell Melville.

She got into bed, meaning to lie and think about him. He was very good-looking, she reflected sleepily, not tall but always so beautifully turned out. He wore his dark hair rather long and his voice was soft and his speech clipped. On the edge of sleep, she found herself comparing it with Professor van Teule's deep slow tones—not a bit alike, the two of them; the Professor was twice the size for a start…

The Professor walked into the theatre at exactly eight o'clock and Rachel, however easygoing his manner was, had taken care to have everything ready. Sidney, the theatre technician, was standing ready, her nurses were positioned where they would be most required, Dr Carr and his patient were there, the latter already nicely under, and she herself stood, relaxed with her trolleys around her. He bade everyone good morning and she watched his casual glance taking everything in; he expected perfection and she took care that he got it. George and Billy had taken up their places and the Professor waited quietly while they arranged sterile sheets round the patient before putting out a hand for a scalpel.

It would be a lengthy operation—a gastroduodenostomy—but since most of the Professor's work was major surgery, involving all the clap-trap modern methods could devise, Rachel went placidly ahead with what was required of her, by no means disturbed by the paraphernalia around her. She sent the nurses in turn to their coffee, and then Norah, and when at last the Professor stood back from the table, she nodded to the nurse nearest the door to warn Dolly that coffee would be a welcome break.

The patient borne carefully away, the other men followed the Professor and Rachel stripped off her gown and gloves, made sure that Norah was laying up for the next case, and went along to her office. There was no room for them all, but somehow they fitted themselves in and left her chair empty. She poured the coffee and handed round the biscuit tin and, since the Professor had already had his, handed him the patient's notes when he asked for them. He sat hunched up on the radiator, writing up the details of the operation, while the others discussed where they hoped to go for their holidays.

'What about you, Rachel?' asked Dr Carr.

George grinned across at her. 'Oh, our Rachel will be on her honeymoon—somewhere exotic.'

She coloured at that although she answered matter-of-factly, 'Chance is a fine thing—I can't very well have a honeymoon without a husband.'

She was aware that the Professor had stopped writing and was looking at her but she didn't look at him.

Although she had to when he asked casually, 'Did you have a pleasant evening, Rachel?'

The look was grateful; it gave the conversation a turn in a different direction. She didn't mind being teased in the least—three brothers had inured her to that—but somehow she was shy of talking about Melville.

'Lovely,' she told him. 'We went to a club—I've forgotten its name—and it was full of beautiful models and the kind of people you see on the TV.' She put down her mug. 'I'll see if they are ready for you, sir.'

He glanced at his watch. 'We're behind time. George, I may have to leave the last case to you, but I'll be in this evening.' He got to his feet and went unhurriedly to scrub.

The morning wore on. The nurses went in turn to their dinners and two of them went off duty. Norah, back from her own dinner, was laying up in the second theatre for the afternoon list, a short one—dentals—which she would take and then go off duty for the evening. Rachel had intended taking an afternoon off, but as the hands of the clock crept towards two, she resigned herself to much less than that. The Professor had changed his mind and decided to do that last case himself—a good thing as it turned out for it presented complications which he hadn't expected. When at last the patient had been wheeled away it was half-past two.

'Sorry about this, Rachel,' he said. 'You've missed your dinner. Do you suppose they would send up sandwiches for us both? I've an appointment in less than an hour and so can't spare the time for a meal.'

George and Billy had already left. Rachel left two

student nurses to start clearing up, went to have a word with Norah, waiting for her first patient, then went along to phone the canteen. She found the Professor putting down the receiver. 'I thought they might be a good deal quicker if I rang—you don't mind?'

She was pinning her cap on to her wealth of hair. 'Not a bit—they'll fall over themselves to get here. Dolly's making coffee.'

Five minutes later they were sitting opposite each other at the desk eating roast beef sandwiches with the added niceties of horseradish sauce and pickles, some wedges of cheese and, for the Professor, a bottle of beer.

'Well,' said Rachel, happily sinking her teeth into the beef, 'is this what you get when you ask for sandwiches? I get two cheese left over from the day before and a nasty snort down the phone as well.'

'That won't do at all. You're no sylph-like girl to exist on snacks; I'll look into it. Did you have a splendid supper last night?'

His voice was quiet but he glanced at her with intentness. There was something about his calm placidity which invited confidences.

'*Crudités*. Melville thought I'd had supper and he'd had dinner anyway.'

'My dear girl, surely you could have hinted...'

She considered this. 'Not really. It was so—so...' She was at a loss for a word.

He said smoothly, 'The surroundings were not conducive to a plate of steak and kidney pudding?'

'That's exactly it. Anyway, I eat too much.'

His inspection of her person was frank and impersonal. 'You're a big girl and you use up a lot of energy; it would be hard for you to eat too much.'

'Oh, good,' said Rachel and took another sandwich.

The Professor passed her the pickles. 'You're on until eight o'clock? Let us pray for no emergencies.'

Perhaps he didn't pray hard enough. Just as Rachel was closing the last of her books preparatory to sending the junior nurse off duty before going herself, the phone rang.

It was Lucy. 'Rachel, there's a gunshot wound coming in and coming up to you as soon as we can manage it. Abdominal and chest. George is here now and intends to ring Professor van Teule. Have you got a nurse on?'

'Little Saunders; Sidney Carter's on call, I'll give him a ring.' It sounded like a case where the theatre technician might be needed.

She went about the task of getting the theatre ready with Nurse Saunders, keen as mustard but easily put off by anything she didn't quite understand, trotting obediently to and fro.

Rachel was checking the special instruments that might be needed when the phone went again. The Professor, coming through the theatre corridor doors, answered it. A moment later, he put his head round the theatre door.

'For you, Rachel. Melville, I believe.'

'Oh, I can't...' she began, and then said, 'I'd better, I suppose.'

Melville was downstairs, phoning from the porter's lodge, something strictly not allowed. 'Put on your prettiest dress, darling,' he begged her, 'we're going to a party. I'll give you fifteen minutes.'

'Melville, I can't possibly. I'm on duty and there's an emergency case coming up any minute.'

'Well, hand over your revolting tools to someone else, dear girl. This is some party.'

She said tartly, 'You'll have to find somebody else, Melville. I'm on duty.'

'It's gone eight o'clock. You told me that you were off duty then.'

'Well, I am usually, but not when there's an emergency.'

His voice sounded cold and faintly sneering. 'Darling, aren't you just the weeniest bit too good to be true?'

He hung up, leaving her shaking with unhappy rage, and the Professor, who had been standing in the doorway, unashamedly listening, took the receiver from her and replaced it.

'Is there anyone we can get to take over from you?' he asked and his voice was very kind. 'Night sister? Norah?'

She gave him an indignant look. 'Certainly not, Professor. I'm on duty, and in any case I'm not in the mood for parties.' She added unhappily, 'I've nothing to wear—I mean, he has seen the dresses I've got at least six times.'

'That is a point,' agreed the Professor gravely. 'I have no doubt that, to a man in his type of job, clothes matter a great deal.'

Rachel nodded. 'Oh, they do, and you see I've never bothered a great deal—I mean, not to fuss, if you know what I mean? Brothers never notice what you're wearing anyway…' She stopped suddenly. 'I'm sorry—talking to you like this; I quite forgot who you were.'

If the Professor found this remark a little surprising, he gave no sign. He said soothingly, 'I am sure you will have an opportunity to go out with, er, Melville again.' He became businesslike. 'This man who is coming up—gunshot wounds at close range—I've had a look and we'll need a lot of luck on our side. How are you off for staff?'

She cast him a grateful look. He never failed to see that she had enough help. 'If Billy is here, I can manage. I've a junior on—very new but eager—and Carter's coming in.'

'He's a good man to have about. Right, I'll take a look at what you've put out, shall I?'

They went over the instruments together and then he went away, leaving her to scrub and get into her gown and mask and gloves and lay up.

Dr Carr would be anaesthetising; she had expected that. The Professor and he had worked together for a year or two now. He appeared with his patient and a nurse from the accident room to attend to his wants and keep an eye on the drip they had set up. The Professor, with George and Billy, followed hard on his heels.

It took a very long time; it was an hour short of midnight when at last the Professor finished his patchwork, meticulously done with tiny stitches and infinite patience. He thanked them all, as he always did, and left George to do the tidying up before the man was taken to the intensive care unit.

Rachel started to clear up, and Nurse Saunders, still

game, toiled with her until two night nurses appeared to help. Things went more quickly then and presently Rachel and Nurse Saunders were able to take off their gowns and masks and go off duty. But not yet, it seemed. As they went down the corridor George came to meet them. 'There's food and drink in the office—we're all having a picnic; come on.'

The Professor had been exerting his charm again. There were sandwiches and a dish of sausages, a bowl of crisps and a great jug of coffee.

'However did you get this lot?' asked Rachel and sat Nurse Saunders down in front of the sausages.

'It's a kind of blackmail,' he explained gravely. 'You see, if the kitchen superintendent keeps me well fed, she feels pretty sure that, should she need my help at any time, I shall give it gladly and with expertise.'

Rachel forgot the time, that she was tired, that she had missed a glamorous evening with Melville. She looked round at her companions, very contentedly munching, and thought of the man they had worked so hard to save. She would have missed a dozen evenings out just for the satisfaction of knowing that the patient would recover, and as for her companions, she couldn't think of any better. She caught the Professor's eye and he smiled at her.

'Not very elegant and none of us look fashionable, but there's a satisfaction…'

She beamed at him, her mouth full. He was right, but then he always was.

Chapter 2

Perhaps it was a good thing that there was a sudden spate of emergencies; Rachel had very little time to wonder why Melville didn't phone her, although the nagging thought that he was angry with her was at the back of her mind. She could, of course, phone him, but even after the four days of silence from him she couldn't bring herself to do that. She loved him, she had no need to tell herself that, but she also held a responsible job and he would have to try to understand that.

It was on the fifth evening, after a gruelling day, that she found him in the entrance hall as she was going off duty. Her tired face lit up at the sight of him although her, 'Hello, Melville,' was uttered in a matter-of-fact voice.

Melville wasn't in the least matter-of-fact. He

swooped upon her, his handsome face all smiles. 'Darling, you're off duty? Nip along and put on something pretty—I've got a table at the Savoy and we'll find somewhere to dance.'

She said uncertainly, 'I'm tired, Melville; it's been a busy day. If we could go somewhere quiet...'

'Nonsense, darling, what you need is some fun and a drink or two. I'll give you fifteen minutes.'

She thought longingly of supper, a hot bath and blissful bed, but what were they compared to Melville? She said quietly, 'All right, fifteen minutes.'

She showered and changed into what she hoped would pass muster at the Savoy and, because she had cut it rather fine, took the short cut past the consultants' room. There would be no one about as late as this, she told herself, but skidded to a halt as the door opened and the Professor came out.

His look of astonishment left her without words. 'My dear girl,' he said. 'You're going out on the town?' His lazy gaze swept over her nicely made-up face and the blue dress she hoped would meet the occasion. 'You were rocking on your feet,' he observed. 'It should have been supper, bath and bed.' He added, 'I've that nephrectomy first thing tomorrow—you'll need to be on your toes.'

Rachel stared up at his placid face. 'He's here—Melville. I've not heard from him all week, ever since... He wants to take me out to dinner and then go dancing.' She hesitated. 'You see, Professor, I can't not go—so often he asks me out and I'm not free, and I'm so afraid he'll...'

A large comforting hand came down on her shoulder. 'Of course—a dry old stick such as myself tends to overlook the first fine raptures of first love. Why not give yourself a morning off? Norah can scrub.'

She said indignantly, 'Certainly not, Professor,' and went on ruefully, 'I'm sorry, I didn't mean to say it like that. It's kind of you to suggest it, but I shall be all right.'

'Good. Run along then, and enjoy yourself.'

She wished him goodnight and almost ran the rest of the way, wondering why on earth she should imagine that behind that placid face he was amused about something.

Melville was impatient although he hid it very successfully. 'They'll keep our table', he assured her as he hurried her out to the car. 'You're wearing that blue dress again—a mistake, darling, you haven't enough colour for it.'

Rachel, indignation for once swamping her love, snapped, 'I've been hard at work all day and I'm tired—I did tell you...'

He had got into the car beside her and now he leaned over and kissed her. 'My poor darling, you'll feel fine after a meal.'

She did her best; the food was delicious and Melville at his most amusing, but her heart wasn't in it. When they had had their coffee she said contritely, 'Melville, do you mind very much if we don't go dancing? I really am tired.'

She was happily surprised when he leaned across the table and took her hand in his. 'My poor sweet, I'll take you straight back. Get to bed and have a good sleep—get someone to bring you your breakfast...'

There wasn't much point in telling him that she would be getting up at seven o'clock, and as for being brought breakfast in bed… There was, she realised, a wide gap between his world and hers, but that gap would disappear in time. She gave him a grateful smile. 'I've spoilt your evening and I'm sorry—I'll do better next time.'

He pressed her hand and smiled at her. A charming smile which made her happy, as it was meant to. She felt happy still as he drove her back to the hospital, kissed her goodnight, and then drove away at once. She opened the door and wandered through the entrance hall on her way to the back corridor leading to the nurses' home. She had almost reached it when she became aware that Professor van Teule was watching her from the massive staircase at the back of the hall.

She crossed the hall and met him at the bottom step. 'Has there been something in theatre?' she wanted to know urgently, quite forgetting the 'sir'.

He smiled and shook his head. 'I came to check on that transplant we did this morning.' He stood there quietly, waiting for her to speak.

'I've had a simply lovely evening,' she said at last, defiantly, just as though she expected him to contradict her, unaware that her pretty face was white and pinched with fatigue. And, when he nodded gently, 'Goodnight, Professor.'

'Goodnight, Rachel.' He watched her go back down the passage and through the door at its end before he crossed the entrance hall and got into his car.

Rachel slept like a log and only her long training in early rising got her out of bed in the morning. She

went down to a breakfast she didn't want, immaculate
as always but her face pale and shadows under her eyes.
She gulped tea, crumbled toast and then went on duty.
Norah was laying up for the nephrectomy and the student nurses were trotting to and fro. Rachel bade them
good morning, cast an eye over what was being done
and went to her office. The usual small pile of paperwork was on her desk. She pushed it aside, checked
with the accident room that there was nothing in the
way of an emergency, then went through to the anaesthetic room to do a final check. Dr Carr was already
there, adjusting his machines; he glanced up as she
went in and then gave her a second longer look.

'Rachel, my dear girl, you look like skimmed milk.
Haven't you slept?'

She managed a bright smile. 'I slept like a top, whatever that means. I'm fine.' She glanced at the clock.
'Shall I phone the ward to send up the patient?'

He nodded. 'If you're ready. Professor van Teule will
be here in about five minutes.'

She swept away and did that and then started to
scrub. She was gowned and gloved when the patient
was wheeled in with Dr Carr at his head. A moment
later the Professor, with George and Billy beside him,
started to scrub. She was on the point of taking up her
usual place behind her trolleys and replied compos-
edly to their good mornings and stood just as calmly
waiting for them to come into the theatre. She didn't
feel calm; she had a nasty headache and it was too late
now to take anything for it.

The nephrectomy wasn't straightforward; the Professor seemed to attract complicated cases like honey

attracts bees; moreover, he didn't seem to mind. Other surgeons in like circumstances would give vent to strong language, not caring who heard them, but he, beyond muttering in his own tongue, which nobody there understood anyway, remained as placid as usual.

He was putting the final touches to his work when he addressed Rachel.

'I should like to do a transplant—kidney—on a young man. Could you arrange things so that you will be available—and such of your nurses as you will need?' He glanced at her. 'It will probably be during the night or the very early morning but I am told that the donor is in a coma and not likely to live for very long.'

'I'll see to it, sir. Is the patient already in the hospital?'

'Yes, I got him in last night. Shall I be treading on anyone's toes if I take over theatre at short notice?'

Rachel tried to forget her aching head and thought hard. 'No, we can manage. Norah can take the second theatre—it's Mr Sims tomorrow morning and Mr Jolly in the afternoon. I'll have Staff Nurse Pepys here with me...'

She caught George's eloquent eye—he disliked Mrs Pepys and Billy was terrified of her, so she added soothingly, 'If you need to operate between eight o'clock and seven in the morning, Professor, there will be the night staff nurse and the runner as well. They're both very good.'

'Sorry to spring it on you, Rachel.' He sounded quite sincere and he seldom addressed her by her Christian name while they were working. 'There's always a silver lining though; I'll be away for a couple of weeks.'

She said, 'Oh, will you, sir?' rather blankly. It was her headache which made her feel so depressed, she supposed.

She took a Panadol with her coffee presently and her head cleared, so that the rest of the list passed off smoothly enough even though they finished late. The Professor might be a stickler for punctuality, she reflected, going down to a warmed-up dinner, but he forgot that there was such a thing as time once he was scrubbed.

The afternoon list with the fourth consultant, Mr Reeves, an elderly man on the verge of retirement, went well. Rachel handed over to Norah just after five o'clock, and went off duty. An early night, she told herself, trying to ignore the hope that Melville would phone her. A quiet evening somewhere, perhaps outside London, where they could have a meal and talk without the constant greetings and interruptions from his friends. Rachel sighed as she got out of her uniform and pottered off to look for an empty bathroom.

But he didn't phone; she took a long time changing into a knitted suit and then, unwilling to spend an evening in the sitting-room with the other sisters, thrust some money into a purse, and went down to the entrance. She wasn't at all sure what she was going to do—perhaps a run in the car...

She was getting out her car key when Professor van Teule loomed up beside her. 'Ah,' he said sleepily. 'Going out, Rachel?'

'Yes—no. I don't know,' she almost snapped at him. 'I just want to get away for an hour.' She added by way of explanation, 'It's a nice evening.'

He took the key from her in his large hand, picked up her purse from the car's bonnet where she had laid it, and put the key into it.

'You sound undecided. Moreover, you don't look in a fit state to drive a car. I'm going for a quiet potter—why not come with me? We can eat somewhere quiet and you can doze off in peace.'

She had to laugh. 'It's kind of you to suggest it, Professor, but I couldn't go to sleep; it would be rude...'

'Not with me, it wouldn't. You need a nap badly, Rachel. You're wound up too tightly; don't you know that? No sign of, er, Melville?'

'You always say "er, Melville", as though you can't remember his name,' she said crossly.

'Well, I can't.' He sounded reasonable. Really, it was impossible to be put out by him.

'He's a very busy man.'

The Professor, hardly idle himself, nodded understandingly. 'If you had a quiet evening out of town, you'd be as fresh as a daisy in the morning and ready to go dancing again when he asks you.'

She stood looking up at him. He was kind and friendly in an impersonal way and it sounded tempting, to be driven into the country for an hour.

She asked abruptly, 'Why do you ask me?'

'You run the theatre block very efficiently, Rachel, and to do that you have to be one hundred per cent fit; my motive is purely selfish, you see.'

She found that his answer disappointed her. 'Well, thank you, I'll come, only I would like an early night.'

'Don't worry, I'll see that you're back by ten o'clock

at the latest. I shall want to take a quick look at that young man later on, anyway.'

The Rolls was ultra-comfortable; she sat back with an unconscious sigh and the Professor suggested, 'Why not close your eyes until we're clear of London? I'll wake you once there is something worth seeing.'

'Don't you like London?' she asked. Somehow she had pictured him, when she had bothered to think about him at all, as a man about town, wining and dining and going to the theatre; having smart friends.

'No. Close your eyes, Rachel.'

She closed them and, although she hadn't meant to, went to sleep at once.

He had turned off the motorway at Maidenhead before he woke her up.

'There's rather a nice pub by the river at Moulsford—the Beetle and Wedge—we'll bypass Henley and go across country. It's charming scenery and it's still light.'

Rachel, much refreshed by her nap, sat up. 'Sorry I went to sleep, but I feel fine now.'

'Good. I hope you're hungry—I am.'

He talked easily as they drove through the country roads and after a while arrived at the Beetle and Wedge. It was an old inn surrounded by trees and with plenty of garden around it. And it was cosy and welcoming inside. They sat by the log fire in the bar and had leisurely drinks and then dined generously; here they hadn't heard of *crudités*. There was watercress soup with a lavish spoonful of cream atop, followed by steak and kidney pie which melted in the mouth, and even more generous portions of vegetables. Rachel polished off the homemade ice cream she had chosen and drank the last of the claret the Professor had ordered—a very nice wine, she had observed, and he had agreed gravely; a vintage 1981 Château Léoville-Lascases should be nice. He had no doubt that she would be thunderstruck if she knew what it cost.

They had coffee round the fire in the pleasantly filled bar and, true to his word, when she suggested rather diffidently that she would like an early night, he got up at once, paid the bill and settled her in the car. This time he took the main road through Henley and then on to Maidenhead and the motorway, so that they were back at the hospital minutes before ten o'clock.

It was unfortunate, to say the least of it, that Melville should have been getting into his car as Rachel got out of the Professor's.

The Professor shut the car door behind her and she heard him say, 'Oh, dear, dear,' in an infuriatingly mild voice. She felt his reassuring bulk behind her as Melville left his car and came towards them.

'Rachel? I came to take you out for a drink.' He smiled but his eyes were angry. 'But I see that someone else had the same idea.' He gave the Professor an angry look.

'Ah, Mr—er—Grant, isn't it? Good evening. My dear fellow, how vexing for you. We have been for a run into the country. Rachel has had a busy day and so have I. We return considerably refreshed.' He smiled gently and made no move to go away.

Rachel touched Melville on his coat sleeve. 'Melville, I'm so sorry to have missed you. You didn't phone—I had no idea.'

'You're not the only one who's had a busy day.' Melville's voice held a sneer. 'Well, I'll be on my way—I'll see you some time.'

He was going, probably out of her life for ever. Rachel swallowed panic. 'Melville, I've said I'm sorry. If only you had let me know… Can't we go somewhere and have a drink now?'

'I left a desk full of work to come and see you,' declared Melville dramatically. 'I'll go back and finish it.'

'Look, can't we talk?' asked Rachel desperately and glanced round at the Professor, hoping that he might take the hint and leave them alone. He returned her look with a placid one of his own and she saw that he had no intention of doing that. There he stood, saying nothing, silently watching and not being of the least help. She said again, 'Melville…' but that gentleman turned without another word and went back to his car, got in and drove away.

'He'll ruin that engine,' observed the Professor, 'crashing his gears like that.'

'Who cares about his gears?' asked Rachel wildly. 'He's gone and I don't suppose he'll ever come back.'

'Oh, yes he will, Rachel. There is nothing like a little healthy competition to keep a man interested; something which I'm sure you know already. Not, I must hasten to add, that in fact there is competition, but, there is no harm in letting, er, Melville think so.'

'Don't be absurd,' snapped Rachel, and then, 'Do you really think so? You don't think he's gone forever?'

Her voice shook a little at the idea.

He was reassuringly matter-of-fact. 'Most certainly not. Men want the unobtainable, and you were unobtainable this evening—you are a challenge to his vanity.' He sighed. 'You don't know much about men, do you, Rachel?'

She said indignantly, 'I have three brothers…'

'That isn't quite what I meant. I dare say you boss them about most dreadfully and take them for granted like an old coat.'

She stared up at him. 'Well, yes, perhaps. But Melville's different.'

'Indeed he is.' His sleepy eyes searched her face. 'You love him very much, do you not?' He added, '*pro tempore*,' which, since she wasn't listening properly, meant nothing to her; in any case her knowledge of Latin was confined to medical terms.

'Go to bed, Rachel.' His voice was comfortably avuncular. 'In the morning you'll think straight again. Only believe me when I say that your Melville hasn't gone for good.'

She whispered, 'You're awfully kind,' then added, to her own astonishment as well as his, 'Are you married, Professor?'

'That is a pleasure I still have to experience within the not too distant future. Run along, there's a good girl.'

Emotion and the Château Léoville-Lascases got the better of her good sense. She stood on tiptoe and kissed his cheek and then ran into the hospital.

She felt terrible about it in the morning; thank heaven he had no list, she thought as she went on duty. She opened her office door and found him sitting at the desk: immaculate and placid, writing busily.

He glanced up at her. 'Oh, good morning, Sister.

Can you fit in an emergency? Multiple abdominal stab wounds—some poor blighter set upon in the small hours. Mr Sims has a list, hasn't he?'

'Not till ten o'clock, sir.' Rachel had forgotten any awkwardness she had been harbouring, for the moment at least. 'I can have theatre ready in fifteen minutes; Mr Sims could do his first case in the second theatre—Norah's on as well as me.'

'"I"' corrected the Professor. 'Very well, I'll give Mr Sims a ring.' He gave her a casual glance. 'I'll be up in twenty minutes if you can manage that.'

She nodded, rather pink in the face, and left him there to go into theatre and warn her nurses.

It was just as though last night had never been. The Professor duly arrived, dead on time as usual, with George to assist him, exchanged a few friendly remarks of an impersonal nature with her, and got down to work, and when he was done and they were drinking their coffee in her office, he maintained a distant manner that vaguely disquieted her. She had felt awkward at first, but now she was worried that the calm relationship they had had been disturbed.

He went presently, thanking her as he always did, and she set about organising the rest of Mr Sims's list, thankful that the transplant had fallen through.

She worried about it all day, feeling guilty because only every now and then did she remember Melville. But once she was off duty, Melville took over. Perhaps he would phone, she reflected, and hurried to shower and change just in case he did and wanted her to go out. But he didn't; she spent a dull evening in the sisters' sitting-room, watching a film she had already seen on

TV and listening to Sister Chalk criticising her student nurses. I'll be like that, thought Rachel desperately, unless I marry and get away from here. She said aloud, breaking into Sister Chalk's soliloquy concerning a third-year nurse who had cheeked her only that morning, 'I'm going to bed; I've had a busy day.'

George had a short list in the morning; Rachel left Mrs Pepys to scrub after the first case and went into the office to catch up on the paperwork. She hadn't been there ten minutes when the phone rang. It was Melville. She had made it plain when they had first met that he must never ring her during duty hours and she felt a small spurt of annoyance because he had ignored that, but it was quickly swept away with the pleasure of hearing his voice.

'Melville…' She tried to sound severe, but her delight bubbled through. 'I'm on duty—I asked you not to phone when I'm working.'

'I'm working, too, darling Rachel, but I can't concentrate until I've told you what a prize moron I was last night. Put it down to disappointment. Say you forgive me and come out this evening.'

She hoped he hadn't noticed the short pause before she answered. 'Yes' was ready to trip off her tongue when she remembered the Professor's words. Men wanted the unobtainable; OK, she would be just that for this evening at least. She was a poor liar for she always blushed when she was fibbing, but there was no one to see now so that she sounded convincing enough. 'I can't. I know I'm off at five o'clock but they're doing a couple of private patients this evening.'

'The quicker you leave that damned place the better—talk about slavery...'

She said reasonably, 'Not really—I shall get my off duty hours made up to me when we're slack.'

'And when will that be?'

'I could get a couple of hours added on to my off duty tomorrow.'

'That'll make it when?' he sounded eager.

'About three o'clock for the rest of the day.'

'I'll be outside at three-thirty. We'll drive somewhere and have a quiet dinner.'

'That would be nice. Melville, I must ring off.' And she did. Usually she waited until he had hung up, but the Professor had given her ideas...

Since only one theatre was in use for dentals the next morning, Rachel had plenty of time to decide what she would wear. Norah was off duty but she and the second part-time staff nurse would be on again at two o'clock. In the meantime Rachel handed forceps and swabs and mouthwashes and wished that Mr Reed, the dentist, would hurry up. When finally he finished and had been given his coffee it was time for first dinner. She left two student nurses to clean the theatre and went along to the canteen.

It was fish pie, turnips and instant mash; although she was hungry she only half filled her plate. Melville was fussy about his food and always took her somewhere where the cooking was superb.

There were half a dozen of her friends already sharing a table and she joined them, pecking at the wholesome food with such reluctance that Lucy asked her if she was sickening for something.

'Just not hungry,' said Rachel, who was. She filled her empty insides with tea and went back to the theatre. Norah had just come on duty and there was little to do. They planned a wholesale cleaning operation, leaving one theatre free for any emergency which might come in, decided that Mrs Crow, the part-time staff nurse on duty for the afternoon, could scrub for the three cases of tonsillectomy, and conned the next day's list.

By then it was three o'clock; half an hour in which to make the best of herself. Rachel raced through a shower, brushed her hair until it shone, plaited it neatly into a bun again, and went to study the contents of her wardrobe.

It would have to be the suit again, but this time she would wear the pale pink blouse with it. She thrust her feet into high-heeled shoes, found gloves and handbag and, with an anxious eye on the clock, went down to the forecourt. She was a little late and she hadn't yet learned to keep a man waiting; indeed, the reverse, growing up as she had with three brothers.

Melville was waiting and his greeting was everything a girl could wish for; she got into the car beside him feeling on top of the world, and she stayed that way for the rest of the afternoon and evening. He had never been so amusing nor so anxious that she should be enjoying herself. They had tea in Richmond and then drove on through Hampshire and into Wiltshire to stop in Marlborough and dine at the Castle and Ball, a pleasant and comfortable hotel, but not, thought Rachel fleetingly, Melville's usual kind of place in which to eat. As though he had heard her unspoken thought, he said lightly, 'I had thought of going to Marlow—the

Compleat Angler—but this place is quiet and the food is good.' His glance strayed over her person making her aware of the suit he had seen several times already.

'I'm not dressed for anything four-star.' She wasn't apologising, only stating a fact. 'This looks very nice.'

That was the only small fly in the ointment. They lingered over the surprisingly good dinner and it was after ten o'clock by the time they got into the car again. It would be midnight before she reached her room and she was on duty in the morning. Not that that mattered; she was so happy she didn't give it a second thought.

Melville drove back to London very fast, not saying much. He was tired, she decided, and so said little herself. They were back before midnight and although he kissed her and declared that he had enjoyed every minute of it, he made no effort to delay her; indeed, he leaned across and opened her door with the remark that he would see her just as soon as he could, and drove away before she could do more than utter the most cursory of thanks.

The poor dear, she found herself reflecting as she went inside, he works too hard. Professor van Teule was crossing the entrance hall; Melville wasn't the only one to work hard, but she didn't dwell on that, she would have found it strange if the Professor hadn't. Come to that, she worked hard herself, but she didn't dwell on that; either. She was remembering the delights of the evening and turned a smiling face to him as their paths crossed. She wished him goodnight in a cheerful voice and he answered her with his usual courtesy, glancing with deceptive sleepiness at her happy face. The night porter wondered why he should look so thoughtful as he went out to his car.

Rachel didn't see him the next day; Mr Jolly had a list and Mr Reeves had the second theatre in the afternoon. She went off duty at five o'clock after a routine day, changed and went to the local cinema with two of her friends. It was a tatty place but showed surprisingly good films, and strangely enough although the neighbourhood was prone to muggings and petty thieving, the staff of the hospital, even out of uniform, were treated with respect. They had coffee and sandwiches at Ned's café, opposite the cinema, and went back to make tea and gossip over it until they decided to go to bed.

Norah had days off and Rachel, going on duty in the morning, remembered with a sigh that Mrs Pepys would be on duty from nine o'clock until three in the afternoon, which meant that the student nurses would be in a state of rebellion by teatime. She could hardly blame them; Mrs Pepys was tiresome at the best of times and not of much use, for the Professor had indicated months ago in the nicest possible way that he preferred not to have her scrub for him. There were three heavy cases and he would be doing them all, which meant that Mrs Pepys would be left with the afternoon dentals and laying up between cases, two tasks she felt too superior to undertake.

She would do them, of course; Rachel had a quiet authority which made itself felt upon occasion.

She checked the theatres, gave the student nurses their allotted places and went to scrub. She had laid up the trolleys for the first case when the Professor put his head round the door. His good morning was genial.

'There's a man downstairs I'll have to patch up when he's fit enough—can we add him to the list?'

She wondered what he would say if she said no; something soothing and courteous and the man would arrive in the theatre all the same.

'Certainly, sir. Mrs Pepys will be on at nine o'clock and can take dentals this afternoon so it won't matter if we run late.'

'Norah not here?'

'Days off.'

'Time you had yours, isn't it?'

'When Norah gets back.'

He nodded and his head disappeared and presently, when they were ready for him, he came back with George and Billy beside him. His 'Ready, Sister?' was calmly impersonal and a moment later he was bending over his patient, absorbed in his work.

It was more than two hours before the patient was wheeled away.

'Coffee?' asked the Professor, straightening his great back, and, without waiting for an answer, he wandered out of the theatre.

Mrs Pepys was on duty by now. Rachel left her to lay up for the next case, sent two of the nurses to their coffee and repaired to her office. Dolly had carried in the coffee tray and the four men were crowded into the small room, waiting for her. She handed them their mugs, took the lid off the biscuit tin and put it on the table where everyone could reach it. They devoured biscuits as though they were famished and she made a mental note to supplement the meagre supply she was allowed from stores with a few packets of her own.

They drank and munched in a pleasant atmosphere of camaraderie, and the talk was of the patient who had just gone to the recovery room and the next case. Dolly came to refill the coffee pot and Rachel slipped away to see what was going on in theatre. The student nurses were back from their coffee and she sent the third, junior nurse to the canteen and suggested that Mrs Pepys should go at the same time. 'And when you get back will you get ready for dentals?' suggested Rachel. 'There's an extra case coming up and we shall be late. Mr Reed's got three patients—you'll be ready well before three o'clock, so clear up as far as you can, will you? I'll need all the nurses I've got as well as Sidney.'

Mrs Pepys gave her a cross look. 'If you say so, Sister.' She flounced away and Rachel turned back towards the theatre to find the Professor standing behind her. She had let out a gusty sigh and he asked, 'Is she a trouble to you, Rachel? Shall I get her moved?'

She looked at him in surprise. 'She's annoying, sir, but she does her work—I've no good reason for her to be moved. It's only her manner.'

'She scares the little nurses, does she not?'

That surprised her, too; she hadn't credited him with noticing that. 'Yes, but I make sure they come to no harm. It's nice of you to notice, though.'

He turned away. 'Well, let me know if you need help at any time.' And, over his shoulder as he went, 'Are you going home for your days off?'

She felt herself blushing, which was silly. 'I—I don't know. It depends...'

'Ah, yes—Melville, of course.'

They didn't talk again that day, only to exchange

necessary words about the patients or the instruments he needed. The list finished in the early afternoon and he went away at once, wishing her his usual placid goodbye. For some reason she felt put out, although she was unable to decide quite why that should be. Something was happening to their former easygoing relationship and she had no idea what it was.

Chapter 3

Rachel forgot her vague disquiet almost at once. For one thing there was the usual upset between Mrs Pepys and one of the student nurses to settle and then, at tea time, an emergency appendix which George did. She went off duty debating as to whether she should go home or stay in the hope that Melville would call her with some plan of his own. He hadn't mentioned seeing her on her days off, but he seldom planned anything in advance. Too busy, she thought fondly. It took her only a few moments to decide to stay, certain that Melville would ring; he knew that she had days off, she had told him and he had said that they must spend them together.

She sat in the sitting-room for an hour, willing the telephone to ring, but, since it hadn't by supper time, she went to the canteen and then, refusing offers to go to the cinema with some of her friends, she went to her room and washed her hair, a long business because of its length and thickness. She followed this by doing her nails and examining her pretty face, searching for signs of wrinkles. Finally, she went to bed. Melville would surely phone in the morning; she slept peacefully on the thought.

She got her own breakfast in the pantry at the end of the sisters' corridor and dressed with care. It was a cold blustery morning, quite suitable for the wearing of her winter coat, recently bought and fashionable and which would allow her to wear a silk jersey dress, so that if they stayed out to dinner she would look all right. She perched a little angora cap on to her braided topknot, and, gloves and bag in her hand, went down to the entrance hall. She was so certain that Melville would have written to her that she didn't hesitate, but went straight to the porter's lodge for her post.

There were several letters for her but only one which mattered. She opened it quickly, vaguely aware that it had been delivered by hand, and read it, and then read it again. Melville knew that she would understand; an American actress had joined the cast of the production he was working on and he had been asked to show her something of London; he had intended telling her on the previous evening but there had been a drinks party which had lasted rather a long while. Lucky that they hadn't had anything planned and he would give her a ring early in the week. He had no doubt that she would have a super couple of days off.

Her instant rage was swallowed up in a wave of unhappiness. He could have told her earlier so that she could have gone home. Now half a day at least had been wasted, for she could have driven down on the previous evening. Here she was, dressed for a smart restaurant and probably a theatre with Melville, who took it for granted that she would understand. She had been silly, she admitted to herself, to expect a man as important as Melville to be free to come and go as he wished, and sillier still to have been so sure of him. She read the letter once again and took comfort from the endearments which strewed it so liberally. He must love her very much to write like that... She became aware of someone standing beside her—Professor van Teule, calmly and unforgivably reading the letter she had still open in her hand.

'Oh, bad luck,' he said placidly, and smiled so kindly that the heated words on her tongue were unuttered. All she said was rather weakly, 'You have no right...'

'None,' he agreed cheerfully, 'but how very fortunate that I should, er, glimpse the contents of your letter. I am about to drive down to Bath and will be glad to give you a lift.'

'But I live miles from there.' She knew that she sounded ungracious, but disappointment was still biting deep.

'I had intended to take the road through Andover, and I seem to remember you telling me at some time or other that you lived in that part of the world.'

If she hadn't been quite so upset she would have remembered nothing of the sort. As it was, she mumbled, 'I told Mother yesterday evening that I was going to stay here...'

The Professor became all at once very brisk. 'Give

her a ring now.' His glance took in her little cap and high-heeled shoes. 'I need ten minutes to talk to George; you can change if you want and meet me here.'

He propelled her gently towards the porter's lodge, but as she was lifting the receiver she said hesitantly, 'We're not allowed to use this phone.'

'Leave that to me.' He turned his back and engaged the head porter in conversation as she dialled her home number.

Her mother answered the phone. 'Now isn't that nice?' she commented. 'Your brothers are home—we'll have a cosy weekend together. Are you driving, darling?'

Rachel explained. 'Oh, good.' Mrs Downing's voice was casual in the extreme. 'You'll be here before lunch. Will he stay, this Professor?'

'Most unlikely—he's going on to Bath.'

She put down the receiver and saw that the Professor was still deep in conversation with Simkins, the elderly head porter, who, if rumour had it right, had been there ever since Victorian times. She went towards them now and the Professor turned his head to ask, 'All right? Good, ten minutes then.'

She went back to her room and changed into a sweater and skirt and a quilted jacket, rammed a few necessities into an overnight bag, got into a pair of sturdy shoes, and hurried back to the entrance hall. The Professor was there, talking to George, who gave her a friendly grin and then walked to the entrance with them both.

'Goodbye, sir. I'll see what I can find you when you get back. Rachel, don't forget it's take-in next week.'

He laughed and raised a hand as the Professor took the Rolls smoothly out into the traffic, joining the steady stream going west.

He had little to say, and that required little in the way of a reply, something which was a relief to Rachel, busy with her thoughts about Melville. They gained the motorway and the Professor put his large, elegantly shod foot down so that the car ate up the miles, but once they were off the motorway he slowed the car and presently stopped at a wayside café.

'Shall we have coffee? We've made good time.'

'Yes, please. But have you to be in Bath for lunch? You'll be late if you take me home first.'

'There is time enough,' he told her in his unhurried way, and for some reason she felt snubbed. Over their coffee she made small talk, feeling guilty because for such a lot of the journey she had said almost nothing. As they got back into the car she tried to put that right. 'I'm sorry I'm such a dull companion, but I wanted to think…'

'Let us say restful rather than dull. And I had the opportunity to think a few thoughts of my own, Rachel.'

Which made her uneasy. Was he hinting that he wanted to stay silent for the rest of the journey, or just being kind?

She played safe and kept quiet, and discovered that their silence was a friendly one. There was no need to make conversation; she felt quite at ease, and so, apparently, did the Professor.

As he drew up before her home it struck her that he hadn't hesitated once on the way, nor had she given him any directions; she was on the point of pointing this interesting fact out to him when her mother opened the door and came out to the car.

Mrs Downing wasn't in the least like her daughter. She was barely middle height, plump, but pretty still, looking incapable of running a house, let alone helping her husband, cooking meals at odd hours, waiting with endless patience for him to come home, and owning three very large sons and a daughter, who if not large, was a good deal taller than herself.

She poked her head through the window the Professor had opened and beamed at them both. 'Darling, how nice. Your brothers are in the kitchen.' She turned still-beautiful blue eyes upon the Professor and Rachel said quickly, 'This is Professor van Teule, Mother; he kindly gave me a lift.'

Mrs Downing offered a hand. 'I've often wondered what you were like,' she told him chattily. 'Not a bit what I expected. Will you stay for lunch?'

He smiled at her. 'You are most kind to ask me, but I have to get to Bath.'

'Charming place, have you friends there?' She didn't wait for him to answer. 'Are you calling to take Rachel back tomorrow?'

Rachel pinkened and frowned and the Professor's eyes gleamed with amusement.

'Certainly.' He turned to look at Rachel. 'About eight o'clock?' he asked.

'You'll have to come out of your way.'

'A few miles. Eight o'clock, Rachel?'

She scowled at him, wishing she could refuse the lift her mother had angled for. She said crossly, 'Very well, Professor, thank you.'

'There'll be coffee for you,' said Mrs Downing happily. 'My husband will be delighted to meet you.'

The Professor replied suitably, bade Mrs Downing goodbye, said nonchalantly to Rachel, 'Tomorrow evening, then,' and drove off.

'What a very nice man,' said Mrs Downing, leading the way indoors. 'Is he married? No? Going to be? What a pity, he would suit you down to the ground, darling. And you told me you'd never really looked at him. How could you not? Such a handsome man…'

Rachel put an arm round her parent. 'Mother,' she said patiently, 'the Professor is someone I work for. We get on well enough, but I don't know anything about him and he doesn't know anything about me.'

'He knows where you live,' said Mrs Downing happily.

No one mentioned Melville until Sunday morning, on the way to church, when Mrs Downing asked casually if he was in London. 'For these important men do get around, don't they?' she added chattily.

'He's having to show some American actress the sights this weekend,' said Rachel shortly, 'and he's very busy.' She added defensively, 'We had a lovely afternoon and evening out last week.'

She was glad that her three brothers joined them then and there was no need to say more.

Sunday passed peacefully; church, one of Mrs Downing's superbly cooked lunches and then a long lazy afternoon sitting round the fire in the comfortable rather shabby drawing-room, with the Sunday papers strewn all over the place and desultory family gossip. They had supper early since Rachel was leaving that evening, and the meal had been cleared away before the Professor arrived, exactly at eight o'clock. Rachel was ready to go but he seemed in no hurry; he accepted her mother's invitation to have coffee and followed her into the drawing-room, where her father and three brothers subjected him to a brief scrutiny as she introduced him. They seemed to like what they saw; over coffee and one of her mother's ginger cakes, the men talked and it was almost nine o'clock when, at last, the Professor asked her, 'Well, are you ready, Rachel?' A remark which she considered most unfair, since she had been ready for an hour.

It took another fifteen minutes to say goodbye to everyone and, to make matters worse, the Professor made no attempt to drive fast. Perhaps Melville had phoned, she thought distractedly, and she hadn't been there—he might have written or called...she'd been a fool to go home.

Her companion, uncannily reading her thoughts, observed placidly, 'Well, let us hope that, er, Melville has phoned or called to take you out.'

'Of all the nasty unkind things to say,' began Rachel fiercely.

'No, no you mistake me. Can you not see that his appetite will be whetted? The unobtainable, Rachel— that is what you have to be,' he added with tiresome conviction. 'Use your wits, girl.'

Rachel almost choked with temper. 'Well!' She paused to think up a scathing remark, and he laughed and said, 'What a pity you don't treat, er, Melville to one of your bad tempers.' His voice changed from mockery to avuncular kindness. 'Rachel, if you want

him you'll need to fight for him.' He sighed soundlessly. 'You have the weapons: youth and beauty and a
pretty voice and, besides these, a good brain and plenty
of common sense.' He was silent for a few moments.
'Don't try and be what he thinks you should be; be
yourself—if he loves you he won't care if he takes you
out wearing a potato sack.'

'You're full of good advice,' she said bitterly.

'I do my best,' he told her placidly. 'Have you had
supper?'

'Ages ago.'

'Good, then we could stop for a sandwich. It will
give me an opportunity to discuss tomorrow's list—
I want to make some alterations. I shall be away for a
couple of weeks; George will cope, but there's a case I
want transferred and added...can we do that?'

He had become Professor van Teule again, impersonal and friendly, with his mind on his work. They
stopped at a service station and drank some awful
coffee and ate sandwiches which looked and tasted
as though they were made of plastic, and talked shop
the whole time.

The Professor wasn't a man to leave a girl to open
her own door, even if it was only the hospital entrance;
he took her overnight bag and saw her into the entrance
hall, but before she could say goodbye the night porter
poked his head out of his cubby hole.

'There's a phone call for you, Sister. I was just ringing round for you.'

'Melville,' uttered the Professor and gave her a little
push towards the porter's lodge. 'Take it here and remember what I said.'

It was indeed Melville. Where had she been? He had called twice already. 'I've missed you so,' he added plaintively.

She was on the point of saying that she'd missed him, too, when she remembered the Professor's advice. She said in rather a cold voice, 'I've been home for the weekend. Just this minute got in.'

'I'll be round in ten minutes—we can go to my club and have a drink.'

It cost her a lot to say lightly, 'Sorry, Melville, I'm on my way to bed. There's an early list in the morning and I'll be needing all my wits.'

What was more, she hung up on him.

'Oh, splendid!' The Professor's quiet voice made her jump; she hadn't known that he was right behind her. Probably he had heard every word. He was, she reflected, quite unscrupulous.

'You have him in the hollow of your hand,' he said. 'Goodnight, Rachel.'

He had gone, while she was still gaping at him.

There was, indeed, a heavy list in the morning; Professor van Teule, since he would be away for two weeks, was intent on getting as much work done as possible before he went. Rachel, after a sound night's sleep despite her doubts as to whether she hadn't been a bit drastic in her treatment of Melville, went calmly through her day. The Professor's list extended far beyond its time limits; they stopped briefly between cases to snatch a cup of coffee and a sandwich and then went on again, with the faithful Norah laying up each fresh case and Rachel scrubbing. It was a blessing that Mrs Pepys wasn't on duty; the routine went smoothly and the student nurses, even the junior one, were lulled into a state of instant obedience and confidence by the Professor's pleasantly casual manner and Rachel's unflappable demeanour.

It was almost three o'clock by the time they had finished his last case and Rachel thanked heaven that Mr Jolly had phoned in to say that he was cancelling his list because he had a heavy cold. Norah, who had gone off duty for the afternoon, came on again at six o'clock, and Rachel, bogged down in paperwork, hailed her with relief. 'What a day! We finished at three o'clock and it took us all of two hours to clear and clean. I've almost finished here. You've got Nurse Walters on. There's nothing in the accident room, so with luck you'll have a quiet evening.'

'Has he gone?' asked Norah.

'Not until the morning,' observed the Professor from the doorway. And, as they turned to look at him, 'Don't worry, I don't want to operate. That last case, I didn't write up the notes. If I might trouble you...'

Rachel got up. 'Sit here, sir. I'm going off duty. Norah will be in theatre if you need anything.'

She found the case book he wanted and laid it ready on the desk. 'I hope you have a pleasant holiday,' she said politely.

'Thank you.' He sat down at the desk and pulled the notes towards him and she had the unpleasant sensation of being shut out. She bade him goodbye in a cold voice, cast a speaking glance at Norah and left the office.

There was no phone call from Melville. Rachel spent the evening in the sitting-room, knitting a complicated sweater which should have taken all her attention but didn't, so that she unpicked almost as much as she knitted. Perhaps she had been too harsh with Melville; perhaps the Professor's advice hadn't been all that good. She pondered the matter at length, giving absent-minded answers to her friends' remarks, not really hearing them.

When she went to bed she was still thinking about it, so that it was all the more surprising that her last thoughts were of the Professor. Where did he go when he went on holiday? she wondered. To Holland? To stay with the girl he was going to marry? Did he have parents like everyone else? And where did they live? These questions and others quite ousted Melville from her mind.

She had to admit after a day or two that she missed the Professor; at least, she missed the bustle and urgency of working for him. George had lists, of course, and so did Mr Jolly and Mr Reeves, and of course there were the dental cases, but, whereas the Professor always worked himself and everyone else to their capacity, the days were now orderly, with everyone going off duty at the right time and the lists finishing exactly when they should. So that, when Melville at last phoned, she was in a mood to agree with anything he might suggest.

A party, he told her; the production he had been busy with had been completed, and they were having a celebration. He would fetch her at nine o'clock the next evening, and she was to wear her prettiest dress. 'I missed you, darling,' he declared. 'It seems ages since I saw you. Thank heaven I'll have nothing important on for a time—we'll see each other as much as possible.' He added dramatically, 'You have no idea how busy I've been.'

Rachel had been busy, too, but she was too happy to say so. Perhaps after all the Professor's advice was bearing fruit.

She gave a good deal of thought to what she was going to wear. She was off duty at six, which gave her ample time in which to change her mind half a dozen times. The women would be smart; more than that, they would be fashionable and expensively dressed and she mustn't let Melville down. She decided on a long black skirt, a vividly patterned silk top which had cost the earth and a wide black satin sash of Lucy's. Not bad, she considered, inspecting her reflection and admiring the black satin slippers she had bought for their last evening out. She had a long black evening cloak which seemed too dramatic for the occasion and Lucy came to the rescue once more with the offer of her short fur jacket: rabbit, and a little on the small side, but it lent a certain cachet to the outfit.

Remembering the Professor's advice again she waited until five minutes past the hour before going down to the entrance; she found Melville waiting for her in his car. He didn't get out but opened the door for her and kissed her warmly when she got in. 'Darling, you're more beautiful than ever. How I've longed to see you. This is going to be some party—in Chelsea—everyone who's anyone will be there.'

Rachel said, 'Oh, how nice,' feeling this to be an inadequate remark, but Melville wasn't listening; he was reciting names to her—important names of the important people they would meet. It took the entire drive to complete and left Rachel, who wasn't at all up-to-date with the latest pop stars, bewildered.

The party was being held in a large terraced house near the river; there were rows of cars in the street outside and lights blazing from every window. 'Hurry up,' begged Melville and leaned across to open the door impatiently.

The house inside was opulent and very warm. It was also brilliantly lit and the huge chandelier in the hall shone down on the rabbit so that there was no hope of passing it off as anything else. Melville gave it a look as she handed it to a haughty-looking maid, then he cast an eye over her person. 'I don't suppose you had time to buy something more suitable,' he began, and then paused at the look Rachel gave him. 'Not that you don't look smashing,' he added hastily. 'You always look marvellous. Let's go in.'

The room they entered was packed and the noise of voices drowned normal speech. Melville seemed to know everyone as he made his way across the room with Rachel close beside him. At the far end standing by a roaring fire was their host, or so she presumed; it was impossible to hear what Melville was saying. She shook hands and smiled and accepted a glass of something and to her dismay saw Melville disappear into a group of people standing nearby. She sipped the drink which she privately decided was sugared petrol, and then looked around her. The women's dresses were fabulous; she stuck out like a sore thumb and her hair was all wrong. Several of the girls there had brightly coloured hair—pink and purple and pale blue and even the normal colours had been coaxed into wild clouds of crimped hair, or spiky hairdos, and there were several with hair so short and sleek that it seemed to have been painted on to their heads. Rachel stood there, entertaining wild ideas about having her hair cut off and buying some shoes with diamond encrusted heels three inches high at least, and was roused from these unlikely happenings by a pleasant voice at her elbow.

'You came with Melville Grant, didn't you? You're his latest girl, aren't you? We've all been wondering what you were like! A smasher, I can see that. But then he always has the best.'

Rachel turned to look at the speaker; if the words had been offensive she was sure that they weren't intended to be. The middle-aged woman beside her had a kind and smiling face, motherly in fact, and was dressed in the kind of frock that one would expect a middle-aged woman to wear. Moreover, her hair was frankly streaked with grey and twisted untidily into a small bun.

'I'm Pat Morris—I write TV scripts and try to do a bit of directing too. Work sometimes with Melville; that's how I got to hear about you.'

She put out a hand and Rachel took it. 'How do you do,' she said politely. 'I'm Rachel Downing and yes, I came with Melville.' She decided to ignore the rest of her companion's remarks. A handsome, sought-after man such as Melville would naturally enough have lots of girlfriends, but they had to come to an end one day and he had told her on numerous occasions that she was the only girl in the world for him. She glanced across the room to where he stood surrounded by a laughing group of people and Pat Morris followed her gaze. 'Always the life and soul of any party,' she commented. 'I don't know how he does it, though his work isn't all that demanding. He's got a secretary, of course, and an assistant, and he doesn't have to work till all hours like some of us.' She took a sip from the glass she was holding, and pulled a face. 'Poison,' she said and went on chattily, 'Away at half-past four every day and not a sign of him until ten o'clock the next morning.'

Rachel said, 'Oh, yes,' in a doubtful voice. Why had Melville told her that he worked far into the night, and, if he didn't, where did he go and what did he do? Something she would ask him.

They were joined presently by a youngish man in horn-rimmed glasses and a thin woman in black draperies and rows and rows of beads. They were introduced as Fay and Murphy and embarked at once on a commentary of the people at the party. Rachel stood and listened. There was no need to say anything; when Fay paused for breath Murphy carried on, cheerfully slandering everyone in sight. They told her, laughing heartily, that they wouldn't say anything about Melville and she said gently, 'Well, I don't suppose there's anything much to say,' which remark left them for the moment speechless.

There was an awkward little silence after that broken by someone offering them tiny sandwiches on a tray. Rachel could have eaten the lot and was horrified when they were waved away by her companions. 'I simply can't eat after dinner,' said Pat and Fay added, 'Food can be such a bore.' She looked at Rachel's nicely shaped person. 'You'll put on weight,' she pointed out, 'eating between meals. As it is you'd photograph on the plump side.'

Rachel decided not to mention that her last meal had been at midday and the next would be breakfast. She said mildly, 'Well, no one photographs me, so I'm not worried.'

'You exercise?' asked Murphy.

'Quite strenuously,' said Rachel gravely.

They were joined by another three persons who were hailed with shrieks of laughter and enquiries as to whether they had had their licences endorsed. A slight accident with their car, explained Murphy rapidly. No one hurt; at least, the driver of the other car had a leg broken, or it could have been an arm, he wasn't sure. But wasn't it a huge joke?

Rachel, a forthright girl, would have had quite a lot to say about that but it struck her forcibly that these people would stare at her uncomprehendingly and label her a prig, and what good would it do anyway? She couldn't get a word in edgeways as it was and besides, she had to think of Melville...

He joined them a moment later, putting a careless arm around her shoulders. 'And how's my girl?' he wanted to know. 'Having a splendid time, I can see that. Have another drink. Toss that one off, darling, and I'll get you something else.'

She handed him her glass. 'No thanks, Melville, it's almost midnight. I must go, but you don't have to come. Could you get a taxi for me?'

'My dear girl, you can't possibly leave yet. Why, the evening is only just beginning.'

She sensed his annoyance and she almost gave in,

but the Professor's advice was still loud in her ear. 'Perhaps it is for you,' she told him cheerfully, 'but I'm a working girl.' She gave him a bewitching smile, nodded to Pat and Murphy and Fay without looking to see if he was following her and made her way to where her host was standing.

She made her farewells charmingly so that he looked after her as she went out of the room and observed to the man standing with him. 'How refreshing to meet a girl like that—I'd forgotten they existed.'

Rachel had a moment of panic when she realised that Melville wasn't going to drive her home, but his explanation was plausible enough, and she, hopelessly infatuated, was ready to accept it and make excuses for him besides. He couldn't leave the party, he explained as they stood in the hall waiting for her taxi. There were important people there he had to meet, to keep in with; it was part of his job. He kissed her with practised charm and put her into the taxi and paid her fare before he stood back on to the pavement with a final wave. It was only as she reached the hospital that she remembered that he hadn't said anything about their next meeting.

It had been a successful evening on the whole; she felt a little uneasy about the people she had met, but perhaps not all Melville's friends were like that; he must have a family, although he never mentioned them, and some kind of home life. She undressed slowly, in a daydream where she lived with him in a charming house in the country with a brood of children and a clutter of animals. The unlikelihood of this didn't strike her at all, and she got into bed and went to sleep, still with a head full of foolish fantasies.

There were flowers for her the next day, with a card: 'My undying love,' tied to them. They had been delivered to her office and she stuck them in a large jug until she could take them to her room at dinner time.

George and Billy both stared and George said, 'He must love you, Rachel; there's half a week's salary there,' and Mr Jolly when he arrived to take his list let out a low whistle. 'My, my—do I smell romance in the air? Rachel, who's the lucky man?'

She blushed. 'They're just flowers from someone I know,' she observed and made haste to get him interested in the first case.

The week wound to its close and, since it was her weekend off, she decided to go home. Melville hadn't phoned or written and even if he did she wouldn't change her mind. She packed her overnight bag, got into sweater and skirt and went down to her car. On the way she looked to see if there were any letters for her. There was one, from Melville. He would call for her that afternoon—there was a preview he knew she would love.

It needed all her resolution not to dash back to her room and unpack her bag. Instead, she went over to the porter on duty. 'If a Mr Melville Grant calls or comes for me, will you tell him that I've gone home for the weekend please?' She hesitated. 'You won't forget, will you?'

'No, Sister. Shall I say when you'll be back?'

'No, no need. I'm not sure myself and I can always telephone.'

She worried as she drove home; Melville might be so annoyed that he wouldn't want to see her again; perhaps she had been too severe—if things went wrong she would never forgive Professor van Teule and his advice.

Common sense took over as she neared her home. Nothing could be gained by worrying so she would forget about it and enjoy her weekend. Which, surprisingly, she did, helping her mother round the house, driving her father to a couple of urgent cases, taking Mutt the elderly labrador for walks.

The hospital looked unwelcoming as she drove the Fiat round to the car park on her return. The thought went through her head that the week ahead would be dull, for the Professor wouldn't be back for another seven days. There was plenty of work but no transplants or complicated surgery; she was a girl who liked a challenge.

There was a letter for her. Melville was disappointed; he had planned a marvellous time for them both and why couldn't she have let him know that she was going to be away? He had spent a wretched lonely weekend, working late into the night. Which reminded her of what Pat had told her. Did he really work so hard? Probably at home, she told herself. She longed to phone him, but stopped herself in time; it seemed likely that the Professor, who, after all, must have had some experience in such matters, had been right.

The week passed uneventfully and, as sometimes happened, there were few emergencies. Rachel saw Norah off for her weekend and settled down to two days of catching up with paperwork, browsing over catalogues of instruments and teaching student nurses.

Melville telephoned her on the Saturday and, since Mrs Pepys was relieving her on the following afternoon, she agreed on meeting him for tea on Sunday. 'But I must be back here by five o'clock,' she warned him, 'so that the staff nurse can go off duty—she's part-time and has a home to run.'

He had sounded eager to see her. The moment Mrs Pepys arrived Rachel hurried to change and then made herself wait so that she wouldn't be too punctual. It was hard when she wanted to spend every second she could with Melville, but she managed it and was rewarded by a warmth she hadn't expected. He drove her to Green Park, and they walked for an hour before having tea in a small, elegant tea-room. He was full of a new series being prepared for television. 'We'll have to go on location,' he explained, 'but not yet. There are weeks of studio work first. We've signed up that actress I took around a short while ago. She'll be marvellous, and the clothes will be gorgeous.'

Rachel listened eagerly; his life seemed so exciting, even though she wasn't sure that she liked his friends. It didn't occur to her that not once during the afternoon did he ask her about her work or what she had done with her days. Only when he told her that he would be free for a good deal of the following week and had planned all kinds of delights for their benefit did she tell him with real regret that Professor van Teule would be back and it was take-in week.

He scowled at that and muttered something about her loving her work more than him.

'No, I don't!' she protested. 'But I can't come and go as I please.'

'You're tied to that tyrant, Professor van Teule; he's got you under his thumb.'

She was a little bewildered. 'That's ridiculous—he does his work, and I do mine. And I'm not under his thumb; he's most considerate, but if a patient needs surgery then we get on with it. If you had to have an emergency operation and had to wait while they found someone to scrub and get the theatre ready, you wouldn't be best pleased.' She added hotly, 'You're being unreasonable.'

'And you are being a righteous little prig.'

He drove much too fast into the hospital forecourt and the Professor, getting out of his car, raised his eyebrows and then stood watching while Rachel got out of the car and without a backward glance hurried into the hospital. Melville turned the car and drove away just as ferociously.

'Now that is interesting,' observed the Professor softly, and he strolled unhurriedly into the hospital in his turn to wander along to the consultants' room and collect his letters. There was a copy of the morrow's list waiting for him—a formidable one; they would all be busy. He doubted if Rachel would get any off duty. 'And a good thing, too,' he murmured and settled himself to read the first of his letters.

Chapter 4

Bad temper sustained Rachel as she tore through the hospital and gained her room. She got ready for bed still seething, but once there, doubts came crowding in. Was she really a prig? Just because she liked her work, did that mean to say that she was boring? And did Melville really expect her to walk off duty regardless of whether she was needed in the theatre or not? Supposing he never wanted to see her again? There were all those glamorous women, too... She fell asleep at last and dreamed that Melville had gone away and would never come back. It was so vivid that she could think of nothing else while she dressed and ate a sketchy breakfast.

But once on duty she had to abandon these troublesome thoughts and plunge into the day's work. She had already seen the theatre list on Saturday; now it lay on her desk, considerably lengthened, and as she studied it the phone rang: George, ringing from the accident room to say that a woman with internal injuries would need surgery as soon as possible.

'But the Professor is starting at half-past eight and the list is bulging.'

'I know. He's seen her and he wants her up first. How soon can you manage?'

'Fifteen minutes. What kind of injuries?'

'Ruptured spleen, internal haemorrhage for a start. I've warned Men's Surgical to delay the first patient.'

She was replacing the receiver when Professor van Teule walked in. His good morning was genial, the glance he gave her sleepy and brief, but long and intent enough to note her pale face and shadowed eyes.

He said placidly, 'Sorry to get us off to such a bad start, Rachel—I've added a couple of cases to the list, too.'

'I've just seen them, sir. Has the patient been cross-matched? Do you want me to send to the Path Lab?'

'I've asked Lucy to see to that. Put out the pedicle forceps and the clamps, will you. Oh, and the curved compression forceps.' He was lounging against the door so that she had to pause before him on her way out. 'Did you have a pleasant weekend?'

'I was on duty, sir.'

'No time off—hard luck on Melville.'

She said stiffly, 'We were able to spend the afternoon together yesterday. Green Park looks lovely—tulips and hyacinths and all the trees budding.' She added, 'I hope you had a good holiday, sir.'

'Delightful, thank you. No one called me "sir" for two whole weeks.'

She blushed faintly. 'No, well, I suppose not—I mean, if you're not in the hospital there's no need...'

'I must remember that.' He stood on one side and opened the door for her.

It was nice to have him back, she reflected, giving quiet instructions to Norah and the nurses. The day bade fair to be chaos before its ending but at least life was never dull. She conferred with Sidney, told Norah to see that the nurses went to their coffee as and when they could be spared, and went off to scrub.

The emergency took a long time. 'Coffee?' asked the Professor mildly, handing over to George and standing away from the table.

Rachel nodded to Nurse Saunders and went on handing things to George and Billy. There was a mass of work ahead of them but the nurses had gone to their coffee, Norah was having hers at that very moment and would lay up for the next case and Sidney would be back within minutes. Rachel reviewed the theatre list and thought that, with luck, they might be done by two o'clock.

They weren't, of course; a second emergency— a perforated appendix in a teenage girl had to be squeezed in between the last two cases and, to complicate matters, Mrs Pepys phoned to say that she didn't feel well and wouldn't be coming in for her usual afternoon duty. Which meant that Norah had to go into the second theatre to take Mr Jolly's list, and take two nurses with her.

They had stopped after the fourth case and had a

hasty meal of sandwiches and coffee and then gone steadily on, reinforced by Nurse Saunders who had had a long weekend off duty and came on at one o'clock, which meant that the junior nurse could take her time off. Rachel didn't need to worry about Sidney; he stayed stolidly doing all he was supposed to do and he wouldn't go off duty until he was no longer needed. He was a tower of strength in theatre and liked by everyone; for his part he admired Rachel and considered the Professor to be the finest man he had ever met.

They worked on steadily, in a comfortable friendly atmosphere, until at length the Professor straightened his back for the last time.

'Thanks, all of you—a good day's work.' He went away, unhurried as usual, to cast an eye on the day's patients.

It was too late to do anything about off duty. Rachel sent the student nurses to their tea, left Norah to clear the theatre after Mr Jolly's list and started on the main theatre with Nurse Saunders. The student nurses, back in half an hour, would finish the clearing and still get off duty and she would stay with Nurse Saunders until the night staff came on. Norah protested at this but, as Rachel pointed out, if Mrs Pepys was going to be off sick, off duty would be chancy; Mrs Short, the second part-time staff nurse, only came in twice a week and was terrified of working with the Professor. 'You take your usual evening,' she told Norah, 'and I'll give myself an extra hour or two when we're slack.'

'You didn't go to dinner,' pointed out Norah.

'Nor I did—I'll have to have a good supper to make up for it. I wasn't going to do anything this evening anyway.' It was just as well that she wouldn't be off duty, she reflected silently, or she might be tempted to phone Melville, and certainly if he had phoned her she would have gone out with him. A kind-hearted-girl, she had already forgiven him for his show of temper, and was only too ready to apologise for her own snappy remarks.

If she had secretly hoped that there might be a phone call during the evening, she was to be disappointed. She went off duty just after eight o'clock, ate her supper with those of her friends who had also had an evening duty, and went along to the sitting-room to watch the television and drink tea until bedtime.

She was tired after her long day; she was asleep almost as soon as her head touched the pillow. It was two o'clock in the morning when a touch on the shoulder sent her upright in bed. The night runner was standing beside her bed, holding a mug of tea and looking anxious.

'Sister, I'm sorry but could you come back on duty? There has been a demonstration, I'm not sure where, and we are admitting. The accident room's full and Professor van Teule and Mr Jolly and Mr Reeves are there and quite a few patients need surgery.'

Rachel gulped the tea, wide awake now. 'Get someone to phone Sidney Carter and get Nurse Walters up, will you please?' It was no use wanting Norah; she lived out, and, besides, if she was going to be up half the night, Norah would have to take the morning's list. Rachel dressed with the speed of long practice, plaited her thick rope of hair into a securely pinned bun, rammed her cap on top and sped silently through the hospital to the theatre wing.

The night runner was there, laying up with the general set, but when she saw Rachel she said breathlessly, 'Oh, Sister, may I go? They're up to their eyes downstairs and Night Sister said if you could spare me…'

'Of course. Many thanks for getting started—it's a great help. Ask Night Sister to let me know what's coming up first, will you?'

'A very nasty multiple stab wound,' said the Professor from behind her. 'God knows what we'll find once we start looking. George is setting up a drip but time is of the essence. Where are your nurses?'

'Nurse Walters will be here at any moment and I've asked them to get hold of Sidney.'

'My dear girl, there are a dozen or more in the accident room—we'll need both theatres. I'll be here, Mr Jolly next door and Mr Sims will use the operating room in the accident room.'

'I'll be here,' said Rachel calmly, 'with Sidney and Nurse Walters, junior night Surgical Sister will be with Mr Jolly and I'm sure that night super will rustle up someone for Mr Sims.' She started to scrub. 'Norah will be on at eight o'clock. If we're not finished she can take over, and there will be two student nurses and the little junior on at half past seven.'

'Nicely organised.' He smiled faintly. 'What a pity you can't organise your own life as efficiently, Rachel.' Before she could do more than open her indignant mouth, he was leaving. 'I'll be up in ten minutes,' he told her over one shoulder.

Nurse Walters came then, pop-eyed with the excitement of being got out of bed in the middle of the night but anxious to play her part. Rachel left her to the manifold tasks around the theatre, and got herself gowned and masked and gloved. She had her trolleys and Mayo table laid up by the time the patient arrived with Dr Carr and a moment later Sidney came quietly in with a laconic, 'Hi, Sister, here's a fine thing. Two o'clock in the morning, too—they ought to know better, getting honest folk out of their beds. What's coming up first?'

Rachel told him as he began to assemble the equipment the Professor might call for, checked her swabs and stood patiently until the Professor with Billy joined them.

'Ready, Sister?' he asked quietly, and then, 'George will come up presently; he's got his hands full downstairs for the moment. The next case is a man with a ruptured kidney.'

He waited while Billy arranged the sterile towels and sheet over the patient and then put out his hand for a scalpel. It was some time later, when he had found and assessed the damage and begun to repair it, that he observed, 'I've asked for some of the day staff to be called on duty at six o'clock—your nurses among them, Sister—no objections?'

'None, sir—thank you for thinking of it.' She passed Billy the intestinal retractor, nodded to Nurse Walters to count swabs, and cast an eye over her trolleys. There was no one to lay up for the next patient, of course; there would be a delay while she cleared theatre with Nurse Walters's help and laid up again. Sidney would help, of course, but they would be a bit pushed. It was almost four o'clock when the Professor took off his gloves and prepared to leave the theatre.

'Finish off, Billy, will you? Sister, I'm going down-stairs to see what's happening. Ten minutes?'

She nodded. Nurse Walters was already clearing; Rachel's painstaking instructing was paying off. She helped Billy with the dressings and wheeled her trolleys to one side as the porters came in to take the patient to the intensive care unit. Dr Carr went too and so did Billy, and she and Sidney and Nurse Walters began to clear and presently to lay up once more.

The Professor did a nephrectomy on the next patient since it was hopeless to do anything else. The man was young and looked healthy and there was no reason why he shouldn't make a good recovery.

'Another multiple stab wound coming up,' the Professor told her towards the end of the operation. 'A teenager—he's in a pretty poor state. Can you cope or would you like a rest until the day staff come on?'

'I'm not tired,' said Rachel, uttering the lie loudly to make it sound more convincing. 'Do you want a break, sir?'

'After this next case. George will be up presently and Billy can go down and do some stitching.' He glanced over at the young man. 'You've done very well, Bill—thanks.'

It wasn't possible to see Billy's gratified face, but they could all see the way he flung out his chest. Just like the Professor, thought Rachel, to remember, even when up to his eyebrows in work, to give credit where it was due.

The Professor took infinite pains with the boy; he

had been severely wounded and lost a lot of blood, but, as the Professor pointed out to George, the lad was young and although undernourished had a good chance of recovery. 'I shall want him on strict observations, though; see to it, George, will you?' He busied himself with tubing and some meticulous stitching and presently cast down his instruments on to the Mayo table. 'He should do now.'

He glanced at the clock. 'Seven o'clock—we'll break for half an hour, Sister.' He looked around him. 'Ah, reinforcements, I see.'

They had been there for the last hour but he had been too engrossed to notice that. Nurse Walters had slipped away in response to a nod from Rachel and Nurse Saunders had taken her place with Nurse Smithers hovering in the background. Rachel asked, 'What comes up next, sir?'

'An internal haemorrhage, but we don't know why at the moment. Put out everything we've got, will you?' He glanced at her, seeing her tired eyes above the mask. 'But you will have breakfast first, Sister.'

She was only too glad to obey him. Norah, always punctual, had come on duty earlier than usual. Rachel handed over to her with a thankful sigh and went down to the canteen, more than thankful to see that Dolly, apprised of the situation by a friend of hers on night duty, had arrived and gone straight to the theatre kitchen to make tea and cut sandwiches. Rachel told Norah to let each nurse in turn have ten minutes for refreshments and warn Dolly that, once they started again, the surgeons would most certainly need something to keep them going.

The canteen was crowded with night staff eating breakfast, day nurses gobbling down a quick meal before going on duty and a sprinkling of nursing staff who, like Rachel, had been got out of their beds during the night. Rachel sank down beside Lucy and one of the canteen staff brought over a pot of tea. 'And I'll bring you a nice boiled egg and a bit of toast, Sister,' she promised. 'Still busy are you with them poor wounded?' She added with relish, 'They tell me they're swimming in blood downstairs.'

'You shouldn't believe all you hear, Ida,' said Rachel. 'It doesn't say much for the hospital staff, does it? Someone has been pulling your leg.'

Ida looked disappointed, so she added kindly, 'But it's very busy in the accident room and we shall be operating for the rest of the day.'

Ida went to fetch the egg and toast and Rachel gave Lucy a tired grin. 'How are things down below?' she asked.

'Well, not quite as bad as our Ida would wish, but bad enough and you're right, you'll be up to your eyes for hours.'

She was right, of course. Rachel couldn't remember such a day; they worked steadily, stopping briefly for coffee and sandwiches. She lost count of time as the day wore on, concentrating on keeping the theatre going without any hitches. She and Norah took over from each other at intervals so that one scrubbed while the other laid up for the next case and then changed over, and with the three nurses on duty as well as Sidney it was possible to send them off for short spells. But the Professor seemed tireless, going ahead with each case with the relaxed air of a man who had slept well and with nothing of an urgent manner to bother him.

The night staff came on early just as the very last case was being wheeled away and, reinforced by extra nurses, they took over at once. Rachel was loath to leave without clearing the theatres, but the night superintendent made it clear that for once she would be overruled. Norah was sent home, the nurses went eagerly to the supper being kept for them and Rachel went to her office. Even if she didn't stay to see that the theatres were closed she still had the books to do. She sat down and pulled them towards her and began to write in her neat hand. She had a good memory, but tonight she was tired and sat frowning, trying to remember the second case. It alarmed her rather that she hadn't an inkling; what was more, the rest of the cases were getting more vague by the minute. She glanced up wearily as the door opened and Professor van Teule came in. He had said goodnight and thanked them all and gone away half an hour earlier and now she cried, 'Oh, not another case...'

He shook his head. 'No. Isn't there anyone else to do that for you?' And when she shook her head, 'I've brought the case sheets along—you can get the names and what was done from them.'

She was so grateful that she could have wept. 'I'll take them back to the wards as soon as I'm finished. Thank you very much, Professor.'

He didn't answer but pulled up the second chair and sat himself down on to its flimsy structure. 'I'll read out the names and details, you do the writing.' He didn't give her time to protest, but began at once so that she had to start writing as fast as she could.

When they had finished he collected the case sheets and stood up. 'Now go and eat your supper and go to bed, Rachel. Are you on duty in the morning?'

She nodded. 'But I'll be fine after I've had a good night's sleep.' She smiled at him faintly, looking very tired. 'I must go and see Night Staff Nurse, then I'll go.'

He opened the door for her and she went along to the theatre with a quiet goodnight. He had worked them all hard all day but he had worked twice as hard himself and he had thanked them and bothered to bring the case sheets. He really was a kind man; she couldn't work for a better one. She conferred with the staff nurse, said goodnight and left the theatre wing.

There was still a good deal of activity in the hospital but she didn't heed the various sounds around her. She wouldn't have supper, she decided as she reached the hall, but would go to bed at once. She was halfway across the wide entrance hall when she saw Melville standing there. She stopped and he came striding towards her, arms outstretched.

'There you are at last. The porter said he thought you would be off duty at any moment—I've only been waiting ten minutes or so. I've a rather special evening planned for us, darling—go and put on something pretty. You can have ten minutes...'

She looked at him dully. 'I'm going to bed.'

'Nonsense—bed at nine o'clock in the evening? That's for old folk.'

'I'm tired.' It was too much trouble to explain and

surely he must have heard about the rioting and the casualties.

He frowned. 'Well, so am I. I've had a hectic day but I don't moan about it.'

She wasn't listening. 'I'm tired,' she said again, and saw him look over her shoulder, his frown deepening.

The Professor had joined them, his vast person unseen and unheard. He said pleasantly, 'Good evening, Mr Grant. Sister Downing has been working since two o'clock this morning with scarcely a break. She is tired. Bed is the best place for her. Very hard luck on you, Mr Grant, but I'm sure that you understand.'

'An hour or two away from this gloomy place in cheerful company will soon put her on her feet. Rachel?'

She didn't speak; she couldn't be bothered. Besides, the Professor was there, doing the talking for her.

Now he shook his head slowly. 'I'm afraid she's rather past that. She's asleep on her feet. Look for yourself.' There was something in his voice which made Melville study her properly. Her face was as white as her cap and, of course, her dark blue cotton uniform didn't do much for her. Her hair was untidy, too. He said sulkily, 'I can't see what business it is of yours.'

The Professor's voice was genial. 'My dear fellow, Sister Downing is responsible for the management of the theatre wing, its staff, its equipment and so forth. She assists me and my registrar and the three other consultant surgeons. She needs to be one hundred per cent fit and on her toes. At the moment she is on her knees. If she doesn't get to bed soon she will be flat on her face—something to be avoided at all costs. I'm sure that you will agree with me?'

While he had been speaking he had moved between Rachel and Melville and the latter found himself being edged neatly towards the door which, when he reached it, the Professor politely opened for him. 'I know you will understand.' The voice was still genial but very firm. 'Goodnight, my dear chap.'

He followed Melville outside and stood on the steps watching him get into his car and drive away, and then he went back inside to where Rachel was standing exactly where he had left her.

He put a hand on her arm, nodded to the interested porter in his box, and towed her outside, across the forecourt to where the Rolls was parked. The cool air of the April evening revived her a little, but when she began uncertainly, 'Why...' he hushed her soothingly. 'I'm taking you to have a meal—you won't sleep on an empty stomach.'

'I'd rather go to bed.'

'And so you shall. You shall be back here and in bed by ten o'clock.'

He stuffed her into the car, got in beside her and drove out into the street, and she sat back without arguing. He had said ten o'clock and she knew him well enough to know that he did what he said.

He was driving west through the city, using side streets, and presently she stopped wondering where they were going, noticing only that they had reached quiet streets, lined by town houses of some size. He stopped at length and when he got out and went round and opened her door she got out, too. They were in a narrow street, quiet too, lined by tall narrow houses. It was dusk by now and there were lighted windows and trees at the pavement's edge, so that London seemed very far away even though they were in the heart of it. The Professor took her arm and urged her up shallow steps to a black painted door. There were orange tulips in the window boxes on either side of it and she said, 'Of course, you live here…'

'Of course I do.' The door opened and, obedient to his hand, she went inside.

The hall was long and narrow with a staircase at one side and doors to the left and right. As they went in, the door behind the staircase opened and a thin elderly man came briskly towards them.

'Ah, Bodkin,' said the Professor, 'I have brought Sister Downing back for supper; she has been on her feet since two o'clock this morning and she's very tired. Could Mrs Bodkin find something light? Soup and an omelette perhaps? As quickly as possible?'

Bodkin inclined his grey head. 'Certainly, sir. Give her ten minutes. If you will go into the drawing room…' He opened a door and Rachel went into the room beyond. A very pleasant room, large and comfortably furnished and softly lighted. She said matter-of-factly, 'If I sit down I'll never get up.'

For answer the Professor pushed her gently into an easy chair and bent down and took her cap off, smoothed her untidy hair back from her forehead and observed, 'That's better. Don't worry, I won't let you go to sleep.' He moved away and came back in a moment with a glass. 'Drink this, it will wake you up just enough for you to enjoy your supper.'

Which it did. Within minutes Bodkin ushered them
into a room on the other side of the hall—smaller but
just as charmingly furnished as the drawing-room—
and this time they had company: a labrador, who came
in with Bodkin and the soup, greeted his master, inspected Rachel and went to sit by the log fire while
they ate. They talked little as they had their soup, and
after the first few spoonfuls Rachel discovered that
she was hungry after all, so that she was able to polish
off the omelette with a good appetite, and the caramel
cream which followed it. She was given lemonade to
drink although the Professor had lager, which, he explained, might make her wake up too thoroughly, and
presently, when they had finished, Bodkin, who had
served them in a fatherly way, asked her if there was
anything else she fancied, for Mrs Bodkin would be
only too glad to get it for her.

Rachel thanked him and said no, but would he thank
Mrs Bodkin for her delicious supper, and when she had
done that, the Professor made no attempt to keep her
there; she found herself back in the car being driven
through the now quiet streets. Once at the hospital he
got out again and walked her through the entrance hall
to the door leading to the nurses' home.

'You will go straight to bed, Rachel,' he told her.
'There's a list in the morning and I want you on duty.'

She gave him an owl-like look from sleepy eyes. 'I'll
be there, sir. And thank you.' It struck her then that he
was as tired as she was—his face held lines she had
never seen before—and he had never said so. She put
out an impulsive hand and touched his sleeve. 'You've

been so kind, and you need to go to bed and sleep even more than I do.'

He smiled a little. 'Sound advice, Rachel—I shall take it.' He opened the door and when she went past him she heard the door close again immediately. It seemed a long way to her room but she reached it at last, undressed, washed her face and fell into bed. Lucy, coming in a few minutes later to see if she was back, found her fast asleep, and crept out again.

A night's sleep worked wonders. Rachel ate a good breakfast, discussed yesterday's emergencies and excitements with her friends and went on duty. There was a list, as the Professor had reminded her; not a very heavy one, she remembered thankfully. She went straight to theatre to see how the nurses were getting on, passed the time of day with Sidney and went to her office. Professor van Teule was there, sitting on her desk. He looked up placidly as she went in; he looked very wide awake, extremely elegant and somehow remote. She beamed at him, wished him good morning and, when he made to get up, shook her head and pulled up a second chair to the other side of the desk. 'Are you altering the list, sir?'

'Yes. The cases I should have done yesterday must be done today. I dislike postponing an operation, for the patient's sake; it's no light matter to screw up one's courage to face a certain day and time only to find that it's all for nothing. Can we possibly do the three from yesterday at the end of the list?'

She said, 'Yes, of course, sir,' without hesitating. Everything would have to be rearranged, of course. Normally there were only dentals in the afternoon, but there were only a few cases for that day anyway. She had planned extra off duty for the nurses—Norah could have gone home an hour early and she would have gone off at five o'clock as the second part-time staff nurse would take over. Now she reckoned that theatre would be in use well into the afternoon; Norah would have to stay until five o'clock, and so would Sidney—she would manage with two nurses and let the other two go after second dinner.

'Thrown a spanner in the works, have I?' asked the Professor watching her face.

'Not at all, sir. We're all on duty, it's just a question of rearranging things.'

He finished his writing and closed the folder. 'Your professional calm isn't easily shaken, is it, Rachel? You should learn to apply it to your own life.' And, at her astonished gasp, 'I speak with the best of intentions.'

There was a knock at the door and Norah came in most opportunely, for Rachel couldn't think what to say to that. They plunged at once into ways and means and presently the Professor went away, remarking that he would return at nine o'clock.

The moment the theatre corridor doors closed behind him Rachel burst out, 'Sometimes he is quite impossible!' and, at Norah's surprised look, 'Oh, just something he said; nothing to do with work. Now, which two shall I send off duty this afternoon?'

The day, busy though it was, went smoothly enough; theatre was empty and pristine in its surgical cleanliness by four o'clock. Dentals had been finished long ago and even if Norah hadn't been able to go off duty early at least she had got away punctually, as had the nurses. It only remained for Rachel to clear up her desk, con the next day's lists for Mr Jolly and Mr Sims and check that CSU had sent up a sufficiency of supplies.

Until she began on this comparatively easy task she hadn't spared a thought for anything other than her work, but now her mind, free from the day's urgencies, roamed free once more, and settled, not unnaturally, on Melville.

She couldn't remember very well what she had said on the previous evening; she had been too tired to think clearly or to remember what she had said. She could remember clearly, however, seeing Melville being ushered out of the hospital by the Professor. She hadn't cared two straws about that at the time, but now she winced at the memory. Melville would be annoyed and she excused the annoyance, for no one had made it clear why she was tired. If he had been working all day at the studio, he would most likely have had no knowledge of the rioting and the number of casualties. She forgave him without a second thought, never doubting that he had forgiven her once he knew the rights of the case.

The part-time staff nurse came on duty, and Rachel handed over thankfully; an early night, she promised herself, but first she would phone home and, after supper, wash her hair. There were no letters for her but she hadn't expected any; Melville would write or telephone when he was free and he would know that she wouldn't want to go out that evening. She had a long satisfying talk with her mother, promised to go home on her next weekend off and went along to the sitting-room to read the papers until it was time to go to supper. Most of her friends were off duty, too, but the talk was desultory. Reaction after yesterday's activity had set in and they sat about, yawning their heads off and scanning the headlines or watching the television. No one wasted much time over supper either; as if by common consent, they all went to their beds. Rachel curled up and, already half asleep, wondered what Melville was doing. Then rather to her own surprise, she found herself thinking about the Professor. Having an early night, she hoped; he deserved one.

The Professor was doing something quite different, however; he was on a flight to Amsterdam. And as for Melville, fortunately for her peace of mind, she had no means of knowing that he was living it up with one of the actresses working on the current production; a pretty, empty-headed girl, a marvellous companion for an evening's fun. She knew how to dress, too, and there was no fear at all that she would want to leave early.

The next couple of days were uneventful, enlivened only by the arrival of red roses from Melville. The card said all his love, but there was no mention of him seeing her. Too busy, Rachel decided, arranging them in a vase she had borrowed from the private patients' wing. Perhaps at the weekend he would be free, at least; if he phoned she wouldn't go home as she had planned.

The Professor arrived for his usual list in the morning, placid as ever, but with little to say. Only when George asked him if he had had a good time in Holland did he reply briefly that yes, he had. Rachel, pouring their coffee after the list, paused with the jug upheld.

'Oh, is that where you've been?' She frowned. 'But you were here at the beginning of the week.'

He spoke briefly. 'It only takes fifty minutes to fly to Amsterdam.'

Somehow she felt snubbed. She continued her coffee pouring; she wasn't in the least interested in where he had been anyway, and she would take care not to ask questions again. Just occasionally she glimpsed a side to him which wasn't placid at all.

Melville phoned that evening; he was desperate to see her but he had to go to Paris—on location, he explained. He would see her the moment he got back; he longed to see her, he added.

She was disappointed, but his job was important to him; she didn't know much about it, but he wasn't quite his own master. She thanked him for the roses, told him not to work too hard, told him with candour that she longed to see him again, and rang off. She had quite forgotten all the Professor's good advice.

Chapter 5

Rachel wasn't unduly worried when she heard nothing from Melville; she had the roses to reassure her and he had told her that he would be away. Besides, she had a lot on her mind. Mr Sims and Mr Jolly both had heavier lists than usual and both theatres were in use. It wasn't until three more days had gone by that she went on duty feeling vaguely worried. Surely Melville would have had time at least to telephone her? She could always ring his office but he disliked her doing that, so even if she knew where he was there wasn't much she could do about it.

It was Professor van Teule's list that morning. It would be a long hard day, for he rarely finished before the early afternoon and although Norah would be there to take dentals, one of the student nurses, Nurse

Smithers, a steady, conscientious worker to be relied upon, had days off and Nurse Walters had asked for an evening, which left Rachel with little Saunders. Mrs Crow would be in to take over at five o'clock and the pair of them would manage well enough. Rachel shut the off duty book and looked out of the window. The view wasn't really a view; the forecourt and beyond it the busy street and a vista of small houses and shabby little shops, but it was a May morning, the sky was blue and the sun shone. It was her weekend off—she would go home even if it meant not seeing Melville. The garden would be lovely and she and Mutt would walk miles and come home to one of her mother's splendid teas…

'Nothing better to do than daydream?' asked the Professor mildly as he came in. He glanced out of the window in his turn. 'And it has to be daydreaming with a view like this one.'

She turned to wish him good morning. 'I was thinking how nice it will be to go home this weekend.'

He raised his eyebrows. 'What about Melville? Surely he will want you to stay in town?'

'He's—he's away…'

'He'll be back,' observed the Professor easily. 'Take him home for the weekend.'

'Oh, well, yes— He might find it a bit quiet…'

'Surely not if you are there, Rachel?'

She eyed him thoughtfully. 'You think so? He might have other plans.'

He sauntered to the door. 'Remember what I told you? Stick to it, dear girl. I'll be up in ten minutes or so.'

He didn't refer to their conversation again. For one

thing there was little opportunity to talk and for another, although he was his usual placid self, he was remote, so that even if she had had the chance to say anything she would have hesitated to do so.

At the end of the day, with him gone and the theatre once more ready for use at the drop of a hat, she had time to think about his suggestion. Going off duty presently she decided to take his advice, if and when Melville phoned, and if he was reluctant she would go home all the same.

There was a phone call for her while she was at supper and, quite forgetful of the Professor's advice, she tore along to the phone in the nurses' home. 'Melville!' She was breathless with delight. 'I'm so glad you've phoned, it seems ages...'

'You've missed me, darling girl?' He sounded pleased, smug almost.

'What shall we do this weekend—I hope you're free?'

'I'm going home.' She said it quickly before she could change her mind. 'Why don't you come too?'

He was silent for so long that she had time to regret her words, then, 'Why not? I could do with a breath of country air. I'll drive you down, darling—Friday evening—but I'll have to get back on Sunday evening.'

'I'll be ready about six o'clock,' she told him happily, 'and I don't mind coming back early. Have you been very busy?'

'I'm exhausted; you have no idea how hard I work— nose to the grindstone and all that—but it's going to be a smash hit when it's finished.' There was a pause before he said, 'Must go, darling, there's a meeting I have to attend—plans for next week and so on. See you on Friday.'

She went back to her supper, cold on the plate by now. She put it on one side and poured herself a cup of tea. 'You look like a cat that's been at the cream,' observed Lucy, eyeing her across the table.

'I'm going home for the weekend—Melville's driving me down.'

'Oh, very nice. Do I hear wedding bells?'

Rachel went pink. 'Heavens, no. He's up to his eyes in some new production; he never has a moment to himself.'

They left the table together and Rachel went to phone her mother.

Mrs Downing expressed herself delighted to be seeing Melville, concealing her real feelings in a masterly fashion; moreover she assured Rachel that her father would be equally delighted.

'What will I be delighted about?' asked Dr Downing, coming into the room as she put down the receiver.

'Melville is bringing Rachel down for the weekend, dear. I said you'd be delighted to see him.'

'Well, I won't,' declared the doctor vigorously. 'I don't like him and never shall—can't think what Rachel sees in the fellow. Conceited pompous ass.' He sat down at the table to eat a delayed supper. 'Why couldn't she fall in love with a man? That Professor who brought her down a week or two ago—nice chap. Got a wife already, I suppose.'

His wife murmured suitably. The Professor would do very nicely for Rachel, she thought fondly, and she didn't believe that he was married; he had looked at

Rachel once or twice... 'Oh, well,' she said comfortably, 'things always turn out for the best.'

Her husband grunted; he didn't think that it would be for the best if Rachel married Melville. He was an old-fashioned man; he couldn't think why they weren't engaged if he was so keen on her—she was keen enough on him, more was the pity.

The fine weather held, Friday was a warm day and it was still lovely as Rachel hurried to the hospital entrance just after six o'clock. Melville was there, waiting for her. He didn't get out of the car. 'Hello, darling. Sling your bag in the back and hop in. Do we stop for a meal on the way or have something when we get to your home?'

If she had expected a rather more love-like remark, she suppressed her disappointment. 'Mother will have supper for us,' she told him and was mollified by his kiss. 'What a heavenly evening—I'm so looking forward to the weekend.'

'So am I. Off we go then.'

Too fast as usual, he narrowly escaped the Professor's Rolls as he turned on to the street. Rachel caught sight of the Professor's face as they shot past. He didn't smile; in fact, he looked so stern that she hardly recognised him.

Melville liked to drive fast. Rachel liked to drive fast, too, but she thought privately that sometimes he took risks, overtaking with no regard for oncoming traffic and getting very impatient when he got held up. She wasn't quite as calm as usual by the time they arrived, but the sight of her mother at the open door quietened her frayed nerves. Melville stopped with a flourish and jumped out, opened her door for her and helped her out, keeping a hand on her elbow as they went the short distance to the door.

Clearly calculated to impress me, thought Mrs Downing, and I'm not impressed. But she greeted him charmingly, kissed Rachel warmly and led the way indoors.

Rachel paused in the doorway though and gave a great sniff of delight.

'Can't you smell everything growing?' she demanded happily.

Melville glanced round him; it wasn't quite dark and a faint breeze rustled through the trees behind the house. 'Absolutely heavenly, darling—paradise after town.'

The doctor was in the sitting-room; he kissed his daughter, shook hands with Melville and offered them drinks. Melville embarked on a witty description of his work—he was good at it and they listened with apparent interest, wanting to hear about Rachel's share in the emergency over the rioting. But there was no chance. Melville held the stage and was of no inclination to allow anyone else on it. He had, allowed Mrs Downing, a certain attraction: an amusing way of putting things, a good line in melting looks, too. My poor Rachel, she thought, don't let her get too hurt.

Rachel was happy. Melville was at his most amusing; surely her mother and father could see what a successful man he was, and how attractive. She followed her mother to the kitchen presently to help carry in the supper and, once there, 'You didn't mind me bringing Melville, Mother?'

'Not a bit,' said Mrs Downing stoutly. 'It was a very good idea of yours, darling.'

'Actually, it was the Professor who suggested it to me,' said Rachel, incurably honest, so that her mother, who had been harbouring gloomy thoughts, suddenly felt quite cheerful.

'The papers were full of that riot.' She withdrew a steak and kidney pie from the oven. 'Were you very busy, darling? You said very little over the telephone.'

Thinking about it it didn't seem quite real. 'Well, yes, I was, but so was everyone else. I got up at two o'clock and we worked right round until the evening.'

'And then you went to bed, I hope,' prompted her mother.

'Well, no.' Rachel was dishing young carrots. 'Melville came round—he didn't know, you see—but I was too tired to go out. The Professor took me to his house and gave me supper and brought me back to the hospital.'

'How kind.' Her mother bent her head over the potatoes she was mashing. Prayers get answered, she reflected vaguely.

'Supper's ready,' she said aloud. 'Will you fetch the men, darling?'

Melville continued to entertain them during supper, and when Mrs Downing managed to insert some remark about the rioting and the subsequent state of emergency at the hospital, he paused only long enough to say lightly, 'Yes, these demonstrations can be so tiresome, Mrs Downing. It's best to ignore them.'

She was too polite to question that; it was Dr Downing who said gravely, 'That's all very well, but if the hospital staff had ignored the casualties, there would have been several deaths—there were some serious injuries, you know.'

'I'm sure you are right, sir,' agreed Melville. 'What would we do without our ministering angels?'

He smiled with charm at Rachel, who smiled back but couldn't forbear from remarking, 'Well, we wouldn't have been much good without the medical staff.'

'Ah, yes, we must give credit where credit is due, but don't let's get gloomy, darling. You're home now in this lovely old house.' Melville took the conversation into his own hands again and the hospital wasn't mentioned again—at least, not until Rachel and her mother had gone up to bed, leaving the doctor to entertain their guest.

Rachel was brushing her hair when her mother came in, sat herself down on the bed and said, 'Now, darling, I want to hear all about what happened that night, and don't leave anything out…'

It was nice to be able to talk about it to someone who listened and was really interested. Rachel started at the beginning and recited the night's events, skating over the bit when Melville had come to take her out for the evening, making the excuse that he had been working all day and hadn't known anything about the rioting. Mrs Downing, who had her own ideas about this, merely said, 'Of course, darling. How kind of the Professor to see that you had a meal and went to bed. You must have been exhausted.'

Rachel put down her hairbrush. 'Yes. I do believe that I was. He's got a charming house in a quiet little street with trees, and a nice man called Bodkin who runs it; his wife does the cooking.'

Her mother bit back the obvious remark that he wasn't married. 'When one has been going full tilt for a long time, it's very nice to have someone there to get one back on one's feet,' she observed. 'Now, jump into bed, love, and have a good sleep. Do you and Melville plan to do anything tomorrow?'

Rachel plumped her pillows into maximum comfort. 'I don't know; he didn't say. I'd like to go for a good walk and take Mutt; I dare say that's what we'll do.'

They went for a walk, but not the kind of walk that Rachel had hoped for. Melville pointed out after a mile or so that he wasn't wearing shoes fit for country lanes. It hadn't rained for several days and Rachel had happily set out along a rutted track, its winter mud turned to a powdery dust, her feet sensibly shod, happily oblivious of Melville's discomfort. She was instantly contrite and led the way back to the road, much to Mutt's annoyance. 'Little Creed is just down the road,' she told Melville. 'It's the prettiest place and we can take the lower road home.'

'Darling girl, what a great healthy creature you are. It sounds lovely but I've just remembered that I promised to phone my producer.' He glanced at his watch. 'Can we get back to your place in twenty minutes or so?' He took her arm and kissed her cheek. 'I'd forgotten all about it but what do you expect when I'm with the most beautiful girl in the world?'

She was far too sensible to believe that, but it sounded delightful all the same. While she whistled to the disgruntled Mutt and turned for home, she thought she would have to get used to Melville's work constantly disrupting his free time, but she quite understood. His was an important job and it had to come first. She left him to his telephoning and went in search of her mother.

'Back so soon?' asked that lady, in the kitchen busy with getting the lunch.

'Well, yes. Melville remembered that he had to phone someone. Shall I make coffee?'

They spent the rest of the day indoors, playing two-handed whist and, after lunch, listening to Melville's amusing conversation. Rachel sat enthralled, taking in every word; it wasn't until she was getting ready for bed that night that she suppressed regret at a wasted day. Well, not wasted, she hastened to correct herself—it could never be that while she was with Melville—only it had been so glorious out and she was able to see so little of the country. Her final waking thought was the hope that he wouldn't mind going to church.

To her surprise he didn't. He had a pleasing tenor voice and sang the hymns with great feeling, listening with great attention to the sermon, his handsome profile uplifted to the pulpit, and when they left the church he took her arm in a protective fashion, smiling at anyone who caught his eye. Her heart swelled with pride as they walked back to the house. Her mother, some way behind with her father, voiced her feelings quite fiercely.

'He is not the right man for her, dear. That was an act in church—all that pious singing and charm. I bet he hasn't been in a church for years. But it was an audience, and he has to have that. My poor Rachel. I can't think what's got into the girl.'

Her husband patted the hand on his arm. 'She's infatuated, my dear, and naturally. She's been working at that hospital for years and the only men she has met have been doctors. Then along comes this Melville with his man-about-town manners and sweeps her off her feet. But it won't last; she's going to come a cropper, poor girl, but she'll be none the worse.'

'That Professor she works for… Do you suppose…'

'Shall we wait and see, my dear?'

It was a warm, sunny afternoon. Rachel pottered in the garden while Melville lay in a deck chair, his eyes closed. He had a busy week ahead of him, he had assured her, and needed to relax. They went back after tea and as they drove he made various plans for meeting her. No definite dates, he warned her, his work wouldn't permit that, but he hoped that when he did manage to get free she would be free, too.

She would do her best, she told him earnestly, remembering uneasily that Norah had a week's holiday and that neither Mrs Pepys nor Mrs Crow could be expected to cover for her at a moment's notice.

'A lovely weekend,' he told her when they arrived at the hospital. 'I enjoyed every moment of it, darling. Life is so empty when you aren't with me.' He kissed her. 'Now I must dash—I've work to catch up on.'

She remembered uneasily what the woman at the party had said and dismissed the thought as disloyal. 'When shall I see you?' she asked.

'As I said, darling, I can't say at the moment. But the minute I'm free I'll give you a ring.' He drove off and she picked up her bag and went through the hospital, back to her room, to phone her mother and then to gather in Lucy's room with such of her friends as were off duty and to drink tea. She had no reason to feel depressed, she told herself; it had been a marvellous weekend and Melville had been simply great. Perhaps it was because they had to meet at odd moments whenever he was free, and so often, when he was, she wasn't. If only they could spend more weekends at her home. But the disquieting thought that he might be bored refused to go away; he was a man who liked living in London; he liked parties and theatres and crowds of people, and she supposed that given time, she would get to like them too. Just at the moment, though, she was homesick for her parents and Mutt and the peace of the country. Bed would be the best place and a good night's sleep.

But she slept badly, waking often with a vague worry at the back of her mind. It was a relief to get up and somehow comforting to eat breakfast in the company of her friends, talking shop, the outside world for the moment forgotten. It was equally comforting to find the Professor sitting at her desk, studying a pile of Path Lab forms. His 'good morning' was friendly and his casual enquiry as to whether she had enjoyed her days off uttered in such a placid tone that she heard herself saying, 'Not very. At least, the weather was heavenly and it was so nice to be at home… It was a bit quiet for Melville…'

'With you there?' He sounded surprised. He abandoned the Path Lab forms and sat back looking at her. 'I have a very strong feeling that you ignored my advice;

you probably agreed to every word he uttered and sat about doing nothing much while all the time you were longing to stretch your legs.'

'Well, yes. You see, he hadn't got the right shoes to go walking…'

The Professor allowed a small sound to escape his lips. 'Ah, that of course might make things difficult.' He examined his beautifully kept nails. 'You will not of course take my advice—why should you? But refuse his next invitation, Rachel.'

'Why? He asks me out because he—he likes me to be with him.'

'That is why.' He got up, sweeping the papers before him into a neat heap. 'I shall be in X-Ray if anyone wants me. We start at nine o'clock, do we not?'

He was gone with a careless nod.

His list was fairly straightforward which, seeing that Norah wasn't there, was a mercy. Nor did he waste much time over his coffee once they were finished, only discussed the cases with George, thanked her with his usual politeness, and wandered away to look at his more recent cases on the surgical wards. Rachel sent Mrs Pepys, who had just come on duty, to her dinner with two of the student nurses, and cleared the theatre with Nurse Saunders's help. George had a couple of minor operations for the afternoon and Mrs Pepys could scrub for them while Rachel got on with the books and forms. When that lady came back from her meal, Rachel went down to the canteen to eat roast lamb and two vegetables and treacle tart for afters. For some reason she had lost her appetite, and her friends sitting with her made sure they lost no opportunity to make pointed remarks about being in love. They teased her gently and didn't believe her when she said that she didn't know when she and Melville would be going out again.

After the ordered urgency of the morning's list, the afternoon seemed dull. She did her books, carried on mild arguments with the CSU and the pharmacy, and a more heated one with the laundry, saw Mrs Pepys off duty and went into the theatre to check any instruments which might need repair. Mrs Crow, coming on duty at five o'clock, sent her thankfully off duty in her turn, to have a late tea in the sisters' sitting-room, and then sit around, gossiping until it was time for supper. A dull evening, she reflected, yawning her head off as she got ready for bed. An evening without Melville… It would have been lovely to go out. Never mind what the Professor said; if he phoned and asked her out, she would go. She lay in bed, deciding what she would wear.

Mrs Crow preferred to have an evening duty, so Rachel was free after five o'clock for the rest of the week, but it wasn't until three days had passed that Melville phoned. He had tickets for a concert, he told her, and how about coming?

Any faint remnants of the Professor's advice flew from her head. Of course, she would love to go; she bubbled over with eagerness and Melville laughed in her ear. 'My goodness, what's come over you, darling? You're usually tied up and here you are bursting with enthusiasm. I'm flattered.'

A tiny doubt had crept into the back of her mind; had she been too eager? But it was too late now; she agreed to be ready by seven o'clock that evening and to meet him in the entrance hall. 'And what shall I wear?' she asked anxiously.

'Oh, something pretty. We'll have a drink first; the concert doesn't start until half past eight.'

'What sort of concert?'

'Oh, a bit highbrow, darling, but everyone who's anyone will be there.'

She wore a silk jersey dress she hoped he didn't remember and arrived at the front door exactly on time—a mistake, because Melville wasn't there. But Professor van Teule was, strolling in, presumably to cast an eye over his patients. She stood there and he stopped when he saw her and shook his head.

'Oh dear, oh dear. I fear you have cast wisdom to the winds again, Rachel. A quiet dinner or is it dancing?'

She caught the amused gleam in his eye and frowned. 'We're going to a concert and really, Professor van Teule, you have no right to question what I do in my free time.'

He didn't answer her, only smiled gently. 'Take-in from midnight, isn't it? But of course you will be back in the hospital by then, and here is, er, Melville.'

Melville's 'darling' was a bit too fervent but Rachel didn't mind; it would give the Professor something to think about. He said so little, she thought worriedly, and yet he disquieted her. She wished him goodnight in a cold voice and smiled brilliantly at Melville, quite certain that the evening was going to be marvellous.

They went to a small bar in Soho and she enjoyed every minute of it, even though Melville remembered the dress, adding kindly, 'But of course it was too short notice for you to pop out and get something new.'

One day, she resolved firmly, she would explain to him that she simply couldn't buy a new dress every time she went out with him. Luckily he forgot it very quickly, plunging into an amusing anecdote about a well-known film star whom he had met that very morning.

The concert was well patronised; the hall was filled with fashionably clad women and men smoking cigars. They had seats in the stalls and Melville didn't hurry to reach them, stopping to greet people as they went. And once they had settled down, he spent the time pointing out the various famous people around them. 'I may have to leave you now and again, darling,' he told her and squeezed her hand. 'Must show my face, you know.'

The orchestra filed in and presently began to play. Rachel liked music, with a bias towards Rachmaninov's concertos and Debussy, Chopin and Grieg, but she was quite unable to understand the weird sounds coming from the orchestra. 'Brilliant composer,' whispered Melville. 'Modern music is the only thing worth listening to. He's all the rage.'

Rachel could hardly bear it. To take her mind off the strange sounds she began to work out the off duty for the next fortnight in her head, and, that done to her satisfaction, did a mental check of the extra instruments the Professor would need in the morning, which led to wondering what he was doing at that moment. Whenever she met him off duty he was either going to or coming from the surgical wards or theatre. Surely he must enjoy some leisure? And he had vaguely mentioned that he hoped to marry... His fiancée must be a

long suffering girl. And a lucky girl; the thought had
flown into her head quite unbidden.

Melville left her during the first interval. 'I shan't
be a moment, darling,' he explained. 'There are one
or two people I must speak to. I'll bring you a drink.'

She sat, feeling lonely, until the lights dimmed and
he reappeared, to catch her hand in his. 'Darling, I'm
so sorry—I couldn't get away. Have you been very
lonely without me? We'll go to the bar after this next
concerto, I promise you.'

The thought of a drink sustained her through the
next half-hour of weird sounds and when the lights
went up at last she followed him to the bar, already
packed with people.

They found a corner and he went in search of drinks,
to come back presently with two glasses. 'Martini, darling,' he told her and she felt a little prickle of irritation
that he hadn't asked her what she wanted; she loathed
martini.

He had taken barely two sips when he exclaimed,
'Good heavens! There's Guy. I simply must have a word
with him.' And he had gone again, disappearing into
the dense crowd around them. She put her untouched
drink down on a convenient ledge and looked around
her. Women in ultra-fashionable dresses hemmed her
in, escorted by men who, unlike Melville, didn't keep
dashing off to see someone or other. She couldn't see
him anywhere, and presently she edged her way out
of the bar and went back to her seat, feeling hard done
by. The evening, from her point of view, wasn't being
a success; the music was frightful and she might just
as well have been on her own. Which wasn't quite true

but she was in no mood for niceties. When Melville rejoined her she said coldly, 'Guy must have had a lot to say.'

'Darling, you're cross.' He took her hand in his. 'And I'm grovelling, really I am. We'll have supper somewhere to make up for it. I'm truly sorry; do forgive me.'

And of course she forgave him. She loved him, or she thought that she did. They sat through the last excruciating medley of sound and then, with only the minimum of pauses while Melville greeted the people he knew, they got into the car and drove to the Ivy Restaurant. It was full of well-known faces, Melville told her gleefully, and presently there would be even more. 'And choose what you like, my angel, I can put it on the expense account.'

A remark which upset her. Would he have taken her to this expensive place if he had had to pay for it out of his own pocket? It was a question which bothered her throughout the meal so that she was rather quiet.

'A bit out of your depth?' asked Melville kindly. 'Rubbing shoulders with the famous is a bit awe-inspiring until you get to know them, as I do.'

She swallowed an oyster patty, not liking it overmuch. 'Do you really? Know all of them?' It was difficult not to be impressed, although she had no wish to meet any of them. 'Do you enjoy meeting them?' she asked.

'My dear girl, of course I do. Success—successful people—they matter.'

She wasn't sure what prompted her to say, 'And people like Professor van Teule, who is very successful as a surgeon, although he never appears in public...'

Melville laughed. 'You don't quite follow me, darling. I'm talking about the success which brings you before the public eye. I dare say your Professor is clever enough in his way, but who wants to know about his work? I mean, it's something one doesn't talk about, isn't it?'

Which, she had to admit, was true.

He took her back to the hospital soon afterwards, kissed her fervently, assured her that he would see her soon, and drove off. She got ready for bed slowly, mulling over her evening. The music had been awful and it had been a pity that Melville had had to spend so much time with his friends and leave her alone, but he had been an attentive and amusing companion and she was quite sure that she loved him to distraction.

'A pleasant evening, I hope?' enquired the Professor suavely as he went to scrub before his list. 'Where was the concert?'

She told him briefly and he said, 'Ah, that new conductor—all the fashion at the moment, I believe. Modern music, was it?'

'Very,' said Rachel and went back to her trolleys, subduing a strong desire to tell him just how awful she had found it. He would have listened and, even if he was a devotee of the stuff, he would have given her his full attention.

The list was an exacting one. The Professor, as he always did, carried on a desultory conversation with his companions, touching on a variety of subjects, but music wasn't mentioned, nor did he refer to it while they had their coffee break. When at length he had finished, he bade them all good day, added his thanks, and went unhurriedly away. For some reason Rachel felt frustrated; she had prepared herself for his observation about her evening, and steeled herself against the advice he gave so readily. It was a bit of a let down.

At dinner Lucy warned her that there was a badly injured child in. 'Fell off a high wall, face downwards. Professor van Teule has had a look and he wants to operate; he was talking to George when I came to dinner. You'll get the good news when you get back.'

He was waiting for her, standing with his back to the office, looking at the chimney pots. He turned round when she went in.

'There's a child for a splenectomy. Can you be ready in twenty minutes or so?'

'Certainly, sir. Boy or girl?'

'A little boy—ten years old—fooling around on a demolished block of flats.'

'Oh, the poor lamb. Is his mother with him?'

'No, she hasn't been traced. There doesn't seem to be a father.'

'Someone must look after him—love him.'

'They're looking for his granny; she works somewhere in the Mile End Road.'

'Doesn't it make you furious?' She had gone to stand by him, sharing the deplorable view. 'Can you keep him as long as possible?'

'Yes. He can go to the country branch when he's fit again and we must see what we can do about Granny. A temporary job close by, perhaps?'

'The world's a funny place.' Rachel was voicing her thoughts, hardly aware that she was sharing them with him. 'All these dressed-up people yesterday evening, listening to that frightful music, and being what they call successful. They're not, you know; they don't do anything that matters.' She gave a great sigh. 'You do.'

She didn't see his slow smile and the gleam in his eyes.

'Thank you, Rachel. But it takes all sorts to make a world. I take it that you didn't altogether enjoy your evening?'

'The thing is,' she told him seriously, 'Melville is so popular. When we go out he meets so many friends he has to stop and talk to.'

'But you must meet a number of famous people?'

'No,' she said slowly. 'You see, he thinks—quite rightly—that I wouldn't have much in common with them.'

'I feel sure that he is right.' He glanced down at her and walked to the door. 'You're off duty at five o'clock?'

She was already unpinning her cap. 'Yes, sir.' She followed him out and went to theatre to make sure that it was ready for use; the nurses had done very well. With that she went to scrub and presently, standing by her trolleys, she watched him, gowned and masked, join those waiting for him round the table. He asked, 'Ready, Sister?' in his unhurried voice and she handed him a scalpel, reflecting how nice he was to work for.

Chapter 6

The splenectomy was followed by a baby girl who had swallowed an open safety pin. The Professor extricated it, his large strong hands as delicate as thistledown, and then went away to reassure the anxious mother. He was back again before Rachel had the theatre just so once more.

'Mr Jolly is taking over until tomorrow morning. Billy will assist him if anything comes in. I'm going over to Welbeck Street.' He had private patients there. 'George and his wife are coming to dinner; I wondered if you would care to join us? I haven't asked you earlier because I wasn't sure if you had a date.' He added, 'You know Rosie?'

Rosie was George's wife of less than a year, a nurse like herself who had been working at another London hospital. Rachel had met her and liked her and an evening out would be nice… Melville had said that he was going to be very busy; it was unlikely that he would want to take her out. She said, 'Thank you, Professor, I should like to come.'

'Good—nice for Rosie to have another girl to chat to. I'll be outside at seven o'clock.'

He had gone his unhurried way before she could reply.

There was time to shower and change at her leisure and spend time on deciding what she should wear. It had been a warm sunny day but now that it was early evening, it had turned a little chilly. She decided on a patterned Italian jersey dress which she had worn only once because Melville had declared it to be totally without eye-catching appeal. She had pointed out at the time that she had no wish to catch eyes anyway, but all the same she hadn't worn it again. It was a pretty dress though, in shades of soft pink with a high neck and long sleeves. She put on a light coat, patted her hair into final tidiness and went down to the entrance. As she went she reflected that she could have kept the Professor waiting for ten minutes—after all, he was always advising her not to be too eager—but somehow she didn't want to do that. For one thing he wasn't Melville… She wondered about the girl he was going to marry—in Holland, presumably, or she would have been at the dinner party and she herself would not have been invited.

The Professor was leaning up against the Rolls's bonnet, talking to Mr Jolly, but he straightened up when he saw her and the two men walked towards her, greeted her pleasantly, passed the time of day for a few moments and then parted, Mr Jolly to go into the hospital and they to get into the car.

'George and Rosie will join us just before eight o'clock.' He started the car and slid out into the street. 'You look nice.' He sounded just like one of her brothers and she felt instantly at ease.

'Thank you. What a lovely evening, even in London.'

'You like the country, don't you, Rachel?'

'Yes—oh, yes. I was born and brought up in Wherwell, and of course the hospital is in the wrong end of London, isn't it?'

'Where it does the most good.' They were nearing his home and she thought it wasn't so bad for him, living in a pleasant street with trees and probably a garden behind the house. In fact, she decided, one could live quite happily in such surroundings, with the park not too far away and the sound of traffic nicely muted.

Bodkin had the door open before they had crossed the pavement and bade her a dignified good evening before closing the door after them and throwing open the drawing-room door. The Professor urged her in, saying to Bodkin over his shoulder, 'Mr and Mrs Cook will be here in a few minutes, Bodkin. Show them straight in, will you?'

There was a log fire in the steel fireplace but the French window at the end of the room was open. 'Come and see the garden,' he invited.

It was larger than she expected, with a little fountain at the end of a stone path and trees all round so that the houses on either side were quite hidden. There were flower beds on either side, crammed with wallflowers and late tulips, and at the end there were roses. Not yet in flower, but she guessed that in a few weeks' time they would be magnificent.

They strolled to the end and back with Toby trotting beside them.

'It's beautiful,' she sighed, 'to come back here after a hard day's work. Do you like gardening?'

'Yes, when I can spare the time. A gardener comes and does most of the work, though.' He looked towards the house. 'Here are George and Rosie.'

The evening was delightful. Not a celebrity in sight, thought Rachel naughtily, and instantly felt disloyal to Melville, but it was so nice to sit quietly knowing that when her companions looked at her it was with detached friendliness and not with the sharp eyes of critics.

No one mentioned hospitals or patients during dinner. The conversation was light-hearted and the food delicious and afterwards, when they had had coffee, the men strolled into the garden, and Rachel and Rosie sat gossiping gently, clothes and holiday plans and the exciting news that Rosie and George were expecting a baby. 'Not until November,' said Rosie. 'I wish I could knit.'

'I can—let me know what you want. It will make a nice change from the sweaters I wade through for my brothers. Does Professor van Teule know?'

'Yes, George told him the moment we were certain. He is a dear, isn't he?'

Rachel said slowly, 'Yes, he is. He is always there.'

An obscure remark which Rosie immediately understood.

'I haven't mentioned your Melville—I wasn't sure if you'd mind, but everyone knows about him at the hospital. He's very glamorous, so I'm told. Is he great fun? You must meet masses of famous people.'

'Well, I've seen them, but I haven't met them—Melville says I'd find it difficult to talk to them. I mean, I don't know a thing about the stage and TV and all that, and they certainly wouldn't want to know about hospitals.'

Rosie made a sympathetic noise. 'When we married I thought, oh, good, no more hospitals. I can be a married lady and keep house and have time to read the paper. Well, it's not like that at all. George comes home and gives me a blow-by-blow account of some super operation Professor van Teule has done; I don't know why I don't wear uniform...'

Rachel laughed. 'You know you wouldn't like anything else and it must be super for George to go home and talk to someone who knows what he's talking about.'

Rosie giggled. 'Yes, I suppose you are right. Professor van Teule must feel awfully lonely sometimes; I mean, no one to unburden himself to. He goes out a good deal—lots of friends—but that's not quite the same thing, is it?'

Rachel agreed that it wasn't, but before they could pursue this interesting topic further the two men joined them and they sat and talked for an hour until George declared that they must go home.

Rachel got up to go too and George said at once, 'We'll give you a lift, Rachel.'

'I'll drive Rachel back,' observed the Professor, at his most placid. Rachel knew from long experience of working for him in theatre that the more placid he was the more determined he was to have his own way. She made no demur for it would have been of no use; besides, she enjoyed his company.

Perhaps rather more than he enjoyed hers, she wondered, when, the moment George had left, he urged her, in the nicest possible way, to get into his own car. It was a depressing thought, but she kept up a cheerful flow of small talk until they reached the hospital, where she prepared to alight without waste of time. The Professor's hand clamped down on hers on the door handle. He said to her surprise, 'I wonder why it is that I am able to know what you are thinking despite the social chatter? And no, I am not anxious to be rid of you; at least not for the reasons you are mulling over.'

He bent his head and kissed her cheek gently. 'Stay there,' he bade her, and got out to open her door and walk her to the hospital entrance.

'I have no idea what you're talking about,' said Rachel in a chilly voice.

'Of course you haven't. Later on, perhaps... Good night, Rachel. It was a delightful evening; thank you.'

She gave a gurgle of laughter. 'You've said my lines. It's me who's thanking you, Professor.'

'What deplorable grammar. Perhaps we both enjoyed ourselves equally.'

'Well, I do hope so. I loved every minute of it and thank you very much.' She added ingenuously, 'You see, the food was delicious and I didn't have to worry about what I was wearing...' She stopped and went very pink. 'Oh, I do beg your pardon. That sounds awful, but it wasn't meant to be. What I meant was, I felt quite at home. You see, I'm not much good at parties.'

She stopped because she could see that she amused him; he must think her very silly and gauche. Apparently he didn't. 'You are a nice girl,' he told her as he opened the door. 'Don't try and change, Rachel.'

She went past him and the door swung to. As she crossed the entrance hall she couldn't resist looking to see if there was a letter or a message for her. There wasn't.

It was four days before she heard from Melville again. A note, dashed off in a hurry; he had been so busy, too busy even to phone her, but he couldn't wait to see her again; he would take her out to dinner that evening and call for her at eight o'clock.

She wondered what she would have done if she hadn't been off duty that evening, but as it was, she was free; the day suddenly became wonderful, her eyes shone with delight, she was bubbling over. The Professor, coming to collect some of his instruments to take with him to the nursing home where he was operating, paused to look at her. After a moment he observed, 'Melville is taking you out; am I right?'

'Yes, Professor. How did you know?' She smiled widely; she couldn't help herself.

He said rather shortly, 'You look happy. I wonder if Melville knows what a lucky man he is...'

She blushed. 'Oh, thank you, but that's not quite true. You see, you only know the sensible side of me, the theatre sister; but me, out of uniform, I'm not sensible at all—or perhaps I'm too sensible, I'm not sure; I think that sometimes I fall very short of Melville's standards.'

The Professor picked up the bundle of instruments she had ready for him, shook his head at her and walked away without a word. An unsatisfactory end to their rather strange conversation. She put it out of her head, though, and fell to thinking about what she would wear that evening.

Not the blue; Melville had said that it didn't suit her. She decided on a pale patterned silk dress, sleeveless and plainly cut. It had been an off-the-peg bargain, chosen for its unassuming good cut, soft colours and excellent fit. Moreover she knew that it suited her and it did a lot for her. She went off duty punctually and spent a long time getting ready. She was pleased with the result and, unheeding of the Professor's advice not to be eager, hurried down to the entrance at exactly eight o'clock. Excitement and happiness had rendered her positively beautiful and Melville, sitting behind the wheel of his car, kissed her with a most satisfactory warmth.

'Darling, how I've missed you and how beautiful you look. We are going to have a wonderful evening. The Savoy, no less, and we'll dance the night away.'

He began to tell her about his work, making her laugh a great deal; she hadn't felt as happy as this for a long time. The happiness was only a little marred as they entered the foyer of the restaurant. Melville, waiting for her while she went to hand in her wrap, watched her coming towards him under the bright lights of the chandeliers.

'That's quite a nice dress,' he told her, 'but, darling, can't you be a bit more—well, eye-catching? You've got a splendid figure but you don't show it. Now if you went to one of the good dress houses they would do you proud.'

She refused to be put out. 'Don't be absurd, Melville, I can't afford those kind of clothes. If you don't approve of what I'm wearing then I'll go back to the hospital.'

He caught her arm, laughing. 'Oh, darling, you look lovely in rags, I'm sure, and now I've got you here at last, I'm certainly not letting you go again. It's only that I want you to look more beautiful than any other girl around.' He gave her a long look. 'You are that already.'

Very extravagant talk, thought Rachel with her usual good sense, instantly swallowed up in delight; the evening was going to be sheer heaven and Melville was the most marvellous man in the world.

Marvellous he was, too, ordering dinner and champagne and dancing with a careless grace, murmuring in her ear, holding her hand across the table. But it was unfortunate that as they danced he should see friends, who came back to their table with them and were presently joined by two more. They introduced themselves by first names, were carelessly polite to her and then, when the talk centred around the studios and their work, inevitably she was forgotten. Even when someone did ask her opinion of some actor or actress or some TV show, she was forced to admit that she didn't know much about those things, so that they looked at her in astonishment. It was obvious to her that any way of life outside their own was of no interest to them at all. She smiled and smiled until her face felt as though it would crack and felt relief when someone suggested that she should dance again.

She found herself partnered by a cheerful young man who danced well and hadn't much to say—or perhaps, she thought guiltily, he thinks I'm too stupid to talk to. But she enjoyed dancing with him and presently she danced with Melville who held her too tightly and murmured in her ear, 'So sorry about this, darling, but you see how it is. They're a jolly lot really.'

She agreed cheerfully. 'They must be nice to work with,' she observed.

'Lord, yes. A damned sight nicer than that lethargic fellow you work for. I can't think how you stick it, Rachel, working in that dreary hospital day after day.'

She didn't answer because he never listened to her when she tried to explain that she loved her work and that the Professor wasn't in the least lethargic. They finished the dance and went back to their table and found the other four on the point of going. 'Promised to pop in on Tommy's party,' said one of them. 'See you around, Melville.' They smiled at Rachel—they had already forgotten her name, but she had forgotten theirs, too.

It wasn't very late. All the same, Melville said as they sat down, 'I expect you want to get back, darling. Shall we go?'

A little disappointing, really. She had hoped that they would have stayed for another hour and danced, but it was thoughtful of Melville to see that she got back in good time. She fetched her wrap and got into the car beside him. It was a warm night, starlit and with a bright moon, and London streets were fairly empty, offering a spurious charm. Rachel had a sudden urgent longing to be at home in the garden, sweet smelling and quiet...

'That was a piece of luck meeting that lot,' said Melville. 'They're marvellous company—never a dull moment when they're around. You were a bit quiet, darling.'

'Well, I haven't seen any of the shows they were talking about or the people in them...'

'Which bears out what I'm always telling you. You should go out more, enjoy life, meet people instead of spending your days and half your nights in that gruesome place. Look, my sweet, give up this job of yours; no one will miss you. I can get you into some show or other; you're pretty enough and with a decent wardrobe you would make the grade.'

'Grade to what?'

'Why success, of course; fame, darling, money, the bright lights.'

She said patiently, 'But Melville, I don't want any of those things. Can't you understand that I'm happy as I am?'

They were in sight of the hospital and its ugly bulk against the night sky put her in mind of the Professor and his advice.

To her own great surprise, she said strongly, 'If you don't like me as I am, then we'll stop seeing each other, Melville.' He had stopped before the door and she got out quickly. 'Thank you for a delightful evening and my dinner.'

She marched away, her head in the air, taking no notice of Melville's angry astonishment, although the temptation to look round was very great. She stalked through the entrance hall to find a group of men in the middle of it. Too late, she remembered that the hospital consultant staff were to have met the hospital management committee that evening. The meeting was over, but a large handful of learned gentlemen had paused to chat on the way home.

They paused in their talk as she went towards them and eyed her with appreciation. Her colour was high, her eyes sparkled, she looked ready to do battle and, if they had but known it, she was ready to burst into floods of tears, too.

She circled the group with a vague, glittering smile, not really seeing any of them. It was the Professor's long arm which gently brought her to a halt. 'Ah, Sister Downing, the very person I wished to see. I was on the point of leaving you a note…'

He excused himself to his companions and said blandly, 'If you will come a little on one side—I shall take up only a few minutes of your time.'

She had no choice. They stood a little apart and he leaned his length against a marble column bearing the bust of the hospital's founder.

'Norah's back?' he asked, and, when she nodded, 'Good. There's not much doing in the morning, is there? The theatre sister at the nursing home has been taken ill and there is a gastroenterostomy which needs to be done. If I pick you up at eight o'clock tomorrow morning, will you take the case for me? I'll arrange things at the office.'

She stared up at him, her head still full of her quarrel with Melville, and he said quietly, 'You're upset.' He took her arm and walked her away to the back of the entrance hall where the centre lights hardly penetrated.

She said woodenly, 'I told him I wouldn't see him again. He wants me to leave here, and I won't. He doesn't understand. I—I said, I...' She gulped. 'I took your advice, for what it's worth.' She looked at him miserably. 'I don't know what I'm going to do.'

The Professor smiled. 'You're going to bed and to sleep and then in the morning you will take my case for me, and I am willing to bet my fees against your salary that there will be roses or a phone call or a letter by tomorrow evening. You see,' he added gently, 'I know a good deal more about men than you do, Rachel.'

He gave her a gentle shove. 'Off to bed with you and don't dare cry.'

He opened the door to the nurses' home for her, wished her a quiet goodnight and went back to his companions. And as for Rachel, she went to her room, undressed, crying her eyes out as she did so, and then tumbled into bed and went to sleep at once.

There was a message for her at breakfast; would she hand over the theatre keys to her staff nurse and accompany Professor van Teule, not forgetting to notify the office upon her return? There was no time to brood over Melville. She explained to Norah, gave her the keys and hurried down to the entrance. The Rolls was there with the Professor at the wheel, reading *The Times*. He opened the door for her, folded the paper, wished her a placid good morning and drove without further ado to the nursing home.

Really it was a private hospital, Rachel decided as she got out before its imposing entrance. 'Do you do a lot of surgery here?' she asked as they crossed the splendid hall.

'Oh, yes. Did you sleep?'

'Yes, thank you. You have a very busy life.'

They got into the lift and he pressed the button for the third floor. 'And a lonely one.'

'But not for long. When you're married...'

'You believe that to be the answer?'

'Well, of course. You'll go home to a wife who loves you and I expect you'll have lots of children and you'll never be lonely again.' The lift stopped. 'I didn't know that you were lonely. You must have heaps of friends.'

'Oh, I have. One cannot marry friends.'

He led the way down a wide corridor and through swing doors. 'Here we are, and here is Staff Nurse White who will show you where everything is.' He gave her a reassuring smile. 'I'll be along in ten minutes or so.'

Staff Nurse White was young and pretty and pleased to see her. 'Gosh, Sister, I'd have died if the Professor had told me to scrub. I can manage an appendix or tonsils or something easy but I've only been here a week or two. I'll show you round.'

The theatre was all that could be desired. Rachel poked her nose into cupboards and shelves, made sure she knew where most things were, and went away to scrub and lay up. There would be another nurse beside Staff Nurse White, and Dr Carr would be anaesthetising. There was a resident house surgeon who would assist the Professor.

There were no problems; Dr Carr greeted her as though he had expected her to be there anyway, the house surgeon was a serious young man and the second nurse seemed sensible. The operation was a lengthy one, but once it was over, Rachel was borne away to have coffee with Staff Nurse White. The Professor had gone, presumably to see his patient in ICU and she wondered if she should make her own arrangements to return to the hospital. But there was no need for that; he came back presently, asked her if she was ready and accompanied her to the car.

'I could have gone back on my own,' she pointed out.

'So you could. There is the devil of a lot of traffic around; you might have got back by tea time. Thanks for your help, Rachel.'

'I enjoyed it.' And she had. It had prevented her from thinking about herself and Melville; she would have leisure enough in which to do that later on. The Professor hardly spoke on the way back. He had a teaching round that afternoon; perhaps he was thinking about that, thought Rachel, and, after a few attempts at small talk, she fell silent.

It was during the afternoon that the flowers arrived, an extravagant bouquet with a card attached. From Melville, just as the Professor had said. She put them in the washbasin in the cloakroom and tucked the card in her pocket, its message already learned by heart. 'Forgive me, darling, I am broken-hearted.'

She was clearing her desk just before going off duty when the Professor poked his head round the door. 'Any flowers yet?' he wanted to know. She paused in her writing.

'Yes, and a card.' She couldn't stop the wide smile.

'Good. You have, of course, forgiven him; he only has to phone and you will rush to meet him where and when he tells you to. Don't, Rachel. Wash your hair or whatever you do in the evenings; have a headache if you prefer something more romantic. Go home for the weekend. He'll still be here when you get back.'

'You're very severe. Just supposing he thinks I don't want to see him again?' She gave him a sharp look. 'Professor, you don't approve of me and Melville—it seems to me that you're discouraging him.'

He came round the door and sat on the side of the desk. 'My dear Rachel, why should I do that? I, who am to be happily married as soon as it can be arranged. My sole object is for you to be happy, because happy people work well. And I like my theatre well run.' He stared down at his beautifully polished shoes. 'You are an excellent theatre sister.'

For some reason this civil comment annoyed her. She would have liked him to have thought of her in a different light, although she was very vague as to exactly what. She thanked him frostily and turned her attention rather pointedly to her books.

The Professor got off the desk and wandered to the door. 'I'm going up to Edinburgh tomorrow,' he told her casually. 'I'll see you on Monday.'

He strolled away with a cheerful nod and presently she finished what she was doing, fetched her flowers, and went off duty, feeling peevish. She put this unusual feeling down to the fact that she wasn't spending the evening with Melville. She missed him, she told herself, arranging her bouquet in a large jug she had purloined from the downstairs pantry in the nurses' home.

Which made it all the more strange that when Melville rang her the following morning she firmly refused to make any arrangements for the weekend. 'I promised to go home,' he was told firmly. 'My brothers will be there and we don't see each other all that often.'

'Am I not to be invited?' he asked sulkily.

She almost weakened. 'Well, there wouldn't be any room for you…'

There would have been, if he were the kind of man one could ask to double up with one of her brothers, but he wasn't and regrettably she was sure that none of her brothers would be prepared to give up a bed for him. They didn't know him well and she was honest enough to admit that they had very little in common with him. She said placatingly, 'I do usually get a weekend each fortnight, Melville, and I'll have days off some time next week.'

'Oh, well, I suppose I'll have to exist without you then.' He sounded mollified and she took advantage of it.

'I miss you, too,' she told him.

'I'll give you a ring after the weekend,' he said, and his goodbye was abrupt enough to worry her.

The weekend came and with it a phone call from Norah's eldest child to say that Norah was in bed with a heavy cold—perhaps 'flu.' It was too late to get either Mrs Pepys—who wouldn't have come anyway—or Mrs Crow. Rachel phoned her mother and resigned herself to a weekend on duty.

Saturday was quiet—an emergency appendix which

George dealt with, a teenager with superficial stab wounds and an elderly woman with a severed artery in her upper arm. Sunday was even quieter; it wasn't take-in, so that road accidents and the like went to another hospital and the minor surgery could be done in the accident room. Rachel sent Nurse Walters off duty, handed over to a staff nurse borrowed from the accident room, and went off duty herself.

The fine evening stretched before her, a waste of several hours which she didn't intend to spend indoors. She could phone Melville, of course... He had said he would ring her after the weekend, but that was because he had thought she would be at home. She showered and changed while the idea of going to his flat and giving him a lovely surprise took shape in her head. The more she thought about it, the better it seemed.

It would mean a long bus ride but it was still early evening. She hurried through the hospital and crossed the courtyard to the street beyond and the bus stop, and the Professor, on the point of turning into the hospital yard, saw her and frowned thoughtfully. She should be at home; he had been pretty sure that she would take his advice, so what had happened to make her change her plans?

George enlightened him. 'She told me she'd be off duty at five o'clock—I dare say she's going to meet that fellow who's always sending her flowers.'

The Professor said carelessly, 'Probably,' and began to talk about his list in the morning. He had a nasty feeling that Rachel was in for an unpleasant surprise but there wasn't much that he could do about it.

Rachel sat in the almost empty bus, thinking about

Melville and how pleased he would be to see her. She had never been to his flat, but she knew where it was.

She was walking down the elegant street where he lived when she saw him. He was mounting the steps to the front door of the flats where he lived, his arm flung carelessly round the shoulders of a willowy girl. Blonde, as dainty as a fairytale princess and dressed in the forefront of fashion. Rachel's eyes didn't miss a single detail; they didn't miss the way he bent and kissed the girl as they reached the door, either.

She was quite close to them by now, but they didn't see her. They went inside the elegant entrance and she stood looking at the empty doorway, not seeing it at all. Presently she turned on her heel and started walking back the way she had come. She walked quite a long way before she realised that she was tired, and got on a bus. She walked into the hospital as the Professor, apparently on his way out, crossed her path.

He took a quick look at her white, stricken face and observed cheerfully, 'Hello. Back early, aren't you? Did you have a nice weekend?'

She was tired and very unhappy but she did her best to answer him.

'I didn't go home—Norah isn't well so I took her duty.' To her mortification her eyes filled with tears. 'I went to see Melville; he was with a girl…such a pretty girl, too.'

She tried to pass him but the Professor was a bulky man, not easily circumvented. Besides, the hand he put out, though gentle, was firm.

'A strong drink will help.' He turned her round and

marched her out of the hospital again. 'I know the very place; you shall tell me all about it while you have it.'

'I don't want…' began Rachel and didn't bother to go on. The rest of the evening had to be got through and the Professor's impersonal concern made him an easy man to talk to, and if she didn't talk to someone she would have hysterics. She had never had them in her life, but she felt sure that they must be a great relief. To lie on the ground and kick one's heels in the air and scream held a distinct appeal.

She got meekly into the car when he held the door open, reflecting that it was getting to be quite a habit; it was nothing short of a miracle that he should appear, large, placid and comforting. She was behaving badly, like a teenager in the throes of first love; he might find her an excellent theatre sister, but she was deplorably lacking when it came to managing her own life.

She sat silent while he drove, so busy with her thoughts that she hardly noticed where they were going: Duke's Hotel, in a quiet cul-de-sac near St James's Park.

She was swept inside the restaurant. 'I'm hungry,' declared the Professor. 'We might eat something.'

It didn't enter her poor worried head that he might have gone home to the meal which Mrs Bodkin would undoubtedly have ready for him. She sat down at a secluded table and obediently sipped the sherry he ordered for her.

When the menu cards were brought, he ordered for her: cold cucumber soup, omelette Arnold Bennett and a water ice. Having done that, he embarked on a conversation about nothing at all, allowing her time to pull herself together.

By the time they had finished their meal, she was feeling much better, sufficiently herself to tell him what had happened. In the telling, she did discover that it wasn't as bad as she had imagined it to be. Bad enough, but there were so many reasons why Melville was with the girl; it was harder to think of reasons why he had been kissing her with such satisfaction, but, as the Professor reminded her, people in show business treated kisses and endearments in a different light to the man in the street.

'What shall I do?' It was the kind of question she might have asked her eldest brother.

'Nothing, and if you have the will-power to be un-available for the next week, be that, too.' He sighed. 'I've told you that already...'

'Yes, I know. You're very kind to help me, Professor. And I really will take your advice this time. Only when he's waiting for me and I see him I—I find it very difficult to be unavailable.'

He looked thoughtful. 'You need to put a few hundred miles between you.' Just for the moment the heavy lids flew open, revealing blue eyes with a decided gleam in them, but she didn't see that; she was looking down at her coffee cup. When she looked up at him again, she saw his usual placid face. 'I feel much much better, thank you.'

'Good. I'll take you back.' Which he did, bidding her a pleasant goodnight when they reached the hospital. She went to bed at once and slept soundly, rather to her surprise.

Norah was back on duty in the morning. Rachel heaved a sigh of relief at the sight of her; there was a heavy list and after midnight they would be on take-in again. She inspected the theatre, allotted jobs to the nurses, left Norah to lay up for the first case, and went to the office. There were the usual forms to deal with and she meant to get them done before the Professor arrived, for once work started she had little chance of getting back to her desk.

She had picked up the first form when the office rang for her to go there at once. She banged the receiver back into its cradle, cross that she was to be interrupted, warned Norah, and went down to the ground floor to see the principal nursing officer.

Miss Marks was middle-aged, imposing and distant in her manner. No one liked her overmuch, although everyone admitted that she was fair, an excellent organiser and a splendid disciplinarian. Rachel stood quietly in front of her desk and waited to hear why she was there.

She was surprised to be told to sit down; relieved, too—it couldn't be anything too awful. What was more, Miss Marks smiled thinly at her.

'I have had a letter, Sister Downing, which I think will be of great interest to you. There is to be an international conference of theatre sisters, to be held in Basle, and you have been nominated to represent our group of hospitals. It is in eight days' time and will last for one week, during which time you will attend lectures, visit hospitals and attend discussions. I will see that you get the details later. You will of course be granted special leave for this.'

Typically she didn't ask if Rachel liked the idea. She bowed her head majestically, said, 'Thank you, Sister, that will be all,' and opened a file of papers before her.

'Do I have to go, Miss Marks?'

Miss Marks looked annoyed. 'Of course, Sister. This is an honour both for you and for the hospital.'

There was no more to be said. Rachel went back to the office and found the Professor there, whistling through his teeth and staring out of the window.

His good morning was casual but his glance was sharp. Rachel took off her cuffs and started to roll up her sleeves. 'Good morning, Professor. Something's come up. I've just been to the office. Miss Marks tells me that I'm to go to a theatre sisters' conference in Basle, next week some time. It seems I have no choice in the matter.' She paused. 'I suppose I do have to go?'

'Well, this certainly is a surprise,' lied the Professor smoothly. 'Presumably you will have to go if you've been nominated. I take it you will be representing the hospital group?'

She nodded. 'Yes, but is it so important? I mean there will be hundreds of us there—am I supposed to pick up useful tips, or something?'

He laughed. 'Well, if you do, don't rush to try them out on me. How long will you be gone?'

'A week. Not take-in, thank heaven. Oughtn't you to have been consulted first, Professor?'

'As it happens, Miss Marks has asked if I could see her later on today. I dare say she thought that you should be told as soon as possible; she would be fairly sure that I can have no objection to you going.'

He strolled to the door. 'The first case may present

complications. Put out my own forceps and the special retractors, will you? I'll be back in fifteen minutes or so.'

Left to herself, Rachel made no effort to tackle the forms. The Professor didn't seem to mind her going and for some reason that upset her, but hard on that thought came another one: Melville. Even if he wanted to see her it would be impossible; besides, she wouldn't be tempted to answer his letter if he wrote, and when she got back again, who knew? Anything could have happened. She was a little vague as to what exactly could happen, but it involved Melville begging abject forgiveness, sending her armfuls of flowers and having a perfectly valid reason for kissing that girl.

Considerably cheered by these naïve speculations, Rachel went along to the theatre to tell Norah the news.

Chapter 7

Even if Melville had got in touch with her—and he hadn't—she would have had precious little time to spend with him. She had a passport but the details of her flight had to be arranged. She was to travel on Monday morning and she would be met at the airport and taken to the Hilton Hotel where the conference would be held. For some reason the programme of the week's events had not been sent but, as her friends were quick to point out, what did that matter? She would be staying in great comfort at an hotel which, according to the brochure, was within a few minutes of the shopping centre, she would doubtless meet a great many people and have a marvellous time and never mind the lectures or discussions. Miss Marks had told her that there would be three other theatre sisters from Great Britain attending, but she wasn't likely to meet them until she got there, for they were from Scotland and the north of England and would fly from different airports.

Busy as she was in her off-duty time, deciding what clothes to take, how much money she would need and the best way to get to Heathrow, she was even busier in theatre, for the Professor's lists were longer than ever and the off-duty rota had to be adjusted to fit in with her absence.

She had rung her mother with the news and, since she was due a weekend anyway, arranged to drive herself home on Friday evening. There had been no letter from Melville and she had thrust him to the back of her mind; time enough to think about him when she got back. Just for the moment there was far too much on her mind.

The Professor showed little interest in her trip. Beyond cautioning her to attend all the lectures and see all she could of any hospitals she might go to, he hadn't much to say. Indeed, he was rather more silent than he usually was and certainly, in his placid way, more demanding in his work. Perhaps he had quarrelled with the girl he was to marry...

His list on Friday stretched well into the afternoon, so that by the time theatre was cleared and cleaned and she had handed over to Norah, it was getting on for six o'clock. But it was a splendid evening and driving would be a pleasure after a week of hard work. She hurried to change and get into the Fiat, puzzling over the Professor's decidedly casual manner as he had left the theatre. Perhaps he was sickening for something. On second thoughts, a ludicrous idea, and why was she fussing so? He had been kind and helpful and she liked him but their friendship was impersonal and revolved round their work.

She started the car and plunged into the evening rush hour.

It was late by the time she got home; getting out of London had taken longer than usual and the traffic on the motorway had been heavy. But there was supper for her and her mother and father were delighted to see her, with Mutt barking his head off at the sight of her. She ate her supper while they discussed her trip to Basle and since she didn't mention Melville no one else did either.

'I dare say the surgeons will miss you,' essayed her mother casually.

'Oh, I don't think so. Norah's there for the big lists and the part-time staff nurse can cope with the small stuff. I've not had time to think about it much, I've been too busy, but I think it's going to be fun.'

'How many will there be?' asked her father.

'I don't know. It's an international affair, so there should be quite a few. I haven't got the programme of events—Miss Marks said I should get it when I get there. There'll be lectures and discussions and demonstrations and visits to hospitals…'

'And enough time for you to look around, I hope,' observed her mother.

It was a lovely peaceful two days, pottering in the garden, driving her father on his rounds, taking Mutt for long walks and sitting in the garden, and in the evenings sitting doing nothing with Everett on her lap. She left after tea on Sunday with the promise that she would telephone when she arrived in Basle, and drove back to the hospital to pack the carefully chosen wardrobe, check her tickets and money, wash her hair and go to bed after a good gossip over mugs of tea with half a dozen nurses crammed into one room.

Rachel had decided to drive herself to Heathrow and leave her car in the garage there. She left after breakfast, speeded on her way by those of her friends who were free to wave her away, and watched by Professor van Teule from the windows of Women's Surgical. The ward sister, flustered at his early arrival, was thrown into a still more nervous state when he bade her a polite good morning and left the ward as suddenly as he had arrived. As she had a lot on her mind it didn't occur to her that her ward overlooked the forecourt and the parking space reserved for nursing staff. And as for suspecting his interest in Rachel, she never gave it a thought; everyone knew that she was head over heels in love with Melville Grant. As for Professor van Teule, she, like everyone else on the nursing staff, liked him, stood a little in awe of him and had no interest in his private life, for the simple reason that he had never given them cause to do so.

It was at the end of the morning's list when the Professor told Norah that he would be away for a week. 'Mr Jolly will deal with anything George considers necessary. Otherwise George will go ahead with Thursday's list—all straightforward cases.'

Norah took the news calmly. 'What a good thing that you and Rachel are away at the same time,' she remarked. 'She won't be back until Monday afternoon. Will you have a list on Monday morning, sir?'

'No. I will not be back until Monday evening or Tuesday morning. George will arrange a list for Tuesday.' He gave her a kindly smile. 'You've enough staff?'

Norah said that yes, she had. Such a nice man; he and Rachel would suit each other down to the ground. She sighed, but here was Rachel hopelessly infatuated with this man Grant, and the professor, from all accounts, about to get married.

Rachel parked the car, took herself and her case through the customs and in due course settled herself in the plane. She didn't care for flying but since she had to do so there was no point in getting worked up about it. She ate the odds and ends on the plastic tray she was handed and took out the booklet on Basle which she had unearthed in a bookshop. It seemed a nice city; she only hoped that she would see something of it.

The airport, after the complexity of Heathrow, was a pleasant surprise. It took no time at all to go through customs and walk outside into the warmth of an early summer's afternoon. She had been told that she would be met and she saw a man bearing a board with her name on it almost immediately. He addressed her in French, to her relief, for she had an adequate smattering of that language, but almost no knowledge of German, and he spoke no English.

The six miles to the city were accomplished in an incredibly short space of time. Rachel, a bit shaken, got out at the hotel entrance, tipped the man and went into the foyer. There were a few people standing about, and at the end of the reception counter was a large board with 'International Theatre Sisters' Convention' written on it. The girl sitting beside the board seemed to know all about her; her name was ticked off on a list, she was given a key to a room on the sixth floor, her bag was handed to a porter, and she was whisked into a lift. All very efficient, but she had no idea what she was supposed to do next. She followed the porter to her room and, when he had gone, inspected it slowly. It was comfortable and the bathroom was more than adequate. There were television and radio, several magazines and a really splendid view from the window. She washed and tied back her hair, then unpacked and, dying for a cup of tea, took herself back to the lifts and down to the foyer.

A large arrow pointed to the coffee shop and she followed its direction briskly. She would have to get a programme and any information there was later but tea was more important.

The coffee shop was pleasant and not too crowded. She drank three cups of tea, ate a mountainous cream cake, and went back to the reception desk.

There was to be an inaugural get-together that evening, she was told, to be held in the reception room on the floor below. When she enquired as to the morrow's timetable, she was told that the day's timetable would be available at breakfast. 'For the first day will be undemanding,' said the clerk. 'The first lecture begins after lunch; you will have the morning in which to integrate. After today, the following day's programme will be given to you each evening.'

There were any number of people in the foyer now, but whether any of them were nurses like herself she was unable to decide. Of one thing she was certain, there wasn't much English being spoken—lots of American accents, French and German, and several languages which might have been from any country. She bought a paper at the hotel shop and went back to her room to phone her mother and then sit down and read the day's news.

The get-together was to be informal, she had been told, and she spent some time debating what she should wear. She decided on an Italian silk jersey dress in various shades of amber, spent an hour lying in the bath and doing her face and hair and, a little after seven o'clock, made her way back to the foyer.

A wide curving staircase led down to the floor below and women of every age, shape and size were going down it. No English, she thought unhappily, exchanging smiles with a stout young woman who addressed her in German and with a delicate little creature, half her size and enchantingly pretty. Rachel, whose ideas about the Orient were vague, put her down as someone from the Far East; she looked far too fragile to be a theatre sister.

A get-together wasn't quite the right word for it, she decided after a few minutes. Everyone there was willing and anxious to be friendly but there should have been someone there to start the ball rolling. It was like a gigantic cocktail party, where no one knew anyone else. And what was the point of it all if they were to be lectured in English when, as far as she could make out, almost everyone there was speaking in their own tongue? She took a second drink from the tray being carried around and addressed the two young women nearest her. They were from Denmark and told her so in an English as good as her own, so that she exclaimed happily, 'Oh, I was beginning to think that nobody spoke English…'

They laughed kindly. 'We all speak and understand English but of course we prefer to speak our own language. Are there no other English nurses here?'

'Oh yes. Three I've been told of, perhaps more, only I haven't met them yet.'

'You should ask. I expect they will tell you at the reception desk what their room numbers are and their names. We always do that.'

She hadn't thought of that; obviously she was talking to old hands at the game of nurses' conventions. It was like being a new girl at school. The drinks were loosening tongues and creating a friendly atmosphere. Several more women joined them, two of them considerably older, the other two French and voluble talkers. Presently they drifted to the long table at the end of the room where the food had been set out. Rachel, quite hungry, tucked into cold chicken and salad and listened to her companions' talk. The two older women were from Austria and had little to say for themselves although they were friendly enough; the talk was carried along on the shoulder of the French girls, who lapsed into their own language most of the time but contrived to be very amusing all the same.

Rachel, anxious to find the English girls if they were there, drifted to and fro without success although she met a nurse from Texas and another from Toronto. It was an opportunity to find out more about the week ahead of them but neither girl knew much more than she did, and anyway, as the American pointed out, they would be told in the morning. 'And I dare say it will be a round of lectures and demonstrations and inspecting instruments and how to deal with student nurses.'

At about ten o'clock they began to drift back upstairs and to their rooms. Most of them had arrived that day and were tired; those who weren't went along to the bar or the coffee shop. Rachel refused several invitations to have coffee and went to her room. Her last sleepy thought was to wonder if the Professor had had a heavy list. Of Melville she didn't think at all.

She woke early to a lovely day and, since breakfast could be had in the coffee shop from six o'clock onwards, she got up, did her face and hair with more care than usual, got into a sleeveless cotton dress and went along to the lifts. There didn't seem to be anyone around, but it was still early and they had been told that they would have the morning free.

She got out of the lift in the foyer and the first person she saw was Professor van Teule, elegant in summer suiting, not a hair out of place and looking, if that were possible, more placid than ever.

He came to meet her. 'There you are,' he said carelessly, just as though they had arranged to meet. 'I thought you might be up early.'

She goggled at him, her pretty mouth slightly open. 'However did you get here?' she asked, and then frowned because it was a silly question.

'On an evening flight.' He smiled slowly and she said sharply, 'You're one of the lecturers—why didn't you tell me?'

'I had the ridiculous idea that if I had done so you would have decided not to come.' He didn't say why, nor did he give her the chance to answer. 'Shall we have breakfast?'

When they were seated in the coffee shop he said, 'I hope you aren't too annoyed that I am here—I only lecture in the afternoons and there will be no need for you to attend.'

'Well, of course I shall come.' She met his eye across the table. 'And I'm not a bit annoyed; in fact, I'm glad. I know I shan't see you except on the platform but I'll know you are here. I feel like a new girl at school.'

The waitress came with coffee and a basket of rolls and Rachel ordered scrambled eggs. The Professor asked for bacon, eggs, sausages and mushrooms.

'I haven't had a programme of events yet,' said Rachel, pouring coffee. 'We're to get it this morning and the first lecture is this afternoon.'

For answer the Professor pulled a folder from a pocket. 'Normally they chalk the events up on a board each morning—I daresay they'll do the same here. But cast your eye over this if you like.'

The first lecture was at two o'clock in one of the smaller conference rooms. And the Professor was giving it. There would be a discussion afterwards, a pause for tea and then a film depicting new theatre techniques. Those attending the conference would be expected to make notes and there would be a room put at their disposal for this purpose. Dinner would be at seven o'clock and afterwards there would be a lecture on modern methods of anaesthesia. Quite a busy day, and, casting her eyes rapidly over the rest of the programme, she could see that all the other days would be busy, too; lectures either in the morning and afternoon and the evening free, or the mornings free and the rest of the day taken up with various studies. Two trips to hospitals, she was glad to see, and since her flight home didn't leave until around lunchtime she would have several hours leisure on the last day.

She heard the Professor observe, 'You must see as much of the city as possible while you're here. I'm at the Basle Hotel. I'll give you a ring each morning before eight o'clock and we'll arrange to meet.'

Rachel eyed him thoughtfully. 'That's very kind of you, Professor, but just because you are lecturing here doesn't mean—that you—you have to entertain me.' She took a deep breath. 'Besides, there are three other English girls here—I haven't met them yet...'

'Don't try to give me the brush-off, Rachel.' He sounded amused and she went pink. 'The three ladies you refer to are very senior members of their profession. I doubt if you would have anything in common save an exchange of views concerning the running of the operating theatre.'

'Isn't that why I'm here?' asked Rachel with a snap.

'My dear girl, of course, but it wouldn't be much use for you to glean information from those who, like yourself, have come to be apprised of modern methods.' He passed his cup for more coffee, his voice as bland as his face.

'I shall phone you each morning,' he observed in the placid voice which she had learnt concealed a steely determination to have his own way.

She said meekly, 'Very well, Professor.'

He went on calmly, 'The evening lecture will finish about nine o'clock; Dr Geller wants to meet his wife who is flying in on an evening plane from Vienna. I'll wait in the foyer for you; we'll go somewhere and have a drink and you can give me your impression of the day's events.'

She agreed readily. Truth to tell, it would be nice to have something to look forward to at the end of the day, and someone she could talk to freely.

The coffee shop was filling up now. The Professor put down his cup and glanced at his watch. 'I've a meeting in half an hour. I'll see you this evening.' He bade her a casual goodbye and wandered away.

She waited for a few minutes. She didn't want him to think that she was anxious for his company, although it would have been rather nice, she thought wistfully, to have explored a little with him. On her way out she met the three nurses from home. The Professor had been right; they were all on the wrong side of forty, probably first-class theatre sisters but slightly intimidating in appearance. One of them stopped Rachel as she passed them.

'You're Sister Downing,' she observed. 'You're very young—which hospital are you from?'

Rachel said, 'Hello,' and smiled, for, despite appearances, they might be rather nice—one never knew. She named her hospital and the youngest of the three said, 'You must be very proud of yourself—you must be very good at your job,' and returned her smile.

'I dare say we're all much of a muchness. It's a splendid chance to be here and get up-to-date, though.'

'I doubt if we'll learn anything new,' said the woman who had stopped her. 'And I don't care for this hotel; it's far too crowded and noisy.'

It seemed a good idea not to answer that. Instead Rachel said, 'I'm going for a walk, it's such a lovely day. I expect I'll see you this evening.'

'Oh, yes we should keep together—there are a great many foreigners.'

Another remark best left unanswered. 'I won't keep you from your breakfast,' said Rachel and made her escape.

She enjoyed her morning. It was a pleasant five minutes' walk to the main shopping street and she spent an hour looking in windows looking for small presents to take home. Everything was expensive and she hadn't brought a great deal of money with her. Chocolates were the obvious choice, and something special for her mother. She strolled back presently, enjoying the sunshine and the strangeness of it all, stopping to study the price list in the window of an elegant tearoom. The cakes looked mouthwatering but after some mental arithmetic she decided that it was wildly expensive. Perhaps her last day she would go there as a farewell treat.

The foyer of the hotel was full of people arriving and departing; there were piles of luggage around and porters darting about, and the hubbub was considerable. Rachel went up to her room, tidied herself and went down again to look for lunch.

It was in the same room where they had gathered the evening before, another buffet, and, with an appetite sharpened by her walk, Rachel filled a plate with salad and cold meat and looked for a table. The Canadian nurse she had met already was sitting at a small corner table and she beckoned Rachel over. 'Sadie will be here in a minute.' Sadie, Rachel guessed, would be the American. 'Have you been out?'

They exchanged views of the city, the hotel and the cost of everything and presently when Sadie joined them, began, inevitably, to discuss their jobs. But not too seriously; they laughed a good deal and her three colleagues from home, sitting close by, sent disapproving looks towards their table.

They all had their day's programme by now and began to drift into one of the conference rooms where the lectures were to be held. It was like being back at training school, thought Rachel, sitting with her two companions well to the back. It occurred to her that she had never heard the Professor give a lecture—this one was to be on organ transplants and was going to last an hour with questions afterwards. No power on earth, she told herself, would make her ask a question.

He was introduced by a Swiss Professor of Surgery and he came on to the small stage looking completely at ease and elegant. The Canadian girl dug her elbow into Rachel and hissed, 'I say, he's just not true—look at him. Every girl's dream, I'd say. Am I glad I came.' And Sadie on the other side whispered, 'What wouldn't I give for a chance to get to know him.' She glanced at her programme. 'Dutch, Professor of Surgery in Leiden and London.' She glanced at Rachel, sitting poker-faced between them. 'Have you seen him before, Rachel?'

'Well, yes, he does work in London.'

It was a good thing that there was no more chance to ask questions. He began his lecture. It was a learned lecture, well thought out and delivered with assurance, but Rachel doubted if many of the women there were concentrating on it; the Professor, she had to admit, was quite something. She studied him carefully, and rather to her surprise realised that she had never really looked at him before.

There was an avalanche of questions when he had finished. Rachel, making herself small between her two companions, kept quiet. Any questions she might have could wait until she got back to London.

He went at last after a protracted period of questions and answers and they all went back downstairs again for tea. She was unfortunate enough to bump into the women from home as she stood, teacup in hand, cake balanced on a plate, looking for a seat. They had enjoyed the lecture, they told her; indeed they had all asked a great number of questions afterwards and found the Professor most helpful. 'He would be a pleasure to work for,' observed one of them. 'If possible it would be interesting to meet any theatre staff who have had that privilege.'

Rachel agreed demurely.

It wasn't worth going out again before dinner; Rachel went to her room, lay in the bath for a long time reading an English newspaper and got into a white crêpe blouse and a rose-patterned skirt before going down to her dinner. This time they were seated at long tables for soup, rather small portions of fish with boiled potatoes and no vegetables, and vanilla ice-cream with coffee after. Rachel's shapely person rose from the table, still hungry.

The evening lecture was interesting and ended just as the Professor had indicated, sharp at nine o'clock. There was a general exodus to the coffee shop and the bar, but Rachel went to the foyer. She saw the Professor at once, sitting in a deep easy chair; he looked thoroughly at ease, as though he were on holiday, and for no reason at all she was glad that she was wearing something that she knew suited her.

He came to meet her, smiling pleasantly. 'You look nice,' he told her. 'I've been sitting here watching a succession of stunning outfits going to and fro, and I mean stunning in the correct sense of the word. You're very restful on the eye, Rachel. Was it a good lecture?'

'Yes, I enjoyed it. I enjoyed yours, too.' She was puzzled to feel shy with him, a quite new feeling. Perhaps it was because they were away from their familiar background.

'Thank you. I was pleased at the number of questions at the end of it.' She saw that he had no idea that the questions were asked by an audience who, almost to a girl, would have liked the chance to get to know him. He must know that he was the answer to a girl's prayer, but she doubted if he ever thought about it. There were a lot of people in the foyer by now; some of them had been in the audience recently and they were frankly staring.

'Are you hungry?' asked the Professor. 'I do hope so, I'm famished—I went to a drinks party, for my sins, and there were bits and pieces on little plates—not at all satisfying.'

She laughed and he took her arm as they went out of the hotel. 'There's a charming little restaurant not too far away...' He nodded to the doorman to get him a taxi. 'What have you got on the agenda tomorrow?'

'Instruments in the morning, open heart surgery in the afternoon...'

'Evening free?'

'Yes.'

'Good. I'll get hold of a car and we'll see something of the country.' They got into the taxi and Rachel said, 'That would be lovely, but you must have other things you'd like to do.'

'Not on my own. We are two foreigners here; we should join forces.'

He told the driver where to go and sat back beside her.

It was still quite light and there were a lot of people about. Somewhere between the hotel and Marktplatz they took a turning off Freiestrasse and stopped in front of a small restaurant and went inside. The Professor had booked a table, tucked away in a windowed corner of the crowded room, and they sat, talking little, sipping their drinks and deciding what to eat. The restaurant was French, and Rachel opted for lobster Cardinal and a salad while the Professor chose sole Colbert and salade Niçoise.

The food was delicious. Rachel popped the last morsel of lobster into her mouth and said, 'What a heavenly meal. However shall I be able to face fish fingers and chips when I get back?'

'Don't think about it. Let us make hay while the sun shines and dine here each evening.'

She blushed. 'Oh, I didn't mean that—that is, I wasn't fishing for another meal, I really wasn't.'

'My dear Rachel, surely we know each other well enough not to consider anything so absurd.'

Which, when she thought about it, made good sense. 'Well, it would be nice to discuss the day's work. Have we been a good audience? I haven't met very many of the other girls yet, but those I have are very keen.'

'Dedicated theatre sisters? It makes a nice change from theatre, though.'

She answered him seriously. 'Well, yes, and some of them have come a long way.' She passed him his coffee cup. 'You're lecturing each day, aren't you?'

He nodded. 'And don't forget the visits to the hospitals. I won't be there, but I know them both; I'm sure you'll find them interesting.'

He went on to talk about Basle after that, and presently, when she said that she should be going back to the hotel, he made no demur but paid the bill and took her back by taxi, wishing her a friendly goodnight in the foyer and waiting there until she had got into a lift.

It had been a delightful evening, she thought sleepily, getting ready for bed. She went to sleep at once without a single thought of Melville.

She was wakened by the phone ringing at half past seven.

'Good morning, Rachel.' The Professor's voice was quiet in her ear. 'I'll be in the foyer this evening—the lecture should be over by half-past seven.' And when she said, 'Yes, all right,' he went on, 'Tomorrow you're free in the morning. I shall be round after breakfast so don't go out.' She said, 'Very well,' because it seemed the natural thing to say, and before he rang off he said, 'I've got a car for this evening. Bring a jacket or something with you, it might get chilly.'

She gave her full attention to the lectures during

the day, taking notes and discussing them during the breaks. There were quite a few instruments for her to follow up, although she doubted if the hospital committee would stand the expense of getting them. And the open heart surgery had been interesting although she hadn't learnt anything new from it; the Professor had been using the techniques talked about for some time.

His own lecture was at half-past six. Peritonitis and how to deal with it. She sat quietly, listening to his calm voice, and found the hour too short. There was a buzz of talk when he had gone and she sat for a moment listening to her companions on either side of her. 'I wonder where he goes?' Sadie wanted to know. 'Do you suppose he's married? Perhaps he's got his wife here—if she is, I wouldn't let him out of my sight if I were her.' She got up and Rachel with her. 'Ah, well, let's see what's for dinner. I shan't bother to change this evening.'

Rachel escaped without appearing to do so. The Professor had said that he would wait for her in the foyer and she simply had to change into another dress. She had brought a stone-coloured jersey dress with a matching jacket with her; she got into it, did her face, tidied her hair and shot down to the foyer.

There weren't many people there; it was getting on for eight o'clock and dinner was in full swing. They went out to the car he had hired and he drove away without delay. They went out of the city through the tree-lined streets and Rachel asked where they were going.

'We'll cross the river and drive to Freiburg—it's on the edge of the Black Forest and the scenery is rather

special. There's a good restaurant in a village just beyond; we'll have a meal there. I think you'll like it.'

'I'm sure I shall. It's such a heavenly evening, too—
it's nice to be out of doors. Have you had a busy day,
Professor?'

'My name's Radmer...'

'Oh, is it? It's Dutch, of course.'

'Certainly not—it's a Friese name. My home is in
Friesland; I was born there. We are as touchy about
being called Dutchmen as a Scotsman would be if one
called him an Englishman, and yet we are united with
the rest of Holland, just as Scotland is to England.'

'You don't mind living in England?'

'No, I've made it my second home for a number of
years and I can go to Friesland easily enough.'

'But when you marry—you said you were going
to—will you stay in England?'

'Yes, for the foreseeable future.'

They had left the last houses behind and he went
on, 'I'm going to take an inner road. It will take a little
longer but it is much quieter.'

A hint nicely put for her to mind her own business.
She said brightly, 'That sounds nice,' and fell to thinking about Melville. If he had been beside her instead
of the Professor he would have been telling her outra-
geous stories about the famous people he rubbed shoulders with—he could be an amusing companion. The
Professor wasn't amusing, although he had a sense of
humour. He was restful, she decided and returned to
her thoughts of Melville. He might not like so much
peace and quiet—the road ran through wooded country with here and there a glimpse of a castle crowning

a hill, and infrequent villages tucked cosily around steepled churches. She said, speaking her thoughts out loud without meaning to, 'I don't think Melville would like this,' and she felt awful the minute she had said it. 'I don't know why I said that...'

'Because he is on your mind—at the back of your head, whatever else you are thinking or saying.' The Professor sounded matter-of-fact and not in the least put out. 'I think you must miss him: the excitement of being taken to dinner at fashionable restaurants, meeting show people, finding flowers waiting for you when you go on duty, living on the heights and then plummeting down to the depths. Have you told him where you are?'

She didn't pause to think how strange it was that she could confide so easily in her companion. 'No, I took your advice and made myself unavailable. It worked before.'

'And will again.' His voice was kind. 'We are almost at Freiburg. We shall not stop there but go on to the restaurant; it's just this side of Emmendingen.'

He knew the area fairly well, he told her, but didn't enlarge on that, only pointed out the minster as they drove through Freiburg and shortly afterwards stopped at a restaurant tucked in among the trees well away from the road.

The restaurant was a charming place and well patronised. Rachel, feeling adventurous, chose sweet wine soup, river trout from the Black Forest with a lettuce and bean salad, and finished with savarin with strawberries and whipped cream.

They ate leisurely, enjoying the warm, light evening and talking comfortably about nothing in particular, drinking the rather dry wine the Professor had ordered and then when they had finished, lingering over their coffee.

'I wouldn't want to live here, but it would be a heavenly place to stay for a while.'

The Professor passed his cup. 'A honeymoon, perhaps? You said that Melville might not like so much peace and quiet, but Basle isn't far away, you know, and Strasbourg is almost as close. There's plenty of night life in both places if one is so inclined.'

'I hadn't thought about—about honeymoons,' said Rachel, who had thought of very little else for weeks—ever since she had met Melville. And then, at his look, she blushed. 'Well, yes, I have, but there's nothing definite... He's so busy, you see, Professor.'

'Radmer. Of course.' His voice was dry.

He drove her back along the road bordering the Rhine and crossed the river by the Dreirosenbrucke, through the outskirts of Basle, past the main hospital and Spelentor because he said that it was something she could see, if only briefly.

The foyer was full when they reached the hotel; he bade her goodnight in the entrance, reminded her that they were to spend the morning together, and drove away. On her way to the lifts she encountered Sadie.

'You didn't come to dinner, honey.'

'No, I went out...'

'Fast worker, aren't you?' Sadie grinned. 'Anyone I know?'

Before she could reply she exclaimed, 'Hey, you're

from London; so is that dream man who gave the lecture this evening. It's him!'

'Well, yes. You see, I'm his theatre sister, but it's not what you're thinking. I'm hoping to marry someone— he's something in television, and Professor van Teule is going to get married shortly. It's just pure chance that we happened to meet.'

Sadie considered this. 'Do you mean to say that you work for him and he never even hinted that he'd be here? He must have known that you'd be one of the crowd.'

'I dare say he forgot. We get on well, but only on a professional footing.' Which wasn't quite true. 'Don't spread it around, will you, Sadie?'

'Not me, honey. I'm no bigmouth. What's your man like?'

Rachel spent the next ten minutes describing Melville in loving detail.

The Professor called for her directly after breakfast the next morning. 'Strasbourg would be the obvious place but I don't think we can do it in the time we've got and in this car. We'll go to Kolmar. It will be packed with tourists but we'll take the road by the river and then cross over and come back on the other side.'

He started the car. 'It's the visit to the hospital this afternoon, isn't it? And my lecture this evening. Only an hour—there's a meeting I have to attend at eight o'clock. I should have liked to have taken you out for dinner but I can't get out of this particular gathering. Will you dine with me tomorrow and on Saturday?'

They were running beside the river and she stared at the splendid scenery. 'Thank you, I'd like to. We go home on Sunday—there's a midday flight.'

'Yes, I'm flying to Schiphol, having a couple of days at my home.'

To see the girl you are going to marry? wondered Rachel. Perhaps she is staying with his family. She wondered if she would phone Melville when she got back; after all, he must have wondered where she had got to. If he was free they might go out for the evening; she wasn't on duty until one o'clock the next day.

'A penny for them?' murmured the Professor.

It didn't enter her head to dissemble. 'I was wondering if I'd ring Melville when I get back.'

He shook his head. 'You'll never learn, Rachel.' His voice was gently mocking. 'But I should think that there will be a letter waiting for you, or at least a bouquet and a phone message.'

They parked the car in Kolmar, attractively mediaeval with vineyards all around it, had coffee and wandered round the market, looked inside the church and then crossed the river and drove back along the highway until the Professor turned off to go inland. 'There's time for a sandwich,' he told her. 'There's a place where we can get something to eat in Badenweiler.'

It was a small inn in the tiny spa, hidden away in the Black Forest. They ate rolls and sausage and cheese and drank lager, and the landlord came and talked to them once he discovered the Professor spoke fluent German. He was a nice old man who smiled and nodded at her and then asked a question of the Professor.

'What's he saying?' she asked.

'He thinks you are a pretty girl,' said the Professor easily.

* * *

She didn't see him to speak to for the rest of that day. The visit to the hospital was interesting and there was a discussion afterwards. His own lecture in the evening tied up with what they had seen that afternoon and when he had finished there was another discussion. She went to bed early after another buffet supper.

There were three lectures the next day and she was a little tired by the evening. All the same it was pleasant to see the Professor waiting for her in the foyer. Sadie had come down in the lift with her and clutched her arm when she saw him. 'Honey, there's the boyfriend. Leap to it.'

'He's not…' began Rachel, but couldn't finish in case he heard.

They went to the same restaurant as before and had the same table and the Professor made no effort to entertain her, only talked gently of this and that and made sure that she ate her dinner. He took her back soon after they had finished and said goodnight at the entrance. 'Tomorrow evening?' he suggested. 'Same place if you like it. You're going to the children's hospital tomorrow, aren't you?'

'Your lecture is first,' she reminded him. 'Your last one.'

The final day was well filled. There were last-minute get togethers, the Professor's lecture and the visit to the hospital and in the evening over dinner they talked about the week's events, but not too seriously.

'Everything has been arranged for you?' he asked as they sat over their coffee.

'Oh, yes. We have to hand in our vouchers and pay

any bills tomorrow morning after breakfast and be ready to leave at midday.' She asked diffidently, 'You'll be gone by then?'

'No, my flight is in the afternoon. I had a chat with George this morning; they haven't been too busy, but he was kind enough to remind me that it's take-in next week.'

He said goodnight at the hotel and she said, 'Thank you for giving me such a nice time, Prof... Radmer. I'll see you next week, I expect.'

She was up early in the morning, but so was the Professor, sitting patiently in a corner of the foyer where he had a good view of the reception desk. He had no intention of letting Rachel see him, only a wish to make sure that she was safely on her way home.

He watched her join the small crowd around the reception desk. There were several of the girls who had attended the conference with her, but the people in front of them had just arrived. The Professor gave them a cursory glance and then stood up and started strolling across the foyer. The man even now stretching out a hand for his room key while his other arm encircled a blonde, very pretty girl was Melville. At any moment he would turn round and Rachel would see him.

Chapter 8

Rachel looked up from checking her modest bills, straight into Melville's face. For a few seconds her whole face lit up, her softly curving mouth half open, then she saw the consternation on his face; more than that, angry irritation and blue eyes, suddenly hard. He recovered quickly.

'So this is where you're hiding,' he observed. 'Have you been here long? I haven't had a chance to ring the hospital; I thought you were still there.'

Rachel hadn't spoken; her mouth was dry and she couldn't get the words out. In any case, she wasn't sure what words to utter. She dragged her eyes away from his face and looked at the girl, the same girl she had seen with him going up the steps of his London flat, ignoring her now, tugging at Melville's arm.

'Darling, hurry up. I simply must have a shower, and you've got the key.'

He patted her arm. 'OK, darling, we're on our way.' He glanced at Rachel and away again. 'Well, see you around, Rachel. It was fun while it lasted. No hard feelings, eh?' He added airily, 'We're here on location,' and winked. 'With a holiday on the side, of course.'

The girl gave his arm another tug and he gave her a careless kiss on her cheek. 'Darling, don't be in such a hurry. Haven't you heard of "Off with the old love and on with the new"? I can't remember who said that but I'm following his advice.'

They had gone. Rachel stood quite still, her face white, looking at nothing in particular. The queue around her had moved on but she hadn't noticed. She didn't notice the Professor either. He said quietly, 'Give me those,' and took the bills and voucher from her hand. 'Go and sit down and don't move until I come.'

She did as she had been told; she didn't take in what had happened and certainly was in no fit state to think for herself. Presently he was back again, sitting beside her, saying nothing, watching the colour creep back into her pale face. He lifted a finger to a page and a tray of coffee was set on a small table before them. There was a glass of brandy there, too; he told her to drink it in a no-nonsense voice, and she did that before drinking the coffee he poured. She hadn't spoken and neither had he but presently she whispered, 'I should like to scream.'

'I've a better idea. We will go to your room—you don't have to vacate it until midday—and you will lie down on your bed and take a nap. Then we will talk.'

'What about?' Her voice was fiercely bitter. 'Being jilted—how to make a fool of a girl in six easy lessons?' The brandy was taking effect. 'I'd like to run for miles and never speak to anyone again. And I've got to go back and everyone will ask…'

For answer he took her arm, whisked her into a lift, took her key from her bag and urged her gently into her room. 'Lie down,' he said. 'I'll stay for a while.'

'There's no time,' she said distractedly, and burst into tears.

He sat quietly while she cried and after a while, when the sobs had changed to heaving breaths and snuffles, he got up, mopped her face dry with a hand-kerchief and studied it.

She looked a fright, her nose was red and her eyes pink and puffy and her hair had come loose from its plait, but somehow it didn't seem to matter that the Professor should see her like that. She said forlornly, 'I'd better wash my face. I'm sorry that I've made such a fuss.'

Two tears ran down her cheeks and she brushed them away with the back of her hand. 'I'll have to get ready. I have to go back to the hospital.'

He put his sopping handkerchief back into a pocket. 'Not necessarily. You're in no fit state to travel on your own and certainly not to go near an operating theatre. I'm going to ring Miss Marks. Will you leave things to me, Rachel?'

She nodded. 'But can I stay on here or could I go straight home—just for a day to—to get used to the idea?'

'I'll take you back with me.' He was matter-of-fact.

'My mother will be delighted to have you and in a couple of days you will be able to face up to things again.'

'But I don't know your mother. I can't possibly... Why should you...?'

He sighed gently. 'Of course you don't know my mother, you haven't met. And you can, you know. And why should I? My dear Rachel, from motives of pure selfishness; I prefer you to scrub for me than anyone else.'

He got up and picked up the phone. 'Go and wash your face while I get things sorted out.'

When she got back from the bathroom he was phoning someone in his own language. He hung up presently and said, 'I told Miss Marks that you had picked up a mild virus and that I would be taking you to my home to get over it. I suggested two or three days off.'

Rachel was jolted out of her misery for a moment by the notion of Miss Marks agreeing to anything so unusual. 'Did she mind?'

He smiled faintly. 'I didn't ask her. She agreed with me that a virus infection in the hospital was to be avoided at all costs.'

'But that's not true—I haven't got a virus.'

'No. I can lie most convincingly when I need to.' He smiled again. 'My mother will be delighted to welcome you.' He looked her up and down. 'That's better. Slap on some make-up and do your hair while I see if I can get a seat on my plane.'

There seemed nothing unusual in sitting down before the mirror and doing what she could to her face and brushing out her hair while he went on with his phoning, booking her a seat and then ringing the reception desk.

She was twisting her plait into a tidy knot by the time he had finished.

'Do you feel up to eating some lunch?—not here. If your luggage is ready you can check out and we'll go to my hotel, collect my case, hand over the car and eat a sandwich.'

Just for a moment she thought she would cry again. He was being so kind—arranging everything, giving her an impersonal sympathy and blessedly not offering good advice.

'Don't dare weep,' he warned her and swept her out of the room and into the lift. In the half-empty foyer he sat her down out of sight behind a mass of greenery, checked out for her and then led her to the car outside. She was trembling when she got in, frightened that she might come face to face with Melville again. The Professor glanced at her shaking mouth and said, 'Now, now,' in a fatherly way, and started the car. By the time they had reached his hotel she had pulled herself together again. She drank the orange juice he ordered for her, said that yes, she would like chicken sandwiches, and, when they came, made a brave effort to eat them. They had coffee afterwards while the Professor, never a chatty man, kept up a steady flow of inconsequential talk. Rachel hardly heard a word of what he was saying, only the sound of his voice soothed her and stopped her from thinking.

Their flight was at five o'clock; they had a cup of tea about half past three, took a taxi to the airport and in due course boarded the plane.

It was seven o'clock when they emerged from Schiphol and almost at once a short stout man came up to them. The Professor shook his hand and drew Rachel forward to meet him. 'This is Bratte—he looks after the family.' He introduced her and added, 'He's brought a car to meet us.'

A Mercedes, drawn up to the kerb close by. Bratte and the porter saw to the luggage while the Professor ushered Rachel into the front seat and got in beside her. He said something to the other man as he climbed into the back of the car and they laughed together before he started the car and drove off.

Rachel sat silent, and the Professor, after one quick look at her sad profile, made no attempt to talk to her. She stared out at the countryside, not seeing it, but only Melville's face, hearing his voice: 'Off with the old love, on with the new.' What a fool she had been; a silly young woman who should have known better. Well, it had taught her a lesson; she wouldn't believe any man if ever one said that he loved her. She had a good job and she was expert at it; the Professor had said so. She would be a career girl and end up on the very topmost rung of the ladder. The thought made her shudder inwardly, but it was the answer.

'Close your eyes and go to sleep,' said the Professor softly without looking at her, and, although she hadn't intended to do so, she did.

When she woke up the day was fading. The country on either side of the road stretched away as far as she could see, wide green fields with here and there clumps of trees. Farmhouses, huge barns at their backs, were dotted around at intervals. Here and there were lights twinkling and there was a narrow canal running beside the road.

'We're north of Leeuwarden—the capital town—going towards the coast. We shall be about another ten minutes. Did you have a good nap?'

'Yes, thank you.' She heard the quiet content in his voice and the sudden nervousness she had felt melted away.

The road curved into a large clump of trees and then, unexpectedly, a village. Small, neat houses bordered the road leading to a cobbled square dominated by a jelly-mould church and surrounded by more houses—some of them quite large and most of them old.

Rachel, wide awake now, stared around her as the Professor circled the church slowly and took a narrow road on the further side.

The road was a brick one, tree-lined and with the canal still beside it. Presently there was a bridge with wrought iron gates at its further end opening into a cobbled drive.

The Professor had perforce to slow down which gave Rachel a chance to look around her. There were thick shrubberies on either side with trees beyond, so that she could see very little to the left or right, but as the drive curved she saw the house ahead of them. The evening was far advanced by now but she could see it clearly enough in the dusk for lights streamed from the windows. It was a square house, like a child's drawing, its windows set in rows on either side and above its massive front door, its roof set squarely upon it without gables or embellishment of any sort. Yet it had dignity and a kind of agelessness.

The Professor stopped the car and got out to open her door and as she got out in her turn she saw the symmetrical flower beds before the house, outlined with foot-high box hedges. She sniffed appreciatively; the air was fragrant with summer flowers. It was very quiet, although somewhere a dog was barking; for the first time since she had seen Melville that morning, she felt that she could cope.

The Professor took her arm and urged her up the steps to the door, held wide by Bratte who had gone ahead. 'Welcome to my home,' said the Professor. 'Come and meet my mother and father.'

They crossed a vast, marble-floored hall and opened double doors into an equally vast room with a lofty ceiling, tall wide windows draped in velvet and a polished wooden floor covered with a silk carpet. The furniture was exactly right: great bow-fronted display cabinets along the walls, a rent table between the windows, a Frisian wall clock above an *armoire*, its marquetry in the style of Berain, flanked by a pair of eighteenth-century armchairs covered in Beauvais tapestry. Nicely blended with these were comfortable chairs, small lamp tables and two well-upholstered sofas each side of the hooded fireplace. From one of these, two people arose: a tall, rather stout lady of late middle years, dressed with great good taste and her grey hair swept back in a severe bun, and an even taller man, some years older and, from the look of him, unmistakably the Professor's father. The lady surged forward, embraced her son and turned her attention to Rachel. 'My dear, welcome. Radmer has told us about you and your splendid work at the hospital and I am so glad to meet you.'

She had seemed formidable at first sight, but she wasn't at all; she had a kind face and twinkling eyes and Rachel liked her. She liked the Professor's father, too, a quiet man of few words who put her at her ease at once.

No one mentioned the reason for her being there. She was swept upstairs by a small stout woman answering to the name of Mieke, who puffed her way up the handsome staircase at the back of the hall and along a wide gallery to one of the doors lining it. Her case was already there. Mieke opened a door, showing her a bathroom, beamed at her and went away, leaving Rachel to make a lightning tour of her room. It was a splendid apartment with a bed of some dark wood she couldn't recognise and a matching tallboy and sofa table. The windows were hung with chintz which matched the bedspread and there was a thick cream carpet on the floor. The bathroom was as luxurious as the bedroom and she prowled round, admiring the soaps and bath lotions and pile of pastel-tinted towels before tidying her person. Her face bore signs of the day's events, for she was pale and her eyelids were still puffy, but she didn't allow herself to think about that; she owed it to the Professor to behave sensibly. He had been kind; how kind she was only just beginning to realise.

The Professor was waiting for her when she went downstairs. 'Hungry?' he wanted to know. 'I am. Mother and Father decided not to dine; they will have supper with us. Come and have a drink first.'

She was grateful to him for being so matter-of-fact; sympathy would undoubtedly have sent her off into floods of tears again. She drank the sherry she was offered and presently sat down in the dining-room, a little overawed by its magnificence. It was a large room, its crimson walls hung with numerous paintings. The oval mahogany table could seat sixteen persons in comfort and the chairs were ribbon-back Hepplewhite. Along one wall was a vast serving table laden with silver and presided over by Bratte. It could have been rather overpowering but somehow it wasn't; Rachel did her best to eat the delicious food set before her and bore her share of the conversation, but it was a relief when they had gone back to the drawing-room and, after a little more desultory talk over the coffee cups, her hostess suggested that she must be tired and longing for her bed. 'We breakfast early, at eight o'clock, my dear, but if you would prefer to have a tray in bed you have only to say so.'

Radmer got to his feet. 'Mother, dear, Rachel speaks no Dutch. She wouldn't know what to say. I'll knock on her door at half-past seven on my way down.'

'Oh, but I'll get up—there's no need...'

'All the same I shall knock.' He waited while she bade her host and hostess good night and walked with her to the door and opened it. 'Sleep well, Rachel,' he said quietly. His eyes searched her face. 'Would you like a sleeping pill?'

She shook her head. 'I'm tired. Beside, I have to think.'

He nodded. 'By all means do that, but remember that ideas and plans are always out of all proportion to the original in the early hours.'

He waited by the open door until she had gone upstairs and, she did her best to walk jauntily up the wide staircase, her back very straight.

She cried herself to sleep, of course. She had enough good sense to know that in time she would get over the hurt of it all, but Melville's words were still very clear in her head and she winced each time she remembered them; it wasn't very much good her telling herself that she would take good care never to fall in love again. The thought that Melville might discover that he had been wrong and loved her after all persisted in the back of her head; it was still there when she finally went to sleep.

A young girl with a round cheerful face brought her tea at seven o'clock, smiling broadly, pulled back the curtains and went away again. The smile had only widened at Rachel's good morning but she had waved an expressive arm at the bright morning outside before she went away.

Rachel nipped out of bed and took a look. Her room was at the back of the house, overlooking a large formal garden and what looked like a shrubbery beyond it. The windows opened on to a balcony. She lifted the sash and stepped outside, only to rush back in at a knock on the door.

'Morning,' said Radmer's voice from the other side of it. 'Coming down or breakfast in bed?'

'Oh, good morning. I'm coming down.'

He said, 'Good,' in a casual way and went, and she hurried to shower and dress, to go downstairs half an hour later in time to meet Radmer coming in through the front door, two Jack Russells at his heels. His 'Hello' was friendly, followed by, 'I hope you slept well?' uttered in an impersonal tone that needed no more than a brief reply. That she had been crying was obvious, but he offered no sympathy. He merely expressed the hope that she was hungry and opened the door to a small room behind the dining-room where breakfast had been set out on a round table at which his mother was already sitting. Her good morning was warm and friendly and her enquiry as to whether Rachel had slept well was as brief as her son's had been. 'Your father is down at the stables taking a look at the new foal. We won't wait for him.'

The meal was a pleasant one, unhurried and enlivened by Mevrouw van Teule's comments on every topic under the sun. She was, Rachel reflected, rather like her own mother, and, despite her somewhat intimidating appearance, just as motherly.

Breakfast over and still no sign of Mijnheer van Teule, she told them not to waste the morning. 'Lunch will be at twelve o'clock but it won't matter if you are late. We'll have it outside on the terrace.'

'Would you like a walk?' asked the Professor. 'There's a river beyond the shrubbery.'

'Well, if there is nothing you want to do…'

'Nothing. Let's go.'

They had crossed the formal garden and were deep into the shrubbery when he asked, 'Want to talk?'

He was strolling along, his hands in his pockets, not looking at her.

'What would be the use?' She tried hard not to sound sorry for herself. 'I've been a fool, haven't I? And now I'll just have to get over it. I don't suppose talking about it will help.'

'If it's any comfort to you, we've all been fools in our time. And of course talking will help. I expect you lay awake for hours wondering just what you would say to him if he were to turn up swearing eternal devotion.'

'He won't.' She was suddenly fierce. 'Not after the things he said. "Off with the old love"—if ever I was a love at all.' She stopped to stare up at the Professor. 'Doesn't it make any difference at all that I loved him?'

'Probably not.' His voice was cool. 'There are so many different kinds of love, Rachel. But you can always try again when you get back to London; I don't suppose they'll be on location for more than a week or so. Go and see him and don't, whatever you do, weep.' He smiled suddenly. 'Come and see the river.'

It was a small river, more a stream, running unhurriedly between green fields where the black and white cows stood about it in the sun.

They sat down on the grass and Rachel said, 'You must be very happy to come here after London and the hospital.'

'Oh, I am, but of course I enjoy my work and there are certain ties in London.'

His fiancée—she had forgotten her for the moment. 'Does she like it, too?' She glanced at his placid face. 'The girl you are going to marry?'

'Why, yes, she does. What are you going to tell your friends when you get back?'

'I won't need to say anything at first, will I? Only that he is out of the country. And—and by the time he is back I'll be able to talk about it without, without...'

'Bursting into tears. Delay the breaking of your heart, Rachel, until you have seen Melville. Chin up, stiff upper lip, squared shoulders; I have always thought of you as a young woman who could face up to things.'

She gave a shaky laugh. 'You sound like my eldest brother giving me sound advice.' She gave a watery sniff. 'Have you sisters, Radmer?'

'Four—all married. So you see I'm quite qualified to take your brother's place.' He said very deliberately, 'I'm a good deal older than you are, Rachel—thirty-five.'

'Oh, are you? I've never thought about it.'

His firm mouth twisted a little. 'You have had no reason to do so, have you?'

'No. Oh, Radmer, I don't know what to do. I always thought I was such a sensible person. What shall I do?'

He was lying back, his hands behind his head, his eyes half shut. 'I think I am the last person to tell you to do anything, Rachel. It is your life and you must decide how you want to live it.'

She felt her cheeks grow hot; it was the gentlest of snubs but it made her feel as though she was a silly girl trying to get sympathy. She said, 'Yes, of course,' and then, 'May we cross the river or is that someone else's land?'

He turned his head to look at her, studying her profile, watching the colour ebb away. 'It's our land. There is a narrow ditch which is the boundary between us and the farm you can see over there. By all means let us walk on the other bank—there is another bridge at the far end of the field.'

Not another word was spoken about Melville, only as they strolled along he told her that he had phoned her mother. A remark which brought her up short, to raise a guilty face to his. 'I forgot—oh, how could I? Thank you for letting her know.' Her eyes looked a question she didn't want to ask.

'I told her that you were tired after your week and would be staying here for a day or so. You can ring her when you get back or from here if you wish.'

'I'll wait, I think. She knows I'm all right... Thank you, Radmer.'

She wanted to say more, to thank him more warmly, but he had offered her an inch of help and she had behaved as though it were an ell. She would take care not to talk about herself, not to really take advantage of his kindness. She asked too brightly, 'When are we going back?'

His voice was as placid as ever. 'Do you feel equal to taking a flight tomorrow evening? We don't need to leave until after tea and we can be at the hospital before midnight. But say if you'd rather wait a day or two. Are you on duty the following morning? Can you remember the off-duty rota?'

Of course she remembered it, although she didn't say so. After all, she had to worry over it every two weeks; by the time it was done to her satisfaction, she knew it off by heart. 'Yes, I'm on at eight o'clock—it should be your list.'

'I'll give George a ring presently. Shall we go back to the house? I dare say you'd like coffee or a drink of some sort.'

His mother and father were on the terrace and the dogs raced to meet them. Rachel sat down beside her hostess, drank her coffee and answered the string of questions, casually asked, which that lady embarked upon. She really was a dear, thought Rachel, explaining where her home was and agreeing that living in the country was so much nicer than in town. 'Though it makes a difference where you live,' she pointed out. 'It's very noisy at the hospital but it's not in the best part of London.'

'Radmer lives pleasantly enough,' observed his mother. 'The Bodkins look after him very well.'

'A good thing, too,' said Rachel warmly. 'He works frightfully hard, you know.'

'I am sure he does, my dear,' said his mother comfortably. 'It will be a good thing when he is married and has a wife.'

Rachel was surprised to discover that she didn't want to talk about that. I'm getting mean, she thought. Just because things haven't worked out for me, there is no reason why he shouldn't be happy. She resolutely shut her mind from her own unhappiness and asked Mevrouw van Teule to tell her the history of the house.

Radmer took her into Leeuwarden in the afternoon and accompanied her patiently round the Frisian Museum. He was very knowledgeable about his country; she listened with interest while he told her about Great Pier's enormous sword and the fourteenth-century drinking horn of the St Anthony Guild of Stavoren and explained the mediaeval costumes and paintings. They went from there to Franeker, so that she might see the planetarium and the beautiful Renaissance town hall before driving back to his house.

They had stopped for tea in one of the hotels and the conversation had been about Leeuwarden and Friesland. Even if she had wanted to, she had been given no opportunity to brood. Once back at his home, she had changed into another dress and joined everyone else for drinks before dinner and after that elegant and leisurely meal, they had sat outside on the terrace and she had found herself beside Radmer's father, who talked at some length about Friesland, shooting questions at her from time to time so that she had to pay attention. There had been simply no chance to think about herself all day, she reflected, tumbling into bed and going to sleep at once.

After breakfast the next morning Radmer stowed her into the car once more and drove north to the coast. The villages here were widespread, the cottages built on either side of dykes, and the roads were narrow and for the most part of brick. They had strange names, too; Radmer laughed at her attempts to pronounce them. Presently he said, 'Here's the sea.'

After a while they stopped at Zoutkamp, a shrimp-fishing centre, where they were served excellent coffee in a small dark café. They drove on, down a narrow country road skirting the Lauwers Meer until they joined the main road again, running close to the sea and then inland to Dokkum and so back to his home.

They were just in time for lunch and in the afternoon, despite her protestations that she must pack, he drove her across country to Oostermeer and then took the narrow brick roads to Grouw, where they had tea sitting by the water, watching the yachts spinning over the lake. They were back by four o'clock, to a second cup of tea, and then it was time for Rachel to pack her case once again.

They drove away with Bratte in the back so that he

could take the car back and the warmth of her host's and hostess's goodbyes ringing in her ears. Two days had never gone so quickly and she had enjoyed every moment of them, she thought guiltily, but only because she had been given no chance to be by herself for one single minute—only at bedtime, and then she had been so pleasantly tired that she had slept at once.

Bratte saw them to the very exit gate, bidding the Professor goodbye and *Tot Ziens* and shaking her hand with the hope that he might see her again. They didn't have long to wait. They went aboard in the darkening evening, and, obedient to the Professor's suggestion, she refused the plastic tray of food and accepted the coffee she was offered. 'We'll eat at Heathrow,' he told her.

It still wanted two hours to midnight by the time they had retrieved their bags and gone through customs. Rachel was surprised to see the Professor's car outside the exit; travelling with him was certainly trouble free, she reflected, settling into the front seat.

But not for long. He drove to the Penta Hotel, parked the car and ushered her inside. 'Don't worry,' he said in answer to her look, 'I said you would be in the hospital by midnight and you will. Let's eat.'

She discovered that she was hungry. They ate steak and a salad and finished with a pot of coffee before they got into the car again and drove the sixteen miles to London. It was ten minutes to midnight when he drew in the hospital courtyard, opened her door, got her case, and walked to the entrance with her. The night porter was in his box, reading the paper; he glanced up and then back to the page. The Professor pushed open the door and they went in. He walked with Rachel across the hall to the door leading to the nurses' home, opened it, put the case inside and said, 'I don't dare to go a step further and certainly not at this hour of night. You are all right, Rachel?'

She lifted a grateful face to his. 'Yes, thank you very much—I can't thank you enough, Radmer—and I must stop calling you that now, mustn't I? I'll see you in the morning.'

She smiled at him, making a brave attempt to behave normally.

'Goodnight, Rachel.' He bent his head suddenly and kissed her hard on her surprised mouth, turned on his heel and walked away.

She picked up her case and started up the stairs. She had been feeling dreadful, rejected, undesirable, not worth a second look, but somehow his kiss had changed that. Somewhere, right at the bottom of her unhappiness, there was a small spark; she wasn't sure what it was, only that her cold insides were warmed by it.

None of her friends were still up. She crept to her room, had a bath, unpacked and got into bed, thankful that there would be a great deal to occupy her in the morning. A wave of misery swept over her, swamped almost at once by sleep.

As is always the case, the misery was easier to bear in the morning. Rachel went down to breakfast, answered the questions with which she was bombarded and hurried along to the theatre wing. Norah was already there, delighted to have her back; the moment the night sister had gone, she produced a fistful of requests and notes for Rachel to deal with. The CSD were cutting up rough again, the laundry had rung to say that they were using too many sheets and towels, two nurses wanted days off for something special and Mrs Pepys had rung to say that she had a migraine and wouldn't be in for her normal duty.

'Did anything nice happen?' asked Rachel and they laughed together.

The theatre list was on her desk. A heavy one, but then it always was when the Professor was operating. Rachel organised the day's work, rang down to Women's Surgical to make sure that the first patient was ready and went along to theatre.

Sidney was brooding over his equipment and was obviously glad to see her. So were the nurses. She checked everything was ready for the first case and went to scrub. She could hear the whine of the lift bringing the patient to theatre and turned her head to wish Dr Carr good morning as he poked his head round the door to see if she was there.

'Better?' he wanted to know, and she remembered just in time that she had had a virus, and said that yes, she was fine again. When the list was finished she would have to go to the office and see Miss Marks.

She was being tied into her gown when the Professor came in to scrub. His 'Good morning, Sister' was uttered with a detached friendliness and he turned away at once to speak to George. She wasn't sure what she had expected but certainly not this polite indifference. She went into the theatre and checked her trolleys and cast an eye around before checking with Norah who should be sent to coffee first and which of the nurses should go into the sluice.

The Professor, with George and Billy, was standing away from the table while the patient was arranged
just so and Dr Carr checked the anaesthetics, and Rachel, with nothing to do for the moment, allowed her
thoughts to dwell on him. He was quite right, of course.
He had helped her when she had needed help, but the
circumstances had been unusual and now they were
back, leading their normal lives once more. At least he
was; she still felt as though she were in a bad dream
and at the moment all she longed for was to recapture
the quiet orderly life she had led before she had met
Melville.

The patient was deeply unconscious. Dr Carr said
'She's ready when you are, Radmer,' and sat back on
his stool, all his attention on the quiet face before him,
the signal for Rachel to hand towels and clips and then
scalpel and forceps, her well-trained mind concentrating on her work.

The list lasted several hours, and when they paused
for coffee half-way through the talk was about the
cases. No one mentioned Basle at all and Rachel supposed that they had already discussed it before they
got to theatre. Only at the end of the list when the men
had gone to the changing room and she was organising the clearing up did Billy poke his head round the
door to ask, 'Did you have a good time, Rachel? You
don't look quite your usual smashing self. Did they
work you too hard?'

She hadn't bothered to take off her mask, only pulled
it under her chin, and she still wore her theatre cap, but
that didn't detract from her pretty face. She gave him a

grin. 'Not a bit of it; just lectures and things, you know, but there were rather a lot of them.'

'It must have been great. Pity about the virus.'

The Professor had lounged into theatre, on the point of leaving. 'Nasty things, virus infections. Billy, I want you to go to Men's Surgical and check on Mr Willis—he's for the end of the week, isn't he? He's been running a temperature.' He looked across at Rachel. 'Sister, I've a kidney transplant lined up as soon as it's possible to do it. Can you get your extra staff at short notice?'

'Yes, sir.' She was pleased with her coolly efficient voice. 'I'll warn the part-timers and the nurses here.'

'Good, thank you.' He nodded with the faintest of smiles and went away. Watching his broad back so impeccably clothed, she found it hard to equate his elegant image with the casually dressed friend who had listened so patiently to her as they sat by the little stream at his home.

She pushed her cap further back on her head and began to bundle the instruments, ready to be collected by the CSD. Best not to waste time thinking; next week she would go home on her days off and sort herself out in the peace and quiet of the country.

Chapter 9

Despite the fact that her days were fully occupied, Rachel found that they dragged. It seemed as if her days off would never come, but at last they did. She flung things into her overnight bag, got into the Fiat and drove herself home. She had hardly spoken to the Professor since they had returned. Beyond enquiring as to whether Miss Marks had accepted her excuse of a virus infection without fuss, he had had very little to say to her except for their normal exchanges regarding theatre lists and the like. It was as though he were standing at a distance, watching her; a silly fantasy she instantly dismissed. She had been sleeping badly, too, waking in the night to remember far too clearly Melville's cruel remarks about being off with the old love. During the day she resolutely put him out of her mind, but at night it was a different matter; at home, perhaps she would sleep soundly.

She had phoned her mother when she got back to England with the Professor but she had said nothing about Melville; that could wait until she and her mother were alone some time during her brief stay at home. As she drove she thought about the Professor, wondering if she had annoyed him in some way, but discarding the idea. It seemed more likely that he regarded her as a possible embarrassment, seeing that he was thinking about getting married; perhaps he was expecting her to take advantage of his kindness while she had been in Basle. 'Well, he's quite wrong,' said Rachel loudly, and then, 'All the same, I wish I knew what was the matter…'

She had left the hospital in the early evening but the traffic was heavy and it was late when she got home at last. Her parents were waiting for her, and over her supper she gave them an expurgated account of her week in Basle, aware that it was only too obvious that she was leaving out a great deal. But her mother and father said nothing to that effect, merely observing that it had been an experience, and that it must have been a tiring week for her. 'Though your brothers are green with envy,' said her mother. 'Edward and Nick are going to Scotland during the holidays camping but they are already talking about hitchhiking round Europe.'

Her room welcomed her: all her childhood furniture, her dolls sitting in a row on the shelf her father had made for them, flowers in a bowl on the dressing-table. She unpacked her few things and went to bed and slept all night, although she hadn't expected to.

She told her mother everything the next morning while they were sitting in the garden, shelling peas. It was easier than she had expected, partly because she had something to do while she talked. Her mother didn't interrupt; now and again she made soothing murmurs and once drew in her breath sharply when Rachel repeated what Melville had said at the hotel. Rachel had finished and was blowing her nose in an effort not to cry when she spoke. 'I'm sorry you're unhappy, love, but look at it this way, you would have been even more unhappy if you had gone on seeing Melville, expecting to marry him, no doubt. Infatuation makes one blind but the nice part is that sooner or later you see again and it becomes something that doesn't matter at all.' She glanced sideways at her daughter's unhappy face. 'Professor van Teule was very kind—I wrote a letter to his mother, just to thank her, and she wrote back saying how much they had enjoyed having you. I suppose he's back at the hospital too?' The question was put so casually that Rachel answered without hesitation.

'Oh, yes. He had a list the morning after we got back.'

'So you've had a chance to talk about the conference...'

Rachel frowned. 'Plenty, but we haven't. You see, Mother, it's all over and done with now, I expect he wants to forget it. He told me weeks ago that he hoped to get married soon.'

Her mother shelled quite a few peas before she said, 'I wonder what she's like…'

'I've no idea. He never talks about himself and no one mentioned her when I was at his home. He did say that she liked his father's house.'

'Ah well, I dare say you'll meet her one day.' There was regret in her mother's voice but Rachel didn't notice it.

'I don't expect so. Actually, we've hardly spoken since we came back.' She sighed soundlessly. 'We've always been on good terms but we aren't any more. He's—he's gone all distant.'

'What a pity,' observed Mrs Downing, and meant it.

Rachel went back on the following evening considerably refreshed. She had walked miles with Mutt, called on friends in the village, driven her father on his afternoon rounds and helped around the house, and she felt content. She refused to think about Melville but she had to admit to herself that she was glad that she wouldn't have to meet any of his friends again. All those clothes in my cupboard, she reflected, and chuckled for the first time in days. And no more agonising over her face and hair either. She remembered then how she had sat at her dressing-table, putting herself to rights while the Professor had sat beside her, telephoning. She hadn't given it a thought then because for some reason she hadn't minded him seeing her looking a mess. She frowned a little over that; perhaps she had been in a state of shock. On the other hand she had to admit that if the same circumstances should arise again, she would think nothing of it. 'Very odd,' she said out loud.

It began to rain as she neared the hospital. It was an ugly building at the best of times; now it looked downright hideous and she would have to live and work in it, probably for years, until or unless she went somewhere else. She would get a post easily enough, she was a good theatre sister and the world was her oyster, but somewhere at the back of her mind was a niggling reluctance to leave the place.

She parked the Fiat and went through to her room, pausing, because she hadn't been able to stop herself, by the letter racks to see if there were any letters for her. There was one envelope, from the Professor, containing a brief note; he hoped that she wouldn't be greatly inconvenienced if he started his list half an hour earlier than usual—abdominal injuries—a man too shocked for immediate operation. It was signed with his initials.

Businesslike in the extreme, she thought, but only to be expected. She turned round and made her way up to the theatre wing and sat down at her desk in the office and checked the off duty book. There would be enough nurses on duty during the morning. She would have her breakfast early so that she could check theatre before she started to scrub. The night staff nurse was on duty; Rachel asked her to get things started ready for the morning's work and then went along to her room, her personal difficulties ousted for the moment by plans for the morning.

The morning went well, just as hundreds of others had. The Professor was his usual calm self, George and Billy cheerfully friendly, the nurses on their mettle. The list was finished by half past one and Rachel

went down to the canteen to consume cottage pie and
cabbage, stewed prunes and custard. This uninspired
menu set her in mind of the previous week's food, way
ahead of what was on her plate at the moment. She
didn't allow her thoughts to dwell on it but drank two
cups of very strong tea and then went back to theatre.

The next day or so were uneventful but fortunately
for her very busy. She had little time to brood and,
to her relief, none of her friends had mentioned Melville once. If she had thought about this she might have
found it strange, but she was almost feverish in her en-
deavour not to think of him at all.

The week had almost gone by when she was warned
at the end of the day's work that there was a real possibility of a kidney transplant within the next few hours.
She set about getting organised, warning in her turn the
nurses she would need, seeing that the second theatre
was ready for use for any emergency, phoning the faithful Sidney. She scrubbed and laid up in readiness and
then went to the sisters' sitting-room to await events.

She had had supper and had gone back to sit curled
up in a chair, reading the day's news, before George
phoned and told her that they would operate in an
hour's time. She put her cap on, slipped her feet back
into her shoes and went back to theatre. The night staff
nurse, whom she had warned, was already there and
there was almost nothing to do. Rachel warned Sidney,
made sure that the path lab, X-Ray department and the
dispensary had been told, told the staff nurse to make
tea and checked the theatre once more.

Half an hour later she gathered her nurses around

her, replaced her cap with a theatre mob cap and went to scrub. If all was going well Dr Carr would be along with his patient within the next ten minutes. Everything was just as it should be as the Professor walked in. He made no apology for there was no need; everyone there knew that transplants took place to no set timetable. The operation started and no one so much as glanced at the clock.

The patient was a teenage boy with little chance of a normal life without a transplant; everyone in the theatre would willingly have spent twice as long there if it had been necessary. It wasn't; the Professor completed his work, pronounced himself satisfied and the patient was borne away to the recovery room and then to the intensive care unit. The Professor thanked his companions, and wandered out of the theatre with George in close attendance. Rachel, already busy with the clearing up, nodded to one of the nurses to go and get the coffee from the kitchen. The men would need a drink; she could do with one herself. When the worst of the clearing away had been done, she sent the nurses off duty, and began on the wearying task of readying the theatre for the morning, now only four or five hours away.

It was another half-hour before she was ready to leave. The night runner was in the sluice; Rachel wished her goodnight and went along to her office.

The Professor was there, standing by the window, looking out into the night. He glanced over his shoulder as she went in. 'Finished?' he asked.

'Very nearly, sir.' She sat down at the desk and began to record the operation in her neat handwriting, suddenly conscious of her capless head and shining nose, made all the worse by the elegance of the Professor's appearance.

She closed the book and he said quietly, 'Go to bed, Rachel.'

She stood up. 'You wanted something, Professor?'

He strolled to the door. 'Oh, yes, but not just at the moment.' He paused at the door and turned to look at her. His smile was amused and tender and her eyes widened. Melville had never looked at her like that and she didn't know what to make of it, and she had no way of finding out because he had gone with a quiet, 'Goodnight.'

She told herself as she tumbled into bed that she had imagined his look; she was tired and still feeling the sharpness of her break with Melville. She was too sleepy to admit that she didn't feel anything of the sort.

She didn't see the Professor the next day and for some reason she felt peevish, ticking off the nurses with unwonted sharpness and even biting Norah's head off over some trivial matter. She apologised immediately, adding in a bewildered manner, 'I don't know what's the matter with me, Norah. At least I don't think so.' She hadn't told anyone about Melville, not even Lucy, but now suddenly it didn't matter any more if everyone knew. 'I saw Melville in Basle—with another girl. He told me plainly that we were finished. It was a blow but I think my pride was more hurt than my heart. It—it was a bit of a surprise.'

'No one ever thought he was good enough for you,'

declared Norah stoutly. 'He'll make a rotten husband—if he ever marries.'

'So why do I feel so wretched?'

Norah preserved a prudent silence, only murmuring nothings. She had her own ideas about that.

Rachel discovered the answer for herself the next morning. She had been to the dispensary to do battle with the dispenser, a middle-aged acidulated man who dispensed his pills and medicines as though they were drops of his life blood. Rachel had spent five minutes of valuable time upon prising a bottle of surgical spirit from the miserly grasp and now, flushed with triumph, started on her way back to the theatre wing. There were several routes she could take; she chose the one which would take her past the letter racks. Tom had told her that he and Natalie were intending to marry quite soon and as soon as they had decided on a date, he would let her know. There might be a letter from him. There was. Tucking it into her pocket, she turned round to find the Professor right behind her.

'Melville?' he asked.

'Melville.' She repeated the name as though she had never heard it before. 'No—my brother Tom, he's going to be married. He said he'd write and tell me the date.'

The Professor's face remained impassive at this news, although his eyes gleamed beneath their lids. He said nothing, just stood there looking at her and she stared back, going slowly pink in the face. Her mother had been quite right; she had said that sooner or later she would see again, and she saw now with a clarity which took her breath away and sent her heart racing.

Melville might never have been; it was this gentle giant she loved, and why hadn't she realised it before? She had always been at ease with him, she had howled her eyes out in front of him and not felt in the least ashamed of it, she had even sat down and done her hair and face without giving his presence a thought. Oh, she had been as blind as a bat and now, too late, she wasn't. A pity she hadn't stayed blind, then she wouldn't have minded in the least that he was going to marry. The appalling thought struck her that he knew exactly what she was thinking.

She said in a high voice not in the least like her usual serene tones, 'I have to get back to theatre... Surgical spirit,' she added inanely, and, because he was smiling now, 'The instrument cupboards,' she babbled and whisked past him, cheeks still hot, chaotic thoughts tumbling around in her head, to get away as far as possible and never see Radmer again. The thought was so agonising that she dismissed it at once. Indeed, if her heart had had its way she would have turned round and run straight back and flung herself into his arms. Which, of course, wouldn't do at all. Common sense took over: she went into theatre, dealt with a difference of opinion between Mrs Pepys and the senior student nurse, threatening to reach alarming proportions, checked that the second theatre was ready for Mr Sims, who had a short list that morning, and went to her office. Norah would scrub for Mr Sims and when he'd finished Mrs Pepys could take the dental list. It was a quiet day workwise; she would get the off-duty rota seen to, catch up on the various forms she was required to fill in from time to time and go off duty at five o'clock, wash her hair and have an early night.

She had been sitting at her desk doing nothing at all for all of ten minutes when the phone rang. It was Miss Marks and at the sound of her voice Rachel hastily reviewed the last few days, trying to remember if anything had gone wrong. Mrs Pepys was always threatening to go to the office about this, that and the other; she supposed it was something to do with her.

'Sister Downing,' Miss Marks's voice sounded severe. 'Will you go to the consultants' room now. Professor van Teule wishes to speak to you.'

'Whatever for?' asked Rachel, forgetting all about being civil to one's superiors at all times.

'I do not know, Sister,' Miss Marks's voice was rebuking. 'I presume he will tell you. Be good enough not to keep him waiting.' She rang off and Rachel got up and went to peer in the mirror to see if her cap was on straight and her nose wasn't shining. At the moment she could think of no reason why the Professor should want to see her and she was to be given no time in which to speculate about it. She went to tell Norah and then made her way to the wide corridor on the other side of the entrance hall where the consultants spent any spare time they had in comfort.

She tapped on the door and went in and the Professor, sitting on the edge of the massive table in the centre of the room, got up and came towards her. She did her best to be her usual calm self; she had become a little pale at the thought of seeing him and her eyes were full of questions, but she had clenched her hands to stop their trembling and when she spoke her voice was almost normal.

'You wanted me, sir?'

He had come to a halt before her. 'I've wanted you for a long time now, Rachel.' He smiled a little at her look of utter surprise. 'But you didn't know that until an hour or two ago, did you?'

He paused and looked at her and she knew that he expected an answer. 'No, I didn't. Mother said…she said that infatuation had made me blind but that one day I'd see again.' She added very worriedly, 'But I don't think we ought to talk like this—you're going to marry, aren't you? I'm not sure what you wanted to see me about, but could we stop now? We've always been good friends and it would be nice to go on being that.'

He said with a good deal of warmth, 'It would not be nice, it would be an untenable situation. I am in love with you, Rachel.'

She closed her eyes for a moment. The sheer joy of hearing him say that made her feel quite giddy, but only for a moment. She opened them again and looked at him steadily. 'I love you, too. I wouldn't have told you of course…' She said loudly, 'Oh, this is a strange conversation in a most unsuitable place. If Miss Marks knew she would have a stroke.'

'Let us forget Miss Marks. You said you loved me, it sounded nice. Will you say it again, my darling?'

'I'm not your darling. Oh, how can I be? Perhaps you're infatuated with me, like I was with Melville, and you'll wake up and look at your fiancée and know that you love her more than anything in the world.'

'I said you were my darling, and you are and you always will be. Listen to me now. Weeks ago I told you that I hoped to get married. From the simple statement you have fashioned a fiancée who doesn't exist. You silly girl, did it never enter your head that I might be in love with you?' He made 'silly girl' sound like an endearment.

'No, never.' She went close to him and put out a shy hand on to his sleeve. 'I thought of you as a friend. I didn't mind you seeing me when I cried or my hair fell down or I was tired, but I know now that it was all part of loving you, if you see what I mean. But you never… That is, I never thought that you loved me. Is that why you wanted to see me?'

His arms were round her, holding her very close. 'Yes, my dearest darling, it was.' He bent and kissed her and then kissed her again. 'Will you marry me, Rachel?'

'Oh, yes, of course I will!' Her pale face was beautifully pink now, and her eyes shone. 'When?'

He threw back his head and let out a bellow of laughter. 'If I had my way, this very minute, but there is the question of the licence. How about a week's time? Can we assemble the families by then, the church, the parson…'

'My dress.' She smiled up at him. 'If we really want to, we can.'

'We'll make it five days.' He kissed her slowly. 'Now we'll go and see Miss Marks.' And, at her look of enquiry, 'So that you can leave, dear heart.'

'She'll never agree…'

'I have a certain amount of influence,' said the Professor with faint smugness. 'And we will invite her to be godmother to our firstborn.'

'She'll have to come to the wedding…'

'As far as I'm concerned, sweetheart, the entire world may come, just as long as you are there.'

She threw her arms around his neck. 'I'll always be there, I'll never want to be anywhere else.' A remark which gave the Professor so much satisfaction that he kissed her again, very thoroughly.

* * * * *

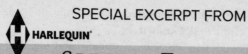
Shania flushed as she raised her eyes toward Daniel. "I don't usually babble like this."

Daniel found the pink hue that had suddenly risen to her cheeks rather sweet. The next second, he realized that he was staring. Daniel forced himself to look away. "I hadn't noticed."

"Yes, you had," Shania contradicted. "But I think that it's very nice of you to pretend that you hadn't." When she heard Daniel laugh softly to himself, she asked him, "What's so funny?" before she could think to stop herself.

"I'm not accustomed to hearing the word *nice* used to describe me," he admitted.

Didn't the man have any close friends? Someone to bolster him up when he was down on himself? "You're kidding."

The lopsided smile answered her before he did. "Something else I'm not known for."

She pretended that he was a student and she did a quick assessment of the man before her. "You know you're being very hard on yourself."

"Not hard," he contradicted. "Just honest."

She had no intention of letting this slide. If he had been one of her students, she would have done what she could to raise his spirits—or maybe it was his self-esteem that needed help.

"Well, I think you're nice—and you do have a sense of humor."

"If you say so," Daniel replied, not about to dispute the matter. He had a feeling that arguing with Shania would be pointless. "But just so you know, I'm not about to chuck my career and become a stand-up comedian."

She grinned at his words. "See, I told you that you had a sense of humor," she declared happily.

Don't miss
The Lawman's Romance Lesson *by Marie Ferrarella,*
available April 2019 wherever
Harlequin® Special Edition books and ebooks are sold.

www.Harlequin.com

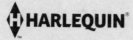

Looking for more satisfying love stories
with community and family at their core?

Check out **Harlequin**® **Special Edition**
and **Love Inspired**® books!

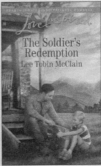

New books available every month!

CONNECT WITH US AT:

Facebook.com/groups/HarlequinConnection

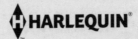

Facebook.com/HarlequinBooks

Twitter.com/HarlequinBooks

Instagram.com/HarlequinBooks

Pinterest.com/HarlequinBooks

ReaderService.com

⬡ HARLEQUIN®

**ROMANCE WHEN
YOU NEED IT**

HFGENRE2018

They'd both just turned back to their work when a familiar loud, croaking sound cut the silence.

The twins shrieked and ran from where they'd been playing into the little cabin's yard and slammed into Anna, their faces frightened.

"What was that?" Anna sounded alarmed, too, kneeling to hold and comfort both girls.

"Nothing to be afraid of," Sean said, trying to hold back laughter. "It's just egrets. Type of water bird." He located the source of the sound, then went over to the trio, knelt beside them, and pointed through the trees and growth.

When the girls saw the stately white birds, they gasped.

"They're so pretty!" Anna said.

"Pretty?" Sean chuckled. "Nobody from around here would get excited about an egret, nor think it's especially pretty." But as he watched another one land beside the first, white wings spread wide as it skidded into the shallow water, he realized that there was beauty there. He just hadn't noticed it before.

That was what kids did for you: made you see the world through their fresh, innocent eyes. A fist of longing clutched inside his chest.

The twins were tugging at Anna's shirt now, trying to get her to take them over toward the birds. "You may go look as long as you can see me," she said, "but take careful steps by the water." She took the bolder twin's face in her hands. "The water's not deep, but I still don't want you to wade in. Do you understand?"

Both little girls nodded vigorously.

They ran off and she watched for a few seconds, then turned back to her work with a barely audible sigh.

"Go take a look with them," he urged her. "It's not every day kids see an egret for the first time."

"You're sure?"

"Go on." He watched her run like a kid over to her girls. And then he couldn't resist walking a few steps closer and watching them, shielded by the trees and brush.

The twins were so excited that they weren't remembering to be quiet. "It caught a *fish*!" the one was crowing, pointing at the bird, which, indeed, held a squirming fish in its mouth.

"That one's neck is like an S!" The quieter twin squatted down, rapt.

Anna eased down onto the sandy beach, obviously unworried about her or the girls getting wet or dirty, laughing and talking to them and sharing their excitement.

The sight of it gave him a melancholy twinge. His own mom had been a nature lover. She'd taken him and his brothers fishing, visited a nature reserve a few times, back in Alabama where they'd lived before coming here.

Oh, if things were different, he'd run with this, see where it led...

Don't miss
Lee Tobin McClain's Low Country Hero,
available March 2019 from HQN Books!

www.Harlequin.com

PHLTMEXP0319